After thirty-five years as a nurse, **Patricia Davids** hung up her stethoscope to become a full-time writer. She enjoys spending her free time visiting her grandchildren, doing some long-overdue yard work and traveling to research her story locations. She resides in Wichita, Kansas. Pat always enjoys hearing from her readers. You can visit her online at patriciadavids.com.

Alison Stone lives with her husband of more than twenty years and their four children in Western New York. Besides writing, Alison keeps busy volunteering at her children's schools, driving her girls to dance and watching her boys race motocross. Alison loves to hear from her readers at Alison@AlisonStone.com. For more information please visit her website, alisonstone.com. She's also chatty on Twitter, @Alison_Stone. Find her on Facebook at facebook.com/alisonstoneauthor.

USA TODAY Bestselling Author

PATRICIA DAVIDS

The Amish Midwife

&

ALISON STONE

Plain Pursuit

❖ HARLEQUIN® LOVE INSPIRED®

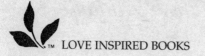 LOVE INSPIRED BOOKS

Recycling programs for this product may not exist in your area.

ISBN-13: 978-0-373-83813-4

The Amish Midwife and Plain Pursuit

Copyright © 2016 by Harlequin Books S.A.

The publisher acknowledges the copyright holder of the individual works as follows:

The Amish Midwife
Copyright © 2015 by Patricia MacDonald

Plain Pursuit
Copyright © 2013 by Alison Stone

www.Harlequin.com

Printed in U.S.A.

CONTENTS

The Amish Midwife

PATRICIA DAVIDS

This book is dedicated with great respect
to my nephew's wife, Terrah Stroda, a nurse midwife,
wife and mother. She has seen the works of God
as few people do. May He continue to bless her
and her family. I wish to thank my brother, Greg Stroda,
for his invaluable information on pumpkin farming.
Thanks, bro. Couldn't have done this without you.
And I want to extend a special thanks
to Te'Coa Seibert for letting me tour her goat dairy
and meet her remarkable animals up close.
They were too cute. And the fresh cheese was great!

Therefore God dealt well with the midwives:
and the people multiplied, and waxed very mighty.
—*Exodus* 1:20

Chapter One

❧

"You miserable *alt gayse*. Oh, no, you don't. Not again!" Anne Stoltzfus shot to her feet when she spotted the intruder working his way under the fence beyond her red barn. She stepped closer to the kitchen window. He was almost through.

"What's wrong?" Roxann Shield remained seated at Anne's kitchen table, her eyes wide with concern.

"It's Joseph Lapp's old goat. He's getting into my garden. I'm not going to lose the last of my precious tomatoes or another prized pumpkin to that thief."

Anne dashed out into the cool morning. Flying down the steps, she raced toward the rickety fence separating her garden plots from her cantankerous neighbor's farm, yelling as she ran. "Out! Get out of there!"

Her nemesis was halfway under the fence when she reached him. Armed with only a kitchen towel, she flew into battle, flapping her weapon in the black-and-brown billy goat's face. The culprit tried to retreat, but his curved horns snagged in the sagging wire. The more he struggled to escape her attack, the more tangled he became. He bleated his misery as loud as he could.

Anne stopped flapping when she recognized his dilemma. He couldn't go forward and he couldn't go back. She rested her hands on her hips as she scowled at him. She heard laughter behind her. Looking over her shoulder, she saw Roxann doubled over with mirth on her front steps.

Anne turned her attention back to the goat. "I should leave you here. It would serve you right to spend the night with your head stuck in the fence."

Feeling sorry for the goat was the last thing she wanted to do, but he did appear miserable sprawled on his belly with his head cocked at an awkward angle. His eyes were wide with fear and his mouth hung open. She looked about for his owner, but Joseph Lapp was nowhere to be seen. Of course he wasn't. Trust her neighbor to be absent when his animal was misbehaving. That was usually the case.

How many times had his goats managed to get in her garden and eat her crops? More than she cared to count. More than she could afford to lose. Each time she drove them out, she bit her tongue to keep from telling Joseph Lapp exactly what she thought of his smelly horde. Her Amish faith required that she forgive grievances, but enough was enough. If the man didn't repair his fences soon, she was going to have a word with Bishop Andy about Joseph's poor stewardship. She didn't want to cause trouble, but she was tired of being on the losing end of the situation.

However satisfying a conversation with the bishop might be, it didn't solve her current problem. The goat continued bleating pitifully. A number of other goats looked over their pens to see what was going on. Anne waited for Joseph to appear, but he didn't. She studied the billy goat for a long moment.

"If you are to be free, I reckon I'll have to do it. Remember this kindness and stay out of my garden."

"Be careful," Roxann called out.

Crouching in front of the goat, Anne put her hand on his head and pushed down so she could untangle his horns. She wrinkled her nose at his stench. Why did he smell so bad? If she had a garden hose handy, she would bathe him before she let him up. Maybe that would deter him from visiting next time. He struggled harder but she was only able to unhook one horn. "Hold still, you wicked animal."

Suddenly, the goat surged forward. His second horn popped free and he made a break for it, barreling into Anne. The impact toppled her backward into her precious tomato plants. Although it was mid-October, the vines still bore huge red fruit, the very last of the summer's bounty and a sure cash crop at her produce stand. She sat in openmouthed shock as the feeling of squished tomatoes beneath her soaked through her dress. So much for a goat's gratitude.

She shook her fist at him. "You miserable, ungrateful beast!"

"Do you need a hand?"

The mildly amused voice came from the far side of the fence. Joseph Lapp stood with his arms crossed on his chest and one hand cupped over his mouth.

He was a tall, brawny man with wide shoulders and muscular arms. A straw hat pulled low on his brow covered his light blond hair. The wide brim cast a shadow across his gray eyes, but she knew he was laughing at her. Again. They rarely shared a conversation, but he was always finding some amusement at her expense. Did he enjoy seeing her suffer?

She scrambled to her feet. "I don't need a hand. I need you to keep your goats out of my garden. Unless you keep them in, I'm going to complain to the bishop."

Joseph walked to the gate between their properties a few yards away and opened it. "Do what you must. Chester, *koom*."

The billy goat snatched a mouthful of pumpkin leaves and trotted toward the gate. He walked placidly through the opening, but Anne saw the gleam in his beady black eyes when he looked over his shoulder at her. He would be back. Well, she wouldn't be so kind to him next time. It wouldn't be a kitchen towel. She'd find a stout stick.

Joseph closed and latched the gate. "I will pay for the tomatoes. Just throw the ruined ones over the fence."

She brushed off her stained maroon dress and glared at him. "I'm not going to reward that mangy animal with my fresh tomatoes, even if they are ruined. He'll only come back wanting more."

"Suit yourself. If I can't have them, I won't pay for them."

"Are you serious?" Her mouth dropped open in shock. She took a step toward him and planted her bare foot in another tomato. The pulp oozed between her toes.

"You sat on them. Chester didn't." Joseph turned to walk away.

Furious, Anne plucked the closest whole tomato and threw it with all her might. It hit Joseph squarely between the shoulder blades, splattering in a bright red blob where his suspenders crossed his white shirt.

Horrified, she pressed her hands to her mouth. She had actually hit the man.

Joseph flexed his shoulders. Bits of broken tomato dropped to the ground. Chester jumped on the treats and gobbled them up. Joseph turned to glare at Anne.

She didn't wait to hear what he had to say. She fled to the house as fast as her shaky legs could carry her. She dashed past Roxann and stopped in the center of her kitchen with her hands pressed to her cheeks.

"What a great throw." Roxann came in, still chuckling. "Did you see the look on his face?"

"In all the years I played baseball as a *kinner*, no one wanted me on their team. I couldn't hit the broad side of the barn when I threw a ball. But today I struck my neighbor."

"You didn't hurt him with a tomato."

"You don't understand." How could she? Roxann was *Englisch*. She didn't have to live by the strict rules of Anne's Amish faith.

Roxann stopped giggling. "Will you get into trouble for it? I know the Amish practice nonviolence, but you weren't trying to hurt him."

"I struck him in anger. That is not permitted. *Ever*. If Joseph goes to the bishop or to the church elders, it will be cause for a scandal. I'm so ashamed."

Roxann slipped her arm over Anne's shoulder. "I'm sure Mr. Lapp will forgive you. You are only human. Put it out of your mind and let's finish these reports. You and the other Amish midwives are doing a wonderful job. Your statistics will help me show the administration at my hospital that our outreach education program is paying off. Our funding is running out soon. If we're going to continue educating midwives and the public, we have to prove the benefits outweigh the cost."

Roxann, a nurse-midwife and educator, was determined to improve relations between the medical community and the Amish midwives, who were considered by some doctors to be unskilled and untrained. It was far from the truth.

Anne allowed her mentor and friend to lead her back to the table and resume the review of Anne's cases for the year. Glancing out the kitchen window, Anne looked for Joseph, but he wasn't in sight. She nibbled on her bottom lip. Was he going to make trouble for her?

A full harvest moon, a bright orange ball the color of Anne's pumpkins, was creeping over the hills to the east. The sight made Joseph smile as he closed the barn door after finishing his evening milking. It had been two days since the tomato incident, but he still found himself chuckling at the look on Anne's face when she'd realized what she'd done. From shock to horror to mortification, her expressive features had displayed it all. She might be an annoying little woman, but she did provide him with some entertainment. Especially where his goats were concerned. Her plump cheeks would flush bright red and her green-gray eyes would flash with green fire when she chased his animals. She was no match against their nimbleness, but that didn't keep her from trying.

Goats enjoyed getting out of their pens. Some of them were masters of the skill. Was it his fault that the best forage around was in her garden plot?

It wasn't his intention to make life harder for the woman. He planned to mend his fence, but there simply weren't enough hours in the day. Now that the harvest was done, his corn cribs were full and his hay was safe in the barn, he would find time to make the needed repairs. Tomorrow for sure.

He was halfway to the house when the lights of a car swung off the road and into his lane. He stopped in midstride. Who could that be? He wasn't expecting anyone. Certainly not one of the *Englisch*.

Most likely, it was someone who had taken a wrong turn on the winding rural Pennsylvania road looking for his neighbor's place. It happened often enough to be irritating. His farm was remote and few cars traveled this way until Anne Stoltzfus had opened her produce stand. Now, with her large hand-painted sign out by the main highway and an arrow pointing this direction, he sometimes saw a line of cars on the road heading to buy her fresh-picked corn, squash and now pumpkins. Since the beginning of October, it seemed every *Englisch* in the county wanted to buy pumpkins from her. He would be glad when she closed for the winter.

He didn't resent that Anne earned a living working the soil in addition to being a midwife. He respected her for that. He just didn't like people. Some folks called him a recluse. It didn't matter what they called him as long as they left him alone. He cherished the peace and quiet of his small farm with only his animals for company, but that peace was broken now by the crunching of car tires rolling over his gravel drive. From the barn behind him, he heard several of his goats bleating in curiosity.

Whoever these people were, they should know better than to come shopping at an Amish farm after dark. Anne's stand would be closed until morning. The car rolled to a stop a few feet from him. He raised his hand to block the glare of the headlights. He heard the car door open, but he couldn't see anything.

"Hello, *brooder*."

His heart soared with joy at the sound of that familiar and beloved voice. "Fannie?"

"Ja."

His little sister had come home at last. He had prayed for this day for three long years. Prayed every night before he laid his tired body down. She was never far from his thoughts. Still blinded by the lights, he took a step forward. He wanted to hug her, to make sure she was real and not some dream. "I can't believe it's you. *Gott* be praised."

"It's me, right enough, Joe. Johnny, turn off the lights."

Something in the tone of her voice made Joseph stop. Johnny, whoever he was, did as she asked. Joseph blinked in the sudden darkness. He wanted so badly to hear her say she was home for good. "I knew you would come back. I knew when your *rumspringa* ended, you would give up the *Englisch* life and return. Your heart is Amish. You don't belong in the outside world. You belong here."

"I haven't come back to stay, Joe." The regret in her voice cut his joy to shreds. He heard a baby start to cry.

After few seconds, his eyes adjusted and he could make out Fannie standing beside the open door of the vehicle. The light from inside the car didn't reveal his Amish sister. Instead, he saw an *Englisch* girl with short spiky hair, wearing a tight T-shirt and a short denim skirt. He might have passed her on the street without recognizing her, so different did she look. No Amish woman would be seen in such immodest clothes. It was then he realized she held a baby in her arms.

What was going on?

He had raised Fannie alone after their parents and his fiancée were killed in a buggy and pickup crash. He'd taken care of her from the time she was six years old until she disappeared a week after she turned sixteen, leaving only a note to say she wanted an *Englisch* life. For months afterward, he'd waited for her to return and wondered what he had done wrong. How had he failed her so badly? It had to be his fault.

It was hard to speak for the tightness that formed in his throat. "If you aren't staying, then why are you here?"

The driver, a young man with black hair and a shiny ring in the side of his nose, leaned toward the open passenger-side door. "Come on, Fannie, we don't have all night. Get this over with."

"Shut up, Johnny. You aren't helping." She took a few steps closer to Joseph. "I need your help, *brooder*. There's no one else I can turn to."

Were those tears on her face? "What help can I give you? I don't have money."

"I don't want your money. I… I want you to meet someone. This is my daughter. Your niece. Her name is Leah. I named her after our mother."

"You have a *bubbel*?" Joseph reeled in shock. He still thought of his sister as a little girl skipping off to school or playing on their backyard swing, not someone old enough to be a mother. He gestured toward the car with a jerk of his head. "Is this man your husband?"

"We're not married yet, but we will be soon," she said in a rush.

"Soon?" Had she come to invite him to the wedding?

"*Ja*. As soon as Johnny gets this great job he has waiting for him in New York. He's a musician and I'm a singer. He has an audition with a big-time group. It could be our lucky break. Just what I need to get my career going."

She looked away and bounced the baby. Something wasn't right. Joseph knew her well enough to know she was hiding something.

Maybe he was being too hard on her. Maybe she was simply ashamed of having a babe out of wedlock and she expected her brother to chastise her.

This wasn't the life he wanted for her, but he was a practical man. It did no good to close the barn door after the horse was gone. He struggled to find the words to comfort her. "If Johnny is the man *Gott* has chosen for you, then you will find a blessed life together."

"Thanks. *Danki.* We will have a good life. You'll see. But in the meantime, I need your help. Johnny has to get to his audition, and I'm going to have surgery. Nothing serious, but I can't keep the baby in the hospital with me." She moved the blanket aside and showed him a cast on her wrist.

"It was an accident," Johnny shouted from inside the car.

"It was," Fannie added quickly, her eyes wide. She nibbled at the corner of her lower lip.

"I did not think otherwise." At least not until this moment. He eyed Johnny sharply. *Nay*, it was wrong of him to think the worst of any man. If his sister said it was an accident, he must believe her. He nodded toward the house. "Come in. We can talk there. I have a pot of *coffe* on the stove."

"No, thanks. Your coffee was always strong enough to dissolve a horseshoe. I can't stay, Joe. Please say you will take care of Leah for me. It's only for a couple of days."

"Think what you are asking. I have no experience with babies."

"You raised me."

"You were not in diapers."

"Please, Joe. If you don't keep her, I don't know what I'll do. I have everything she'll need in a bag for you. I've even mixed a couple of bottles. Keep them in the fridge and warm them in a pan of hot water when you need them. That's all you'll have to do. If you run out, there's powdered formula in here." She set a pink-and-white diaper bag down by her feet.

"Hurry it up, Fan, or I'm going to leave without you." Johnny's snarling tone made her flinch. Joseph scowled at him. Johnny sank back behind the wheel muttering to himself.

Joseph shook his head. Why was she with such a fellow? "This is not a good idea, Fannie. You know I would help if I could."

She moved close to him. "I'm desperate, Joe," she whispered.

Glancing at the car, she kissed the baby's forehead. "She will be safe with you. I won't worry about her for a single minute. Please. I know this sounds crazy, but it's what's best for her." She thrust the baby into his arms and hurried away.

Stunned, Joseph froze and then tried to give the baby back, but his sister was already getting in the car. "Fannie, wait!"

The moonlight showed her tear-streaked face and her hand pressed to the window as the car took off with a spray of gravel. He stood staring after it until the taillights disappeared.

"Don't do this, sister. Come back," he muttered into the darkness.

The baby started crying again.

Chapter Two

Startled awake from a sound sleep, Anne tried to get her bearings. It took her a moment to realize someone was pounding on her front door downstairs.

She threw back the quilt and turned on the battery-operated lantern she kept on her nightstand. As a midwife, she was used to callers in the middle of the night, but only Rhonda Yoder was due soon. Anne lived so far away from them that the plan was for Rhonda's husband to use the community telephone when she was needed. Anne carried a cell phone that had been approved by the bishop for use in emergencies. She checked it. No calls had come in.

After spending the previous day and night delivering Dora Stoltzfus's first child, Anne was so tired it was hard to think straight. Maybe Dora or the baby was having trouble.

The knocking downstairs started again.

"I'm coming." After covering her head with a white kerchief, she pulled on her floor-length pink robe, making sure her long brown braid was tucked inside.

She hurried down the stairs, opened the door and

gazed with sleep-heavy eyes at the man standing on her front porch. She blinked twice to make sure she wasn't dreaming and held the lantern higher. "Joseph?"

Why was her neighbor pounding on her door at two o'clock in the morning? He shifted a bundle he held in the crook of his arm. "I require your help, woman."

That didn't make any sense. Joseph was a confirmed bachelor who lived alone. "You need the services of a midwife?"

"That is why I'm here." He spoke as if she were slow-witted. Maybe she was. What was going on?

It had been almost a week since she'd hit him with a tomato. This wasn't his way of getting back at her, was it? Suddenly, the most probable answer occurred to her.

She reared back to glare at him. "Don't tell me it's for one of your goats. I'm not a vet, Joseph Lapp."

She was ready to shut the door in his face. Joseph's passion was his annoying goats. They were practically family to him. He preferred their company to that of his human neighbors. She often saw him walking in the pastures with the herd surrounding him. The frolicking baby kids were cute in the springtime, but it was the adults, Chester in particular, who saw her garden as a free salad bar.

"She's sick and I don't know what's wrong." The bundle Joseph held began whimpering. He lifted the corner of the blanket and uncovered a baby's face.

Anne's stared in openmouthed surprise. Her lantern highlighted the worry lines around his eyes as he looked at the infant he held. This wasn't a prank. He wasn't joking.

"Joseph, what are you doing with a *bubbel*? Where's her *mudder*?" The babe looked to be only a few months old.

"Gone."

"Gone where? Who is the *mudder*?" None of this made sense. Anne felt like she was caught in a bad dream.

"It's Fannie's child."

"Fannie?"

"My sister."

Anne had heard that Joseph's sister had left the Amish years ago. It had broken his heart, or so everyone said. Anne wasn't sure he had a heart to begin with.

"Can you help her?"

His terse question galvanized her into action. He had a sick child in his arms and he had come to her for help. She stepped away from the door. "Come in. How long has the babe been ill? Does she have a fever?"

Shouldering past Anne, he entered the house. "She has been fussy since her mother left her with me four nights ago, but it got worse this morning. No fever, but she throws up everything I've given her to drink. Tonight she wouldn't stop crying. She has a rash now, too."

The crying was more of a pitiful whimper. "Bring her into my office."

Anne led the way to a small room off the kitchen where she met with her mothers-to-be for checkups and did well-baby exams on the infants as they grew. She quickly lit a pair of gas lanterns, bathing the space in light. She pulled her midwife kit, a large black leather satchel, off the changing table and said, "Put her down here."

He did but he kept one hand on the baby in case she rolled over. At least he knew a little about babies. That was something of a surprise, too, in this night of surprises. His worry deepened the creases on his brow. Sympathy for him stirred inside her.

Joseph Lapp was a loner. He was a member of her Amish congregation, but he wasn't close friends with anyone she knew about. When there was trouble in the community or someone in need, he came and did his part, but he never stayed to socialize, something that was as normal as breathing to most of the Amish she knew. He didn't shun people. He just seemed to prefer being alone.

They had been neighbors for almost three years and this was the first time he had been inside her home. A big man, he stood six foot two, if not more, with broad shoulders and hammer-like fists. He towered over Anne and made the small room feel even smaller. She took hold of the baby and tried to ignore his overwhelming presence. He took a step back, thrust his hands in his pockets and hunched his shoulders as if he felt the tightness, too.

Anne quickly unwrapped and examined the little girl. The baby was thin and pale with dark hollows around her eyes. She looked like she didn't feel good. "How old is she?"

"I don't know for certain."

This was stranger and stranger. "I would guess three or four months. She's a little dehydrated and she is clearly in pain." The baby kept drawing her knees up and whimpering every few minutes. The sides of her snug faded yellow sleeper were damp. It was a good sign. If the baby was wet, that meant she wasn't seriously dehydrated.

"She needs changing, for one thing. Do you have a clean diaper?" Anne glanced at him.

"At the house, not with me."

"There are some disposable diapers in the white cabinet on the wall. Bring me one and a box of baby wipes, too."

He jumped to do as she requested. Anne took off the sleeper that was a size too small as well as the dirty diaper, noting a bright red rash on the baby's bottom. "Bring me that blue tube of cream, too."

When Joseph handed her the things she'd asked for, she quickly cleaned the child, applied a thick layer of aloe to the rash and secured a new diaper in place. It didn't stop the baby's whimpering as she had hoped. She carefully checked the little girl over, looking for other signs of illness or injury.

Joseph shifted from foot to foot. "Do you know what's wrong with her?"

Perplexed, Anne shook her head. She didn't want to jump to a faulty conclusion. "I'm not sure. Her belly is soft. She doesn't have a fever or any bruising. I don't see anything other than a mild diaper rash and a baby who clearly doesn't feel well. I reckon it could be a virus. Is anyone else in the family sick?"

"I'm fine."

Anne wrapped the baby in her blanket, lifted the child to her shoulder and turned to face Joseph. "What about her *mudder*?"

"I don't think so. She wasn't sick when I saw her last, but I only spoke to her for a few minutes."

The baby began sucking noisily on her fingers. Anne studied the child as she considered what to do next. A cautious course seemed the best move. "She acts hungry. I have some electrolyte solution I'd like to give her. It's water with special additives to help children with sick stomachs. Let's see if she can keep a little of that down. What's her name?"

"Leah."

"*Hallo*, Leah," Anne crooned to the child and then handed the baby to Joseph. He took her gingerly, clearly unused to holding one so little. The babe looked tiny next to his huge hands.

Why would Leah's mother leave her baby in the care of a confirmed bachelor like Joseph? It didn't make sense. There were a lot of questions Anne wanted to ask, but first things first. "I need to see if Leah can keep down some fluids. If she can't, we'll have to consider taking her to the nearest hospital."

That would mean a long buggy ride in the dark. It wasn't an emergency. An ambulance wasn't needed. Anne glanced at Joseph to gauge his willingness to undertake such a task. He nodded his consent. "I will do what you think is best."

He put the baby's welfare above his own comfort. That was good. Her estimation of his character went up a notch. "Let's hope it doesn't come to that. I'll put the wet sleeper in a plastic bag for you. It's too small for her, anyway."

"It's the only clothing she has." He gently rocked the child in his arms.

"Nothing else?"

"*Nay*, just diapers."

"She's been wearing the same sleeper for four days?"

His eyes flashed to Anne's, a scowl darkening his brow. "I washed it."

Why wouldn't Leah's mother leave him clothes for the child? That was odd and odder yet. A baby could go through a half-dozen changes a day between spitting up and messing their diapers. "I have some baby clothes you can take home with you. I buy them at yard sales and people give them to me so I have some for mothers who can't afford clothing." Not all of her mothers were Amish. She had delivered two dozen *Englisch* babies during her time in Honeysuckle. The clothes had come in handy for several of the poorer women.

Anne pulled open a lower cabinet door and gave Joseph a pink gown from her stash of baby clothes. She put several sleepers and T-shirts in a spare diaper bag for him, too.

He dressed Leah while Anne fixed a few ounces of electrolyte water in a bottle. When it was ready, Anne took Leah from him and settled in a rocker in the corner. He took a seat in a ladder-back chair on the opposite side of the room. He leaned forward and braced his massive arms on his thighs. Even seated, he took up more room than most men. Her office had never felt so cramped.

The baby sucked eagerly, clutching the bottle and holding it while watching Anne with wide blue eyes. Leah belched without spitting up and smiled around the rubber nipple, making Anne giggle. What a cutie she was with her big eyes and wispy blond hair.

Anne stole a glance at Joseph. He had flaxen hair, too, cut in the usual bowl style that Amish men wore. It was straight as wheat straw except for the permanent crease his hat made over his temples. His eyes weren't blue, though. They were gray. As dark as winter storm clouds. When coupled with his dour expression, they were enough to chill the friendliest overture.

Not that she and Joseph were friendly neighbors. The only time she saw him other than church was when she was chasing after his miserable, escape-happy goats and trying to drive them out of her garden, while he was laughing at her from the other side of the fence. He didn't laugh out loud, but she had seen the smirk on his face. She thought he secretly enjoyed watching her run after his animals. "How are your goats, Joseph?"

He frowned. "What?"

"Your goats. How are they? They haven't been in my garden for days."

A twitch at the corner of his mouth could have been the start of a smile, but she wasn't sure. "They're fine. I reckon they got tired of you flapping your apron or your towels at them and decided to stay home for a spell."

"Or it could be because I fixed the hole in your fence."

He looked surprised. "Did you? I'm grateful. I've been meaning to get to that. How is she doing?"

Anne looked at the quiet baby in her arms and smiled. The scowl on the baby's face was gone. She blinked owlishly. "She's trying to stay awake, but her eyelids are growing heavier by the minute. She seems fine right now. All we can do is wait and see if she keeps this down."

He let out a heavy sigh. "At least she isn't crying. It near broke my heart to listen to her."

So he did have a heart, and a tender one, at that. Her estimation of his character went up another notch.

"You said this started this morning. Was there anything different? Do you think she could have put something in her mouth without you seeing it?"

"I don't think so."

"Has there been a change in her food? Did you make sure and boil the water before mixing her formula?" Most of the Amish farms had wells. Without testing, it was impossible to tell if the water was safe for an infant to drink. She always advised boiling well water.

"*Ja.* I followed the directions on the can I bought yesterday. Her mother left me some mixed bottles, but I went through them already. The can of powdered formula in the bag was nearly empty."

"You bought a new can of formula? Did you get the same brand?" That might account for the upset stomach.

He shrugged. "I think so. Aren't they all alike?'

"Not really."

"She hasn't spit up your fancy water. She seems fine now. *Danki.*"

Anne gazed tenderly at the babe in her arms. Babies were all so precious. Each and every one was a blessing. Times like this always brought a pang of pain to her heart. She wished her baby had survived. Even though she had been only seventeen and pregnant out of wedlock, she would have loved her little boy with all her heart.

But God had other plans for their lives. He'd called her son home before he had a chance to draw a breath here on earth. She didn't understand it, but she had to follow the path He laid out even if it didn't include motherhood.

She refused to feel sorry for herself. She would hold her son in Heaven when her time came. She loved her job as a midwife and she was grateful she could help bring new life into the world and comfort families when things went wrong. Her own tragedy left her well suited to understand a mother's grief.

Anne stroked the baby's cheek. "She does seem to be better, but let's give it an hour or so before we celebrate."

"One less hour of sleep is fine with me as long as you don't mind."

Anne looked up, surprised that he would consider her comfort when he looked as tired and worn-out as she felt. She had never seen him looking so worried. "Where is Fannie? Why did she leave Leah with you?"

He was silent for so long that Anne thought he wasn't going to tell her anything. He stared at his clasped hands and finally spoke. "Fannie brought the baby to me four days ago. She said she had to have surgery and couldn't keep the child with her in the hospital. She asked me to watch her for a few days."

"What about the baby's father? Why couldn't he watch the child?"

"He had to get to New York for a job interview."

"Which hospital is she in?"

"She didn't say. She'll be back soon. Probably this morning."

"It seems strange that she didn't tell you which hospital she was going to. Did she leave a phone number or a way to contact her?"

He rose to his feet. "I should go. It's not right that I'm here alone with you. I'm sorry. I wasn't thinking straight. If the bishop hears of this, it could mean trouble for you. You have your reputation to protect."

"I'm sure Bishop Andy would understand. You were only thinking of the baby."

Speaking of the bishop reminded Anne of her regretful behavior toward Joseph. "I want to beg your forgiveness for my grave lapse in manners the other day. I've never done anything like that before. I'm humiliated and so very sorry that I acted as I did. You would be within your rights to report me to the church elders for discipline."

"It's forgiven. The babe seems fine now. *Danki*. I should go home." He reached for the baby, and Anne let him take her.

"Feed her the electrolyte water if she wakes up hungry again tonight. Tomorrow you can mix a little formula with it. One part milk to three parts water. If she tolerates that, mix it half and half for the next feeding."

"I understand. *Guten nacht*, Anne. You've been a great help. I appreciate the loan of the clothes, too."

"Tell Fannie she can keep them if she wants. Good night, Joseph," Anne called after him, but he was already out the door.

Was he that concerned about her reputation or was he reluctant to answer any more questions about his sister? At least he had forgiven her for striking him. That was a relief. Shaking her head over the whole thing, Anne put out the lights and climbed the stairs to bed for what was left of her night.

Waking at her usual time, Anne fixed a pot of strong coffee and made her plans for the day. She didn't have any mother's visits scheduled, so her whole day could be devoted to getting her pumpkins up to her roadside stand. After two cups and some toast, she was ready to get to work.

Outside, she took her old wheelbarrow out to her patch and began loading it with ripe pumpkins. Her white ones and the traditional orange carving pumpkins were her bestsellers, but she did have a number of cooking pumpkins ready to be picked. She added three of them to the top of the heap in her wheelbarrow for her own use. Having planted a new cooking variety, she was anxious to see if they were as good as her tried-and-true heirloom ones.

A crooked front wheel made pushing the wheelbarrow a chore, but getting it fixed would have to wait. If she came out ahead on her produce stand this fall, she was definitely investing in a new pushcart. Leaving the barrow at the front steps, she carried her cooking pumpkins in and put them in the sink to be washed. She stood contemplating another cup of coffee when she heard someone shouting her name.

She opened the front door. Joseph came sprinting toward her with Leah in his arms.

Chapter Three

"Joseph, what's wrong?" Anne held the door wide for him.

He rushed inside looking frazzled and more exhausted than the last time she had seen him. "I did as you told me. She was fine the rest of the night. When I gave her some of the formula this morning, she threw up again and her face got all blotchy. Now she won't stop crying."

Anne could see that for herself. Joseph's blue shirt had a large wet streak down the front. The unmistakable odor of sour milk emanated from him. Leah continued to wail. It was hard to tell if she was red in the face from crying or from something else. Anne began to suspect the child had an intolerance to milk.

She took the baby from him, sat down in a kitchen chair and unwrapped the blanket Leah was swaddled in. The baby was wearing the long pink gown that Anne had given Joe last night. She untied the ribbon from around the hem and pulled up the material, exposing Leah's kicking legs and belly and more red blotches. Anne had seen this kind of reaction before and was almost sure she was right. "I think she may have an allergy to the formula."

He shook his head. "I checked the can her mother gave me. It's the same brand I got for her. How can a baby be allergic to milk?"

"Some babies just are." It was possible the rash was from something else, but it seemed too coincidental that it appeared immediately after she'd had the formula. Anne needed more information.

Joseph ran a hand through his hair. "She can't live on water."

"*Nay*, she can't." Anne pulled the gown down and wrapped the blanket loosely around her. Lifting the baby to her shoulder, she patted the fussy child's back until she quieted.

"Then what do I feed her?" Joseph sounded like a man at the end of his rope. Looking as if he hadn't slept a wink, he raked a hand through his disheveled hair again. He hadn't bothered putting on his hat. If Anne needed proof of how upset he was, she had it. Joseph never left his house without his straw hat unless it was to wear his black felt hat to Sunday services.

She shifted the baby to the crook of her arm. "You may need to switch her to a soy formula. I need to know what brand you gave her. It could be that you just need a different kind of milk."

"I'll get it." He rushed out of the house, leaped off the porch without touching the steps and sprinted toward his home a few hundred yards to the south. Anne watched as he vaulted the fence at the edge of his property instead of using the gate and kept running. She didn't know a man his size could move so fast.

She struggled not to laugh as she gazed at Leah.

"You're certainly showing me a different side of my neighbor. Do be kinder to the poor man. I think he's having a hard time adjusting to you."

It was clear that Joseph was deeply concerned about his niece and determined to do whatever it took to help her. Anne watched him rush into his house and wondered what else she would learn about Joseph Lapp while he cared for his niece.

Did his sister have any idea how much she had disrupted her brother's life? Anne didn't know Fannie, but she found it hard to picture anyone leaving a baby with Joseph, even for a few days. Still, his sister would know him better than Anne did. She'd seen him bottle-feeding young goats in his pen. Maybe he knew more about infants than she gave him credit for knowing.

Leah buried her face against Anne's chest and began rubbing it back and forth. She whimpered and then started crying again, pulling Anne's attention away from her thoughts of Joseph.

Anne stroked the baby's head. "You poor little thing. That rash itches, doesn't it? I have something I think will help."

Joseph came sprinting into Anne's house and skidded to a stop on her black-and-white-patterned linoleum. The baby had stopped screaming. Leah sat naked, splashing and giggling in a basin of water in the center of the kitchen table. Anne cooed to the child as she supported her and poured a cupful of the liquid over her slick little body. Leah wagged her arms up and down in delight.

He took a couple of gasping breaths and held out the cans. "This is what I gave her and this is what her mother left me."

"Just set them on the table." Anne didn't even look at him. She was grinning foolishly at the baby and making silly noises. Leah seemed mesmerized by Anne's mouth and the sounds she was making.

He put the new formula on the tabletop along with the empty can he'd pulled from the trash. Thankfully, he'd been too busy to burn his barrel yesterday. He dropped onto a chair as he waited for his racing heart to slow. It seemed his mad dash was for nothing. Both Anne and Leah were enjoying the bathing process. He soon noticed the communication they seemed to share.

Leah was attempting to mimic the shape of Anne's mouth. When Anne opened her mouth wide, Leah did, too. When Anne pursed her lips together, Leah tried to imitate her. Although the baby couldn't produce the sounds Anne was making, it was clear she was trying to do so. She flapped her arms in excitement.

After a few minutes, Joseph realized he was staring at Anne's mouth, too. She had full red lips that tilted up slightly at the corners in a perpetual sweet smile. He liked her smile. He hadn't paid much attention to her in the past but now he noticed her sable-brown hair glinted with gold highlights where it wasn't covered by her white *kapp*. It was thick and healthy looking.

She was a little woman. The top of her head wouldn't reach his chin even if she stood on tiptoe. Apple-cheeked and just a shade on the plump side, she had a cute button nose generously sprinkled with ginger freckles and wide owlish gray-green eyes. She wasn't a beauty, but she had a sweet face. Why hadn't he noticed that about her before? Maybe because he usually saw her when she was running after his goats, when she was furious.

He'd been leery when a single woman moved into the

small house next to his. It had been an *Englisch* house before Anne bought it. It took her a while to convert it to meet their Amish rules, but the bishop had been tolerant of her progress because she was single.

She hadn't set her sights on Joseph the way some of the single women in the community had over the years. He wasn't the marrying kind. Apparently, Anne wasn't the marrying kind, either. She had to be close to thirty, if not older. He'd never seen her walking out with any of the unwed men in their Plain community. The only fellow he'd seen hanging around her had been Micah Shetler. He was known as something of a flirt, but she'd never shown any interest in return and Micah had soon stopped coming around.

Anne minded her own business and let Joseph mind his. If it wasn't for the traffic her produce stand brought in and her dislike of his goats, he would have said she was the perfect neighbor. She was proving to be a godsend today. He pulled his gaze away from her and concentrated on Leah. The baby looked happier than he'd seen her since she arrived. "She seems to be enjoying her bath."

"I put some baking soda in the water to soothe her itching skin. It will help for a little while. Grab that towel for me, would you, please?" Anne lifted the baby from the water. Joseph jumped up and held the towel wide. He wrapped it around the baby when Anne handed her to him.

"Should I bathe her this way?" How much baking soda? How often? He didn't want to show his ignorance, so he didn't ask.

"If her rash doesn't go away, you can. We need to find

out what is causing the rash in the first place. I'm pretty sure she has an allergy to something."

When he had the baby securely in his arms, Anne picked up the two formula cans. "This is odd."

"Did I buy the wrong thing?"

"*Nay*, it's nothing you did. This is soy formula. It's often used for babies that are sensitive to cow's milk–based formulas. I wish I could ask Fannie why Leah is on it. Was it her first choice, or did the baby have trouble with regular formula and so she switched her to soy? It's puzzling."

"What difference would it make?" He laid the baby and towel on the table and began drying her. She tried to stuff the fingers of both hands in her mouth.

"If Leah had trouble tolerating regular formula, there isn't any point in giving her what I have on hand. Do you or Fannie have a milk allergy?"

"Not that I know of."

Anne stepped up and took over the task of drying and dressing Leah. He happily stood aside.

Leah quickly became dissatisfied with her fingers and started fussing again. He glanced at Leah. "Have you more of that special water?"

"I do, but I think I want to try something else. Do you have any fresh goat's milk?"

"*Nay*, the truck collected my milk yesterday evening. I haven't milked yet this morning. Are you planning to give her goat's milk?"

"It won't hurt to try it."

He had heard of babies being raised on goat's milk, but he wouldn't have thought of it. "I can bring you some fresh as soon as I catch a goat. How much do you need?"

"A quart to start with. I'll have to cook it first. I don't want to give her raw milk."

He bristled at her insult. He ran a first-class dairy. "My goats have all been tested for disease and are healthy. I have a permit to sell raw milk and my operation is inspected regularly. I drank raw goat's milk when I was growing up and it didn't hurt me."

She looked him up and down. "I can see it didn't stunt your growth. I'm not questioning the sanitation of your dairy. I feel babies shouldn't have raw cow's or goat's milk until they are much older than Leah is. I grew up drinking raw milk, too."

"Cow's milk? Maybe that's what stunted your growth."

"Very funny," she snapped, but he detected a sparkle of humor in her eyes.

He folded his arms over his chest. "You don't like my goats."

"I'm sure they are wonderful animals."

"My does are some of the finest milk producers in the state."

"Joseph, I don't have to like your goats to make a formula from their milk. Let's hope Leah can tolerate it. Are you going to go catch a goat or do I have to?"

"I've seen you herd goats. You'd still be chasing them tomorrow. I'll be back in a few minutes."

"Make sure you use a very clean container to put the milk in."

He shook his head as he walked out of her house. If she knew anything about his work, she would know his pails were stainless steel and cleaned with soap, water and bleach twice a day. He took good care of his animals and his equipment. How could she live next door to him and not know that?

Maybe the same way he'd never noticed how pretty her smile was. He hadn't been inclined to look closely. Until now.

As he crossed the ground between his house and Anne's, he looked her property over with a critical eye. Some of the siding on her horse barn was loose and the paint was faded. It could use a new coat. The pile of manure outside the barn was overdue for spreading in the fields. Two of the vanes on her windmill clacked as they went around, proving they were loose, too.

He hadn't noticed things were slipping into disrepair for her. He hadn't been a very good neighbor. They were all things he could fix in a day or two. As soon as Fannie came for Leah, he would see to the repairs as a way to thank Anne for her kindness to the baby. It was the least he could do.

When Fannie came back.

She would be back. She was later than she'd said she would be, but he was sure she had a good reason. He just wished he knew what it was. Why hadn't she contacted him? He'd checked the answering machine in the community phone booth out by the highway twice a day for the past two days. He knew she had that number.

Her whispered words, the memory of her tearful face in the car window had flashed into his mind when she didn't return as promised. The pain and sorrow he had seen in her eyes gave rise to a new doubt in his mind. Had she abandoned her child with him? Each passing hour without word made him worry that she might have done so. It wasn't right to suspect her of such a thing, but the doubts wouldn't be silenced.

As always, his goats were happy to see him and frolicked in their pens as he approached. In spite of what Anne thought, his goats were all as tame as kittens. They came when he called them, with Matilda, the oldest female, leading all the others in a group behind her. He selected Jenny from the milling animals and opened the gate leading to his milking barn.

"Jenny, up you go."

The brown-and-black doe knew the routine. She trotted up the ramp onto the waist-high platform and put her head in the stanchion. He gave her a handful of alfalfa hay and closed the bar that would keep her from pulling her head out if she was finished eating before he was finished milking her. He didn't bother hooking her to his milking machine. His church allowed the limited use of electricity in some Amish businesses such as Joseph's dairy. The electric milking machines and refrigeration allowed him to sell his milk as Grade A to *Englisch* customers for more money. Today he milked Jenny by hand. In less than five minutes, he had a frothing pailful of milk.

After giving Jenny a quick scratch behind the ear to let her know he was pleased, he opened the head lock and allowed her to rejoin the herd. Holding the pail high, he waded through the group of younger goats vying for his attention and went out the gate before making sure it was latched securely. They bleated until he was out of sight.

The sound of a car on the road caught his attention. He looked hopefully toward the end of his lane, but it was only the mailman. The white truck stopped at Joseph's box.

Maybe there would be a letter from his sister explaining everything. He put down the pail and strode toward his mailbox at the end of the drive. He refused to think about how many times he'd made this trip praying to find a missive from her in the past. She didn't have a baby then. She had to be concerned about her child.

The mail carrier drove away before Joseph reached him, but he didn't care. He wasn't in the mood to visit with the talkative fellow. Opening his mailbox, Joseph pulled out a bundle of envelopes and flyers. Leafing through them, he found they were advertisements and junk mail until he reached the final envelope.

Immediately, he recognized his sister's handwriting, although he hadn't seen it in years. The letter was addressed to Joe Lapp. For some reason, she insisted on calling him Joe, when no one else did. Relieved, he tore open the letter and asked God's forgiveness for doubting his sister. As he read, his relief turned to disbelief.

When Joseph entered Anne's kitchen, he presented the pail of milk to her without a word. He had a strange dejected look on his face. Had one of his beloved goats kicked him? Knowing how much he'd been through, she decided not to tease him about it.

She gave him the baby to hold and took the pail to her stove. Their Amish church allowed members to use propane-powered appliances in the home. Her hot-water heater, refrigerator, washer, stove and some of her lighting all ran off propane.

Anne transferred the milk to a large kettle. "It will take a while to heat this through. She got fussy when you left, so I gave her some more electrolyte solution. I can bring the formula to your house when I'm finished."

Anne glanced at him. He held Leah close, gazing intently at her face. He rubbed his eye with the back of his hand and sniffed.

"Is something wrong, Joseph?"

"Nay."

She could see that wasn't true, but she didn't press him. She glanced covertly at him as she went back to measuring and mixing ingredients together. She referred frequently to a paper on the counter beside her. Her mother had come up with a goat's milk formula years earlier after consulting with a local doctor. Anne was grateful for her mother's thorough record keeping. She added molasses to a glass measuring cup that held a small amount of coconut oil. It didn't look appetizing. "Have you had breakfast, Joseph?"

He cleared his throat. "I'm fine. You go ahead."

She looked his way and noticed he was staring at her concoction. She grinned. "This isn't breakfast, but I could make you some eggs. There is still some coffee in the pot, too."

"Just the *coffe* sounds good. What is it that you're making?"

"Formula."

"I thought you were going to give her the goat's milk."

"I am. Goat's milk is perfect for baby goats, but it is lacking some things that a human baby needs. I don't have all the ingredients here, but if she tolerates this milk, I can give you a list of things you'll have to buy."

"Like what?"

"Liquid whey. Molasses or Grade B maple syrup. Cod liver oil and extra-virgin olive oil plus coconut oil and liquid vitamins. There are a few other things, as well."

His frown deepened. "How often will I have to do all this?"

"Every other day at least. The milk needs to be fresh, but it can be kept refrigerated for two days. What I'm making now will last through today unless Leah can't tolerate it. You said Fannie would be back today, didn't you? Send her over when she comes to pick up the baby, and I'll show her how it's made."

"You had best show me how to do it. I'll be the one taking care of her from now on."

Confused, Anne turned to him. "What about her *mudder*? Isn't she coming? What's happened?"

Chapter Four

The anguish on Joseph's face told Anne something was very wrong. She watched him struggle to compose himself. What had happened to his sister?

He sank onto one of her chairs and gazed at the baby for a long time. Finally, he whispered, "Your *mudder* is not coming."

"She's not coming today?" Anne waited for him to elaborate.

He shook his head. "She's not coming back at all."

Anne cupped a hand over her mouth as a horrible thought occurred to her. "She died?"

"*Nay*, but that would be easier to explain."

"Please, Joseph, tell me what has happened."

"Fannie lied to me."

Anne took a seat beside him. "In what way did she lie?"

"When she left Leah with me, she said it would only be for a day or two. She deliberately lied to me."

"I don't understand."

He pulled a letter from his coat pocket. "This came in the mail this morning. It's from Fannie. I was happy when I saw it. I thought it would explain why she was late returning. Instead, she wrote that she didn't have surgery. That was a lie she made up to get me to keep Leah. Fannie was going to New York City with Johnny. She said her baby was better off growing up in the country rather than in the city."

"Oh, Joseph, I'm so sorry." It was clear he was hurting and she didn't know how to help.

He looked at her, his eyes filled with confusion and pain. "What kind of mother would do that? I tried to raise my sister to be a God-fearing woman of faith, but I failed. I don't know what I did wrong. I knew my duty. I kept us fed and together with a roof over our heads. I dried her tears. I took her to church. I made sure she said her prayers. Then she does this, and I think I never knew her at all."

He put the letter away and adjusted the blanket so it wasn't covering Leah's mouth. "Why couldn't she be happy among us? Is this life so terrible?"

Anne laid a hand on his arm. "We can't know what is in another person's mind or the reasons why they behave as they do, unless they share that with us." Her heart ached for the pain he was going through. He had suffered a terrible betrayal of trust.

"How can I raise another child after I failed so miserably with my sister?"

Anne wished she could offer him the comfort he needed. She searched for the right words. "We do what we must. We depend on *Gottes* grace to see us through. Leah will be a blessing to you."

He pressed his lips into a tight line and shook his head. "*Nay.* She will grow to hate me and abandon her faith as her mother has done."

"You don't know that." He was upset, not thinking straight. Anne didn't blame him. This was a terrible shock.

He surged to his feet. "I know I can't raise a baby. I can't! You know what to do. You take her! You raise her." He thrust Leah toward her. The baby started crying.

Anne jumped out of her chair and backed against the counter as she held up both hands. "Don't say that. She is your niece, your blood. You will find the strength you need to care for her."

"She needs more than my strength. She needs a mother's love. I can't give her that. I couldn't give Fannie that."

Anne covered her eyes with her hands. He had no idea what he was offering. For years after she lost her son, she'd suffered a recurring dream. In it, she found a baby alone in some unlikely place. In the barn or out in the garden. She was always alone, and Anne rejoiced because she could keep the unwanted child. Yet every dream ended exactly the same way. The moment she had the baby in her arms, someone would take it from her. She woke aching with loss all over again.

Joseph had no idea what a precious gift he was trying to give away. He didn't understand the grief he would feel when his panic subsided. She had to make him see that.

Lowering her hands, she stared into his eyes, willing him to understand. "I can help you, Joseph, but I can't raise Leah for you. You're upset. That's understandable. Fannie has wounded you deeply, but she must have enormous faith in you. Think about it. She could have given her child to an *Englisch* couple or another Amish family. She didn't. She wanted Leah to be raised by you, in our Amish ways. Don't you see that?"

He rubbed a hand over his face. "I don't know what to think."

"You're tired. You haven't had much sleep in the past four days. If you truly feel you can't raise Leah, you must go to Bishop Andy and seek his council. He will know what to do."

"He will tell me it is my duty to raise her, just as the bishop before told me it was my duty to raise Fannie. Did you mean it when you said you would help me?" His voice held a desperate edge.

"Of course I meant it. Before you make any rash decisions, let's see if we can get this fussy child to eat something. Nothing wears on the nerves faster than a crying *bubbel* that can't be consoled."

He needed a break. Anne could give him one. It was the least she could do. She took the baby from him.

He raked his hands through his thick blond hair again. "I must milk my herd and get them fed."

"That's fine, Joseph. Go and do what you must. Leah can stay with me until you're done, but I have to get my pumpkins up to my stand before long. Customers will be arriving soon. It's getting late." It was nearly nine o'clock.

He stepped back and rubbed his hands on the sides of his pants. "I reckon I can take your load of pumpkins up to the roadway for you before I milk."

"That would be *wunderbar*, Joseph. *Danki.* But I should warn you that the front wheel is loose and it wobbles."

He gave her a wry smile. "So do your windmill blades. There are tools to fix those things."

She leveled a hard stare at him. "Are they the same tools you could use to fix a fence so your goats don't get out? What a pity neither one of us owns such wonders."

He had the good grace to look embarrassed. "I may have a few tools lying around somewhere. If you can get Leah to eat without throwing up, I'll fix your wheelbarrow and your windmill."

"I would do it without a bribe, but you have a deal." At least he seemed calmer. The look of panic had left his eyes.

"*Danki*, Anne Stoltzfus. You have been a blessing. You have proven you are a good neighbor. Something I have not been to you." He went out the door with hunched shoulders, as if he carried the weight of the world upon them.

Anne looked down at Leah. "He'd better come back for you. I know where he lives."

The baby continued to fuss softly, trying to suck on her fingers, trying to catch anything to put in her mouth.

Anne shifted Leah to her hip, freeing one hand to finish mixing the formula, and went to her stove. When she was done with the milk and it had cooled enough, she poured some in a bottle mixed with her electrolyte solution and sat down in the rocker in her office. Leah latched onto the bottle but spat it out and fussed louder.

"Don't be that way. I know it tastes different, but give it a chance." Anne offered the bottle again. Leah began sucking, reluctantly at first, then with gusto. She managed to clasp the bottle in her tiny hands and pulled it closer, hanging on to it for dear life.

"Not so fast. You'll make yourself sick." Anne took the bottle away. A tiny scowl appeared on Leah's face, reminding Anne of the one that normally marked Joseph's brow. She had to smile. "You take after your mother's side of the family."

What a beautiful child she was. Anne sighed heavily. "It's not that I don't want you. You understand that, don't you? To have a babe of my own, I would love that, but I have stopped thinking it is possible. I only met one man I wished to marry and he didn't want to marry me. I'm not a spring chicken anymore. I'll be thirty-four in June."

Leah didn't comment, but she was watching Anne intently.

Anne closed her eyes as she rocked the child. "I stopped having dreams about finding babies when I turned thirty. I'm not sure what my age had to do with it, but that's when it stopped. Your poor mother. This had to be the most difficult decision of her life. She may yet change her mind and come back for you. I'll pray for her. And for your *onkel*, who needs comfort, too."

Only God knew if Leah would be better off with her mother or not. Either way, Joseph was going to need Anne's support and the support of the entire community. He faced a difficult time and a hard choice. The person she needed to talk to was Naomi Beiler, the woman in charge of the local widows' group. Naomi would know what to do and how to do it.

Joseph stood on Anne's steps for a long time staring out at his yearling goats in the pasture across the fence. They moved slowly, grazing quietly, their white-and-brown coats contrasting sharply with the grassland. A few of the young ones frolicked briefly and a mock battle broke out between two young bucks. They butted heads a few times, but they soon stopped and went back to grazing. The sky overhead was clear, but Joseph's mind was in a fog. He couldn't make sense of what had happened. The letter sat like a stone in his pocket. He pulled it out and read it again, hoping for a different answer. It hadn't changed. It still said Fannie wasn't coming back for Leah.

He couldn't accept that.

Fannie would change her mind. She couldn't leave her babe without a thought, not the girl he knew. Not his sister. She would return. It was just a matter of time before she realized what a terrible mistake she'd made. He tucked the letter away again. What he had to do now was take care of Leah until then. He would find a way.

Anne's wheelbarrow full of pumpkins sat off to the side of the porch. He grasped the handles and began pushing it up her lane. He almost dumped it once, but managed to right it in time. Her front wheel was more than a little crooked. When he reached her produce stand, he marveled at the assortment of vegetables, gourds and pumpkins that she had for sale. The vegetables and gourds were displayed in small bins. The pumpkins were lined up along the roadside. Tucked among the produce were pots of mums in a rainbow of colors. She had a green thumb, it seemed. He was unloading the wheelbarrow when a silver car pulled up beside him.

The window rolled down, and the woman driver spoke. "How much are the white pumpkins?"

He wanted to ignore her, but it wouldn't be right to offend one of Anne's customers. He looked around for a sign or price list but didn't see one. Finally, he shrugged. "I don't know. I'm just delivering these. The woman who runs the place will be here shortly."

"I can't wait. What if I gave you twenty dollars for three of them? Would that be enough?"

If the woman drove away, Anne wouldn't get anything. Hoping he was making the right decision, he nodded. "I reckon it would."

"That's wonderful. I'll take the three large ones in your wheelbarrow." The trunk of her car lifted. She got out and offered him the bill. Joseph pocketed the money, loaded her pumpkins and then walked away quickly before he had to deal with anyone else.

His milking goats were lined up along the fence watching for him and bleating. They knew something was up. He was never this late with the milking. He waded through them and opened the gate that led to the milking parlor. The first dozen goats hurried through, and he shut the gate after them, stopping the rest. He could milk only twelve at a time. The others would have to wait their turn.

Inside the barn, the animals went up the waist-high ramp and followed each other to their places. He latched the stanchions around each of them and put their feed in the trays in front of them. When they were happily munching, he jumped down off the platform and moved to clean and dry the udder of each doe and attach the suction nozzles. As he did so, he examined each animal, looking for signs of injury or illness. When he was sure they were all sound, he turned on the machine and began the milking process. The milk flowed from the animals through clear plastic hoses to a collection tank that would keep the fresh milk refrigerated until a truck arrived and collected it three times a week. Joining a co-op of goat dairy farmers had allowed him to increase the size of his herd and have a steady market for his milk. He was almost at the point that he could afford to expand the herd again, but one man could only do so much.

Joseph went through his chores without really thinking about them. His mind was still focused on Fannie. How could she have left her baby? Why had she done it? Was a child that much of a hindrance to the career she wanted, or was there another reason she wanted him to keep Leah?

I'm desperate, Joe. She will be safe with you. I won't worry about her for a single minute. Please. I know this sounds crazy, but it's what's best for her.

What did his sister's words mean? Were they simply part of the lie she had concocted, or had she meant them? Shaking his head, he had to admit that his sister had become a stranger. He no longer knew what to believe.

Try as he might, he didn't see a way he could care for Leah alone. Not while she was so little. He was out of the house from sunup to sunset most days. Even with electric milking machines, milking eighty goats twice a day took hours. Besides his goats, he had a small farm to run. Growing his own feed reduced his milk production costs and made sure his animals received the best nutrition possible. With winter approaching, he wouldn't need to spend time in the fields, but this was when he caught up on equipment repairs and got ready for the spring kidding season. What would he do with the baby when he was out in the pastures all day and all night when the does were birthing? He couldn't be in two places at once. It would be different if he had a full-time helper. Or a wife.

He glanced out the barn window toward Anne's house. She said she would help him. Had she meant only today, or would she be willing to do more? He wouldn't know unless he asked, but he wasn't sure he should.

After finishing the milking, he returned to Anne's

house. He pulled the twenty-dollar bill from his pocket. "I sold three of your white pumpkins to a woman when I took your wheelbarrow up there. I didn't know how much they were. When she offered this, I took it because she couldn't wait."

"That's fine. A little more than I would have asked, but I'm not complaining. *Danki*."

He looked around the room. "Where is Leah?"

"Sleeping. I made a bed for her in the other room. I'll show you." She led the way to her office, where she had lined a large plastic laundry hamper with a quilt. Leah lay on her back making tiny sucking motions with her mouth. A trickle of drool glistened on her chin.

Joseph squatted on his heels beside the basket. He couldn't believe the difference between the screaming child he had shoved at Anne and this little dear. "She liked the milk?"

Anne smiled. "She loved it. I mixed it half and half with the electrolyte water just so it wasn't such a drastic change for her. Sometimes switching to a new formula can upset a baby's tummy unless you do it gradually. She hasn't spit up or fussed since she finished her bottle."

He breathed a quick prayer of thanks that Leah wasn't screaming or hurting. He was more grateful than ever for Anne's knowledge and skill. "You have worked a wonder here."

"I'm glad she tolerated the goat's milk. I had no idea what to try next if she didn't. We would have had to take her to see a doctor."

Now was the time to see how much Anne was willing to do for Leah. Rising to his feet, Joseph hooked his thumbs under his suspenders and took a deep breath. "I have a proposal for you, Anne Stoltzfus."

Chapter Five

"I'm listening," Anne responded, waiting for Joseph to explain his odd statement.

A proposal. What did that mean? Was he going to ask her to take Leah again? Anne hardened her resolve. As much as she liked the babe, she couldn't be Leah's mother. What if something happened to her? The thought scared Anne to death.

Joseph shifted uneasily from one foot to the other. "I will help you get your fields harvested and fix what needs fixing around the farm in exchange for your help with Leah."

She folded her arms. "Exactly what kind of help?"

"Like a mother would do."

"I've already said I won't keep her."

"*Nay*, you mistake my meaning. Like a *kindt heedah*. Feed her, bathe her, watch her while I'm working."

"You mean you will harvest my pumpkin crop if I will be Leah's nanny?"

"*Ja*. That is what I want. Would you accept such a bargain?"

"I don't know. I'll have to think it over."

It was a tempting proposal. Hauling her large pumpkins out of the field was backbreaking work. Some of them weighed over twenty pounds. As strong as Joseph was, he could do it easily. He could probably carry one under each arm and one in his teeth and still push a loaded wheelbarrow. She had only another week to get them all picked unless an early freeze hit, then she wouldn't have anything to harvest. His help would be a blessing.

But taking care of an infant? What would she be getting herself into? She had a produce business to run. She had mothers coming for prenatal and postnatal appointments. There was no telling when an expectant father would show up wanting her to come deliver a baby. She had three mothers due before Thanksgiving. What would she do with Leah then? Run her back to Joseph's home? Amish women didn't call for the midwife until they were ready to give birth. She wouldn't have time to waste.

Still, the idea of Joseph raising Leah alone was as hard to imagine as her raising his goats. If she agreed to his proposal, she would be able to keep an eye on the baby, make sure she was thriving. The big question was, could she do it without becoming too attached to Leah?

The memory of losing her baby lingered in the back of her mind. Loving a child meant risking heartbreak. She shook her head.

Joseph sighed deeply. "You don't want the job. I understand. May I take your laundry basket with me until I can get a crib for her?"

"What has she been sleeping in?"

"A cardboard box that I lined with a blanket."

"Of course you can use my basket. I'm sure the

church will provide the things you need when they learn of your situation."

He picked up the hamper. "I can make do without their help. I will manage until Fannie comes back."

Anne frowned and tipped her head slightly. "I thought the letter said she wasn't coming back."

His face turned stoic. "She will. She'll see what a mistake she has made and she'll be back. I know my sister."

Anne held her tongue. She wasn't so sure. She fetched a half-dozen bottles of milk she had made from the refrigerator. "These pink bottles are half milk and half my fancy water. The rest are plain goat's milk formula. If she keeps the first ones down, give her full-strength milk tonight."

"Will you write down the recipe for me if she does well on this?"

Anne's conscience pricked her. She wasn't doing enough to help him. She could tell by the look on his face that he was unsure of himself. It had to be confusing and frightening for a bachelor to suddenly find he was in charge of a baby. "I'll make all the formula for you if you bring me fresh milk every other day."

"*Danki*. I'm not much of a hand at cooking."

"Why does that not surprise me?"

A grin twitched at the corner of his mouth. "I appreciate all the help you've given me."

"You're *willkomm*."

He walked out with Leah in the basket. Anne closed the door behind him, determined not to feel that she'd made a mistake. She couldn't accept his offer of a job. She delivered babies. She didn't raise them. What she did raise was produce. And right now her stand was unattended.

While most people knew they could leave their money in her tin can and take the pumpkins or the vegetables that they wanted, some *Englischers* would simply drive by if no one was minding the stand. She needed to get up to the road. The last two weeks of October were her biggest sale days. Today, Saturday, would be especially busy.

She grabbed a sweater from the hook beside the door and walked out into the chilly morning. The smell of autumn was in the air as the wind blew fallen leaves helter-skelter down the lane in front of her. The good Lord had blessed her with a bountiful crop and kept the heavy frost at bay. Only He knew how much longer the good weather would last.

Her pumpkins were larger than usual this year and thick under the still-green leaves in the field, but a hard frost would put an end to all of them. She said a quick prayer for continued favorable weather and walked quickly toward the small open-fronted shack she had built at the edge of her property.

If her land had fronted a busy highway, she would have seen more business, but the village of Honeysuckle was small and off the main state roads, so traffic was generally light. Her idea to post a sign out by the highway was paying off, though. She'd had twice as many customers this fall as last. Only Joseph had complained about the increase in cars on the road.

A horse and gray buggy sat parked beside her stand when she reached it. Anne immediately recognized the animal and looked for the owner. Dinah Plank was inside the shack inspecting some of Anne's white pumpkins displayed in a wooden crate. Anne called to her, "Morning, Dinah."

"Wee gayt's," Dinah answered with a wave. "A good day to you, too. I thought you would be in town at the farmers' market, selling your produce there."

"I took a load of vegetable and pumpkins in yesterday and Harvey Zook's boy is selling them for me. I thought it might be better to be open at both places today."

"Goot thinking."

"Can I help you find something?" Anne smiled at her friend. Barely five feet tall, the cheerful plump widow was an energetic gray-haired woman. Dinah lived in Honeysuckle above the Beachy Craft Shop, where she worked for Anne's friend Ellen Beachy. Soon to be Ellen Shetler. The wedding was planned for the first Thursday in November.

Dinah picked up a creamy white pumpkin and thumped it. "I wanted to make a few pies for Ellen's wedding. There's nothing like the taste of a warm pumpkin pie fresh out of the oven piled high with whipped cream. I get hungry just thinking about it."

"I agree. You will want some of my heirloom cooking pumpkins for that. They make the best pies." Anne gestured toward a smaller crate inside her stand.

"What about these white pumpkins?"

"I've tried them and they are okay, but I don't think they have as much flavor."

"I'll be sure and tell my friends as much. Naomi wanted to try some whites."

Naomi Beiler, the widow of their church's former bishop, was the unofficial leader of the local widows' group. The group planned benefit suppers and the like for people in need within their Amish community. They had recently held a haystack supper to raise funds for Mary and David Blauch after their son was born prematurely. The baby had had to be hospitalized for several months and the couple faced a huge medical bill. The Amish didn't carry health insurance but depended on the rest of the community to aid them in times of need. If their local church wasn't able to cover the cost, a plea would go out to neighboring churches to help. The way everyone looked out for each other was one of the most comforting things about living in an Amish community.

Anne thought about Joseph and Leah. Joseph didn't feel he needed outside help, but Anne knew he did. "Will you be seeing Naomi this morning?"

On most Saturdays, Dinah went early to the farmers' market in town, where she met friends from her widows' club for breakfast. "I think so. Why?" Dinah cocked her head to the side.

"I have a small project I'd like help with. Joseph Lapp's sister recently paid him a visit and left her infant daughter with him."

"What?" Dinah's eyes widened behind her glasses and her mouth dropped open. "He's a bachelor."

"Exactly. He has nothing for the child. No crib, no bottles, only a few things he borrowed from me."

"What is his sister thinking? How long is he going to have the child?"

"I wish I knew. She may not be back."

"How sad. Fannie has been out in the *Englisch* world a long time. It must be three years now. You never met her, did you?"

Anne shook her head. "She left before I moved here. Joseph has lived alone for as long as I've known him."

"I'm sure he isn't an easy neighbor to get along with. He's not a friendly fellow."

"We'd get along better if he kept his fences fixed. He

came over three weeks ago to tell me my produce stand was bringing too many cars down the road."

"I can see why that would bother him. His parents and the girl he planned to marry were all killed when a truck struck their buggy right at the end of his lane. Joseph and Fannie were thrown clear with barely a scratch. It was very sad."

Anne's heart contracted in sympathy. "I didn't know."

"It was *Gottes* will."

All things were the will of God, but knowing that didn't dull the pain of losing a loved one. Anne tried to imagine Joseph as a brokenhearted young man. "Was she a local girl?"

"Her family lives near Bird-in-Hand. She was the eldest daughter. I'll speak to Naomi, but all we need to do is talk to a few of the mothers at church tomorrow and ask for donations of baby items. I know my daughters-in-law have clothing they can spare. How old is the child?"

"About four months."

"I can pick up some formula for her in town today and bring it by this evening."

"That won't be necessary. It appears that Leah has a milk allergy. We are giving her goat's milk."

Dinah chuckled. "Joseph should have plenty of that. How many goats does he have these days?"

"I have never tried to count. All I do is shoo them out of my garden."

"Looking at all these pumpkins, I'd say you've done a good job of keeping them away. I'll take six of your best cooking ones, and I'll share your concerns about Joseph's niece with my friends. I'm sure we can come up with the things he needs. Who is watching the child while he is out working with his goats and in the fields?"

"No one. He wanted to hire me as a nanny, but I said no."

"Why? I would think taking care of a baby would be your cup of tea."

Anne turned and began rearranging the gourds she had on display. "Of course I like babies, but… I don't know. I'm busy with the stand. Besides, I could get called out for a delivery at any time. It would be hard to have a baby underfoot."

"I see." Dinah didn't sound convinced. Anne glanced her way. The sharp-eyed little woman didn't look convinced, either.

Sighing heavily, Anne folded her arms and admitted the truth. "I'm afraid I would become too attached to her. She is an adorable *bubbel*. I may never have children of my own and caring for someone else's child every day would be a reminder of that."

"Sounds as if you are already attached to her."

"*Nay*, I'm simply worried Joseph won't be able to take care of her."

"Then you should find someone to be the *kindt heedah*. You must know of several girls who would do well at that."

"I can't think of anyone offhand. Who could get along with Joseph? He is an odd fellow."

Dinah chuckled. "I'll check around and give him a few names tomorrow after the prayer service."

"That is a fine idea. I'll tell Joseph." It was a good solution. Leah needed someone to look after her and Joseph could easily find someone. It didn't have to be her. Then she could stop worrying about them both.

After a busy day at her produce stand, Anne made her way home. The western sky was ablaze with purple, pink and gold-tinged clouds fanned out along the horizon. The air had a decided nip in it as the day cooled. She hoped it wouldn't freeze tonight.

She pulled her sweater close and hurried up the steps, but she stopped on the porch and glanced toward Joseph's house before she went inside. She cocked her head in that direction, but she didn't hear any crying. How was Leah tolerating her goat's milk? The question had been at the forefront of Anne's mind all day.

"At least he didn't come running over. She must be doing all right."

Anne shook her head. Now she was talking to herself. It was not a good sign. If she was going to sleep a wink tonight, she would have to see for herself that the baby was doing better.

Crossing the strip of brown grass that bordered her flower garden, Anne paused at the gate between her place and Joseph's. Was there really a reason to go to his door? If he needed her, he would come and get her. He had already proved that. Anne bit the corner of her lip.

"Checking on them is the neighborly thing to do." As Anne battled her indecision, she saw a light come on in his barn. He was with his goats. Where was Leah?

Anne took a deep breath. She would just ask about the baby and leave. Before she could go any farther, the light went off. She waited a few moments. He appeared at the barn door with her laundry basket in his hands. It seemed Leah would learn about goats from the cradle.

He caught sight of Anne and stopped. After a brief pause, he headed toward her.

"How did she do?" Anne asked when he was close enough.

He stopped at the fence and rested the basket on the

top board. "She did fine. Slept most of the day. The rash is gone. *Danki*."

Anne peered in the basket. Leah lay with her eyes closed, but she was making tiny sucking motions with her lips and then smiling in her sleep. Anne's heart turned over. She touched the baby's soft hair. "She's dreaming about her bottle."

"You solved her problem. I'm grateful."

Anne drew her hand back and clenched her fingers together. "I saw Dinah Plank this morning. She thinks she can find a nanny for you. She said she would give you a few names tomorrow after church."

"I don't need anyone. Leah sleeps while I work."

"She won't sleep this much for long. Then what?"

He scowled and lifted the basket off the fence. "Then she will be awake while I work. We'll be fine until my sister returns. Do not concern yourself with us. *Guten nacht*," he said sharply and turned away.

Anne watched him walk off and wished she had another fresh tomato at hand. First he wanted her help and now he didn't. He was the most irritating man she'd ever met.

Chapter Six

Anne drew several stern looks from Naomi Beiler during the three-hour-long church service on Sunday morning. She tried to concentrate on the hymns sung, on her prayers and on the preaching, but she couldn't. Joseph wasn't among the worshippers.

Where was he? What was wrong? Was Leah okay?

Anne glanced over again, covertly checking the rows of men seated on the backless benches across the aisle. Joseph's size made him a hard man to miss. Although there were close to fifty men and boys all dressed in dark coats and pants with their heads bowed, she knew she could pick him out easily. He simply wasn't there.

Her friend Ellen elbowed her and Anne straightened. Naomi was looking her way again. Her stern look had changed to a definite scowl. Naomi was the unofficial monitor of proper behavior among the church members, particularly the young men and women.

Fastening her gaze on the large black hymnal in her hands, Anne started to join the singing only to realize she was on the wrong page. Blushing bright red at her blunder, she turned the page and joined in on the correct verse in a subdued tone. When the service was ended, she closed her book thankfully.

"What is wrong with you today?" Ellen leaned toward Anne as they filed out of the Hochstetler's barn. Each Amish family in the congregation took turns hosting the prayer meetings that were held every other Sunday in their home, workshop or barn, depending on where there was adequate room to seat the congregation on the wooden benches that were brought in for the day. This Sunday was the Hochstetler's turn. The congregation had outgrown the family's small house, but the wide hayloft of the barn had more than enough room. The meal that would be served afterward would still take place in the house, although the members would have to eat in shifts.

"Nothing is wrong with me." Anne stood on tiptoe to see over the women grouped together beyond the doorway. Maybe Joseph had remained outside with Leah rather than risk her disturbing the worshippers.

"I'm the one who should be nervous, but you are like a mouse on the kitchen counter watching for the cat."

Anne relaxed at Ellen's teasing and put her concerns aside. "Are you nervous? The wedding date is almost here."

"Only a little over a week away. We wanted to be the first wedding in the area, but now I wish we had planned it for later. There is so much to do."

"You have many friends who will lend a hand. It will all get done."

Smiling sheepishly, Ellen nodded. "You're right."

Anne looked over the worshippers again as the men came out of the barn carrying some of the benches that would be stacked and turned into seating and tables for the meal. "I was expecting to see Joseph Lapp today. He's not here."

"Maybe he has gone to visit someone."

"Maybe so. I saw his horse and buggy hitched and waiting in front of his house when I left home this morning. I thought he was coming here." She had almost stopped to inquire about Leah, but she thought Joseph wouldn't appreciate her concern. He hadn't last evening.

Ellen touched Anne's arm. "I see *mudder* looking for me. We'll visit later." She left without waiting for Anne's reply.

Anne spied Lizzie Fisher beckoning to her and walked her way. The young widow of Abraham Fisher had recently suffered a miscarriage only weeks after her husband's death. Anne knew the pain of losing the baby would lessen in time, but the memory of her lost child would never go away. Happily, God had placed a new joy in Lizzie's life. She had fallen in love. The young man was her deceased husband's brother, Zachariah Fisher. They planned to marry next month, too. November was the time for weddings in Amish country and the announcements for several couples had been made in church that day. "Hello, Lizzie. How are you doing?"

"I'm doing well. I just wanted you to know that I took your advice about doing something in memory of my baby. Zach and I chose to plant a dogwood tree beside the house. He has fond memories of playing beneath one when he and Abraham were small. It will be a special place to both of us."

"I'm glad. I hope it brings you comfort."

"It already has. Dinah Plank mentioned that Joseph Lapp was looking for a girl to babysit his niece. I didn't even know he had a sister, let alone a niece. My oldest stepdaughter, Mary Ruth, is interested, but I wanted to ask if you think she would be right for the job before Zach approached Joseph with the offer. I know he hasn't been the best neighbor to you. I've seen his goats in your garden."

Anne understood Lizzie's concern. "Joseph is not the easiest fellow to get along with. I think an older woman would be better. I'd hate to have him hurt Mary Ruth's feelings with his gruff ways."

"Then I'm sure glad I asked. She can look for a job that will suit her better. *Danki.*"

After visiting for a few more minutes, Lizzie left to gather up her stepchildren and take them in to eat. Normally, Anne would have joined the others in a light lunch and then an afternoon spent visiting and watching the children at play. Today she couldn't get her mind off Joseph and Leah. She had to find out why Joseph hadn't been in church.

She found Dinah and explained why she was leaving early. Dinah sent one of her sons to get Anne's horse and buggy, but before he returned, Naomi Beiler approached Anne, followed by a number of the women in the widows' group.

Naomi crossed her arms over her chest. "I understand Joseph Lapp is caring for his niece. Dinah tells me the child is only a few months old."

The woman had a voice that carried. A number of people nearby stopped talking and turned to listen. Anne suffered a niggling of regret at sharing Joseph's story so publicly, but their community was small and tight-knit. She took comfort in knowing his situation would become public knowledge sooner or later. "It's true. His *Englisch* sister left the babe with him. At first Fannie said she would be back for the child. But later she wrote to say she wanted him to raise Leah."

She saw and understood the disbelief on the faces around her.

"We will pray for Fannie," Lizzie said. "It must have been a heartbreaking decision to make. No mother could give up her child without enormous pain."

Anne knew exactly how true those words were.

Nodding to the women gathered near her, Naomi said, "Our group has decided to help."

"That's wonderful." Over the growing crowd, Anne saw Dinah's son had her horse hitched and waiting.

"As this won't require a fund-raising effort, I'm asking those families with infant items they can spare to bring them to the Beachy Craft Shop on Monday. I'll personally deliver them to Joseph as soon as we have some." Naomi frowned and looked about. "Where is he? I didn't see him in the service."

"The baby has been sickly. I'm on my way to check on them now." Anne hoped nothing was wrong.

Joanna Miller glanced at her husband, Wilmer. "We have a crib and dresser we can loan him and plenty of baby clothes that our youngest has outgrown. What do you think?"

Her husband nodded. "I reckon we could."

One by one, the families around Anne began offering to bring various items to the Beachy Craft Shop the following day. Anne's heart swelled with gratitude. Everyone was stepping up to help. It was always this way in their Amish community. People helped each other.

Anne smiled at her friends and neighbors. "*Danki*, I know Joseph will be grateful."

Naomi's eyes grew sad. "I often wish I had done more

for Fannie when Joseph was raising her. She needed a mother's influence in her life, but he didn't see it that way and my husband was ill, so I wasn't able to help as I should have."

"We can only do so much," Anne said to comfort her.

"You are right. The past is the past. It can't be changed. Are you seeing my niece Rhonda Yoder this week? Her babe is due in another three weeks. She's nervous because it's her first child."

"I am seeing Rhonda on Friday. She's doing fine. I don't anticipate any problems, but I know how scary it can be for new moms."

"You have a way with them. Rhonda thinks the world of you and so does her husband," Naomi said.

Anne chuckled. "Rhonda will do fine. I'm more worried about Silas. He's the bundle of nerves in the family. I told him if he fainted, I was going to tell everyone. I think he's as concerned about that as he is about dropping his new baby."

The group broke apart after that as the women went to get the midday meal ready. Anne thanked Dinah's son and climbed into her buggy. She wanted to rush home, but she didn't push Daisy to a faster pace. The mare was getting older and would soon need to be put out to pasture to enjoy her final years. She should have been retired last year, but Anne didn't have the money for a new horse. She would have to come up with it soon. A midwife without a fast horse was one who risked not catching a baby.

Twenty minutes later, she passed Joseph's lane and soon reached her own. Pulling to a stop in front of her barn, she saw that Joseph's horse and buggy was still hitched and waiting in front of his house. Something was definitely wrong.

Anne jumped down from the buggy. Leaving the mare hitched in case she was needed, Anne hurried through the gate and up to Joseph's porch. In spite of the fact that they were next-door neighbors, she had never set foot inside his home. Gathering her courage, she knocked. When he didn't answer, she opened the door and walked in. Joseph, like most Amish, didn't lock his doors.

The kitchen was empty. The sunny room had large windows that let in tons of morning light, but it was a mess. There were dirty dishes on the table and some piled in the sink, too. Several pots on the stove held the remnants of Joseph's recent meals. She called his name and heard a muffled sound from the doorway to her left. She peeked in the room.

Joseph was sprawled in an overstuffed chair. He was wearing his Sunday suit, but he had one shoe on and one shoe off, as if he hadn't quite finished dressing. He had a patch of tissue on his upper lip and one on his neck that bore small bloodstains. He must have cut himself shaving. His head lolled to one side, his hair was mussed and he was snoring softly. Leah lay snuggled tightly in the crook of his left arm. An empty baby bottle was sitting on a small table beside his chair.

Anne pressed a hand to her mouth as a tug of pity pulled at her heart. Joseph's exhaustion had clearly caught up with him. There were dark circles under his closed eyes that even his thick lashes couldn't obscure.

Leah stretched in her sleep and brought her tiny fist to her mouth. She nuzzled her fingers, frowned and screwed up her face, getting ready to cry. She was adorable, no two ways about it. Anyone who took care of her was sure to fall in love with the child. After all, Anne was halfway there already.

This wasn't her baby, but Leah was a baby in need. And Joseph was a man in need, too. It was wrong to pretend they should be someone else's problem. The good Lord had brought Joseph to her doorstep. Anne would not turn them away.

She stepped to Joseph's side and gently shook his shoulder as she called his name.

Joseph heard a voice coming from a long way away. It was a woman's voice. Fannie?

He tried to force his eyes open. They felt as if they were full of sand and he let them fall shut again. Just a few more minutes of sleep. That was all he needed. Just a few more minutes.

"Joseph, wake up."

"I'm up," he muttered. He wasn't, but sleep was fading.

"I'm going to take Leah from you. She's getting hungry."

Who was talking to him? Someone lifted the baby from his chest. He tried to hold on to her, but his arm was numb and it wouldn't move. He raised his head and blinked. Anne Stoltzfus stood in front of him with a silly grin on her face.

"What's so funny?"

"You are." She turned away.

Why was she laughing at him?

He let his head fall back. It didn't matter. He was too tired to care. Sleep tugged at his mind, but his numb arm was waking up. Pins and needles stabbed him. He rubbed his arm from elbow to wrist, trying to ease the discomfort. The sound of Leah fussing penetrated his mind. Where was she? He raised his head again.

Anne had her. Only she was in his kitchen.

His kitchen!

He sat bolt upright. "What are you doing here?"

She held a bottle of milk and tested its temperature by sprinkling it on her wrist. "When you didn't come to the prayer service, I got worried, so I came to check on you."

"I missed church?"

"*Ja*, you did." There was that silly smile again.

He drew his hands down his cheeks. "I must have fallen asleep. What time is it?"

"One o'clock."

He'd been asleep for almost four hours? It was the most rest he'd had since Leah arrived. Yawning, he rubbed his stiff neck. "I don't know why you thought you had to come barging into my home. We are fine."

"I can see that." She laughed, a sweet light sound that sent the blood rushing to his face.

Okay, he wasn't fine, but he would be. If only he could close his eyes for another half hour. Just a half hour. That was all he needed.

Anne came to stand in the doorway. Leah was sucking contentedly on the bottle she held. "Has she been fussing again? Is that why you aren't getting any sleep?"

"She wants to eat every two hours."

Anne nodded. "She's making up for lost time. You can finish your nap. Leah will be at my place when you get up."

"Okay. Wait. What?"

"I'm taking her for the rest of the afternoon and you're welcome."

"*Nay*, this isn't right. She's my responsibility."

"Don't be stubborn and prideful, Joseph. Leah is going to spend the day with me and when you come to pick her up, we'll talk about my salary."

"What salary?" He couldn't keep up with her. His mind was a complete fog.

"The one you will pay me to be Leah's nanny."

"I thought you didn't want to do that."

"I've changed my mind. I'll see you later. Have a nice rest. I suggest you lie down on the sofa. That way, your neck won't be so stiff."

He opened his mouth to reply. There was some argument he needed to make, but he couldn't summon the wits to figure out what it was. He heard the door close and silence filled the house. Blessed silence.

Leah was being looked after. Anne could take care of her better than he could.

Anne with the sweet laugh and the funny smile who hated his goats and threw tomatoes at him.

He'd go and get Leah in a minute. It was his last thought as he dropped off to sleep again. Oddly, he dreamed about Anne walking among his herd with a little girl at her side. They were both laughing at the antics of the baby goats leaping around them. He smiled in his sleep.

Chapter Seven

It was barely an hour later when Anne looked up to see Joseph standing in her doorway. He wore a sheepish expression, but he looked as if he'd finally gotten enough rest.

"I've come for Leah," he said quietly.

"She's sleeping at the moment. I was about to have some pumpkin soup. I didn't stay for the meal after church. Would you like some? It's a new recipe, so I'm not sure how good it will be." Anne stirred the bubbling contents of her pot, tasted it one last time and nodded in satisfaction. It was okay, but not as good as her mother used to make.

"I reckon I could eat a bite if it's not too much trouble." He continued to stand by the door.

"*Wunderbar.* Have a seat." She gestured toward her small table.

He was still wearing his Sunday best. Anne realized she'd never noticed what a handsome fellow he was until now. Normally, they were having a disagreement over the fence or she was throwing tomatoes at him. She blushed at the thought.

"First I want to apologize." He shifted from one foot to the other.

"For what?"

"For being asleep in the middle of the day when you came to my house. I'm not a lazy person."

"Don't apologize for falling asleep with a babe in your arms. You aren't the first person to do that and you won't be the last. I tell all my new mothers to sleep when the baby sleeps. If mothers try to get their housework done when the babe is asleep, they wear themselves out in no time. Babies take a lot of work. That's why mothers need helpers. It's tough to get up and feed a child every two to three hours night and day for weeks on end."

"I've only been doing it a week." He sat down at the table.

"She seems to be tolerating the goat's milk well. She'll start sleeping for longer periods now."

"That's good to know. Did you say you were willing to be her nanny or did I dream that?"

Anne poured the hot soup into two bowls and carried them to the table. "I said I would."

"What made you change your mind?"

"I saw how exhausted you were and I realized I was being selfish not to help." She would simply have to keep in mind that Leah wasn't her baby. Anne would take care of her, but she wouldn't fall in love with her any more than she fell in love with the babies she delivered. Caring for mothers and babies was the calling God had chosen for her. She would do her best to honor that gift. Anne took her place at the table. It was small, and sitting across from Joseph had an intimate feel.

"Danki." Joseph bowed his head for silent grace. Anne did the same.

When he was finished, he picked up a spoon and took a sip of the soup. "Not bad. It could use a little more ginger."

She took a sip. As much as she hated to admit it, he was right. "I'll increase it to a half teaspoon next time."

He blew on the next spoonful. "My mother used to make pumpkin soup in the fall. I've tried to duplicate her recipe, but I've never managed to make a batch as good as hers."

"That is exactly what I was thinking when I made this today. Is it that our mothers were better cooks, or is it that we remember things tasting better because they are no longer with us?"

"A bit of both, I'm sure."

She thought of the pile of dishes in his kitchen. "Do you find it hard to cook for just yourself?"

"I don't cook anything fancy. Mostly, I warm up things from cans."

That made sense. She tended to do the same thing. Sometimes she ate standing at the sink because sitting alone at the table was…lonely. It had been ages since she'd shared her table with a man. Her brother lived in the next county and rarely visited. Occasionally, the bishop and his wife would stop in. Mostly, she ate alone.

"I do make my own chèvre cheeses," he said between spoonfuls.

Anne looked at him in surprise. "You make goat cheese? What kinds?"

"Soft cheeses mostly. They're easy to make and you can flavor them any way you like. Garlic, chives, spices, even chopped walnuts and dried cranberries. It's great on toast."

"I'd love to try some."

It was his turn to look surprised. "You would?"

"If I show you how to make Leah's formula, can you show me how to make goat cheese?"

Anne was delighted to see a true smile spread across his face. "If you have cheesecloth and lemon juice or vinegar, I'll show you how after I milk this evening."

"That would be perfect. I can make up a big batch of formula for Leah then, too."

"She sure likes that stuff. I'm glad you thought to try it. It was right smart of you."

"It was really more a process of elimination, but *danki*." Pleased with his compliment, Anne continued to eat her soup and the conversation ended. They ate in companionable silence until he sopped the last bit from his bowl with a piece of bread and popped it in his mouth.

"Would you like some apple pie for dessert?" Anne had intended to sell it at her stand tomorrow, but Joseph still looked hungry.

"I won't say no to apple pie. It's my favorite."

Anne rose to fetch the pie from the pie safe. "My favorite is strawberry-rhubarb. I have plans to start a large rhubarb patch in the spring."

"Rhubarb leaves are poisonous to goats."

"I didn't know that. I knew they were poisonous to dogs." In that case, she might start her patch by his rickety fence. Maybe that would get him to mend it once and for all.

"Where were you thinking of putting it?"

"Just south of my barn. If it makes them sick, won't they avoid it?"

"Not the young ones. If you plan on planting rhubarb there, I'll for sure have to put up new fencing."

Anne hid a smile as she sliced her pie. How easy was that? She sensed it was as close to an apology as he was willing to make, but it signaled the beginning of a truce between them. She slipped two slices of pie on white plates and carried them to the table.

He accepted the dish from her. "*Danki*. What are your plans for your pumpkin fields when the harvest is done?"

"I'll rake the dried foliage and burn it and then I'll plant corn there next year." She took a bite of her pie. The tart sweetness of the apples and cinnamon in her flaky crust was a perfect ending to the meal.

"I thought your pumpkins were your bestselling items."

"They are, but you can't plant pumpkins in the same field two years in a row. It's best to wait three years."

"Why?"

"Pumpkins produce fusarium fungus in the soil. It causes the fruit to rot if you plant in the same ground too soon. The fungus dies away after two or three years."

"Rather than raking it and burning it, how would you feel about letting my goats graze it?"

She couldn't help needling him a little. "I guess we already know they like pumpkin vines and the leaves don't make them sick."

"Goats like to explore and they often find ways out of their enclosures."

"I've noticed, and they normally find their way through your rickety fence into my garden."

He scowled. "Are you a woman who forever harps on old injuries?"

Okay, maybe not a truce. She glared at him. "Are you a man who won't admit it when he's in the wrong?"

His scowl deepened but he didn't say anything. The

sound of Leah crying in the other room broke their staring contest. Anne pushed away from the table. "I'll get her."

Joseph stood, too. "I'll warm her bottle."

"It's in the refrigerator."

"I figured it would be."

Anne rolled her eyes but didn't reply. At least he was being helpful even if he wasn't going to admit his fences were in poor repair.

After changing the baby and soothing her, Anne carried Leah into the kitchen. Joseph stood at her stove with a bottle of formula warming in a pan. When he saw her, he picked up the bottle and tested the milk by sprinkling some on his wrist. "It's still too cold."

Sitting in her chair, Anne noticed his half-eaten dessert. "You didn't finish your pie."

"I will. It's too good to waste. I wanted to get Leah's bottle ready first." He came back to the table and sat down across from her. He picked up his fork and took a bite.

"I'm glad you like it," Anne said. The atmosphere was strained. Leah seemed to notice and started fussing.

Joseph looked up from his plate. "Do you want me to hold her?"

"She's fine."

"She likes to be up on your shoulder."

Now he was going to tell her how to hold a baby! Why on earth had she said she would work for him? Wanting to prove to him that no matter how she held Leah, the child was still going to fuss until she got fed, Anne lifted the babe to her shoulder. To her surprise, Leah quieted immediately.

"I figured out that she likes to look around."

Leah was holding her own head up. It bobbed slightly, but her eyes were wide and interested. "I think you're right," Anne admitted.

"That was hard to say, wasn't it?" He swallowed the last piece of his pie and returned to the stove.

Choosing to ignore his jab, Anne took the opportunity to finish her own pie. After testing the formula again, he brought the bottle to her. "Have you any chores that need doing?"

Only essential work was done on Sunday. Anything in her garden would have to wait until the next day. "If you could feed Daisy, I would appreciate it."

"Daisy?"

"My horse." Anne gave Leah the bottle. The baby grabbed it with both hands and began sucking vigorously.

"I can take care of your animal. I'll be back after the evening milking."

"All right. Leah and I will see you then."

He started out the door, but paused and looked over his shoulder. "The lunch was good. *Danki.*"

As a compliment, it wasn't much, but she accepted it at face value. She smiled brightly at him. "You're welcome, Joseph. I'm glad you enjoyed it."

Nodding to her, he left and closed the door behind him.

Anne grinned at Leah. "He's a hard man to like, but I think he's growing on me."

Anne Stoltzfus was an annoying woman.

Striding toward her barn, Joseph tried to get the picture of her smiling at him out of his mind. The sight of her pretty lips parted just so and the sparkle in her eyes sent an awareness shooting through his chest and made his heart beat harder. It was an uncomfortable sensation.

He wasn't a foolish youth. He'd had women smile at him before. Ellen Beachy, Elizabeth Fisher, Saloma Hochstetler, they were neighbors and single women. They smiled at him whenever they chanced to meet, but they didn't make his head swim like this. What was different about Anne?

He opened the barn door and stepped into the dark interior.

Maybe it wasn't Anne. Maybe he was coming down with something. He pressed the back of his hand to his forehead and was disappointed by the coolness of his skin. He wasn't sick. He couldn't blame it on a fever.

Offering her a job might have been a mistake. He found a pitchfork and began throwing hay to her elderly mare.

"*Nay*, Leah needs a *kindt heedah*." He couldn't do it alone. Not until Leah was older.

He stabbed the fork into the ground. What was he thinking? Fannie would return soon. She would be back for her child. He had to believe that.

Anne was the most logical choice for the job until then. She lived close by. She knew as much about babies as anyone. Anne with the pretty smile.

Stop thinking about her lips.

He lifted the fork and began pitching hay with a vengeance. He wasn't attracted to Anne. "I'm tired. That's all. I'm imagining things."

They had lived next door to one another for three years and he'd never once had a romantic thought about her. Just the opposite, in fact. She was annoying and fussy. She hated his goats.

He couldn't like a woman who hated his goats.

After finishing with Anne's horse, he went home and cleaned his kitchen. A neat house was something he enjoyed. Everything had a place and he liked everything in its place. Since Leah's arrival, he hadn't found a moment to tidy up. Anne must think he was a slob. He'd have to have her over soon so that she could see he wasn't.

He shook his head. It didn't matter what Anne thought of him. Her job was to take care of Leah.

He took full advantage of the baby's absence and scrubbed the floor and counters, consoling himself with the thought that it was necessary work on a Sunday and all good housewives would agree.

Necessary to keep his mind off Anne and how she was getting along with the baby.

After he was done, he sat down to read from the Scriptures and from his well-worn copy of the *Martyrs Mirror*, a book that documented the stories and testimonies of Christian martyrs from the time of Christ to the 1600s. The trials endured by those people of faith gave him the courage to face the difficulties in his own life. Normally, he could immerse himself in the pages of the Holy Book or the *Martyrs Mirror* for several hours. But not today. He kept glancing at the mantel clock.

He milked at six o'clock in the evening, but by four thirty he gave up trying to read and went out to his milking shed. The goats filed into their stanchions, happy to see him even if he was early. By five thirty he had milked all eighty does, cleaned his equipment and made sure he had two gallons of fresh milk to take to Anne.

He retreated to his small office, a room partitioned in one corner of the barn where he kept his records, medical supplies and a propane-burning stove to warm the room in the winter. A brown leather office chair with the arms worn bare sat in front of a scarred metal desk and two filing cabinets. He made notations about the day's milk production and tallied his total gallons for the week. The herd's overall production was staying steady in spite of his neglect.

He left his office and carried the pails to the gate leading to Anne's property. As he opened it, he caught sight of Chester working his way under the wire near the back of Anne's barn. Leaving both pails by the fence, Joseph moved to stand over Chester until the animal had wiggled through. Taking the buck by the horn, he scolded him and led the culprit home. Instead of putting him back in his pen, Joseph shut the animal inside the barn in an empty stall.

"You stay in this time. I don't want that woman harping about your damages again. I've heard enough."

Chester bleated once, turned around twice and lay down in the straw. His attitude said he was home for the moment but not for good.

"Okay, I will put up new fencing but only to keep you alive. She's going to plant rhubarb."

Chester bleated again.

Joseph returned to his milk pails and carried them the rest of the way to Anne's house. He opened the door and paused at the sight of her rocking Leah in her arms and singing. She hadn't heard him enter. The soft smile on Anne's face, the light in her eyes, cut his breath short and made his heart flip over.

He couldn't like a woman who hated goats. He couldn't.

So what was this feeling?

Chapter Eight

Anne glanced up to see Joseph standing at the door with a steel pail in each hand. He had the oddest expression on his face. As if he'd never seen her before and didn't know who she was.

"You're back already?"

His expression quickly changed to his normal frown. "I finished early. What do you want me to do with this milk?"

"Set it on the table. Are you still willing to show me how to make cheese?" She wasn't sure what was wrong, but she sensed he was upset about something. Had she done something wrong or was he always this grumpy?

He took a deep breath and managed a half smile. "If you're willing to teach me how to make Leah's formula."

"Absolutely. Hold her while I get my pans ready."

After putting the milk on the table, he turned to her and she gingerly transferred the baby to his arms. Standing close to him brought a rush of heat to her face. Stepping back quickly, Anne regained her composure. She didn't normally react this way. She'd handed dozens of men their newborn babies. Why did being near Joseph fluster her? Perhaps it was because she felt sorry for him.

That had to be it. He was ill equipped to take care of the baby. His only sister had disappointed him again and was making his life difficult. If becoming Leah's father was the path God had chosen for Joseph, Anne would do all she could to help him.

"Shall we make cheese first, or shall we make formula?" she asked without looking at him.

He sat down in the rocker. It creaked under his weight but held. "Makes no difference to me. The cheese is probably simpler."

"How do I start?"

"You need four quarts of goat's milk and a good pinch of salt. I like to use minced or dried onions to flavor mine. Then you add one-third cup of distilled white vinegar or lemon juice. It doesn't matter which. I like using lemon juice."

"That's it?" Somehow she'd imagined it would be much more complex.

"I told you it was easy. Bring the milk to a slow boil at 180 to 185 degrees. Be careful not to scorch it. Add the dried onion and salt. Once the milk really starts bubbling, turn off the heat and pour in the vinegar. After that, you wait for the milk to curdle, then pour it through a colander lined with two layers of cheesecloth. Wrap the ends of the cheesecloth together and let it hang for an hour and a half or until all the whey drips off."

"What about saving the whey?"

"I close the ends of the cheesecloth with a rubber band and then slip a long-handled wooden spoon through it and suspend my cheese in a big jar. I keep the whey to make soup stock. Once the cheese is cool, you can add any spices that you like, shape the cheese into a ball or a log and refrigerate it. It will keep for a week."

"I'm anxious to try some." She set about heating the milk and before long she had her cheesecloth-and-curd bundle suspended and dripping into a widemouthed jar. By this time, Leah was sound asleep, so Joseph laid her in the laundry-basket crib and joined Anne by the stove.

Anne gave him an apologetic look. "I wish the formula making was as easy."

"I'm not afraid to learn something new. I will master it."

He had the right attitude. She laid a sheet of paper on the counter. "You have to heat the milk and add a number of ingredients such as cod liver oil, vitamins, blackstrap molasses, yeast and others. I've written down the recipe and the steps. I'll let you go ahead and make it while I watch. If you are confused or need help, I'm here."

It was dark outside and for the next hour, they worked by lantern light in Anne's kitchen to finish the project. Even she had to admit that he mastered the process quickly. After cleaning and boiling the baby bottles and nipples, they filled a dozen with eight ounces of liquid each. Joseph glanced at the clock. "It's getting late."

"I know it is time-consuming, but you can make enough to last her three days in a single batch."

"I meant I should be getting home. It isn't proper for me to be in your house this late."

It wasn't likely that anyone would see them together, but he was right. She appreciated his thoughtfulness. "I will keep Leah with me tonight."

"Are you sure?"

"You could use an uninterrupted night's sleep."

"What if you have to go out on a call?"

"Leah can go with me."

Joseph shook his head as a chill raced down his spine. "I don't like the idea of her traveling in a buggy at night. The *Englisch* drive too fast. It's dangerous."

"Were your parents killed at night?"

So she knew about that. It shouldn't have surprised him. It had happened before she moved in, but it was common knowledge. "*Ja*, it was dark. The truck didn't see us until it was too late."

"I am sorry for your loss."

"It was a long time ago. It was *Gottes* will."

She laid a hand on his arm. "Knowing that doesn't ease the pain of losing someone you love."

Joseph felt the warmth of her touch even through the material of his sleeve. The kindness and understanding in her eyes brought a lump to his throat. "It should help. We must believe in *Gottes* plan."

"We do believe, but we must also grieve, for that is how He made us. There is no shame in our tears."

"You have lost someone?"

He sensed her hesitation. Finally, she said, "My mother and my father have been called home, too. They lived long and devout lives and they were ready to face *Gott*."

He didn't know if his parents and Beth had been ready or not. He hoped they had been. He'd simply frozen when the headlights blinded him. He hadn't thought about God. His only thought had been that he didn't want to die. He swallowed hard to clear his throat. "I was driving that night."

"It would not have mattered, Joseph. It wasn't your time."

It should have been.

The moment the thought crossed his mind, he pushed it aside. God was not finished with him. He still had an unknown purpose to fulfill. Maybe it was to raise Leah. He hoped not. Leah needed her mother. He was a poor substitute.

"I must go. *Guten nacht*, Anne Stoltzfus. I will move more pumpkins to your stand for you in the morning if you'll show me which ones you want." In spite of his discomfort at being near her, he didn't want to leave. She had a peaceful quality that eased the ache in his soul.

Chuckling, she said, "Just pick the orange ones, Joseph. As many as you can find."

She was laughing at him again. He hardened his heart, determined not to like her.

He was meant to be alone. He had accepted that long ago in the months after Fannie left the first time. To care for someone was to invite heartache. It was better to keep the world at bay. Especially a pretty *maidel* with a kind heart and a smile that lit up her eyes like stars twinkling in the night sky.

Angered at the direction of his thoughts, he turned and left. Later that night, as he tried to make his tired mind stop spinning, he found himself remembering each moment of their evening together. Sighing, he punched his pillow into a more comfortable position and turned over. The moonlight bathed his room in a pale glow. The box he had used as a bed for Leah sat empty. He missed her presence. Was she keeping Anne up?

He rose and stepped to the window that overlooked her home a few hundred yards to the north. It was dark. Leah must be sleeping and he should be, too.

He was about to return to bed when he saw a light come on in Anne's upstairs window. After a few moments, the lantern light moved down to the kitchen. He watched until the first-floor light went out and the upstairs window grew bright again.

It was easy to imagine Anne holding Leah and singing to her in a low sweet voice as the baby gobbled up her nighttime bottle. Leah would be making faces and Anne would be grinning at her. Anne had the patience he lacked. She was good with the child.

Why hadn't she married? Why wasn't she a wife and a mother? Was it because of her job? Most Amish women stopped working outside the home once they married, but the local midwife was often the exception to the rule. They were nearly always married women or widows.

He'd lived next to Anne for three years and yet he knew next to nothing about her. Maybe it was time he put aside his need for privacy and got to know her better. She would be caring for Leah until Fannie came back. In the dead of night, he couldn't push aside the fear he kept at bay during daylight. The fear that Fannie wouldn't return. Ever.

He didn't want to believe the words she'd written. He needed to believe she would have a change of heart. He'd never give up on her. Not even now. As he did every night, he prayed for her. Bowing his head, he asked God to send her the comfort she needed. It was with a heavy heart that he returned to his bed, but he had the consolation of knowing Leah was being cared for by someone with a kind, gentle nature.

The next morning, he finished his milking early and headed to Anne's place. He opened the front door and was greeted by the smell of cinnamon toast and frying bacon. Leah lay on a bright quilt in the center of the kitchen floor. Holding herself up on her elbows, she kicked her feet as she tried to reach a pair of yellow plastic measuring cups in front of her. She was making little cooing sounds.

"You can wash up at this sink. Breakfast will be ready in about five minutes. Do you want coffee or orange juice or both?" Anne asked over her shoulder.

"I didn't expect you to feed me."

"There are a lot of pumpkins to move. You will need your strength. Besides, it doesn't take much more effort to make breakfast for two instead of one."

He washed his hands and then squatted on his heels beside Leah. He moved one of the measuring cups closer. She grasped it in her chubby fingers and pulled it to her mouth. "Just *coffe* for me. She seems happy this morning."

"*Ja*, she does. She only woke up once last night and she went right back to sleep after she ate."

Leah rolled onto her back and grinned at him as she chewed on the handle of her prize. "Is that tasty?" he asked. The baby gurgled in reply and he smiled. "I think she is trying to talk to me."

"Babies this age like to interact with others."

"I thought they just ate, slept and needed their diapers changed."

"They do that, too. I have sweetened some of the cheese we made with honey and lemon peel. It tastes wonderful on warm toast." She carried a platter of bacon to the table.

"I told you it was good."

He took a seat and lifted Leah to his lap. She kicked in delight and cast her plastic cup aside. He retrieved it and gave it back to her. Grinning, she dropped it again. He picked it up. "You did that on purpose."

She gnawed on the lip for a second, then dropped it again and giggled. Anne sat down at the table. "You two seem to have discovered a new game."

"I can't believe the difference in her. She did nothing but whimper and cry and fuss for me."

"It wasn't you. She was hungry but in pain every time she ate. She was miserable. Hopefully, those days are behind her."

He settled Leah in his lap and folded her hands inside his as he said a silent blessing before eating. It was the way Amish parents taught their children to behave at the table. Although Leah was too young to understand, she would come to know that sitting quietly with her hands folded was expected of her. When he finished praying, he shifted her to the crook of his left arm. The baby discovered his suspenders and began trying to bring the stretchy material to her mouth.

"I can take her," Anne offered.

"*Nay,* she is fine where she is. What are your plans for today?" He enjoyed watching Leah struggle with the elastic material. An adorable frown formed on her face when it got away from her, but she grabbed it again.

Anne said, "The last week of October is my busiest time. I will sell the bulk of my pumpkins in the next few days, so I have to be at the stand as much as possible. I need you to bring all my pumpkins out of the field. I'll take Leah's laundry-hamper bed up to the shack and she can stay there with me as long as the weather stays decent."

"I heard it may rain tomorrow."

"I hope not. Bad weather means fewer shoppers. The leaves and vines are very prickly, so wear gloves when you go into the field. It will keep you from getting itchy."

"I appreciate the advice. Anything else I should know?"

"When you cut them off the vines, leave a stem about four to six inches long, but don't try to carry them by the stems. They'll break."

"Got it."

Leah gave up on his suspender and threw her cup on the floor again. Joseph sighed heavily as he picked it up. He hesitated but decided to give it to her. She grinned and cooed her delight. For such a smile, he could pick up her toy all day long.

Please, Lord, let her remain as happy and contented as she is at this moment.

After breakfast he helped Anne move the supplies she and Leah needed up to the small shack she had at the end of her lane. There were already two cars parked at the side of the road and a number of small children examining the pumpkins. He left Anne to deal with her customers and took her small wheelbarrow out into the pumpkin patch. She hadn't been kidding about the prickly vines and leaves. What she'd forgotten to mention was how easy it was to get tripped while trying to carry a ten- or fifteen-pound pumpkin out of the vines to the wheelbarrow. By his third foray into the field, he decided he would use his own pushcart the following day. It was larger and easier to move.

The next day went by much like the day before, although he fixed his own breakfast. He had agreed to work in her fields in exchange for her services as Leah's nanny. He hadn't agreed to be fed. He left Leah with Anne before sunup while he did his chores and then he returned to help her move more pumpkins and produce to her stand.

Anne cleaned and polished the orange fruit and arranged them according to size on several tables. Traffic was light but steady throughout the morning. With each large pumpkin Anne sold, she gave away a small one and a sheet of paper.

"What are you handing out?" he asked when her latest customer drove away.

"It's my recipe for homemade pumpkin pie and for roasted pumpkin seeds. I'm hoping folks will enjoy them and come back for more of my cooking pumpkins next year."

"That's a *goot* idea. A way to provide customers with more than they expected and a way to encourage repeat business. I'm impressed."

"Danki." She smiled her thanks at him and blushed sweetly.

A flutter of pleasure deep in his chest caught him by surprise. When had this foolishness overtaken him? He had been fetching toys to make Leah smile at him and now he was handing out compliments in order to make Anne smile, too.

He had to admit he was beginning to like Anne. There was something about her that made him want to please her. It was more than her care of Leah. It was the way she seemed to care about him, too. A smile spread over his face. He sensed a friendship growing between them and he liked the feeling.

A pair of buggies approached, so he wiped the grin off his face. Leah started to fuss as she woke up. He and Anne both dropped down to pick her up and bumped their heads together in the process.

He shot to his feet. Anne did, too, but she stepped on the hem of her long skirt and stumbled forward into him. He caught her in his arms. He steadied her until she regained her balance. She stepped back quickly, her face flushed a bright red. He apologized. "I'm so sorry."

Rubbing her forehead, she said, "It's okay. I'm not hurt. Much."

He caught a glimpse of Preacher David Hostetler and his sons scowling at him as they drove past. He chose to ignore them. "I've been accused of having a hard head."

Anne chuckled. "So have I, but I think you win. I'm going to get a bottle for Leah. You can hold her."

He picked the baby up. As Anne walked down the lane, his gaze followed her. There was a soft sway in her walk that he found attractive. There were a lot of things he was finding attractive about his neighbor. Why hadn't he noticed them before?

He bounced Leah in his arms, keeping her occupied by making faces at her until he saw Anne returning.

Before she reached him, a horse and wagon came down the road and drew to a stop in front of the stand. Naomi Beiler was driving, but two other women sat beside her. He recognized them as widows from his church group. Behind her came Simeon Shetler driving his two-wheeled cart loaded with boxes and baskets. Dinah Plank sat beside him. Simeon had lost a leg in an accident as a young man. Now a grandfather, he got along well on his crutches. He could often be seen driving his cart and palomino pony named Butterscotch, the only animal in the area more notorious for escaping his pen than Chester.

Naomi leaned toward Joseph. "Is that your niece? What a pretty *bubbel*. Anne has told us all about your wayward sister and how she has burdened you with her child. You have our sympathy, brother."

Humiliation burned like acid in Joseph's belly. Gritting his teeth until the muscles in his jaw ached, he snatched the bottle from Anne's hand as he glared at her. "You didn't waste any time spreading gossip about me behind my back, did you?"

Chapter Nine

Anne saw the fury in Joseph's eyes, but underneath his anger, she saw his pain, too. She had hurt him. How could she fix this? "It wasn't like that, Joseph. I wasn't spreading gossip. These women have come to help."

"I told you I don't need anyone's help." He stomped away and Anne realized what a dreadful mistake she had made.

Naomi stepped down from her wagon. "Is everything all right? Have I said something that I shouldn't have?"

"*Nay*, this was my mistake. I didn't tell Joseph that you were coming. I meant to, but I just didn't expect you so soon. Joseph is embarrassed by his sister's behavior. I think he feels he is to blame for raising her poorly."

"We all feel shame when our children disappoint us. Even a child raised in a righteous household can stray. *Gott* granted every man and woman a free will, and so they must use it to find their way to Him or to reject Him. What do you want us to do with the things we have collected? Our community has been very generous."

"They always are. Let's take the things to Joseph's

house. He will soon realize our intention is to help, not to criticize."

Anne walked to Simeon's cart. "Dinah, if you could stay here at the stand and take care of any customers, I'll show the others where to put things."

"Of course, dear." The widow smiled warmly at Simeon and got out of his cart.

Anne accepted his hand and took Dinah's place on the front seat. "One pretty gal after another riding in my cart today. I'm a blessed man."

Simeon was known as a bit of a flirt, but he was a kind man and he would never cross the lines of propriety. Like some others, Anne had begun to suspect Simeon and Dinah were becoming more than friends. It would be a good match for the widow and widower. After turning his pony around, Simeon led the small procession down Joseph's lane and stopped in front of his house.

Joseph and Leah were nowhere in sight. Anne helped everyone carry in the supplies and furniture. To her amazement, the inside of Joseph's home was spotless. All the dishes had been washed and put away. She could tell the kitchen counters and floor had been scrubbed. It was quite a change from the last time she had stepped inside his home.

She directed the women to put the crib and a small dresser in Joseph's living room. He could move it elsewhere if he didn't like the placement. The women folded and placed all the baby clothes and blankets in the dresser drawers and put clean sheets on the crib mattress. The basket of a dozen baby bottles and rubber nipples was left on the kitchen counter. A second basket, a woven Moses basket made to carry the baby around, held an assortment of infant toys. Rattles, colored stacking blocks and a teething ring were but a few of the items in it.

There were also a half-dozen boxes of infant rice cereal and baby food that Leah wouldn't need for a few more months, but when she did, Joseph would be well supplied. Looking over the generosity of the community moved Anne to add something of her own.

She went home and climbed up into her attic. She opened a chest there, withdrew a paper-wrapped parcel and returned to Joseph's place. After everyone filed out of the house, Anne pulled off the wrapper and laid her contribution, a beautifully stitched baby quilt, over the end of the oak crib. She gently smoothed the wrinkles from the material. As she did, her thoughts turned to her own baby. For a minute her regret and grief were so intense she almost broke down. Joseph had no idea how blessed he was to have Leah, but she did. Blowing out a deep breath, she straightened her shoulders and went outside.

She walked over to Naomi's wagon and spoke to the women seated there. "*Danki.* I'm sorry Joseph isn't here to thank you himself, but he will soon realize what a wonderful community he lives in. I hope your generosity opens his heart to the goodness that surrounds him."

Naomi nodded. "I will not let him struggle to raise this child alone as I did when Fannie was small."

"We will all do better," Simeon said as he held out a hand to help Anne into his cart again. She climbed up. He turned the pony and sent the animal trotting up the lane. At her roadside stand, she thanked Dinah for taking care of her customers and waved as the group drove away.

The early part of the afternoon went by slowly. With

only two customers in the next two hours, Anne was left
with plenty of time to think about Joseph. She would
find a way to apologize to him. She should have listened
to that small voice of unease that tapped on her shoulder after the church service, but she hadn't. She hadn't
felt that she was betraying his trust when she shared his
story, but it was clear he felt she had gossiped behind
his back. Had she lost his trust for good?

Would he let her continue to care for Leah? Or would
he find someone else? Anne was distressed to realize
just how much she would miss the baby if he decided to
replace her with a different *kindt heedah*.

And that was exactly why she shouldn't have taken
the job in the first place.

Maybe it would be for the best if he did find someone else. The longer she took care of Leah, the harder it
would be to let someone else take over.

"Can you watch her while I milk?"

Anne spun around at the sound of Joseph's voice. She
hadn't heard his approach. He wore a wary expression
and held the baby in his arms. She was wide-awake but
content to suck on her fingers.

"Of course I can. That was our agreement."

"Danki." He handed the baby to her.

Anne struggled to quell the rush of breathlessness
being close to him inspired. He stepped back quickly
and shoved his hands in the pockets of his dark jacket.
He wouldn't look at her.

The easy camaraderie they had shared that morning
was gone. Only an awkward silence remained.

"Joseph, I'm sorry. I didn't mean to embarrass you.
I wanted to help you and Leah."

"You should have told me to expect them."

"*Ja*, I should have. I honestly intended to do so. I wasn't expecting them to show up this morning. Naomi can move mountains when she sets her mind on something. She feels very badly that she wasn't around to help you with Fannie when she was young."

"We managed."

"I know you did, but you deserved more help than you were given. I know Bishop Beiler was ill then, but did he visit you?"

"I went to see him."

"What did he say?"

"The truth."

"I don't understand."

Joseph sighed deeply. "The driver that hit us claimed the accident was my fault. He said he wanted me to pay for the damage to his vehicle or his insurance company would take my father's farm. My farm. I didn't have that kind of money, but I agreed to pay him over time. I took a second job working for him to pay off the debt. It was hard to keep food on the table in those first months. I went to the bishop to ask if Fannie could be placed with another family until I got on my feet. Bishop Beiler told me raising Fannie was my duty. She was my responsibility and I wasn't to foster her off on someone else so that my life would be easier."

Anne flinched. It had been a harsh thing to say to a grieving young man. "I'm sorry he misunderstood what you needed."

Joseph drew himself up straight. "I know my duty. I will care for Leah until her mother returns."

"And I have agreed to help you. That hasn't changed… unless you wish to fire me."

Watching the struggle going on behind his eyes was

painful for Anne. It wasn't pride that kept him from seeking help. It was a misplaced belief that he needed to do it alone.

She wasn't going to let him. If he needed to believe she was helping only because of their business arrangement, so be it.

Gesturing to her display, she said, "I will need at least two dozen of the biggest pumpkins brought up here first thing in the morning. Do you think you could build a shelf to display them? Something at eye level for the children. The *Englisch* parents seem to want the *kinner* to pick out their own pumpkins. Do you have any ideas?"

He studied her for a moment, then pushed his hat back with one finger and surveyed what space she had. "If I brought up some straw bales, I could lay a couple of planks across them. That would put your pumpkins about waist high. Would that work?"

"That would be perfect. Finish the milking, Joseph, and I'll bring Leah to your house when I'm done here. Have you been inside the house since noon?"

The wary expression returned to his eyes. "*Nay*, I've not."

"The church ladies left some infant items for you to use. Just until Fannie returns. They'll be back to pick them up when you don't need them anymore. It's a loan, Joseph."

"I still wish you hadn't said anything."

She gave him an apologetic look. "I shouldn't have spoken without your permission. I'm sorry I upset you, but it was for Leah's sake."

His scowl remained, but he didn't comment. Could he forgive her interference? Anne gazed at the baby in her arms. "She deserves a better bed than my laundry basket, and now she has one."

"Until Fannie returns."

"Until her *mudder* returns," Anne agreed. She saw a car slowing down as it approached and knew she was about to have another customer.

Joseph pulled a bottle from his coat pocket and held it out. "I thought she might get hungry again before my chores were done."

"Danki." Anne's fingers brushed across his as she took the bottle.

Her soft touch sent a wave of warmth flooding through Joseph. As much as he wanted to stay angry with her, he couldn't. He knew she had Leah's best interests at heart. She didn't believe he could care for the baby alone and maybe she was right. Wasn't that what he feared? He'd certainly done a miserable job so far.

Maybe if she had been around when Fannie was small, things would have turned out differently for his sister. Fannie had needed someone like Anne. Someone to be a mother to her. Maybe he should have married for her sake.

He pushed the thought aside. He couldn't change the past.

When a car pulled to a stop beside them, he left Anne to speak with her customer and went to milk his goats for the second time that day. He'd spent very little time with his animals in the past few days and they gathered around him now when he entered the pen. Matilda rushed to his side and butted him gently in greeting. He paused to scratch behind her ear and murmur a few kind words. More of the young does came seeking attention, too.

He knew each one of them by name, who their dames were and who their grandmothers had been, and how much milk they produced each day. The goats had kept Fannie and him fed during the lean times after their parents and Beth were killed. Then the goats became his life after Fannie left. He'd lavished his affection on them because there'd been no one else to receive it. Until now. Now he had Leah. The thought made him as frightened as he had been when he realized he would have to raise Fannie. More so. A babe Leah's age required almost constant attention.

Matilda butted him again when he stopped petting her. He gave her a wry smile. "You are right to be jealous, but don't worry. Leah will soon be big enough to visit you and bring you apples and cereal when I'm not looking."

Just as Fannie had done. Did she miss them at all?

He couldn't imagine his life without the goats' playful, happy personalities greeting him each day. Their affection never wavered. They might wander away, but they always came home.

In a nearby pen, the young rams started showing off, jumping on the large boulders he'd piled together for them to climb on and play around. He would sell them in the spring. Their mothers were among his best milk producers and that bloodline would command a good price from other goat dairymen looking to expand their herds. Joseph hated to sell any of his goats for meat, but sometimes he had to do so.

He spent an extra thirty minutes with his animals, checking for any injuries or illness he might have overlooked in the past hectic week. They were all healthy. Only Chester was sulking because he was still penned in the barn. He refused to greet Joseph until fresh hay appeared over the stall door. Where food was concerned, Chester had a forgiving nature and he sprang to his feet and rushed to be fed. Joseph scratched the old fellow behind his ears, too.

When he couldn't put it off any longer, Joseph walked up to the house. Anne was there ahead of him. She was holding Leah on her hip as she stirred something on the stove with her free hand.

"I had some leftover vegetable soup that I thought you might like for supper."

"You don't have to feed me. That wasn't part of our bargain."

"I know, but I hated to throw it out. Normally, I'd take it into the Beachy Craft Shop and store it in my freezer there, but I didn't feel like making a trip into town this late in the evening."

As excuses went, it was a little lame, but the delicious smell was enticing enough to keep him from complaining further. "I have electricity in my barn. If you ever want to move your freezer closer, you could put it out there."

"With the goats?" She wrinkled her nose.

"I have an office in there. The goats don't go in that part of the barn."

"I thank you for the offer. I'll consider it."

He noticed the basket on the counter beside her. "Is this what the church donated?"

"Some of it." She kept her eyes averted.

Her friendly smile was missing and he hated that. Shame kept him from apologizing, as he knew he should.

Being the object of charity stung. It was vain pride and he knew it. He opened the lid of the basket. "I reckon I'd better see what they provided to this poor, needy man."

Pulling out the bottles, he counted them. Twelve. It would be easy to make enough formula to fill them and have them handy in the refrigerator. A second large box sitting beside the counter was full of disposable diapers and several packages of cloth ones, as well as baby wipes. A true blessing. He opened a third box and held up a package with the picture of a grinning baby on it. "What is this?"

"Rice cereal. She's too young for it yet. Most *mudders* start cereal when the babe is six or eight months old."

"And the baby food in jars?"

"Also when she is about six to eight months old. It varies. Always start with a single food in case she has a reaction to it."

"Do you think she'll have trouble with these since she can't tolerate cow's milk?"

"There isn't any way to know. She might outgrow her problem or she might not. There are some more items in your living room." Her tone was clipped, professional, as if she were talking to a stranger. She wasn't smiling. He missed her smile.

He entered the living room and saw a beautifully crafted sleigh-style baby crib against the wall by his sofa. A dresser of the same rich oak finish sat beside it. They had both been polished to a high sheen. A bumper pad and sheets in pale yellow completed the set. Over the end of the bed hung a small puffy crazy quilt with blocks and triangles in primary colors. He ran his fingers lightly over the padded fabric and marveled at the tiny neat stitches.

"There are some extra sheets and clothes for her in the dresser drawers," Anne said from behind him.

He swallowed against the lump in his throat. "This is more than I expected. It was a nice thing for folks to do. I'll take good care of it all."

"I know you will, Joseph," she said quietly.

He was afraid to meet her gaze. Afraid he wouldn't see her smile. He wanted to apologize for his harsh words earlier that afternoon, but something kept him silent. Anne didn't understand. Leah was his responsibility, not hers, not the church's, his.

Anne slipped past him and laid Leah in the crib. They stood side by side watching the baby drift off to sleep. When Leah was settled, Anne said, "Good night, Joseph."

She left the house before he could think of some way to stop her.

He ate his supper alone, already missing Anne's presence. There was something special in the air when she was near. The autumn evening was cooler without the warmth she radiated.

Later that night, as he stood at his bedroom window and watched the lights go out in her home, he wondered what she thought of him. Was she angry? She had the right to be. He'd accused her of spreading gossip behind his back. If only he could call back those words.

He didn't want his relationship with her to return to the way it had been. Distant. Cool.

He didn't have many friends. He didn't want to lose Anne's friendship. How could he earn it back?

Chapter Ten

The following morning, Joseph found it was easier to care for Leah when he could safely leave her in the crib while he prepared his breakfast and got her morning bottle ready. She was delighted with the new toy he'd found for her, hard plastic keys that clacked when she shook them. They kept her occupied and quiet for the twenty minutes he needed.

After feeding her, he put her in the stroller on his front porch and pushed her to Anne's house. Dawn was just breaking. The eastern sky was streaked with bands of high pink clouds. The forecasted rain was holding off, but it was already cooler than the day before. Anne wasn't in the kitchen and there was no answer when he called up the stairs. Had she gone out to deliver a baby?

Stepping back on her front porch, he saw her mare in the corral, so he knew she hadn't driven anywhere. Maybe she was already up at her roadside stand. Or was she avoiding him?

He dismissed the thought. She might choose to dodge him, but not Leah. He knew she genuinely cared for the baby. Movement out in her garden caught his eye, and he saw she was loading her rickety wheelbarrow with dried stalks of corn. He walked in her direction, unsure of his reception. She wore a dark blue jacket over a dress of the same color and a black apron. The ribbons of her white prayer *kapp* were tied behind her neck.

"Good morning, Joseph, and good morning to you, too, Leah," Anne called out when she caught sight of them. Her smile seemed a little forced, but he was relieved to see it, anyway.

"What are you doing with those?" he asked, gesturing to the corn.

She brushed her gloved hands together. "I'm making some decorative bundles to sell. A woman who came by late yesterday asked for some. I told her I would have them ready this morning and she promised to be back."

He shook his head. "Decorative bundles of corn. It seems like a waste of good livestock feed to me."

"To me as well, but who can fathom the ways of the *Englisch*?" She began pushing the wheelbarrow toward the house.

He fell into step beside her. The large wheels of Leah's stroller rolled easily over the dry ground. "I should be able to gather the rest of your pumpkins this morning."

"I'm thrilled with how many I have sold, but I need to sell many more. Thursday is the last day of the month and the last day I will be open this season. I'm not sorry to see the end of October, but November will be busy, too."

"With produce?"

"*Nay*, with weddings and babies. I have three mothers due next month. Speaking of babies, how did Leah do last night?"

"We had our best night yet. She woke once, at two in the morning, took her bottle and went right back to sleep. I think she likes her crib."

"That's good to hear." Anne cast him a covert glance, but he saw it.

"I like it, too. It makes it easier to change her and I don't have to worry about her turning the laundry hamper over and rolling out."

"Has she done that?"

"Once," he admitted. "She rolled to one side and it tipped." He didn't mention that he'd had her on the sofa at the time and had barely caught her before she'd tumbled off.

"Then the crib is safer. I didn't realize she could turn over that well."

"She's strong." He stopped by Anne's porch. "I'll take your corn to your stand and then I'll get the rest of your pumpkins."

"I'll take Leah to the stand with me later. I have a mother coming for a checkup soon. Has Leah eaten this morning?"

"*Ja*, she had her bottle. We'll need to make more formula this evening. She's going through it fast."

"I'm just happy we discovered what was wrong with her." Anne crouched down to wipe the drool from Leah's face with the corner of her apron.

It was past time for his apology. He crossed his arms over his chest. "You have done a lot for us."

"Only my Christian duty."

"And I have been remiss in mine. I was wrong to accuse you of gossip. I know you thought you were doing what was best for Leah."

Anne rose to her feet. Her cheeks grew bright pink.

"I'm glad you realize that. I wouldn't hurt you for the world, Joseph."

"I reckon I can be stubborn as my goats sometimes. I see that I should have asked the community for help instead of struggling on my own."

"You have given to others many times in the years that I've known you. When John Beachy had that fire, you came to help. When Mary and David Blauch needed money for their son's medical bills, you gave. There's no shame in accepting help in return. It is what binds us together, our faith and knowing our church and neighbors will rally around us in times of need. We all need help at some point. We all give help when we can."

When she put it that way, it felt less like charity. "You're right. I was wrong."

Her eyes widened as she slapped a hand to her cheek. "Did I hear you correctly?"

He struggled not to smile and lost the battle. "Gloat if you must. You'll not hear that from me often."

Chuckling, she tickled Leah under the chin. "There is hope for your *onkel* yet. It's a wise man who admits his faults."

"It's a wiser woman who does not point them out," he shot back.

Laughing, Anne pushed the child toward her house. She glanced over her shoulder and he saw the bright smile he had been missing. It blew away the chill of the autumn morning and brought warmth to his heart.

Joseph lingered a moment as Anne went inside. She was a wise and kind woman. Hardworking and devout in her faith, she would make a fine mother and wife for any man. Once again he thought it was a shame she had never married. Although he wondered why she remained single, he didn't question her. That was too personal a subject.

After taking her corn up to the road stand for her, he returned to milk his herd and finish his morning chores. He rushed through his milking and cleaning. As he fed the bucks, he saw one of the young ones had a foot caught in the fence. It took a while to free him. By then the milk tanker driver had arrived and Joseph helped him empty the holding tank.

With that done, he went out to Anne's field and got to work. A short time later, he saw a buggy drive up to her house. A woman with a couple of children went inside. That had to be one of her mothers. He wasn't able to tell who it was. He was too far away. When he had the wheelbarrow full, he pushed it up to the house. He wasn't sure where Anne wanted the pumpkins stacked, so he stepped into the house to speak with her.

A little girl about five years old was trying to open Anne's large black leather satchel. She jumped away from it when she heard him come in, clasping her hands behind her back.

"What are you doing?" he asked.

"Nothing."

"It looks to me like you were getting into something that didn't belong to you."

She shook her head vigorously, making the ribbons of her *kapp* dance wildly. "I wasn't going to take anything. We already have one."

He eyed her suspiciously. "You already have what?"

"A new *bubbel*. Anne brought a little *brooder* to me last week. I just wanted to see how many more she had in her bag. I would rather have a sister if she has an extra one."

Joseph burst out laughing. "I'm afraid she doesn't have any more right now. You are going to have to keep your brother."

"Are you sure?"

"I'm sure."

The door to Anne's office opened, and she came out with a young woman who held a baby in her arms. He didn't recognize her. "I need to see the baby again in three weeks. Until then, enjoy him and have someone fetch me if you need anything else."

"I will, Anne. Have a nice day, and thanks for everything." The woman took her daughter by the hand and they left.

"I heard you laughing. What was so funny?"

"The little girl was trying to see how many more babies you have in your satchel."

Anne giggled. "Since Amish women don't discuss their pregnancies, the sudden appearance of a new sibling is sometimes confusing to children. I've had more than one try looking in my bag to see if I have others."

"I just stopped in to ask where you wanted your pumpkins stacked."

"Anywhere you want. It doesn't matter as long as they are close at hand for me. Can you bring a second load up, too?"

"I can." He left the house, unloaded what he had by the road and hurried back to the field. He was finally able to take a breather when he returned to the roadside stand with a second wheelbarrow full of freshly picked pumpkins. Anne was already there. He stopped in front of her and mopped the sweat from his brow on his sleeve.

* * *

Sitting inside the stand with Leah on her lap, Anne tipped her head as she regarded him. "Did you have trouble finding enough pumpkins?"

"*Nay*, only a little trouble with a goat this morning." He began unloading the wheelbarrow and stacked the pumpkins below the shelves in her stand.

"Nothing serious, I hope."

That made him pause in his work. He straightened with his hands on his hips. "Now you are worried about my goats? That's a switch."

She grinned. "Leah needs their milk. I will tolerate them because of that."

"You would like them all if you made the effort to get to know them."

"I'll take your word for it. Here comes a car. It's the first one all morning. I thought I would be busier, but maybe the folks that want pumpkins already have them." She was starting to worry that she wouldn't sell enough to cover her expenses for the season.

"Did the lady who wanted corn come back?"

Anne shook her head. "Not yet."

"Looks like your cornstalks will become livestock feed, after all. My goats will enjoy it."

"I'm not giving up on the lady. Keep your goats away until after November 1."

The car drove past without stopping. Anne's spirits drooped. "Don't bother picking more for now. We'll just have to haul them back if we don't sell them."

Sitting down on a straw bale beside her, he reached for Leah. "Don't give up. It's early yet."

She appreciated his encouragement. It was pleasant having company with her. Manning the stand was often a lonely task between customers. Having Joseph with her for companionship made the slow morning bearable.

More than bearable, Anne admitted. It was nice. They talked about a dozen different subjects. She had no idea he was interested in so many topics or that they liked so many of the same activities. He fished and so did she. He read books by many of the same authors she enjoyed. His goats might be his passion, but he was well-read and had an inquiring mind that surprised her. She was learning more than she ever thought possible about her reclusive neighbor. God had opened a door to Joseph using Leah as the key.

Two of their Amish neighbors drove past in their buggies. They waved but didn't stop. Anne waved back. Joseph didn't. She couldn't expect him to change completely overnight, but she was happy with the progress he had made.

The next vehicle that came down the road was their rural mail carrier. He leaned out his window with Anne's mail in his hand. "Morning, Miss Stoltzfus. I thought I should tell you that your sign by the highway is down. The county is working on the bridge just east of this road. It looks like they moved your sign to get their bulldozers down into the creek bed."

"Oh, dear. Perhaps that's why I haven't had any customers this morning. Thanks for letting me know, Mr. Potter."

"Don't mention it. Joseph, if I had known you were here, I would've brought your mail along."

Joseph perked up. "Was there a letter for me?"

"Nope. Just your newspaper and your *Goat World* magazine."

Anne watched the hope fade from Joseph's eyes. He

was still waiting to hear from his sister. It was a letter Anne feared would never come.

"Have a nice day, folks." With a wave, the mail carrier drove off.

Anne sat beside Joseph and held out her copy of the paper for him to read. "I wonder if I should shut down early."

He handed Leah to her and took the paper. "I think that would be hasty. The sign has been there since the spring. People will have seen it before. If they want fresh produce, they will come this way."

"I reckon you're right. I will just have to wait and see how it goes."

She spent the next half hour playing with Leah before the baby grew tired and slept in her arms. The lady who wanted cornstalks returned just before noon. She took all the ones Anne had cut, explaining that they were being used to decorate a grade-school classroom with a harvest theme. She took an assortment of gourds and pumpkins, too, making Anne grateful that she hadn't closed the stand.

Joseph finished reading the paper and folded it neatly. "Do you have a cell phone?"

"I keep one in my midwife kit in case of an emergency. Why?"

"I wanted to make a call, but I'll go down the road to the Mast farm and use theirs."

Their *Englisch* neighbor lived less than a quarter of a mile away. A kindhearted elderly man, he was always willing to let the Amish use his phone. He was the one who kept Anne's spare cell phone batteries charged for her.

Joseph took off down the road without an explanation

with the paper folded tightly in his hand. Anne spent the next hour cleaning the seeds from several of her over-ripe and damaged pumpkins. It was messy work, but she didn't mind. It was easiest to separate the seeds from the strands and mush by soaking them in a pail of water. The seeds floated to the top.

When Joseph returned, he grasped the handles of her wheelbarrow. "I'm going to gather a few more. You only have several dozen left in the field."

"You can if you wish, but I haven't sold a single one since you left."

"I think you'll sell all that you have." He had such a sly smile on his face that she had to wonder what he was up to.

By late afternoon Joseph had delivered three wheelbarrow loads of the orange fruit to the roadside. Anne chafed at wasting her time waiting for customers who didn't show up. She had plenty to do to keep her busy in the house. "I think we should close, Joseph."

"I'd like to wait a little longer."

"Suit yourself, but I'm ready to go back to the house and so is Leah." The baby had been good all afternoon, but she was growing restless. Anne picked her up.

"Here come your next customers." Joseph took Leah from her.

Anne saw two pickups headed toward them. She was surprised when they both stopped. A teenage boy rolled down the passenger's-side window. "Is this the Stoltzfus pumpkin patch?"

"It is," Joseph called out.

"Sweet. This is it, guys. Load them up and be careful. We can't chunk broken ones. Make sure they're within the weight limit. If you have a doubt, Ben has a scale."

Anne watched in amazement as five young men swarmed her stand and began loading the trucks with her pumpkins.

"Are you taking them all?" This was astonishing. She wasn't sure what to think.

"All that we can find between eight and ten pounds," the one they called Ben said.

"What are you going to do with so many pumpkins?"

"We're going to chunk them."

She looked at Joseph. "Do you know what that means?"

He smiled and nodded. "It means they are going to load them onto a trebuchet and into air cannons and shoot them as far as possible."

Puzzled, she looked to the young men for an explanation. "What is a trebuchet?"

"It's a catapult," Ben said, weighing one of the questionable pumpkins on a small bathroom scale he had produced from the floor of his truck. "Half pound light. We can't take this one. You should come and watch. I hold the county record for the longest air-cannon shot."

Anne still wasn't sure what they were talking about.

Joseph chuckled. "I saw an article in the newspaper that said the Pumpkin Chunkin' Festival was getting under way in a few days. I called the number they had listed for information and asked if they needed more ammunition. It turns out they did."

"We're mighty glad you called. We need all the practice we can get. The big competition in Delaware is coming up in a couple of weeks. We plan to take home the grand prize," Ben said as he counted out the bills and handed them to Joseph.

Joseph held up one hand and nodded toward Anne. "The money goes to her. Keep us in mind for next year."

"We will, man. Good chunkin' pumpkins can be hard to find. Thanks for calling us." They all climbed into their trucks and took off.

As the dust settled, Anne stared in amazement at the money in her hand. It was far and above what she had expected to make for the entire season. She would be able to get a new wheelbarrow and order more seeds. She looked at Joseph. "You did this for me? How can I thank you?"

Without blinking an eye, he said, "You can help me milk the goats tomorrow."

"Are you kidding me?

The I-dare-you look in his eyes forced her to reconsider the answer hovering on the tip of her tongue.

Chapter Eleven

Joseph watched the play of emotions across Anne's expressive face. She didn't want to have anything to do with his goats, but she wasn't about to back out of her offer, either.

Her eyes narrowed and she crossed her arms tightly. "Very well. I will help you milk for one day."

"Both morning and evening."

She bowed her head in resignation. "I'll be there."

"Don't look so excited."

She shot him a sharp look. "I'm not."

He laughed heartily. Something he hadn't done in years. What was it about this woman that made him happy when he was talking to her, teasing her, just being near her? Had he avoided people for so long that the simplest exchange with a woman felt out of the ordinary and exciting?

Anne raised her chin. "Shall I take Leah now, or do you want to bring her over when you milk tonight?"

He grinned at the baby. "I'll keep her for a few hours."

"*Goot.* That will give me time to close up the stand.

Shall I make her formula, or are you going to try making it yourself?"

"I reckon it's time I took over the task."

"I don't mind doing it."

"Are you sure?" He knew he could do it, but the chance to spend the evening with Anne was too good to pass up.

"You bring the raw milk and I'll have the rest ready, including supper. No arguments." She shook the money in the air. "This is cause for celebration. Pumpkin chunkin'! I never heard of such a thing."

After returning to his house, Joseph put Leah down for her nap and got started on the laundry that had piled up over the past week. When he had the last of it pinned on the clothesline, he fixed himself a cup of coffee and sat down to read his magazine. As interesting as the articles were, he couldn't keep his thoughts on supplement feeds with essential macro- and microminerals. His mind kept going back to the joy on Anne's face when she realized how much money her pumpkins had earned.

He enjoyed making her happy. Seeing her smile made him want to smile, too. The feeling was something he hadn't experienced in a long time. Not since Beth had died.

Was it really almost thirteen years now since the accident? In a way, it felt as if it were only yesterday. So much of his life had changed in an instant.

He and Beth had been giddy teenagers, in a hurry to get started on a life together. Looking back, he realized now that he hadn't really known her. They had met at the wedding of a cousin in Delaware. For him it had been love at first sight. Beth had been as eager as he to marry. She'd come from a big family and wanted a home of her own.

She would've made him a good wife, and he would have been a good husband to her, but God had other plans for them.

Joseph realized he'd never looked for love again after her death. He didn't believe it could happen twice. He had been wrong about a lot of things. Maybe he was wrong about that, too.

He glanced at the baby sleeping in the crib beside his chair. If it hadn't been for Leah, he might have lived his whole life without getting to know Anne. What a shame that would've been.

Lord, You do move in mysterious ways. Help me to see the goodness in life and in the people around me. Make me a better servant to Your will.

When Leah woke from her nap, he changed her diaper and dressed her warmly. There was a distinct chill in the air. He noticed the wind had switched to the north as he carried the baby to Anne's house. She was waiting at the door for them. "The approaching winter is ready to make itself felt," she said, holding open the door.

"The paper had a hard freeze warning for this area."

"*Gott* has surely blessed me by holding off until now. I'm ready for some quiet days without weeds to hoe or produce to pick, sell or can."

He glanced at the array of pumpkins she had lined up along the wall of her kitchen. "It doesn't look to me like you are done."

"A few dozen quarts of pumpkin puree won't take that long to make, but it sure will taste fine in soups, breads and pies this winter."

He eyed the pie pan on the counter. "Are we having a pie with supper?"

"Indeed we are. What better way to celebrate than with the fruits of our labors?"

"Sounds *goot*. I'll be back right quick."

Joseph left her house and hurried through his evening chores. At one point he found himself whistling. He paused in his work and gazed at the lights glowing in Anne's windows. He hadn't been this happy in a long time and she was the reason. If only Fannie would come home, his heart could truly be content.

Anne used a pair of thick hot pads to pull her pie from the oven. The mouthwatering aroma of pumpkin and spices filled the air. She took a deep breath and savored it. After setting the pie on the counter to cool, she checked the pork steaks simmering on the back burner and turned the heat down. All she needed now was to heat some of her freshly canned green beans and supper would be ready. She opened the pantry and pulled out a pint jar of them. She heard the front door open and a thrill of excitement jumped across her skin. "Come in. Supper will be ready in a few minutes."

"*Danki*, but we can't stay." It was a woman's voice.

Anne leaned back to look around her pantry door. Naomi Beiler and Bishop Andy stood inside her doorway. There was something in Naomi's expression that killed Anne's excitement.

"*Willkomm*. What brings you out here this evening?"

"I wanted to check on Joseph and the baby," the bishop said.

"After his less-than-cordial reaction to my last visit,

I thought it was best that we check with you before we went to his home," Naomi added.

"They are both fine." Anne clutched the jar to her chest.

The bishop nodded but didn't take his eyes off her. "That's good to hear. This is an unusual situation."

Anne moved to the counter to open her green beans. "It is unusual, but Joseph is making the best of it. I watch the baby for him when he has to be away from the house."

"So he is paying you to be his *kindt heedah*?"

"Not paying exactly. He is doing some farmwork for me in exchange. He picked most of my pumpkins and that was a blessing."

"Several people mentioned seeing him with you at your roadside stand. Including Preacher Hostetler. I understand Joseph was there for several hours."

"*Ja*, he was." The jar lid came off with a pop. Anne poured the contents into a pan and set it on the burner. "Are you sure you can't stay for supper? I have plenty. Joseph will be here soon to pick up Leah. You can ask him then how he is doing."

"Your *karibs* pie smells *wunderbar*, but we have another visit to make yet tonight. They are expecting us to have supper with them."

"I see." She turned around and smoothed her apron. Joseph was standing behind the bishop with two pails of milk in his hands. He towered over the smaller man.

"*Guten owet*, Bishop. Naomi." Joseph set the buckets aside and pulled off his hat. He held it to his chest like a shield.

The bishop turned to him with a smile. "Good evening to you, too, Joseph Lapp. We were just talking about you. How are you doing, my boy? I hear you have a niece staying with you."

"I do. Things are much better for us thanks to Anne and to the good ladies of Naomi's group who brought many fine gifts for us to use. You have been a true blessing, Naomi. *Danki.* Please share my thanks with the others."

The woman's face softened. "I'm glad to hear we have helped. It is what *Gott* wants us to do in His name."

Joseph looked at Anne. "Is Leah ready?"

"*Ja*, she is asleep in my office."

"*Danki.*" He put his hat on, went through to the other room and returned a few moments later with the baby in his arms. "I will see you the same time tomorrow, Anne."

He wasn't staying for supper. "That's fine. I have to make a prenatal visit on Friday morning. I'll need you to pick Leah up by eight o'clock after your morning milking. Will that be a problem?"

"Not at all."

The bishop held the door open for him and the two men went out together.

Naomi stayed behind. She clasped her hands together. "You do not have a mother to tell you these things, so I hope you do not take it amiss that I am standing in her stead. You and Joseph can easily become food for gossip if you are seen being too familiar with one another."

Anne folded her arms tightly across her chest. "We haven't done anything improper."

"I'm sure of that. Just take care. A good reputation is easy to lose and hard to regain."

"People who gossip need to examine their own motives."

Naomi shook her head. "Do not be flippant, Anne. This is serious business. I'm looking out for you and for Joseph. He doesn't need to run afoul of public opinion. For now, he has the sympathy of many, but that can change. I'm sure the bishop is telling him the same thing I'm telling you."

"What would you have us do? He's my neighbor. I'm caring for his niece. We will see each other daily."

"Be circumspect. Don't be overly friendly, especially when you are in public. Limit your time together."

Anne bit the corner of her lip. She had encouraged Joseph's friendliness and enjoyed it more than she should. Maybe Naomi was right.

Naomi arched one eyebrow. "Unless he is courting you. In that case…"

"*Nay*, it is nothing like that," Anne added quickly.

"A pity. It would be a good match for the two of you and for the child. Tell my niece Rhonda when you see her that I will visit this coming Sunday. *Guten nacht*, Anne."

"Good night." Anne closed the door behind her and leaned against it. This wasn't the way she'd expected to end her evening. There would be plenty of leftovers for lunch tomorrow. She spied the pails of milk beside the door and carried them to a counter. Leah needed her formula whether her nanny was in trouble or not.

Anne slept poorly that night. She went over every moment she had spent in Joseph's company, looking for things that others might see as improper and wondering why she resented Naomi's advice. Naomi had her best interest at heart. Anne knew that.

When morning finally came, the light revealed heavy frost on the windowpanes. Was Joseph still expecting her to help milk his goats? She had no way of knowing.

She would have to go ask. A sense of dread hung over her as she bundled up to go outside. Ending their friendship was the last thing she wanted to do.

She was almost to the gate between their properties when she saw him coming her way. He had Leah bundled in the baby quilt she had made. A pang of grief took her aback, but she suppressed it. The quilt had been made with love to keep a child warm. She was glad that child was Leah.

Joseph stopped on his side of the gate and spoke first. "I was bringing her to you."

The cautious expression in his eyes and his flat tone brought Anne's spirits to a new low. It seemed that the visit by the bishop and Naomi had indeed put an end to their budding friendship. She should take Leah and return to the house. That would be the circumspect thing to do.

Except Anne wasn't feeling particularly circumspect today. Joseph needed a friend. Asking her to turn her back on him was wrong. Would she rather have Joseph's friendship or Naomi's approval? "I thought you were going to teach me how to milk goats this morning."

"I don't think it would be a good idea."

"That's funny. I didn't think it was a good idea yesterday, but today I really want to learn."

He shook his head. "It wouldn't be proper. I don't wish to damage your reputation. The bishop is unhappy with us. Someone mistook our stumble into each other as a kiss. I set him straight."

That shocked her. "A kiss in public? You and I? That's ridiculous! Why would anyone believe such a tale?"

"I'm sure they don't any longer. I explained what happened."

"I should hope so."

"Now you see why helping me milk isn't a good idea."

"Joseph, I'm sure you received the same lecture that I did, or a very similar version. Goat milking wasn't mentioned to me. Was it mentioned to you?"

"You're splitting hairs, Anne."

"Am I? What if something were to happen to you? What if you fell and broke your leg? Who would take care of your goats? It's perfectly reasonable that I learn how." She softened her tone. "Besides, I really want to learn."

He stared at her for a long minute. Finally, he rubbed his chin with one hand. "It does make sense that someone should know what to do if I'm laid up."

"Exactly."

"It might as well be you since you live closest."

Anne threw her hands wide. "*Ja*, I'm the logical choice."

"Except that you don't like my goats." A twinkle appeared in his eyes as a smile twitched at the corner of his lip.

Her heart grew light. This was the right thing to do. "All *Gottes* creatures deserve my respect and my care. Even goats. Even Chester."

She was rewarded with a bark of laughter from Joseph. "That's putting it on a little thick, Anne."

"I didn't sound sincere?"

"*Nay*, you didn't. Not at all." He handed her the baby and opened the gate so that she could come through.

"I'll work on it." She cast him a sassy look. Was he blushing?

They fell into step together as they walked toward his barn. He glanced her way. "You surprise me."

"Sometimes I surprise myself." Like now. Who would believe she was willingly going to milk a goat?

"I kind of like that about you."

Warmth flooded her and drove the cold from her cheeks. She was finding a lot of things she liked about Joseph, too, but she wasn't brave enough to tell him that. Not yet. He opened the gate to his pasture and Anne followed him in. He put his fingers to his mouth and whistled one piercing note. Seconds later dozens of animals came galloping toward them from all corners of the field.

They were about to be mobbed. Anne clutched Leah tightly to her chest and closed her eyes.

Chapter Twelve

When the expected impact didn't happen, Anne opened her eyes. She was surrounded by goats. Some were spotted, a few were snowy white, but the majority of them were brown with black markings. They milled around Joseph bleating softly. Some of them butted against his leg gently. Anne had seen them all in his pastures and a few of them in her garden, but Chester was the only one she'd been this close to.

One of the smaller white ones stood on her hind legs to investigate Anne. Another one tried to nibble on Leah's blanket. Anne held the baby higher. "Do they eat cloth?"

"Goats are browsers. They will sample about anything. They don't eat tin cans, though. That is a myth, but they do enjoy eating the paper labels."

Anne noticed two of them had no ears. "What happened to these poor things? Did their ears freeze off? I've heard it can happen to animals in bad winters."

"Nothing happened to them. They are Lamanchas. They're an earless breed."

"How strange. Can they hear?"

"*Ja*. They have an ear canal same as any other. Ruby girl, *koom*." He held out his hand and one of the white earless goats trotted over to nibble at his fingers.

"How many do you have?" Anne couldn't begin to count them, for they were all milling around.

"Over one hundred. I milk eighty of them. The rest are my breeding rams and a few of my kid crop from last spring that I haven't sold yet. I'm a seasonal pasture-based dairy. That means my does are bred in the fall and have their kids in the spring. Goats produce milk for about nine months. My milking season begins in March and ends in December each year. It gives my girls a two-month break to rest up before the next round of kids arrive. As soon as they freshen, I start milking again."

He scratched the head of the tall brown goat with a black line down her back. "This is Matilda. She is the matriarch of the group. They all follow her."

"Do they all have names?" A second goat tried to sample Leah's quilt. Anne pushed her away.

"*Ja*, I know them all by name. This is Jenny. She is my best producer. She gives me a full gallon morning and night. Matilda is her mother. The small buckskin-colored one chewing on your shoelace is her daughter Carmen. This is Zelda. This is Betsy. This is Cupcake. Over here is Yolanda." All of the females had heavy udders.

Anne cocked her eyebrow. "I'm not required to learn their names, am I?"

Joseph shrugged. "I reckon not, but they respond better when you call them by name."

Anne realized the musky odor of the does wasn't as strong as Chester's stink. "Why do the male goats smell so bad?"

"You don't want to know. They only smell bad to us. The female goats find the odor quite attractive."

"Then Chester must be a very popular fellow."

"He is," he said with a chuckle.

A pale brown doe with a white blaze on her face and droopy ears sniffed at Anne's hand. She was cute as a button. Anne smiled and tentatively petted her head. "Who is this?"

Joseph shifted his weight from one foot to the other, looking oddly ill at ease. "I thought you didn't want to learn their names."

Anne scratched the pretty doe behind the ear and the animal leaned into her hand, her eyes closed in bliss. "Not all of them. Just this one."

"It's Anne," he muttered so softly she almost didn't hear.

Anne's mouth dropped open. "Joseph Lapp, did you name a goat after me?"

"Not exactly. I try to go through the alphabet when I'm giving the new kids names and it was time for an *A* name."

"Annabel. Abigail. Arlene. There are lots of names that begin with *A*."

"I already have an Annabel and an Abigail. I picked Anne. It was no reflection on you."

She wasn't so sure, but she let the subject drop. "Show me how to milk."

"It's easy." He led the way inside his metal barn and flipped a switch.

The hum of a generator started up and in a few seconds, the lights came on. The building was large and airy with a high ceiling and white painted walls. Anne was amazed at how clean everything was. She didn't think of goats as clean animals.

"I noticed you use electricity."

"I have permission from the bishop to use it in my barn. I don't have it anywhere else on the farm. I use a propane-powered generator. It's cleaner than a diesel-fuel-powered one and less noisy. My goal is to produce the best goat's milk I can. An important part of that is keeping the milk clean and chilling it as soon as possible."

His milking parlor was a raised platform with twelve stanchions. The panels were painted royal blue and each place held a small blue tub in front of it. He climbed onto the platform and began filling the tubs from a small wheelbarrow. "I feed grain at milking time. The gals don't mind being milked, because they get fed."

When he had filled each tub, he opened the door at one end of the parlor. "*Koom*, girls. Up you go."

The goats filed in quickly. They walked up one ramp to come into the parlor. Another ramp led down and out of the barn. The first doe walked all the way to the end of the line before stopping and putting her head in the stanchion. Each one did the same until all the places were full. As each goat began eating, Joseph closed the latches that would keep their heads locked in place.

He hopped off the platform and stood beside Anne. "It's important to clean their udders thoroughly with an iodine solution and dry them well before putting on the suction tubes. The milk goes directly from the goat into the milker, then into a pipeline, through a filter and finally to the milk tank in the next room, where it is chilled in a holding tank. A truck comes three times a week to pick up the milk."

"How long does it take?"

"To milk all of them? It takes me about two hours."

"How do you clean all this tubing?"

He began washing the udders of each doe and attaching the milkers. "I'll show you when I'm done. The pipeline system gets cleaned after each milking, morning and night. Warm water flushes the leftover milk out of the lines. That is followed by a hot-water detergent rinse and then a mild bleach rinse. Like in the house, I have a propane hot-water heater here. The milk lines are sanitized just prior to each milking."

This was a much more complex operation than she had imagined. "Joseph, none of this looks easy except opening the door and letting them in."

"It looks more complicated than it is. You'll get the hang of it in no time."

She shifted the baby to her other hip. "I agreed to help do this for one day."

He leaned on the parlor ramp. "I remember. When do you want to start?"

"Haven't we started already?"

"I'm showing you how it's done. You haven't helped me do anything yet. Are you backing out of our deal? I did manage to sell almost all your pumpkins." He moved toward her and took Leah from her.

"You did and I'm not backing out. I'm grateful for your help. I will attempt milking one evening, with your supervision, of course."

"Of course. I don't trust my gals to just anyone. Isn't that right, Leah?" He bounced the baby and smiled at her. She grinned back at him.

Anne cocked her head to the side as she watched him interact with Leah. He was a much different man from the sour, reclusive neighbor she had lived next to for so many years. It did her heart good to see such a positive change in him.

Joseph caught Anne looking at him with a soft smile on her lips and tenderness in her eyes. His heart started beating faster. His logical mind quickly quelled the sensation. Her tender smile was aimed at the baby and not at him. He shouldn't read more into her friendliness than was there. He knew he had to keep their relationship casual or he'd risk running into problems with the church community. He wouldn't do anything to jeopardize Anne's reputation.

"I've shown you how the milking is done. I reckon that's good enough. Why don't you take Leah back to your house? I think she's ready for a nap." He didn't mean to sound brusque, but his words came out that way. He handed her the baby.

Anne's smile faded. "I will see you later."

He didn't want her to go, but he had no reason to stop her. He waited until she reached the door. "Anne?"

She turned back to face him. "Yes?"

He wanted to say, *Don't go.* Instead, he asked, "What do you think of my goats now?"

Her smile reappeared. "I still like them much better when they are on your side of the fence."

"Now that the growing season is over, would you consider letting me graze them in your fields? For a price."

"How much of a grazing fee are you offering?"

He gave her a price that was less than what it would cost him to buy the same amount of feed.

"I'll think it over."

"What's to think about? You get your fields cleared and I get low-cost feed for my gals that's right next door."

"If you want to graze it, there may be others in the area who would like to graze it, too. Maybe someone else will pay me more. As I said, I'll think it over. Cows and sheep will eat the broken and blemished pumpkins that are still out there. They will eat the leaves and vines, too."

If she was looking to foster the appearance of a business relationship with him for propriety's sake, he understood. "Ask around. I doubt you will get a better price."

"I *will* ask around. If I decide not to let your goats graze it, will you complain about me?"

"Loudly, and to everyone who will listen."

"That settles it," she said primly and left without giving her answer.

He chuckled as he returned to work. Anne certainly wasn't a boring woman. Her self-sufficient streak might have been what kept her single all these years. Each day he seemed to discover something new and intriguing about his bossy neighbor.

And each day he liked her more.

He pushed the thought aside. For Leah's sake, he valued Anne's friendship, but he knew there would never be anything more between them. He was a bachelor set in his ways. She was bent on remaining single. It wouldn't work between them.

So why was he even thinking about it?

He gave himself a sharp mental shake and went to feed Chester. To his chagrin, he discovered the buck was missing. Again. Somehow he had escaped from the stall.

A quick check of the outbuildings showed the goat wasn't on the farm. Joseph headed to Anne's, praying the goat wasn't causing any new damage. His prayer went unheeded. He found Chester in the corral chasing Anne's mare away from her hay. The old goat was leaping and kicking happily in the crisp morning air, making the frightened horse dash from one end of the enclosure to the other.

"Chester, *koom*! Before Anne sees your mischief and I end up in her bad graces again." He managed to shepherd the goat home, found where he had worked a board loose to get out and fixed it.

As he hammered the last nail in place, he glared at Chester. "At least Anne wasn't the one to find you. You have to stop giving her a bad impression of goats. Behave. We want her to like us."

Joseph straightened as soon as the words were out of his mouth. He did want Anne to like him because he cared about her. A lot.

It was a scary thought.

On Friday morning Anne walked out to hitch up her horse a little after eight o'clock. When the mare came limping toward her, Anne frowned in concern.

"You poor thing. What's wrong?"

Anne slipped into the corral to examine Daisy's right front leg. Her knee was swollen and hot. Anne patted the mare's neck. "You aren't going to carry me to the Yoder farm this morning. You are going to have to rest for a few days. I'll fix up a poultice for you as soon as I get back."

Leaving the corral, Anne headed to Joseph's house. She found him mending a pair of socks at the kitchen table. "Good morning, Joseph."

"*Wee gayt's*, Anne. What can I do for you?"

"I'm sorry to bother you, but I wonder if I might borrow your buggy horse this morning. My mare has come up lame."

He laid his mending aside. "Do you want me to look at her for you? Maybe it's just a loose shoe."

"It's her right knee. She has had some trouble with it in the past. She must have twisted it while she was out in the pasture because I haven't used her since last Sunday. I won't be gone long. Rhonda Yoder is expecting me at nine o'clock. Prenatal visits normally take about thirty minutes."

"You can't borrow my horse."

Stunned, she drew back. "Oh."

"I'll drive you." He got his coat and hat.

"That's not necessary."

"Duncan is temperamental. I wouldn't want him to run away with you. If you will get Leah ready, I will go hitch him up."

"All right."

Within ten minutes Anne had the heavily bundled baby in her Moses basket and was standing outside waiting for Joseph. She handed him the baby and then climbed in. Once she was settled, she took Leah and placed the basket next to them on the seat.

Joseph flicked the reins and set the horse in motion. "You will have to tell me how to get there. I haven't been to their place since they moved."

"They live on the west side of Honeysuckle now."

"Okay." He turned the horse in that direction when he reached the end of the lane.

Anne enjoyed riding beside Joseph until they reached the edge of town. Several of the women from Naomi's widows' group were gathered in front of the Beachy

Craft Shop. Their curious looks and furious whispering made Anne realize how odd it must look for her to be riding out with Joseph only a day after Naomi and the bishop had come to call. She resisted the urge to pull her traveling bonnet low across her face.

"I should have come alone," she muttered.

"Why?"

"People are staring at us." It was one thing to defy Naomi's suggestion to be more circumspect with Joseph when they were alone on their farms. It was another thing to brazenly disregard that advice in front of her church members.

"They will soon find other things to talk about."

Anne wasn't so sure. She may have opened herself up to criticism for no reason. Duncan was behaving perfectly. She could have handled him easily. Why hadn't she thought about being seen with Joseph?

Because she wanted his company and that was as far ahead as she had been thinking.

Joseph glanced at her. "It will be fine. You'll see. We will explain what happened. After everything you have done for me, it's nice to be able to do something for you in return. Besides, it's sort of my fault that your mare is lame."

"How can that be?"

"Yesterday one of my goats got in with her and was chasing her. That may have been when she hurt her leg."

Anne narrowed her eyes at him. "Let me guess. It was Chester."

"Ja," Joseph admitted with a hangdog expression.

"That miserable animal. I don't know why you put up with him."

Duncan chose that moment to shy violently as a dog

ran across the road in front of them. Anne toppled into Joseph. He threw his arm around her and pulled her to his side to steady her. She looked up in gratitude. Her heart hammered in her chest, not from fear but from his nearness. *"Danki."*

Another buggy topped the rise in front of them. Anne knew exactly who it was before they got close enough to see the driver. She struggled out of Joseph's embrace, pushing his arm off her shoulder. It was the bishop's buggy.

Joseph acknowledged him with a tip of his hat. The bishop's countenance remained set in disapproval.

Anne wanted to sink through the seat. "Just so you know, I'm going to plant rhubarb the entire length of our property line in the spring."

"I can't say that I blame you."

She could tell from the tone of his voice that he was worried now, too.

Chapter Thirteen

The road remained free of traffic for the next mile as Anne and Joseph traveled on. It should have been a pleasant morning drive through the rolling hills of Lancaster County. Autumn colors splashed the tree-covered hillsides with scarlet, golds and flaming oranges. The harvest was finished. The land and the people who worked it were ready to rest. Shocks of corn lined up like brown tepees across the fields, waiting to be used when snow covered the ground. The orchards were bare. The pasture grasses were turning brown, though the cattle and horses still foraged there.

The air had a nip to it and held the scent of wood smoke rising from the Amish farms they passed. The sun shone brightly, promising a warm afternoon. There wasn't a cloud in the sky.

Joseph glanced at Anne several times, but she refused to look at him. "I will go see the bishop first thing tomorrow morning and explain that this was an unusual occurrence. I was simply doing my Christian duty by offering you assistance."

"I should've had you stop at the Beachy Craft Shop.

I should have asked one of the women there to take me out to the Yoder farm. I wasn't thinking. I know what's proper."

"There's no harm done. Tongues may wag about us for a day or so, but when we give them nothing else to talk about, this will be forgotten."

Anne sat up straighter. "You're right. We aren't doing anything wrong. I have nothing to be ashamed of this time."

This time? What did that mean? Had she done something to be ashamed of in the past? Sadness stole over her features as a faraway look entered her eyes.

"Is something wrong, Anne?" He wanted to help, to comfort her, but he didn't know how.

She shook her head and the distant look disappeared. "Nothing's wrong. About a mile farther on, you'll cross a bridge. The Yoder home is on the south side of the road."

They soon caught up to a wagon loaded with hay traveling in the same direction. When he could safely do so on the hilly highway, Joseph passed it, urging Duncan to a burst of speed. The moment the black horse came neck and neck with the draft horses, he broke trot and tried to gallop ahead of them.

Anne clutched Leah's basket with white knuckles until Joseph was able to regain control. Her eyes were wide with fright. "I see what you mean about your horse being hard to handle."

"He came from a racing farm. He does well most of the time, but now you see why I didn't want you to drive him alone."

"I do, and I'm grateful you insisted on coming."

They rode in silence for a while longer. Suddenly he asked, "Do you like being a midwife?"

"I don't like it. I love it. I love mothers and their incredible strength. I love babies and their amazing resiliency. It's a humbling part of life and I'm blessed to play a role in it."

"Did you have to have a lot of training?"

"I am what is known as a direct-entry midwife. I am not a nurse. I don't have a nursing license, but I am a CPM. That stands for *certified professional midwife*. It means I have met the requirements for those credentials. My mother was a midwife for many years in Ohio. I apprenticed with her. After I moved here, I joined an association of midwives that work to improve the training and practice of midwifery. They hold workshops and classes several times a year. Although I do mainly home births, I can do deliveries at the birthing center attached to the hospital."

"I don't know much about midwives."

"I'm not surprised. I follow the Midwives Model of Care. That means I monitor the physical, emotional and social well-being of women during their childbearing years. I provide individualized education and prenatal care. I'm there to provide continuous hands-on assistance while a mother is in labor, during delivery and in the months after the baby is born. My goal is to help a woman understand that birth is a natural process that does not require technological intervention except in very rare cases."

"How many babies have you delivered?"

"Thirty-six in the last three years," she said, pleased with her success.

"That's not so many. I was at the delivery of forty-four kids last spring alone. I'd hate to try to count the number since I raised my first goat."

She shook her head in disbelief. "I think goats are a little different from human mothers and babies."

"Nope. We're more alike than you want to believe."

She didn't rise to his bait. He wanted to get her mind off the bishop's disapproval, but she wouldn't let him.

They reached the Yoder farm without further incident. Anne went inside while he waited in the buggy with Leah. The baby was still sleeping. It was warm in the sun and he wasn't worried about her getting a chill. Silas Yoder came out of the barn. He waved when he saw Joseph and came over to speak to him. The two of them had attended all eight grades together in the one-room schoolhouse not far from the outskirts of Honeysuckle, but Silas had joined a different church district when he married Rhonda. The two men rarely saw each other now.

"Long time no see. What brings you to my place today, Joseph?"

"I brought Anne Stoltzfus to see your wife. Her horse came up lame this morning. She wanted to borrow my buggy horse so she wouldn't be late, but Duncan is temperamental. I decided it was safer to drive her."

Silas winked. "As good an excuse as any to take a *maidel* out for a drive on a nice day. Anne is a sweet one. I've often wondered why she remains unwed. She's not hard on the eyes. Who is that you have with you?" He leaned in to get a better look at the baby.

Joseph tensed. He had been dreading this. He knew he would have to introduce his niece to the community and tell her story sooner or later. He was surprised that Silas hadn't already heard about his sister's actions. News traveled amazingly fast among the Amish in spite of their lack of telephones. "This is Leah. She is Fannie's daughter."

"You don't say? How is your sister? Has she returned?"

It had been more than three weeks since Fannie had dropped Leah in his lap and over two weeks since her only letter arrived. It should have been more than enough time for her to come to her senses and return for Leah. Or at least to write and ask how the babe was doing.

He didn't want to believe she could abandon her child, but how much longer could he pretend she was coming back?

"My sister has left our faith. I do not know when I will see her again."

"I'm sorry to hear that, Joseph. I will pray for her. She has a pretty *bubbel*. I can't believe I'm going to have one of my own in a few weeks. Do they really wake up and cry every two or three hours through the night?"

"They do. Through the day, too."

"Every night?"

"Every night until they decide otherwise."

Silas shook his head. "I don't think I'm ready for this, Joseph. How can I be a *vadder*? I'm not a smart man, not like my *daed*. He knows a little about everything. There's nothing he can't fix. I tell you, I'm worried about bringing a child up who will embrace our faith. What if my son or daughter is as wild during their *rumspringa* as I was during mine?"

Joseph thought of all Anne had taught him about caring for Leah. "I reckon you must pray for guidance. You have a good wife, Silas. Listen to her. She will help you become a *goot vadder*. If your children give you gray hairs, it is only right. I remember how your *mudder* worried over you."

Silas grinned. "She still does."

"It's the way of the world."

Silas glanced toward the house and his smile faded. "I'll be glad when this pregnancy is over. Rhonda worries me more every day. She thinks something is wrong with the babe, and I can't convince her otherwise."

Anne could see that Rhonda wasn't feeling well as soon as she entered the house. The young mother-to-be wore a pained expression and rubbed her stomach almost constantly. Anne sought to calm her and find out what was wrong.

It didn't take long for Rhonda to voice her concerns. "The baby isn't moving much. Shouldn't the baby be more active now?"

Warning bells went off in Anne's mind but she kept her face calm. "The quarters are getting tighter for your little one. He or she may not have as much room to wiggle. Let's get you checked out. You may be closer to your delivery date than I thought."

Anne weighed Rhonda on the bathroom scale she carried with her and jotted down the numbers on the record book she kept for each of her patients. She also checked her blood pressure and her pulse. It was all normal. "Your weight has stayed the same."

"I don't know how it can. I feel as big as a cow. I had to have Silas help me out of the bathtub the other night. It was so embarrassing."

"I'm sure he didn't mind."

"*Nay*, he's been a great help and so understanding. I've been blessed with a wonderful husband."

Anne pulled out her stethoscope. "I agree. Lie down on the bed for me and let me take a listen to your little one."

"Do you think it will be a boy or a girl? *Mam* says I'm carrying the babe low, so it will be a boy. Is that true?"

"It is about fifty percent of the time," Anne said with a wink and a grin. She put the bell of the stethoscope to Rhonda's belly. Her grin faded. The heartbeat she heard was much too slow. She listened in a different place and found the same results.

"Turn on your left side, Rhonda."

"Why? What's wrong?" She rolled over.

Anne listened again. The heartbeat was a shade faster, but not normal. "Stay on your side for a few minutes."

"Something is wrong. I can see it on your face. What is it? Tell me!" Tears welled up in Rhonda's eyes.

Anne knew that overwhelming sense of panic and fear as well as she knew her own name. She drew a deep breath. "You must keep calm. It's important. The baby's heart rate is slow."

"But it's there?"

"*Ja*, it's there. It gets better when you are on your side. I want you to stay this way while I talk to Silas. I'm going to suggest that you go to the hospital."

"But I want my baby born at home," she wailed.

Anne grasped Rhonda's hand and gave it a reassuring squeeze. "I know you do and going to the hospital now doesn't mean that can't happen. But I'm concerned. I think you should see a doctor. He can take a look at the baby with an ultrasound and see what is causing the problem."

"Talk to Silas. We can't afford a hospital bill. Is *Gott* taking my baby away?"

"I pray that is not His plan." She didn't want any young mother to suffer the pain of a stillborn child.

"You know I can't make this decision, Anne. I must be obedient to my husband."

"I understand. I'll be right back. Okay?"

Rhonda nodded and Anne hurried outside.

This can't be happening. Please, God, don't let this baby die. Not the way my baby did.

She saw Silas talking to Joseph and rushed to him. She hated to frighten the young man, but she had no choice. "Silas, I must speak with you."

He grew instantly somber. "What is it?"

She had to keep calm. Everyone was depending on her. She prayed for strength. "I have examined Rhonda, and I discovered that your baby's heartbeat is slower than normal."

"What does that mean?" Worry filled his eyes.

"It means the baby is in distress. Something isn't right. I'm going to urge you to take Rhonda to the hospital."

"Is she losing our baby?" Fear replaced the worry on his face.

"I can't say for sure, but that may happen."

He pulled off his hat and raked a hand through his hair. "If it is *Gottes* will to take my child back to Heaven, I must accept His will. *Gott* help me to be strong."

She clutched his arm. "Silas, listen to me. Every minute counts. If it is *Gottes* will to call your babe home, nothing we do will change that. But *Gott* in His wisdom brought me here today for a reason. Maybe that reason was to see the danger and send you both to the hospital. I need your permission to call the ambulance. The church will help with the hospital bills. You know that."

"I don't care about the money. Call the ambulance." He ran toward the house.

Anne staggered toward the buggy and felt her knees give way.

Joseph jumped down in time to catch Anne as she slumped against him. "Are you all right?"

She nodded but didn't speak as she clutched his arms.

"Tell me what you need me to do. How can I help?"

She focused on his face. "I'm so frightened for them."

"*Gott* is with us all. We can bear what must be borne. Rhonda and Silas, too."

"I know." She drew several deep breaths.

"Shall I call for the ambulance?"

She shook her head. "I can do that. I need you to go out to the highway and direct them here when they arrive."

He leaned forward to peer into her eyes. "Are you sure you don't need me here?"

She managed a wan smile. "I'm okay now. I have a patient to take care of."

"*Goot* girl. Make the call. I'll go out to the highway as soon as I know they are on their way."

Leah woke and began to fuss. Joseph picked her up to quiet her. Anne pulled a cell phone from her apron pocket and flipped it open to dial 911. When the dispatcher answered, she explained the situation and gave concise medical information about Rhonda, answered the dispatcher's questions and provided directions. When she was finished, she closed the phone. "I'm going back inside. The ambulance should be here in ten minutes."

"Then I'm on my way. I will keep Leah with me so you are free to do what you need."

"Bless you, Joseph. I'm so glad you are here."

"I wish I could do more." He settled Leah in her Moses basket again, climbed in beside her and slapped the reins against Duncan's back. The horse jumped forward and Joseph guided him down the road to the highway. After that, he had to sit and wait. Thankfully, Anne had packed a bottle for Leah and he was able to feed the baby. She was almost finished when he heard the sound of a siren in the distance. He climbed out of the buggy, then walked to the edge of the roadway and began waving his arm when he saw the flashing lights crest the hill.

The ambulance slowed. He motioned toward the Yoder farm. The ambulance driver nodded that he understood and turned onto the dirt track. Joseph got back in his buggy and followed them.

The paramedics were already pulling a gurney from the back of the ambulance when he arrived. Knowing he could help by staying out of the way, he waited and prayed for everyone in the farmhouse. Twenty minutes later the paramedics brought Rhonda out on a gurney and loaded her into the ambulance. She lay on her side. Her face was pale and streaked with tears. She had a green oxygen mask over her nose and mouth. Silas was at her side holding her hand. He looked every bit as pale and shaken as she did. He climbed in the ambulance when they had her loaded, and the doors were closed.

Three additional buggies drove into the yard. Joseph wasn't surprised. The unusual sound of an ambulance in the normally quiet farm country would bring neighbors hurrying to see if they could help.

Then the ambulance pulled away, leaving Joseph to answer the many questions of Silas and Rhonda's friends. He waited for Anne to appear, but she didn't come out of the house. When the last of the curious neighbors departed to spread the word of what was going on, Joseph walked up to the house, looking for Anne. Inside, he found her huddled in a rocker with her arms clasped around her knees, sobbing.

Chapter Fourteen

"Don't cry. Please don't cry, Anne. You did everything you could."

The sound of Joseph's voice penetrated Anne's sorrow. She opened her eyes to see him kneeling in front of her. Through the blur of her tears, she saw the concern etched on his face. How could she tell him the tears weren't for Rhonda and her baby but for a baby boy, stillborn and laid to rest years ago? They were tears she had kept at bay for many long years, but today's events brought back every bitter, sad memory of that time in sharp detail. It was exactly what had happened to Anne, but her mother had never called for the ambulance.

Anne tried to but couldn't speak. She reached out and laid her palm against Joseph's face. He cupped his hand over hers and held it tight.

"We should go home now," he said softly. "Are you ready?"

Her hiccuping sobs slowed. Finally, she nodded.

Joseph helped her to her feet and kept one arm around her. She cherished his strength. Although she was used to standing alone, today she needed someone to lean on. She needed him.

He helped her into the buggy after scooting Leah over to make room so that Anne could sit beside him. She should have objected, but she didn't. She was emotionally spent. The comfort of Joseph's touch meant more to her than proper behavior.

Picking up the reins, he set the horse in motion. Anne kept her eyes closed as she leaned against him.

"Is there any hope for Rhonda's babe?" he asked a short time later.

Sighing, Anne sat up. Immediately, she missed the warmth of his body. "The baby's heartbeat improved when they put the oxygen mask on Rhonda. I imagine the doctor will do an emergency C-section when they reach the hospital. If *Gott* wills it, the child will live."

"I'm relieved to hear that. From the force of your weeping, I thought the babe had perished."

She wanted to tell him about her baby, but shame kept her silent. It was a shame she had hidden for many years. Only her mother and the maiden aunt Anne had stayed with in Ohio knew about her unwed pregnancy. Anne had been seventeen at the time. Seventeen, headstrong and in love. As it turned out, she couldn't marry the *Englisch* boy she adored. He hadn't loved her. He hadn't wanted to be a father. He'd urged her to give the baby up for adoption. Her mother had thought it would be best, too.

Brokenhearted, she had agreed to give her baby to a childless Amish couple in her aunt's church. She'd never imagined she would have to give him back to God. A single question haunted her still. If she had been brave enough to keep her son, would God have allowed it?

Joseph watched her closely. She wouldn't share her story, not even with him. "I was just overwrought. I keep thinking I must have missed something. I didn't foresee Rhonda having any problems. I was frightened, but I tried not to let them see that. I'm sorry I fell apart."

"Are you better now?"

"I am. I'm fine." She scrubbed her face with her hands to erase the signs of her tears and sniffed once.

"You don't seem fine." He pulled her close again.

Laying her head on his shoulder, she relaxed in his embrace. Did he know how wonderful it felt to be cared for? Did he have any idea how firmly he was planting himself in her heart?

It was time to admit she was falling for this man. She understood he offered the kindness of a friend, but the feelings swirling through her were more than friendship. Unless she was very careful, she would find herself in love with another man who didn't love her in return.

She sat up straight, determined to put their relationship back on proper footing. "We should stop and let Naomi know what has happened."

"That's a *goot* idea. You can explain why we were driving out together this morning, too. Naomi will put a stop to any gossip about us if you fill her in on the details."

"You might be right about that. What about the Yoders' bishop? Should we tell him what's going on?"

"A number of neighbors came by when the ambulance was there. I'm sure he already knows."

Anne had to chuckle. "There's nothing quite as fast and efficient as the Amish telegraph."

And sometimes completely inaccurate, as in the case

of their "kiss." Casting a quick glance his way, she wondered, *What would it be like to kiss him?*

It was best not to think such thoughts. She lifted Leah's infant carrier to her lap, scooted away from Joseph and placed the baby between them. They remained quiet for the rest of the trip. The streets of Honeysuckle were empty, so Anne didn't have to face any of her friends again. For that she was thankful. She knew her blotchy, tear-streaked face wouldn't go unnoticed.

Joseph turned the horse into Naomi's driveway and stopped in front of her house. Her fourteen-year-old daughter, Abigail, was sweeping the front steps. She smiled brightly. *"Wee gayt's."*

Anne stepped out of the buggy. "Good day to you, too, Abigail. Is your *mudder* about?"

"Ja, koom in." Abigail's eyes filled with concern. Anne knew she must look a sight with her red eyes and blotchy cheeks.

"I'll only be a minute." She glanced at Joseph.

He nodded. "I'll wait here."

She followed Abigail inside and found Naomi at her quilting rack. Naomi smiled. "Anne, I wasn't expecting you. Come in. Pick up a needle. Child, have you been crying?"

"I'm afraid I bring you some unhappy news."

Concern furrowed Naomi's brow. "What is it?"

"I saw Rhonda today. I've sent her to the hospital. Her baby wasn't doing well."

"Oh, my poor child. I must go at once to see what I can do." She slipped her needle into the fabric and got up.

"I thought you would want to know right away. Can you get word to Silas's family?"

"I can. *Danki*, Anne. It was good of you to stop.

Would you like a cup of tea or coffee? I'll have Abigail fix something."

"*Nay*, I can't stay. My mare came up lame this morning and Joseph was kind enough to drive me to see Rhonda. He and Silas went to school together. I've already kept Joseph from his work long enough. I must go."

"Thank you again for stopping. Please tell Joseph I'm grateful for his kindness to you."

"I will."

Anne left the house knowing she had done all she could to quiet the gossip about Joseph and herself and to let Rhonda's family know what was happening. Joseph held out a hand to help her into the buggy. He had Leah in his arms. She was crying.

"I'll take her," Anne said, letting him have free hands to drive.

"I couldn't find another bottle."

"I only packed one. I thought we'd be home long before this." She cuddled Leah close. The baby stopped crying and grabbed the ribbon of Anne's *kapp*. She pulled the material to her mouth and gurgled happily.

Anne smiled at her. If she was in danger of falling for Joseph, she had already gone over that cliff with Leah. It would be impossible not to love such a sweet child. Anne kissed the baby's hand. Leah was becoming as dear to her as her own babe would have been. Why had Fannie chosen to give her baby away? Anne wanted to know. She wanted to understand.

Yet forgiveness did not require understanding. She forgave Fannie and prayed that Joseph had forgiven her, too.

Joseph kept a close eye on Anne as they traveled home. It was distressing to see her so sad and not be able to help her. He could believe she was upset by Rhonda's emergency, but he didn't believe that was all that was troubling her. There was something else. Something she didn't want to share with him. He noticed that she held Leah close, stroking her face, holding her hand, kissing her tiny fingers. It was as if only Leah could give Anne the solace she needed.

He drove her up to the front door of her home. She remained seated, as if she didn't want to be parted from the baby. "Anne, could I ask you a favor?"

"Of course." She glanced at him. There were still traces of tears on her cheeks.

"I'm going to be working late tonight. I have to take apart all my milking lines and replace some of the O-rings. I've noticed that I have less suction than I should. I'm just not sure where the trouble is. Would you keep Leah overnight for me? I know that's not our usual arrangement."

Anne stared at him intently. A tender smile appeared on her face. "You are a good friend to me, Joseph Lapp."

He didn't mind that she saw through his ruse. He would work late. One of his O-rings did need replacing. It wouldn't hurt him to catch up on his paperwork, either. "You are a good friend to me, too. Can you keep her?"

Anne kissed the baby's cheek. "Of course I will."

"Danki." He leaned over and placed a gentle kiss on Anne's cheek. Her eyes widened, but she didn't pull away. He tried to tell himself it was a gesture of friendly comfort, but he realized he was only lying to himself. He had come to care deeply about Anne. Much more deeply than he should care about someone who was simply his neighbor.

She placed Leah in her basket. He got out and lifted

her down. He set the baby on the ground and reached for Anne. His hands easily spanned her waist. She rested her hand slightly on his shoulders as he lowered her to the ground. She gazed up at him with wide eyes. It took a strong act of willpower not to kiss her again.

He reluctantly stepped away. Anne picked up the baby carrier and walked up her steps. At the door, she turned to look back at him. "Thank you again for everything you did today."

He tried to make light of it. "It is my Christian duty to help my neighbor."

"This neighbor is grateful that she lives next door to a kind and caring man."

"Even if he is a goat farmer?"

That brought a little smile to her lips. "*Ja*, even if he is a goat farmer. With poor fences."

"I can see my welcome is just about worn through. I'll talk to you tomorrow morning." He tipped his hat and led his horse toward the gate between their properties. As he closed it behind the buggy, he noticed the hinge was loose and the wire was starting to sag. If she believed him to be a kind and caring neighbor, then he had better start living up to her expectations.

Anne fed Leah and put her down in a small playpen Joseph had provided her from the donated items at his place. As soon as she was done, she sat down in the kitchen and pulled out her cell phone. She hesitated but finally dialed the number to the obstetrical unit at their local hospital. Anne was relieved when her friend Roxann answered the phone. Roxann was a nurse-midwife who taught classes for the Amish midwives in the area.

Anne had learned a lot from Roxann and valued her as
a friend.

"*Hallo*, Roxann. This is Anne Stoltzfus. I'm calling
to check on my patient Rhonda Yoder. She was brought
in by ambulance this morning. Can you give me an update?"

"Let me check to make sure she has signed a release
to give you information, Anne. You know how picky the
HIPAA laws are. Yes, it's here on her chart. I'm happy
to say that mother and baby boy are both doing well.
We did a crash C-section for low heart tones as soon as
she arrived. The baby had the cord wrapped around his
neck three times. He was very fortunate that you saw
his mother today. The proud papa has been singing your
praises to everyone who will listen."

Ann clapped a hand to her chest as relief brought
tears to her eyes again. *Thank You, God, for sparing
this woman and child.*

She had prepared herself to hear the worst. Instead,
she was overcome with gratitude and joy. "I'm so thankful. *Gott es goot.*"

"I don't speak *Deitsch*, but I get your meaning, Anne.
Our new obstetrician was impressed with the medical
records you sent along with the EMS staff and your handling of the patient. You did exactly the right thing. He's
one of those doctors who think Amish midwives don't
know how to read or write, let alone deliver babies."

"Was there anything in my records that I missed?
Should I have known this might be a problem?" The
day had shaken her belief in her calling. Was she meant
to be a midwife?

"A nuchal cord doesn't normally have warning signs
until the baby drops lower in the birth canal and the cord

gets tight. You didn't miss anything. You did good getting Rhonda into a position that took pressure off the cord and in sending her to the hospital as soon as you discovered there was a problem."

It made Anne feel better that she hadn't missed something, but her spirits remained low. What about the next time a mother had problems? Would she be skilled enough to handle it?

"Rhonda and her baby should be dismissed in about three days," Roxann said.

"I will follow up with them as soon as they get home."

"Thanks for making our direct-entry midwife program look good. We still have some resistance in the medical community, but you and I both know home births are every bit as safe as a hospital birth. If they weren't, there wouldn't be so many Amish babies in Pennsylvania. Rhonda was the exception to the rule, but a sharp midwife knows when to call for help. You are a sharp midwife, Anne."

"It was in *Gottes* hands. I only did what I have been trained to do. I appreciate the information, Roxann. Call me if anything changes."

"I will. How many of your mothers are due in November?"

"Only two in November now, but four in January."

"You're going to be busy. Have a happy Thanksgiving, if I don't talk to you before then."

Anne closed her phone and tucked it into her case. Now that the crisis was over, she felt weak as a kitten. She fixed herself a cup of tea and went to sit in the rocker in her office. She stayed there for an hour watching Leah sleep. In her heart, Anne knew Rhonda would be doing the same thing. She would be watching her baby slumber and giving thanks to God for His mercy.

She wasn't surprised when Joseph showed up as daylight was fading. Leah was awake. Anne was holding her and reading her a story. He stepped into her office and pulled off his hat. "Have you heard anything?"

"They had to do a C-section but mother and baby are fine. I should have come to tell you that. I'm sorry."

Relief filled his eyes. *"Gott es goot."*

"Ja, Gott is good. He showed us all His power and His mercy today. Would you like some supper?"

"Nay, I've eaten. I don't want to intrude on your evening. I just wanted to know how things turned out. You look better."

"Was I haggish before?"

His gaze softened and he shook his head. "Only tired and worried looking. I doubt you could look haggish if you tried."

"That is sweet of you to say." Her grumpy neighbor wasn't so grumpy, after all. She was coming to depend on him, on his kindness and his insight.

A flush crept up his neck and he ducked his head to avoid her gaze. "It's the truth, that's all. Would you like me to take Leah home?"

She gazed at the baby on her lap. Leah was grasping at the colorful pictures on the pages of the children's book. "If you don't mind, I would like to keep her with me."

It was sad to admit, but she needed company tonight. She didn't want to be alone. Even if there was only a baby to fill that role.

Joseph crouched down beside them. "I don't mind

missing her three a.m. feeding. You can keep her overnight anytime you wish."

Leah grew excited at the sight of him. He gave her his finger to hold. She immediately pulled it to her mouth. He looked at Anne. "Don't worry. I washed my hands after I milked my goats."

"I should hope so. Why don't you pull up a chair and listen to this story. I think you'll enjoy it."

"Is it about goats?" He pulled a chair over and sat down. He offered his finger to Leah again and she grabbed it.

"It's about a little girl who has lost her puppy. Leah likes it." At least, she liked the pictures.

"She would like it better if it was a story about goats."

Anne struggled not to smile. "When she is at your home, you can read to her from your *Goat World* magazine. When she is here, she is going to learn that there is more to life than goats and milking machines."

"And you think a story about a puppy will do that?"

"This is about a very naughty, adventuresome puppy who learns that home is the best place of all."

"Okay. As long as there is a good moral, I guess she can hear the story even if it doesn't have a goat in it. Start at the beginning. I don't want to miss anything."

Anne smiled and turned back to the first page. She put more animation in her voice as she retold the tale. Several times she caught him chuckling at the story. A month ago she never would have imagined that her neighbor had an adorable sense of humor or that his laugh could make her warm all over.

It was nice having him to keep her company. It was wonderful to see the affection in his eyes as he played peekaboo with Leah while she read. Having him there felt comfortable. It felt right. It felt like they were a family.

They weren't. She knew that. But just for a little while, it was wonderful to pretend they were the family in the book, rejoicing over the return of their missing puppy. Was that so wrong? Or was she setting herself up for heartbreak?

Chapter Fifteen

Dora Stoltzfus stood at Anne's side while she weighed Dora's baby boy at his checkup. He was Dora's first child. She and her husband had been nervous wrecks during the pregnancy, calling Anne out several times on false alarms. Always late at night. But as a new mother, Dora was proving to be a natural. Her husband, Wayne, was a distant cousin of Anne's. It had been his mother who'd written to Anne asking her to consider moving to the area after the community's last midwife passed away.

Dora leaned closer to Anne. "I heard a rumor that you are walking out with Joseph Lapp."

Anne could barely contain her dismay. "Where did you hear such a thing?"

"My mother-in-law was at McCann's Grocery last evening when Alma Miller came in. Alma said you and Joseph were out for a buggy ride yesterday morning and she saw he had his arm around you. In broad daylight. Alma was shocked. It's not as if the two of you are silly teenagers. You are both baptized members of the church. So what's the story?"

Anne decided to stall until she could think of a plausible explanation. "Mrs. Miller got it wrong. Nine pounds and ten ounces. Your son is growing like a weed." She handed the squirming naked baby back to his mother.

"That's because he eats all the time. I'm lucky to get anything done around the house."

"Isn't your husband helping?" Anne was happy to change the subject.

"With housework? Not a chance. His mother is staying with us, though. I don't know what I would do without her. Lovina has been wonderful. When I first married her son, I thought she didn't like me. But she sure likes her grandson. She calls him *Gottes Shenkas*."

God's gift. Anne smiled. The feeling of being close to God was one of the things she loved most about delivering babies. She took a seat at her desk and began writing her notes in Dora's chart. "Babies have a way of bringing people together. They are pure and simple love from our Lord above."

"*Ja*, they are." Dora kissed her son's forehead and began to dress him. "So how did Alma Miller get it wrong? Was Joseph with someone else? Or were you with someone else?" she asked with renewed interest.

Since the truth was generally the best way to go, Anne replied, "Joseph and I were together. My horse came up lame and Joseph offered to drive me to see Rhonda Yoder. That's all. We are not walking out together."

"Then he didn't have his arm around you?"

She closed her eyes and shook her head. Stick to the facts. "Actually, he did, but only because the horse bolted and I was thrown sideways. He saved me from being dumped off the seat."

"Interesting." Dora didn't appear completely convinced. "I thought it was strange because I didn't think you liked him. I thought you were sweet on Micah Shetler."

"I'm not sweet on Micah and I never said I disliked Joseph. I disliked the fact that he wouldn't keep his goats out of my garden. I was ready to complain to the bishop about it."

"Is that why he's putting up a new fence today?"

Anne looked up from her notes. "He is?"

"I saw him unloading a wagon full of mesh wire and T posts when I drove up."

"Really." She rose from her chair, walked through the house and looked out the kitchen window. Sure enough, Joseph was out in his pasture driving T posts into the ground. He had a row of them about ten feet apart along his existing fence. Leah sat in her stroller several yards away from him. A few of his goats were standing around sniffing her. Anne hoped they wouldn't start eating the sweater the babe was wearing. Surely, Joseph would notice that.

"Is it true that his sister just left her baby with him?"

"Sadly, that is true. I have been helping him take care of Leah, and he has been doing chores for me in exchange."

"It makes it easy that the two of you live so close together."

"It does, but it also makes us food for gossips since we are coming and going between the two houses often. I hope you'll set anyone straight who mentions we are walking out."

"I will do that, but it's a shame you aren't seeing him."

"Why do you say that?"

"A baby needs a mother. Joseph should marry if he

intends to raise the child. It's not right to let her grow up motherless. I hope he knows that. Has he said anything about taking a wife?"

"*Nay*, he hasn't." She frowned at the idea of another woman taking over Leah's care. Was it something Joseph was considering? He hadn't mentioned it.

"If he doesn't wish to wed, my sister and her husband have been trying to have a baby for seven years. They would adopt that little girl in a heartbeat."

Anne shook her head. "I don't think he would give her up."

"He would if he realized it was best for the *bubbel*. When do you want to see me again?"

"As long as you are feeling good and the baby is doing well, a month from today."

"Sounds fine to me. You were a wonderful labor coach, Anne. You made the whole experience something Wayne and I will always remember and cherish."

"You did all the work, Dora. Don't give me the credit." The two women hugged and Dora left with her son in her arms. Wayne sat in the buggy outside waiting on them. He waved at Anne and helped his wife into the buggy. They settled close together and he touched his son's face lovingly.

After they left, Anne walked across her field to where Joseph was putting up the fence. She hated to tell him what she had heard, but she knew he needed to know. He'd taken his coat off and was working with his shirtsleeves rolled up. His forearms were tanned and muscular. He handled the heavy posts and sledgehammer with ease. Was Dora right? Should he marry to give Leah a mother?

"*Wee gayt's,*" he called out as she drew near.

"Good day. I see you have been busy since you picked Leah up this morning. Why didn't you leave her with me?"

He glanced at the baby trying to grab the closest goat. "I was missing my girl. She's not been a bit of trouble. In fact, she put in the first six posts for me."

The image of a baby driving a six-foot steel post into the ground made Anne giggle. "That explains why they're crooked."

He turned to look down the line. "They aren't crooked."

"And they weren't put in by a baby, either. I can't believe you are doing this."

"It was time."

She almost said "Past time," but she held her tongue. "Dora Stoltzfus told me something I thought you'd want to hear."

"Oh? What was that?"

"Alma Miller has been telling people that we are walking out together."

"How would Alma Miller know such a thing?"

"She saw us riding together in the buggy."

"That's not a crime."

"You had your arm around me in broad daylight, which seems to be a crime in Alma's book."

Joseph came to stand opposite Anne at the fence. "I hope you set Dora straight."

"I did. I explained the circumstances, and I told her there was nothing between us. I'm taking care of Leah and that's all there is."

She waited to see his reaction because a part of her was beginning to hope that what she said wasn't true.

There was an attraction growing between them. At least on her part. Did he feel the same way?

Joseph cringed inwardly. Anne spoke so adamantly when she insisted there was nothing personal to their relationship. When he heard her put it so strongly, the words hurt. Maybe there wasn't for her, but there was for him. He had started to care about Anne. How did he tell her that when she was trying to convince others of the exact opposite?

"I'd like to believe we are friends, you and I," he ventured, waiting to see her reaction.

She plucked at a weed that had grown through the fence. "Of course we're friends, but I'm not sure others will understand that."

At least that was something. Her friendship was better than nothing, but he realized it wasn't enough. Maybe in time she would come to think of him as more than a friend.

Was he foolish to hope her feelings would change? The only thing he could do was continue to offer his friendship. And that meant getting the rest of the posts in. "I should get back to work."

Anne remained at the fence. He could see she wanted to say something else. "Is there more?"

"More talk about us? Not that I know of. I need to ask you a favor, but in light of what I just told you, I'm not sure if I should."

"I can't say yes or no until I hear the question."

"I'm out of several of the ingredients I need to make Leah's formula. Daisy is still limping and I can't drive her to town. Is there any chance you could drive me? I see that you're busy. If you can't, that's okay. I think I can handle Duncan if you will allow me to borrow him, but Leah has to stay with you."

He brightened at the chance to do something else for her. "You can't take my horse. I would feel awful if something happened to you and I had to find a new nanny for Leah."

He was rewarded with a tiny smile from her. "Only because you would have to find a new nanny?"

He rolled down his sleeves and pulled on his coat. "Should I have another reason?"

"Because you wouldn't want to cause your friend pain and suffering?"

He moved to stand in front of her. Softly, he said, "That's true. I would never want to hurt you, Anne."

Her cheeks grew pink. "*Danki.* I would never knowingly hurt you, either. That's why I wasn't sure I should ask you to take me to town. What if there is more talk about us?"

"People will always talk. Leah needs her formula. Come to think of it, I need to pick up a few things, too. Shall we go to McCann's Grocery or Miller's General Store?"

He began pushing Leah's stroller toward the gate. Anne walked along on her side of the fence. "McCann's should have everything I need. What about you?"

"Miller's. I need some small-gauge wire to fasten the fence to these posts. I don't have enough on hand. We need to stop at the Beachy Craft Shop after that."

"Why?"

"It's a gathering place. We need to put out the word that you require the loan of a buggy horse until Daisy gets better so I don't have to keep driving you places."

Her expression fell. "I'm sorry it's an inconvenience."

He stopped to face her. "It's not. But if others believe that to be true, our being seen together won't be so remarked upon, and you will soon have a drivable horse."

"That's a good idea."

"Don't sound so surprised. I have them once in a while." He started walking again. When they reached the gate, he opened it and pushed the stroller over to her side.

Anne looked the gate over with a puzzled expression. She swung it back and forth. "Did you fix my gate?"

"How come it is my poor fence, but it's your fixed gate?"

She rolled her eyes. "Very well. Did you fix *your* gate?"

"I did, and I added a weight to it so that it will close on its own and swing in either direction."

"You have been ambitious today."

He enjoyed the admiration in her tone. He started making a mental list of other projects that might please her. "I'll be back with the buggy in a few minutes."

"Leah and I will be ready."

The ride into Honeysuckle didn't take long. They stopped at McCann's Grocery first because it was closest. Anne got out. Joseph stayed put. "Aren't you coming in?"

"I thought I would sit here looking annoyed and bored."

She giggled. "In other words, normal for you."

He started to smile but quickly smothered it. "I don't want it to look like we are enjoying each other's company. Now hurry up. And you're right, annoyed and bored is normal for me."

Anne chose to take Leah with her. Inside the store,

she set the infant carrier inside one of the shopping carts and started down the closest aisle. It didn't take her long to find what she needed, but it did take her a while to get out of the store. She ran into three different women she knew and had to explain to each one of them who Leah was.

By the time she got out, she thought Joseph would truly be annoyed with her for keeping him waiting so long. To her surprise, he was busy talking to the husbands of the women she had encountered. Five men were gathered around one of the buggy horses. Joseph caught sight of her and beckoned her over.

"What do you think of this mare?" The horse was a sturdy-looking black-and-white pinto.

Anne looked her over carefully. "She's a very pretty animal."

"Her disposition is just as sweet," Calvin Miller said. His wife, Alma, was the one who had been spreading gossip about Anne and Joseph.

"Would you be willing to rent her to me for a week or two?" Anne asked.

"I'll loan her to you for a week. No rent needed. Joseph was just telling us how his old goat lamed your mare."

"She hates that goat," Joseph added drily.

"Because he's a menace and you won't keep him locked up," she snapped, rounding on him.

Joseph folded his arms and scowled. "I was putting up a new fence when you decided you needed to come to town today. Don't complain if he's in your garden tomorrow because I didn't get it done."

A couple of the men snickered but quieted when Anne shot them a sharp look. She turned to Calvin. "I would deeply appreciate the loan of your mare. Can you bring her by soon? I would hate to tear Joseph away from his fence building if I need to deliver a baby again. Although I am grateful he found the time to take me out to see Rhonda Yoder yesterday."

Calvin stroked his long beard. "I heard it was a near thing with her babe. The little fellow had a cord around his neck three times. It was *Gottes* mercy that saved him."

All the men nodded and murmured in agreement. How did he and his wife gather so much information in such a short period of time? It was truly amazing.

Calvin patted the mare's neck. "I'll bring Pocahontas along to the church service tomorrow and you can take her home from there."

"That would be *wunderbar*."

Joseph unfolded his arms. "*Goot*. Can we go now? I need to pick up that wire at Miller's General Store before they close."

"I'm ready when you are," she said with a stiff smile.

They walked away from the group and Joseph helped her up into his buggy. He whispered, "How was that?"

"You almost convinced me we don't like each other."

"Then we should confound them even further. It is getting late. How would you like to have dinner with me at the Mennonite Family Restaurant?"

"What reason will we give for going there?"

He rubbed his stomach. "Anne, I'm hungry. I haven't had lunch or dinner today. I've been putting up fence and running you all over town."

"Oh, in that case, *danki*. I'll be happy to join you. They have a very nice buffet on Saturdays."

"Sounds perfect."

Anne waited in the buggy with Leah while Joseph

purchased his wire. He was out of the store in record time. They left the buggy where it was and walked to the restaurant. It was busy inside, but the waitress was able to seat them at a small booth in the back corner and brought them two large glasses of sweet iced tea.

Most of the patrons were Amish families enjoying a special night out. A few were *Englisch* folk, tourists, from the way they gawked at those in Plain dress. The room was cozy with green-and-white-checked table-cloths and curtains on the windows. The benches in the booths were covered in solid green vinyl to match them.

Joseph stayed with Leah while Anne filled her plate. When she came back, she sat down and waited for him to return. He came back with two heaping plates of food.

Anne looked at him in amazement. "Can you really eat all that?"

"This will be a good start. Did you see the dessert bar? I'm hankering for a big piece of that carrot cake."

"Poor Margaret." Anne shook her head.

He began to salt his mound of potatoes. "Who's Margaret?"

"She's the owner of this place and she's going to lose money on you."

He gestured toward Anne's plate. "*Nay*, she won't. You eat like a bird. We will balance each other."

Anne coveted the warmth spilling through her veins. They did balance each other in many ways. She dropped her gaze to her hands folded on the table. Was she being foolish to believe it could lead to something more?

What did the soft expression on Anne's face mean? Joseph knew she wasn't indifferent to him. If she liked him, maybe she cared more than she let on.

Leah kicked and cooed in her basket. Anne picked her up, but Joseph said, "I'll take her."

He settled her on his lap, took the baby's hands and held them between his own as he bowed his head to pray. Leah protested only briefly before keeping still. Joseph began silently reciting the *Gebet Nach Dem Essen*, the Prayer Before Meals.

O Lord God, heavenly Father, bless us and these Thy gifts, which we accept from Thy tender goodness. Give us food and drink also for our souls unto life eternal, that we may share at Thy heavenly table, through Jesus Christ. Amen.

He followed it with the Lord's Prayer, also prayed silently, knowing he had much to be thankful for but still asking God to bring Fannie home soon.

Joseph lifted his head, signaling the end of the prayer for Anne. He patted Leah's check and told her what a good girl she was. Anne looked pleased with both of them as she took Leah from him and settled the baby on her shoulder.

The smell of baking bread and pot roast filled the air. Joseph thought back to the food his mother used to make. Roast beef and roast pork, fried chicken and potatoes, schnitzel with sauerkraut, all served piping hot from her stove with fresh bread smeared with butter and vegetables from her garden. He hadn't given a thought to how much work his mother had done without complaint until she was gone.

Cooking was a struggle after that. Fannie eventually grew up and learned enough to take over the kitchen, but she never found the joy in it his mother seemed to have. Maybe it was because his mother had a husband she wished to please and *kinner* to watch grow big and strong on the meals she gave them.

Anne would be like that. He could see her making sure all her children ate their vegetables and drank their milk. She should have little ones.

To do that, she would have to marry.

"Anne, I'm surprised to see you here."

Joseph looked over his shoulder to see Micah Shetler approaching with a friendly grin on his handsome face. Joseph's enjoyment of the evening started going downhill.

Chapter Sixteen

Anne was pleasantly surprised to see Micah Shetler approaching. She had wondered how he was doing now that his brother was about to marry the woman Micah had been courting only a few weeks ago.

"*Wee gayt's*, Micah. How have you been?"

"Busy."

"I'm sure you are with your brother's wedding approaching." She gave him a sympathetic smile. Both Micah and his brother, Neziah, had been walking out with her friend Ellen Beachy. Their father and Ellen's father had decided it was time Ellen married and she was expected to choose one of the brothers. At first it had looked as though Micah would be her husband, but then Neziah had won her heart. She'd fallen in love with him and they would marry in a few days.

If Micah was suffering from a broken heart, it didn't show, although there was something different about him now. She couldn't put her finger on what it was.

"I drove by the other day and saw your stand was closed for the season. I stopped in but you weren't home."

"I'm sorry I missed you."

He gestured toward Leah. "Are you keeping the babies that you deliver now?"

"*Nay*, this is Joseph's niece."

"Anne is acting as her nanny until her mother returns." Joseph's annoyed tone made Anne glance at him sharply. Why was he upset?

Micah noticed, too, but it seemed to amuse him. "You couldn't find a more caring and capable woman than Anne to look after the child. I would let her take care of all my *kinner*. Of course, I don't have any. But who knows? That may change one day."

"One day soon?" Anne teased.

"You'll be among the first to know. It was good seeing you, Anne. I may stop in again one of these days."

"I'm always happy to see you." She wondered with dismay if he was going to ask her to walk out with him. He was a fine, good-looking man, but she wasn't on the hunt for a husband. Why else would he want to speak to her?

He walked away and stopped at another table where a young Amish woman sat with her parents. Anne didn't recognize them. They weren't from her church district. She noticed the way the girl pointedly avoided looking at Micah as he spoke to her father. What surprised Anne was the warm way Micah's glance rested on the young woman. Was there a new romance blooming in his life?

"Joseph, do you know the family Micah is speaking with?"

"Henry Hochstetler. He owns a harness shop over in the next town. He's done some work for me."

"Is that his wife and daughter?"

"*Ja*. Why do you ask?"

"No real reason."

"Micah is a friend of yours?"

She glanced at Joseph and found him watching her intently. "I guess you could say that. He's always been nice to me."

"He's nice to all the women." Joseph stabbed his slice of meat loaf with his fork.

"True," she admitted. Micah was known as something of a flirt, but the same could be said for his father, Simeon Shetler. Anne knew neither of them meant any harm. As Micah walked away from Henry Hochstetler and his family, the daughter finally looked up. When she did, her eyes followed Micah with poignant longing.

"Why would he be coming to visit you?" Joseph asked.

"I have no idea. His brother is marrying my friend, so perhaps it has something to do with the wedding plans."

"That's not likely."

"Is there a reason you dislike Micah?" she asked, intrigued by the hostility she sensed.

"I never said that."

"Sounds that way to me."

"You're wrong. I've nothing against the man."

"I'm sorry I misunderstood." She wasn't wrong. He did dislike Micah. She decided to change the subject. "How's that meat loaf? I might get a piece."

"It's *goot*. How's your salad?"

"It's okay, but I don't care for the dressing."

"Try the pickled okra. It's great."

"Yuck."

"You don't like okra?" He looked stunned.

She shook her head. "Not pickled. Fried is okay, but not pickled. I don't care for pickled anything."

"Pickled beets?"

"Nope."

"Sauerkraut? Everyone likes sauerkraut."

"Not everyone. What food do you dislike?"

He shrugged. "I don't know. I haven't tasted it yet."

"When you marry, your wife is going to find you very easy to cook for."

"What makes you think I'm going to marry?"

"I just assumed you would when you met the right woman."

He grew somber. "I did meet her. A long time ago."

"I'm sorry. I heard about your loss." He didn't mention her name. The Amish rarely spoke about those who had passed away.

"It was *Gottes* will," he said.

"All is the will of God," Anne agreed, thinking of the baby whose name she never spoke aloud but would carry in her heart forever.

What would Joseph say if he learned her story? Would he be forgiving? Or would he decide to find another woman to look after Leah? One without a blemished past. No one in Honeysuckle knew about her unwed pregnancy. That secret had remained in Ohio, known only to a few members of her family.

Joseph would never learn about that part of her life unless she decided to share it with him and she had no reason to do so.

The following day was Church Sunday, which was held at the home of an Amish family who lived less than two miles from Anne. Her mare, Daisy, was still limping, but Anne was able to walk the distance easily. She would've walked much farther to avoid riding to the prayer meeting with Joseph. That would really set tongues wagging.

Joseph arrived with Leah a short time after Anne reached the farmhouse. His arrival generated a number of comments from the women who were bringing food into the home and preparing to feed the congregation later. When questioned, Anne assured those who would listen that she was not romantically involved with Joseph. Some of her friends winked and smiled as if they didn't believe her. She wasn't surprised that she had to defend herself, but she was surprised by the number of older women who voiced their concerns about Leah being raised without a mother. By a man who wasn't her father. That Joseph was her uncle seem to carry little weight with them.

From her place among the unmarried women during the service, Anne could see Joseph and Leah from the corner of her eye. She didn't dare turn her attention to him. Halfway through the three-hour-long prayer meeting, Leah's patience evaporated and she began to fuss. Joseph took her outside. Anne followed as unobtrusively as she could. She found them at the rear of his buggy. "Do you want me to take her for a while?"

"She needs to be changed and fed. I can manage."

"I know you can. But now that I have come outside, it might be best if I returned in the role of a nanny."

"I reckon you're right. Has there been more talk?"

"Not about us so much." She wasn't sure how to broach the subject the women had been discussing.

"About Fannie?" He looked braced to hear the worst.

"*Nay*, it's nothing. Idle chatter. Go back and I'll bring Leah in when she is finished with her bottle. I'll keep her with me until after the preaching is done." Maybe if the women saw Leah was getting adequate attention from Anne, they would be less critical of Joseph. She wasn't Leah's mother, but she would do her best to provide the child with a role model.

She kept the baby with her for the rest of the morning. Once the service was over, she carried Leah outside, happy to show off the good-natured baby to those who admired her.

It wasn't long before Joseph approached. "I'm leaving now."

"You don't intend to stay for the meal?" she asked, wishing he would make an effort to join in with the community.

"I have two sick goats I need to tend. I'll take Calvin Miller's horse home for you."

Anne handed over Leah, and he left without another word. She glanced at the women around her and saw disapproval on several faces. Joseph needed to realize he wasn't alone. He was part of a large and caring community. All he had to do was reach out to them to be accepted. The more he distanced himself, the less they were able to know and understand him.

"He would be a good match for you, Anne," Rhonda whispered in her ear. She and her husband had chosen to attend services with Anne's church since they were staying with Naomi until Rhonda's mother arrived to help the young couple with their newborn son.

"I'm not looking for a match."

"I wasn't either when I found Silas. Now look at us."

Dora joined their group. "I agree. The babe needs a mother. You should marry him."

"I can hardly marry a man who hasn't proposed to me." Anne reined in her irritation.

"I think Micah has his eye on you," Rebecca Yoder added. She was Rhonda's sister-in-law and still single. She glanced across the way to where the young men were gathered in groups.

Anne shook her head. "Micah can put his eyes back in his head. I'm not going to marry anyone!"

She left the group to visit with Naomi for a while, then headed home. She was happy to have the long walk alone with her thoughts.

Joseph was working on his last section of fence posts when he saw Micah drive up to Anne's home on Monday morning. Joseph didn't pause in his work. He knew Anne was gone. She had been called out two hours ago to attend a delivery. He had Leah in the stroller at his side as he worked.

"Good day, Joseph," Micah called cheerfully as he approached after he realized Anne wasn't home.

"Good enough, I guess." Joseph drove in the last stake.

"Do you happen to know where Anne is?"

"Gone to deliver a baby."

"So there is no telling when she will be back?"

"Nope."

Micah looked disappointed. "I guess I can stick around for a while in case she comes back soon. Would you like some help?"

"The stakes are all in."

"I can help stretch the wire. It's a two-man job."

It was easier with two. Joseph shrugged. "Suit yourself."

Micah came into the pen and waded through the goats to Joseph's side. "Friendly bunch, aren't they?"

"I think so." Joseph pulled a roll of wire off his wagon and began unrolling it.

Micah grabbed the loose end and pulled it to the corner post. "Do you mind if I ask you a question about Anne?"

"What about her?" Joseph fastened the fencing to the post with small strips of wire that he tightened with a pair of pliers.

"There's some talk going around that you are walking out with her. I was wondering if that's true."

"What difference does it make to you?"

"If you aren't seeing Anne, then I'd like to ask her to walk out with me."

"She is my niece's nanny. That's all. She watches the baby while I work and I help her with her garden and fix things around the farm."

"That's good to know. I didn't want to step on anyone's toes."

They finished stretching the fence and securing it by early afternoon. Joseph was grateful for the help, but he was happier when Micah finally gave up and left without seeing Anne.

Would she walk out with him? There was no reason she shouldn't. Micah was a well-liked member of the community. Joseph had no reason to dislike the man, but he did.

And in a moment of honesty, he realized it was because Micah was interested in Anne. Not as a nanny or as a midwife but as a woman and a potential wife.

Why did the thought of Micah and Anne together irritate him so? Joseph never imagined himself as the dog in a manger, but apparently, he was. He wasn't interested in her as a wife. He enjoyed her friendship. He liked her smile. He wanted to see her happy.

He took the handles of Leah's stroller and began pushing her toward his house. Just because he was happy being single, didn't mean Anne was happy being single. Women were different. They wanted different things in life. If she wanted Micah, then he would be happy for her.

Maybe.

Matilda came to his side. The rest of the herd followed along. She looked up at him with wise brown eyes. Joseph had to admit the truth. "Maybe I wouldn't be happy about it."

It didn't seem right. He couldn't imagine Anne and Micah as a couple. Being married. Matilda bleated softly.

Joseph nodded. "*Ja*, I know. They don't fit together."

The more he thought about it, the more upset he became. Anne would be a wonderful mother and wife, but she deserved someone who loved her. Not someone who decided to take a wife because his brother was marrying the woman he truly wanted. Anne wasn't second best. She deserved better.

Matilda paused to scratch her ankle with her nose. He paused and looked down at her. "I know. It's none of my business what she wants."

"What who wants?"

His gaze shot from Matilda to the new gate, where Anne stood waiting for his reply. "Nothing."

"Joseph, were you talking to the goat?"

"I was. What of it?"

Anne's eyebrow rose a fraction. "Did she answer you?"

"*Nay*, she was no help at all."

Anne pushed open the gate. "That's a relief. *Hallo*, Leah. Are you ready to come to my house while your *onkel* gets the milking done?"

He pushed the stroller out of his pen and up to Anne. "Micah dropped by to see you."

"He said he might." She began walking toward her house.

Joseph glanced at her as he fell into step beside her. She didn't look particularly excited by the news. "He waited for several hours."

"That's too bad. Did you tell him what I was doing?"

"I did. He wanted to wait, anyway. He helped me finish my fence. We spent a lot of time talking."

"I noticed you had the fence up. Alvin and Mary King had a healthy baby girl."

She didn't act like a woman smitten with a fellow. Joseph stopped walking. "That's good to hear. Don't you want to know what Micah and I talked about?"

She kept walking. "Not really."

"We talked about you."

"That wouldn't take up several hours."

"You underestimate your attraction, Anne."

She rounded on him. "What are you talking about?"

"Micah is interested in walking out with you."

She planted her hands on her hips. "Did he ask you to be his go-between?"

Chapter Seventeen

Anne knew it was common practice for a young Amish man to have a member of the girl's family or one of her friends find out if she would be receptive to his courting. She considered it something bashful teenage boys engaged in. Not grown men.

Joseph stared at his feet. "Not exactly."

"Then what *exactly* did he say?"

"He wanted to know if you and I were walking out."

"I'm getting very tired of answering that question. I hope you set him straight."

Joseph held up both hands. "I told him you were Leah's nanny. Nothing else."

That didn't exactly flatter her. "*Goot.* What else did he say?"

"I reckon I should let him tell you."

She closed her eyes. "I knew it. He wants to ask me out again, doesn't he?"

"You don't sound very happy about it."

"I'm *not* happy about it. I'm not interested in walking out with Micah. He's a nice man, but he isn't the one for me."

Joseph sighed in relief. "I'm glad to hear you say that."

"What does that mean?"

He looked taken aback. "Just that he doesn't seem right for you."

She planted her hands on her hips again. "Since when do you get to decide who is the right man for me?"

He dropped his gaze to his boots. "That's not what I meant."

She took Leah's stroller from him. "I am in charge of my own life. If I wish to walk out with Micah, I will do that."

"I only said that he didn't seem right for you. You are free to choose. You would make any man a fine wife."

He looked so contrite that she began to feel she had overreacted. "I'm sorry. It's not you. My friends are all telling me who to go out with and who I should wed. No one is asking me what I want."

"What do you want, Anne?" he asked quietly.

Anne met his gaze. There was genuine concern in his beautiful stormy-gray eyes.

She bent to unbuckle Leah from her stroller and lifted the babe to her shoulder. "I don't know."

That was a lie. She did know. She wanted the man with the stormy eyes to want her. Not as a nanny, a friend, a neighbor, but as a man wants a woman he has come to cherish. It was a foolish thought, but it had taken root in her heart and she couldn't weed it out. Her head said it wasn't possible but her heart wasn't ready to give up.

He stepped close and placed a hand on Anne's shoulder. "When you do know, I hope God grants you all that you desire."

How was that to happen when Joseph was blind to anything but her friendship?

The next few days passed in a comfortable pattern for Joseph. He rose early, got Leah up and dressed her for the day. He carried her to Anne's house, had a cup of coffee with her, then did his milking and chores. He took care of his horse, fed and watered Anne's horses, cleaned the stalls and made sure the animals were all in good health. Daisy's leg improved, but he knew it was time for her to retire from pulling a buggy. Anne would have to buy a new horse soon.

In the late morning, Anne would bring Leah to his place when he was done working outside. Leah stayed with him until the evening milking, when Anne came to pick her up again.

After he was finished, he walked the hundred yards to Anne's house again. On Wednesday night he found her in a flurry of activity.

"What's the occasion?" he asked, noting the array of baked goods on the counter.

"The wedding," she said happily.

He frowned. "What wedding?"

"Ellen Beachy and Neziah Shetler."

"I forgot all about it. Are you going?"

She glanced over her shoulder. "Of course I'm going. Aren't you?"

"I hadn't thought about it."

"You got an invitation, didn't you?"

"I don't usually go to these things."

She stopped stirring something on the stove and turned to face him. "You should start."

"Why?"

"Because people need to see that you are raising Leah according to our ways."

"I take her to church."

"Our community is much more than a church service. It's about fellowship and friendship. It's about being able to depend on each other. Almost from the time an Amish child is born, they know where they belong, that they are loved and cherished. By everyone, not just their families. Leah needs to be a part of that. She needs to form bonds and friendships."

"She will when she goes to school." He picked her up from her playpen.

"She won't feel that she belongs if you don't feel that way, Joseph."

He wouldn't look at Anne. "You will take her to the weddings and picnics and haystack suppers. She will learn what she needs from you."

Anne sighed heavily. "I'm a temporary nanny. I'm not her parent."

"Neither am I. I didn't want this responsibility. I didn't ask for it. Why is it up to me?" He took Leah and left, letting the door slam behind him.

Regretting his outburst the minute he stepped outside, Joseph walked toward home with lagging steps. He hadn't gone far when he heard her voice behind him.

"Joseph, wait."

He stopped. "I wasn't cut out to be a parent. I know it. You don't need to point it out."

"I wasn't trying to do that."

"All I want is to be left alone and to raise my goats. Why can't I do that?"

"Because you belong among us. You are part of the whole that is the fabric of this place and our people."

"Am I? Maybe Fannie had the right idea. Leave and have done with it. Why pretend to be something I'm not?"

Anne laid a hand on his arm. "You don't believe that."

"I'm not sure what I believe anymore."

He expected more arguments from her, but she simply said, "All right. I'll take Leah to the wedding with me if you will permit it. You don't have to come."

It was what he wanted, wasn't it? "*Danki.* I'll have her ready."

As Anne walked away, Joseph knew he had failed some test in her eyes. He went home, but he slept fitfully that night. When morning came, he had Leah ready before Anne drove up in her buggy. He walked out on the porch with the baby asleep in her basket.

He handed Leah up to Anne. "She had a bottle a half hour ago."

"Okay. I'll be home before dark."

"Enjoy yourself."

"I will. You can come later if you feel like it. For the dinner or for the supper. You'll be welcome."

"I doubt I'll make it."

She nodded but didn't speak. Picking up the reins, she turned the spotted mare around and drove away.

As he watched them go, a bitter sense of loss settled in his chest. He had gotten his wish. He was alone and it wasn't what he wanted, after all. The only person he had to blame was himself.

Anne put another dozen plates in the dishwater and added a small squirt of soap to the waning suds in the tub set up on a sawhorse at the side of the house. As a friend of the bride, she was doing her part to help Ellen's family during the massive undertaking. The wedding had gone off beautifully and the dinner was winding down. Anne had no idea how many people had been fed, but she guessed it was over two hundred. She began scrubbing the plates. Once the dinner was done, the preparations for the evening meal would get under way. Amish weddings were an all-day affair.

She glanced beside her. Leah was finally asleep again in her Moses basket. She had been held and passed around by the older girls responsible for watching the younger *kinner* for most of the morning. As far as Anne could tell, Leah had enjoyed every minute of the attention.

She heard a buggy rolling in and washed faster. They would need the plates to feed the newcomers. Glancing in the direction of the sound, she let a dish slip back into the soapy water. Joseph stepped out of his buggy looking very handsome in his dark Sunday suit and black hat. His suit fit snuggly over his broad shoulders. The dark material made his gray eyes look brighter. He pulled his hat off and smoothed his thick blond hair with one hand. He wasn't smiling, but Anne's heart skipped with happiness at the sight of his dear, sweet face. She knew how hard this was for him, but he was making the effort for Leah.

After handing his horse over to the young man parking the buggies, he walked toward the house. He stopped when he saw Anne. He gave her a brief nod and walked inside.

She was so happy for him that she wanted to sing for joy. It was a start. If he wanted, he could find his way back into the tight-knit community and he wouldn't have to be alone. And best of all, Leah wouldn't grow up in his self-imposed isolation, as Anne feared she might.

Anne didn't mention his attendance at the wedding when Joseph saw her the next day, but he knew she was pleased with him. She was smiling and happy, singing as she worked in the house. He took his time finishing his coffee. He liked the sound of her voice floating down the stairs as she stripped the sheets to wash them. It was hard to leave and get his own work done but he finally tore himself away. She brought him lunch when she brought Leah back after the morning milking. Thick slices of ham and cheese on homemade bread. It was a rare treat for him.

That evening, he wondered if she would bring supper, too, but she showed up on his doorstep with only Leah.

"I decided that it's time," she said brightly.

A half smile tugged at his lips. "Time for what?"

"To prove my friendship, and because I agreed to it as a way to repay you for getting my pumpkins sold, I will do the milking this evening."

He clapped a hand to his chest. "Be still, my happy heart. Are you serious?"

She handed him the baby. She was wide-awake. He held her to his shoulder. Anne started walking toward the barn. "The house is clean. Supper is in the oven. I find I have some free time this evening. You will have to watch Leah."

"I think I may need to sit down. I never thought I would see this day."

"You already know I can do this. You showed me how. I'm reasonably sure I remember everything you told me." She pulled open the barn door.

"On second thought, I won't sit down. I'm coming with you."

"That sounds like you don't trust me." She shot him a saucy grin.

"I absolutely trust you but this is some very expensive equipment."

She flipped on a switch. He heard the generators start up. A few seconds later, the lights came on. She smiled. "So far, so good. This isn't hard at all."

Joseph gave a bark of laughter. She raised her chin and walked to the door that opened to the goats' pen. "Here, girls. Up you go!"

The goats came in and they kept coming. She tried to close the door but they squeezed past her. Those in the lead ran to their stanchions. Those that didn't have a place began crowding the others out of the way. Several of them fell off the platform and tried crawling underneath to get at the feed in the wheelbarrow on the other side. Anne struggled desperately to get the door closed, but another goat got her head through and Anne couldn't latch it. "Joseph, help me!"

"You're right. It's not hard at all. You are doing fine."

Anne could have cheerfully chucked another tomato at him. Maybe even a pumpkin. Why did he have to be enjoying himself at her expense? "What do I do?"

Chuckling, he walked to her side. He put his hand on the goat's nose and pushed her back. "Wait your turn, Abigail."

The goat backed out, and Anne was finally able to shut the door. She looked at the mass of goats milling about inside. "Now what?"

He pointed to the ramp leading down from the milk-ing platform. "Open the out door."

Anne made her way through the herd and opened the door he indicated. The goats reluctantly began to leave. They expected to be milked and fed and they were con-fused. Joseph hurried them along with slaps on their rear ends. After a few minutes, the area was clear.

"Do you want to try this again?" He was struggling not to laugh as he balanced Leah on his shoulder.

Anne shuddered. "Not particularly, but how else am I going to learn?"

"*Goot* girl. Open the in door only wide enough for one goat at a time. Count them as they come through. We can only milk twelve. Shut the door on the thirteenth goat. If she gets her head in, a thump on the nose will make her back out."

Anne gathered her resolve and returned to the door. She slid it open a little way, using her knee to keep it from being fully opened by the rush. When she had twelve, she pushed the door shut. Just like last time, one more goat got her head in. Anne pushed her back. "Wait your turn, Abigail."

"That is Jenny," Joseph said.

"I don't care what her name is—I want her to get back!" The goat complied and Anne slid the door closed. She dusted her hands off, feeling pleased with her effort.

That soon faded. It took her four hours to finish milk-ing. It normally took Joseph just under two. When the last goat went out the door, he showed Anne how to clean the milkers and tubing and then said, "You're done."

Her *kapp* had come off in her struggles at the door and hung by a single bobby pin from the back of her bun. Her feet were bruised from the multitude of hooves walking over them and her arms ached from reaching above her head to clean udders and attach milkers. The platform that was waist-high on Joseph was shoulder level for her. She leaned against the metal barn wall. "I'll never do this again."

Joseph came up and put his arm around her, gave her a hug and kissed her forehead. "You did great for your first time."

She was so flabbergasted by his display of affection that she simply stood there with her mouth open while he walked out.

If goat wrestling got her this much attention, she would definitely do it again.

Chapter Eighteen

The next morning started out as well as the previous day. Anne seemed happy, if a bit stiff after her milking ordeal. Leah was happy, too, after sleeping through the entire night for the first time. Smiles, laughs, gurgles and coos greeted Joseph when he picked her up in the morning. She quickly grabbed a handful of his hair and tried to put it in her mouth. Joseph liked the direction his life was taking. Thanks to Anne, it was all working out.

In the early afternoon, he picked up the mail before loading the last of his yearlings to take to market. He found the usual assortment of junk mail and a single letter that made his heart freeze for an instant before it began hammering wildly.

It was from Fannie, but there was no return address. He tore it open.

> Dear Joe,
> I'm writing because I know you have been wait-
> ing for this letter. I know you, Joe. You think I
> will change my mind and return to your little goat
> farm, but I won't. I wised up and left Johnny. He

wasn't much of a boyfriend and he certainly wasn't father material. I have to get my life straightened out. I'm in some trouble, but it's nothing you can fix. I have to do this myself. I can't have Leah with me, as much as I want to hold her again. I hope you'll tell her that her mother loves her. I know it doesn't seem that way, but it's true. The best life I can give her is a life with you. I didn't know what a good thing I had when I lived in Honeysuckle until it was too late.

None of this is your fault. Don't blame yourself. I made my own choices and now I have to live with them. Maybe that means I've finally grown up. This is my last letter, brother. Don't look for another one from me. I will only disappoint you again.

Your baby sister always,

Fannie

Joseph crushed the single page into a tiny ball as grief gripped his heart. She was wrong. It *was* his fault. He had failed her somehow. He hadn't given her what she'd needed.

Smoothing out the letter, he carried it to the house, where he went to his family Bible. It sat in a place of honor on an ornately carved stand that had been made by his great-great-grandfather. He opened the book and leafed through it until he found the story of Moses. Tucking the letter between the pages, he closed the book. Someday he would let Leah read her mother's letter. It might help her understand why her mother had left her. He prayed it would comfort her. It didn't comfort him.

He walked outside and saw he had a visitor. Bishop Andy stepped down from his buggy.

"*Wee gayt's*, Joseph. How are you this cold morning?"

"I'm fine, Bishop. What brings you out this way?" It was unusual for the spiritual leader of the congregation to come calling. Unease settled between Joseph's shoulder blades.

"It has been a while since I've spoken to you. You didn't stay long after the last service. I thought I would see how you are doing."

"I'm fine."

"How is your niece? I understand she was sick."

"Leah is fine now that she's drinking goat's milk. She is with Anne until I finish my chores."

"I won't keep you from your work. Is it true that your sister does not plan to return for the child?"

He couldn't pretend anymore that Fannie would be back. "That is what she said in the last letter I had from her."

"You are a good man, Joseph. Not friendly with your neighbors but always willing to help when there is a need."

"I hope that I do my part."

"And I must do my part for the spiritual health of the congregation God has entrusted to me. Raising a child is a sacred duty. I find myself in an unhappy position, Joseph."

"How so?" He didn't like where this was heading.

"Several members of our community have expressed concern about your niece. They feel it is not right for a bachelor to rear an infant alone. I am in agreement. A baby needs a mother's touch, a mother's love."

"I would gladly return her to her mother if I knew where she was," he said drily.

"I'm sure that is true. It is a sad thing for a man to lose his sister to the outside world. My worry is about your niece."

"Anne is taking good care of Leah. She is a kind woman, and she loves the child."

"But is it enough? Is the care of a nanny a substitute for a mother? *Nay*, it is not. I am here to urge you to wed, Joseph. Take a wife and give this baby a mother."

"I don't want a wife. I don't need a wife. I can manage on my own. I raised Fannie by myself."

"She was not an infant at the time your parents died. She had known a mother's love and care. It might have been better had you taken a wife, for it is clear Fannie has wandered far from our teachings. Some will lay that at your door and say it is proof that this babe is better off in a home with both a mother and a father."

Wasn't that what he believed, too? That his failure had led to his sister falling away from their faith.

"If you cannot in good conscience marry one of the suitable women in our community, I urge you to consider allowing one of our childless couples to raise Leah."

"And if I refuse?"

"This is a very serious matter. I have prayed on it, and I believe I'm only asking what is best for the child. You must pray on it, as well. We will talk again in a few days. It is my fervent hope that you will have reached a decision by then. I don't want to take the child away from you, but I will do what I must."

When the bishop had left, Joseph sank onto his porch steps and put his head in his hands. "What do You want from me, Lord? What do You want? Do You want someone else to raise her? Why leave her with me in the first place and let me grow to love her?"

He couldn't give Leah up. He couldn't. She was more than his only connection to Fannie. She was the child he was learning to love as a father would love a daughter. That left him only one option. Find a wife.

The list of women he would consider was short. There was only one name on it.

Joseph rose to his feet, settled his hat on his head and walked toward Anne's place. She might not know it, but she held the answer to Leah's future. He had to make her understand that. He didn't try fooling himself. It wasn't going to be easy. Anne was set in her ways just as he was, but she loved Leah. That was the key. She loved the child. He saw it every time they were together.

Somehow he had to convince her that they belonged together permanently.

Anne was surprised to see Joseph so early in the day. "I thought you were taking some of the young bucks to the livestock sale in town."

"I've changed my mind. I'll go next week. There is always another sale."

"True. Would you like some coffee? I'm afraid it's getting old. I made it early this morning."

"*Nay*, I'm fine. Where is Leah?"

"She's sleeping in my office. I thought I would get these jars washed so I can start making pumpkin puree." She gestured toward the assortment of gourds lined up along the wall. "I'm a little tired of the pumpkins decorating my kitchen."

"You are always finding something to do."

"That's because my work never ends." She plunged

her hands into the hot soapy water in her sink and began washing her small canning jars and lids.

"There is something I need to talk to you about."

"And what is that? Has Chester eaten my windmill or my buggy?"

"Anne, we've gotten along well together these last few weeks. Don't you think?"

She chuckled. "Compared to the past three years, I'd say you are right, Joseph."

"I'm being serious now. Please come and sit down. I can't talk to your back."

Anne stopped washing the dishes and dried her hands as she turned to face him. The look on his face frightened her. "What is it? What's wrong?"

He managed a half smile with some effort. "Nothing's wrong. I just want to talk to you."

"All right. I'm listening."

She waited, but he didn't say anything. He had his hands deep in his pockets as he shifted his weight from one foot to the other. She folded her arms, giving him her complete attention.

He glanced at her face and suddenly crossed to the stove. "A cup of *coffe* would be *goot* right now. Would you like one?" He pulled a mug from her cabinet and began filling it from her coffeepot.

"*Nay*, I'm fine. Help yourself. What is it that you wanted to talk to me about?" Something was very odd. She had never seen him look so nervous.

"*Koom* and sit at the table." He settled in a chair.

She pulled out the one across from him and sat down. "All right, I'm sitting. Joseph, what is going on?"

He took a sip of his coffee and then gripped the mug between his fingers. His knuckles stood out white. "My farm is small, but I have room for expansion in my milking parlor. I could double my goat herd if I had someone to help me."

"Twice as many goats next door? Ack, I would not be overjoyed. No wonder you wanted me to sit down." She didn't bother to hide her sarcasm.

He cleared his throat. "I'm trying to tell you that I can support a family."

"That's good, since you already have one child."

"You have hit the nail on the head. I already have a child."

"And?"

"You love Leah. I can see that. You are like a mother to her. She will never remember Fannie."

Anne dropped her gaze to stare at her hands. "I do love Leah, with all my heart."

Joseph reached across the table and took Anne's hand in his. Startled, her gaze shot to his face. "You want what is best for her. So do I. I think it is best that she have a *mudder*."

"She has a *mudder*."

"*Nay*, she does not. I received a letter from Fannie this morning. She is never coming home. She wants me to raise Leah. I can't do that by myself. I need a helpmate. Someone who will love Leah as a mother loves a child."

Anne had no idea where this conversation was going. "Are you trying to tell me that you have decided to marry?"

Relief filled his eyes. "*Ja.* That is exactly what I'm trying to say."

Anne blinked hard as his words settled in her mind. He was going to take a wife. That would change everything. He wouldn't need a nanny. He wouldn't need her.

When he married, she would have no part in Leah's life except as the kindly woman next door. Of course, she expected Leah to grow up. In a few years, she would have no need for a *kindt heedah*. She would start school and soon be old enough to take care of herself.

Tears stung the back of Anne's eyes. She'd thought she would be able to hold her darling girl and sing her to sleep until that time. She'd thought she had years to enjoy her baby, to watch her grow up. Now Joseph was telling her another woman would take her place.

How would she bear being alone again without her baby to brighten each day?

She fumbled for the right words to say. "I wish you every happiness, Joseph. Who have you chosen?"

"I've chosen you."

Anne snatched her hand away from him. Was he out of his mind? "What do you mean by that?"

"I knew I wouldn't do this right. I'm sorry. Anne, will you do me the honor of becoming my wife? Will you become Leah's *mudder*? My farm is small, and so is yours. If we combine them, we will have more than enough for one family."

"You want me to marry you so that you can have my farm?" She drew back to glare at him. She didn't know if she was outraged or simply floored by his audacity.

"Not for the farm, but you must admit it makes sense. You are a reasonable woman."

"I thought I was until this minute."

It seemed to dawn on him that he had made a mistake. "Please, Anne. Hear me out. I like you a great deal. I hope I have not offended you. I think that you like me, too. We have become friends. *Goot* friends. Many a marriage has started with less and prospered. We both love

Leah. Together we can give her all that she needs. Will you consider my offer?"

He liked her, but he hadn't said that he loved her. Her feelings for him had grown by leaps and bounds in the past few weeks. It hurt that he didn't return them. "Friendship isn't enough to hold a marriage together."

"Isn't it? It's what binds a man and woman together. Love is like a bonfire. It burns bright and hot, but it dies down. The glowing embers of the fire are what give the warmth that lets a person draw near and use the fire. To heat a home. To cook a meal. To forge iron. Friendship is like those embers. It sustains us."

Anne rose to her feet and crossed the kitchen to the sink. She gripped the edge and bowed her head. Would it be so wrong to accept him? She loved him, but could she spend a lifetime with a man who didn't love her in return?

She would have Leah, too, as her very own babe to love and care for her entire life.

Joseph might not love her now, but perhaps he could learn to love her over time. If she said no, he would look elsewhere for a wife and she would have to watch another woman become the center of his life. How could she bear that?

He came to stand behind her and placed his hands on her shoulders. He was so close she could feel his warmth. If she leaned back, she would be in his arms. Wasn't that where she wanted to be?

She had been given a choice. She could move into his arms or remain alone for the rest of her life and grow old with no one to care for her or about her.

Leah began fussing in the other room. The overwhelming urge to go comfort the child made up Anne's mind.

But before she agreed to become Joseph's wife, she needed to tell him about her shameful past. She dreaded the look of condemnation that would fill his eyes, but it wasn't fair to try and keep her secret from him now. Not even if it cost her everything.

She drew a deep breath and turned around.

"Before I give you an answer, there are some things you need to know about me."

A half smile tilted his lips. "I know as much about you as I need to know. You are kind. You are hardworking. You are a woman of faith. A little bossy perhaps, but you love Leah."

"You must listen to me. There was a time when I was not such a good woman. I was a foolish teenage girl who fell in love with the wrong man."

His grin disappeared. "Was this during your *rumspringa*? Before you were baptized?"

"Ja." She closed her eyes as shame burned in her chest.

"Have you violated the Ordnung, the rules of our church, since you took your vows?" he asked softly.

She opened her eyes so he could read the truth in them. *"Nay,* I have not."

He laid a finger to her lips as his gaze softened. "Then there is no need to speak of the past."

"You have a right to know."

"That is between you and God. The sins of your past were forgiven. I have made mistakes, too. I have done things that displeased the Lord, but I sought forgiveness and it was given to me. Our souls were made new through baptism."

Anne's heart swelled with love. She could not ask for a better mate in life. Joseph was a good man in every sense of the word. She would be blessed to be his wife. Was this God's plan for them? How could she know? How could she be sure she was doing the right thing?

She prayed for an answer and felt it deep in her soul. She placed a hand on his chest and felt the heavy thud of his heart against her palm.

"I will wed you, Joseph Lapp. I'll strive to be a good wife to you and a good mother to Leah."

He covered her hand with his own. "Leah needs us both. This is the best thing for her."

Anne nodded and bit her lip as trepidation filled her heart. Was a marriage without love between the parents really the best thing for a child?

Chapter Nineteen

Their intention to marry was published in church the
Sunday after Joseph proposed. Simeon Shetler and
Dinah Plank's intentions were published the same day
and caused more of a stir than Anne and Joseph's an-
nouncement. Anne's wedding would take place a week
before Thanksgiving. Dinah and Simeon would marry
the first Tuesday in December.

Anne expected her friends to be surprised by her engagement, but most of them weren't. Ellen Beachy Shetler expressed it best. "The gossip about you and Joseph
has been circulating for weeks. We all knew something
was up. We're all happy for you."

A whirlwind of activity began for Anne the next day.
Invitations were sent to her far-flung relatives. She didn't
have a big family, only a few cousins in Ohio. She didn't
expect many of them to come, but she hoped they would.
She sent another set of invitations to her friends and Joseph's friends in Honeysuckle. She also sent them to a
few of the nurses at the hospital in Lancaster, including Roxann. They had been instrumental in helping her

improve her midwifery skills and in caring for Rhonda Yoder and her son.

Naomi Beiler offered the use of her home for the wedding ceremony and Anne gratefully accepted since her mother was gone. The horse Pocahontas was returned to Calvin Miller, and Daisy returned to pulling the buggy, if slowly.

Anne's days were soon filled with sewing her wedding dress, cleaning, cooking and preparations for the big day. She chose a deep blue material for her gown and hoped that Joseph would approve. She saw little of him. He brought Leah over as usual when he was doing his chores, but he didn't stay long. They rarely found time to be alone. It seemed that she always had company.

The day before the wedding, a dozen of her married friends and members of her church arrived to prepare the wedding feast and the house for the bridal party. There would be a generous meal served following the wedding, but the celebration would continue until supper time, when a second meal would be needed for all the guests.

When the day finally arrived, Anne was up at four-thirty in the morning. Six of her cousins from Ohio had arrived the night before and were helping her get ready. It was wonderful to see the women she had grown up with and to share stories about old times. It had been a long time since Anne felt so connected to her family.

She was standing at the window looking toward Joseph's house and wondering what he was feeling when Ellen and Lizzie came in to hurry her along. Both of them were newlyweds and the light of happiness in their eyes gave Anne courage. She was doing the right thing, wasn't she? If she married Joseph, he would never have the chance to find a woman he loved. What if he was settling for Anne and regretted it later?

Ellen took Anne's hand. "It's time. Micah has the buggy here for you."

Anne had asked Ellen and Neziah to be members of her bridal party. Micah, Neziah's brother, was acting as *hostler*, the driver for the group.

Anne nodded. She was ready, but her fingers were as cold as ice. Was Leah reason enough to wed Joseph and be bound to him for all time?

Ellen squeezed Anne's hand. "It will be fine."

Anne took a deep breath and her panic retreated. Leah was only part of the reason for this day. She might have been instrumental in bringing them together, but it was Anne's love that would make them a family. With God's help, she would be a good wife and mother.

Joseph was waiting for her at the foot of the stairs. He looked every bit as nervous as she felt, but he also looked incredibly handsome in his new black suit and bow tie. Her husband-to-be had Leah in his arms. He smiled and held out his hand. "Are you ready?"

She grasped his fingers tightly. "I am. Are you?"

"Maybe."

"Now is the time to run," she suggested.

"*Nay*, you are stuck with me."

"*Goot.* Are Rhonda and Silas here?" She and Joseph had asked them to be their second bridal-party couple.

"They are outside in the buggy already," Neziah answered. He slapped Joseph on the back. "Better get going."

The trip to Naomi's home didn't take long. The wedding-party couples rode in a second buggy while the bride and groom rode alone. Anne sat stiffly beside

Joseph. She was grateful to have Leah on her lap because she wasn't sure if she should hold his hand or not. Her wedding day was something she would remember all her life. She didn't want it marred by these doubts.

As if he could read her thoughts, he leaned toward her and whispered in her ear. "Smile. You look like you're going to a funeral."

"I'm sorry. I'm not sure how to act."

He took her hand between his own. "Act like yourself."

"You mean throw a tomato at you?"

He threw back his head and laughed. "That was a *goot* throw. You sure did surprise me that day."

Micah glanced over his shoulder at them but didn't comment.

Anne lowered her voice. "I was so mad at you. I hope you have forgiven me."

"I have. And I hope you have forgiven me for causing you so much extra work and worry. It was my responsibility to keep my goats out of your garden and I failed. I will not fail you again, Anne. I promise this."

She gazed into his eyes. "We're going to be all right, aren't we?"

"I think so. I really think we are."

She believed him.

It was just after seven o'clock when they arrived at Naomi's home. The pocket doors between her rooms had been pushed open to make room for all the guests, and the benches were being set up.

Abigail came to take charge of Leah while Anne and Joseph greeted the early guests as they arrived. The ceremony wouldn't take place until nine. By eight thirty the wedding party took their places on the benches at the front of the room where the ceremony would be held, Anne with Rhonda and Ellen on one side of the room, Joseph with Silas and Neziah on the other.

Their *forgeher*, or ushers, four married couples from their church group, made sure each guest had a place on one of the long wooden benches. When the bishop entered the room, he motioned for Anne and Joseph to come with him as the congregation began singing.

Anne and Joseph glanced at each other and quietly followed the bishop. It was customary for the bishop or ministers to counsel the couple before the ceremony took place. One of Naomi's bedrooms had been prepared with chairs for them all. Anne's knees were shaking.

Holding open the door, Bishop Andy said, "Sit. Be of good heart, for I promise not to keep you long."

He took a seat in front of them. "Anne, your place will now be at your husband's side. You will be his counselor, his helpmate. God willing, you will bear his children and raise them to love and serve the Lord."

"That is my hope," she said softly. The thought of having more children filled her with joy, but being a true wife to Joseph filled her with concern. Her hands grew cold.

The bishop cleared his throat. "Joseph, you must provide for and cherish your wife. Anne's love and God's love will be your strength in times of trial. As happy as you are today, it is hard to imagine the sorrows you will face together and alone. We are but travelers through this world on our way to eternal joy at the foot of God's throne. No matter how great is the sorrow or joy that this life brings, it will pass away and the glory of God will shine all around you. Do you understand this?"

Joseph nodded. "I do and I accept what God wills."

The bishop smiled at him and turned to Anne. "*Gottes* love is never wavering, never changing and never ending. Remember this in times of trouble."

"I will," she said quietly.

"Marriage is not easy, but it can be wonderful. I pray God will bless you both. Shall we go back in?"

Anne reached for Joseph's hand. He gave her fingers a quick squeeze. Soon they would be joined as husband and wife. She wanted the man with stormy eyes to be hers alone and it was about to happen. Her heart soared with excitement and happiness as they followed the bishop into the main room and returned to their places.

The singing continued, punctuated by sermons from the ministers, for almost three hours. Anne tried to keep her mind on what was being said, but she could only think about the coming days and nights when she would become a true wife to Joseph.

Finally, Bishop Andy stood to address the congregation. "Brothers and sisters, we are gathered here in Christ's name for a solemn purpose. Joseph Lapp and Anne Stoltzfus are about to make irrevocable vows. This is a most serious step and not to be taken lightly, for it is a lifelong commitment to love and cherish one another."

As the bishop continued at length, Anne glanced at Joseph. He was sitting up straight, listening to every word. He didn't look the least bit nervous. The bishop motioned for Anne and Joseph to come forward.

As Anne stood before him with Joseph at her side, she knew the questions that would be asked of her.

Looking at them both, the bishop said, "Do you confess and believe God has ordained marriage to be a union between one man and one woman? And do you believe that you are approaching this marriage in accordance with His wishes and in the way you have been taught?"

She and Joseph both answered, "Yes."

Turning to Joseph, the bishop asked, "Do you believe, brother, that God has provided this woman as a marriage partner for you?"

"I do believe it." Joseph smiled at her and her heart beat faster.

The bishop then turned to her. "Do you believe, sister, that God has provided this man as a marriage partner for you?"

"I do."

"Joseph, do you also promise Anne that you will care for her in sickness or bodily weakness as befits a Christian husband? Do you promise you will love, forgive and be patient with her until God separates you by death?"

"I do so promise," Joseph answered solemnly.

The bishop asked Anne the same questions. She focused on Joseph. He was waiting for her answer, too. Taking a deep breath, she nodded. "I promise."

The bishop took her hand, placed it in Joseph's hand and covered their fingers with his own. "The God of Abraham, of Isaac and of Jacob be with you. May He bestow His blessings richly upon you through Jesus Christ, amen."

That was it. They were man and wife.

A final prayer ended the ceremony and the festivities began. The couple returned to Anne's home, where the women of the congregation began preparing the wedding meal in the kitchen. The men had arranged tables in a U shape around the walls of the living room.

In the corner of the room facing the front door, the

honored place, the *eck*, meaning the corner table, was quickly set up for the wedding party.

He was married. It was hard to wrap his mind around the fact. When the table was ready, Joseph took his place with his groomsmen seated to his right. Anne was ushered in and took her seat at his left-hand side. It symbolized the place she would occupy in his buggy and in his life. A helpmate, always at his side. Her cheeks were rosy red and her eyes sparkled with happiness. There would be a long day of celebration and feasting, but tonight would come, and she would be his alone. Could he make her happy? Under the table, he squeezed her hand. She gave him a shy smile in return.

Joseph released Anne's hand and began to speak to the people who filed past. The single men were arranged along the table to his right and the single women were arranged along the tables to Anne's left. Later, at the evening meal, the unmarried people would be paired up according to the bride and groom's choosing, as Amish weddings were where matchmaking often got started.

Although most Amish wedding feasts went on until long after dark, Joseph still had a dairy to run and goats to milk. He and Anne bid their guests good night before dark and walked toward his home. He carried Leah, who was worn-out and sleeping after such a long day.

His heart filled with trepidation as he glanced at the woman beside him. She was not just his neighbor. She was now Mrs. Joseph Lapp. His wife. His helpmate, until death did part them. His soul mate for eternity. Had he done the right thing in convincing her to marry him?

He believed so. Together they would build a good life together. She would be a loving mother to Leah.

He would do his best to be a good husband to her and show her just how much he cared for her. The thought made him smile.

Anne gripped his hand. "What are you smiling about?"

"What are *you* smiling about?" he countered.

Her smile trembled. "I asked you first."

"I was thinking about adding another milking parlor in the barn." He glanced to see if she was buying his story.

"Why would we need another milking parlor?" She looked at him askew.

"So you can have your own herd to milk."

"Me? I've no wish to have my own herd. Yours is trouble enough."

"After all this time, you still don't like my goats? Maybe we should have discussed this before the wedding." He wanted to see her smiling a bright smile, not this scared, timid one.

"The young ones are cute. The does are sweet natured, but I will never be fond of those smelly bucks."

"Not even Chester?"

"Especially not Chester. If you wish to give me a bridal gift, you can give Chester away."

He laughed out loud. She wasn't going to be a boring wife, that was for certain. He saw her relax.

A growing nervousness suddenly replaced his humor. Would he be a good husband? Could he make her happy? Could he give her children? Could he grow old beside her and still care for her?

He prayed that he could do all within his power to make her happy. She had married him for Leah's sake, but he prayed she would grow to love him in time. Even just a little.

As they walked through the gate, he saw a car parked in front of the house. He didn't recognize it. "Anne, do you know them? Are they some of your *Englisch* friends?"

"I don't think so, but it could be someone from the hospital in Lancaster. I sent several of the obstetrical nurses there an invitation."

"There's no one in the car. They must be making themselves at home."

He smiled at her. "Did I tell you what a pretty bride you made?"

She blushed a charming shade of pink and took the baby from him. "*Nay*, you didn't mention it."

"I reckon I had a lot on my mind."

She gave him a saucy grin. "Like how to bolt before the knot was tied?"

"I can honestly say that never crossed my mind."

At the sound of the door opening, Joseph glanced toward the house. Fannie came running out. "Leah! Oh, my beautiful baby! I thought I would never see you again." She pulled the child from Anne's arms.

Chapter Twenty

Anne stood frozen with shock. This was her nightmare come to life. She held the baby in her arms, ready to love her for a lifetime, and then the child was torn away from her.

Was this Fannie? Leah's mother? She looked to Joseph for confirmation.

He looked as stunned as she was. "Fannie, what are you doing here?"

So it was his sister. Anne saw her dreams of a lifetime with Leah and Joseph crumble to dust.

Fannie looked at her brother with a trembling smile. "I couldn't do it. I couldn't stay away from her. I tried. I tried so hard. But it's okay. I can take care of her now." She gestured to a young man standing behind her. "This is Brian. He wants us to be a family. He knows I need my baby to make me happy."

Anne wrapped her arms tightly across her middle to ease the crippling ache. She wanted to snatch Leah back. She wanted to take her and run far away. What right did Fannie have to show up and expect Joseph to give the child back to her?

"Don't do this, Fannie." His voice wavered. His hands were shaking. Anne took hold of one. She needed something solid to hold on to or she would scream.

Fannie tipped her head to the side. "Don't do what, Joe?"

"Don't take her away from us."

Taking a step back, Fannie held Leah tightly. The baby started to cry. "She's my daughter. I need her. I wanted you to look after her for a little while. That's what I told you."

"Your letter said you weren't coming back. I didn't want to believe it, but then you sent another letter telling me I would never hear from you again. She is ours now, Fannie. This is my wife, Anne. We love Leah. Please don't do this to us. Don't take her away."

"I'm sorry. I was mixed up. I didn't know what to do."

The man she called Brian stepped up and put an arm around her shoulders. "Johnny was a real piece of work. He broke her wrist. He even shook the baby. Fannie gave her baby to you to protect her. Now she's safe. They are both safe with me. I'm gonna take care of them."

Fannie looked at him. "Johnny didn't mean to hurt me. It was just that Leah cried all the time. She wouldn't stop."

"She was allergic to her formula," Anne said. "That's why she cried so much. She has to have goat's milk now."

Brian sneered. "Goat's milk? Who ever heard of that? We'll take her to a pediatrician. There are all kinds of formulas out there. There has to be something better than goat's milk."

"There's nothing wrong with it, Brian. I grew up drinking it." Fannie tried to comfort Leah, but the baby only cried louder.

"You didn't know any better because you belonged to a backward religious group who thinks we should all live in the Dark Ages."

"No, we don't," Anne countered.

"Whatever. We should get going, Fannie. Can't you make her stop crying?"

Anne pressed her hands to her heart. It was over. She was losing another beloved child. Why was God doing this to her? She could feel her heart withering inside her. Why wasn't Joseph doing something to stop it? She glanced at his face. His gray eyes were blank. His face looked as if it had been turned to stone except for the tracks of his tears. She had never seen such pain.

Leah continued to cry. Anne needed to help her. "She's just hungry. I will get a bottle for her. Come inside, everyone. Fannie, you can feed her while I pack her things."

"We don't need your cheap homemade stuff," Brian said. "I can buy her whatever she needs in a real store."

Fannie turned pleading eyes to him. "Let me feed her, and then we'll go. She'll sleep in the car the whole way if she gets something to eat first."

"All right, but don't let these hicks talk you into leaving her. You're easily persuaded to make the wrong choices. That's why I'm here for you. To be your backbone."

"I won't let them change my mind."

Anne forgave Brian for his insults but she wanted to shake Fannie. What was she doing with such a man? Why was she letting him insult her family? Anne turned to Joseph. "Come inside. Visit with your sister for a while."

"I don't have a sister. She is dead to me."

"*Brooder*, do not say that. Please!" Fannie reached for him.

Joseph jerked away from her and walked out to the barn.

"Speak English, honey. This is America. Is that the shunning thing the Amish do?" Brian asked.

Fannie's eyes filled with tears. "He didn't mean that. I know he didn't mean that."

Anne took her by the elbow and led her inside Joseph's house. Brian paused in the doorway. "I'll wait in the car."

Fannie sat down at the kitchen table. "Did I hear Joseph right? Did he say you are his wife?"

"*Ja.*" Anne forced herself to go through the motions of warming a bottle for Leah one last time. She began filling up a pan with hot water.

"That's good. He needs somebody. It has to be lonely out here all by himself."

She took a bottle from the refrigerator and placed it in the pan. "Your brother was lonely. He missed you very much. He has his animals—you know how much he likes them—but he loves you."

She turned to face Fannie. Leah was arching away from her mother and reaching for Anne. Anne bit her lip so hard she tasted blood. How could this be happening?

"Joseph did his duty by raising me, but he never really loved me."

"How can you say that?"

"He was always gone. He left me alone all the time. It was my fault Beth was killed. I made her trade places with me so I could sit beside him. I loved my brother. I was jealous of her."

"Joseph didn't blame you, Fannie. He was gone so

much because he was trying to save this farm. The driver who hit you threatened to sue and take the farm if Joseph didn't pay for the damages to his vehicle. Joseph believed the accident was his fault."

"I didn't know that. Why didn't he tell me?"

"You were a child. He didn't want to worry you." Anne checked the bottle's temperature by shaking a few drops on her wrist. It was warm enough. She handed the bottle to Fannie, although she longed to hold Leah once more.

"*Danki.* I mean, thanks. Brian doesn't like it when I speak *Deitsch.*"

"Are you sure he is the man for you? He doesn't speak kindly to you. It makes me worry. We are sisters now. We must look out for each other."

"Brian doesn't hit me. But I'm not very bright. I'm not educated. That frustrates him."

Anne couldn't believe she was sending Leah into such a poor situation. How could she bear knowing her beautiful child would be raised by that unkind man?

Fannie gave Leah her bottle. After fighting it briefly, the baby latched on and drank eagerly. "Wow, she really likes the goat's milk. She would never eat like this for me. I felt like such a failure as a mother."

Anne sat beside her and laid a hand on her arm. "It wasn't anything you did, Fannie. Eventually, your doctor would have figured out what was wrong."

"Johnny never let me take her to the doctor. He said they were a waste of time and money."

"Johnny doesn't sound like a very smart man."

Fannie chuckled. "He wasn't and he wasn't a good musician, either."

"Where are you staying? I would love to keep in

touch. Find out how Leah is doing, you know. We wanted to send you an invitation to the wedding, but your letters didn't have a return address."

"I would have liked to come. I'm not sure Brian will let me write to you. Besides, Joseph says I'm dead to him. He won't read my letters, even if I write."

"I'll read them. You haven't been shunned by the church. You aren't under the Ban. Can you at least tell me which city you live in?"

"Lancaster."

"That's not too far away. I have a friend there. Let me give you her name." Anne found a piece of paper. Quickly, she wrote Roxann's name and phone number. "Roxann Shield works at Lancaster Medical Center. She's a midwife like I am, only she's a nurse-midwife. If you ever need medical advice or if Leah gets sick, Roxann will see you free of charge."

Anne knew Roxann wouldn't be able to do that, but she would forward the bill to Anne.

"That's nice. Thanks. Leah, you little piglet, you're almost done with this bottle."

Tears pricked the back of Anne's eyes. *Slow down, baby. When you're done, I may never see you again.*

She cleared her throat and began gathering items to put in Leah's bag. "I'm going to put a few things in here for her. Diapers and such. I know you'll buy new clothes, but this will get you home. I'll put in the recipe for her formula, too. You can buy goat's milk in most stores. In case you can't find another formula that works."

Brian appeared in the doorway. "I'm getting tired of waiting. How long does it take two Amish women to feed a baby?"

"She's done." Fannie jumped to her feet.

Anne closed her eyes. This couldn't happen. "Please don't take her. We'll give her the best possible home. We love her."

"I love her, too. I've got to go." Fannie started out the door.

Anne switched to *Deitsch*. "Little sister, you will always have a home with us, even if you remain *Englisch*. You are loved by us and by God. Never forget that. Do not fear to come to us."

Brian frowned. "What is she jabbering about?"

"She's just wishing me a safe journey. It's a tradition. Let's go."

Anne's heart broke into a million pieces. She followed them to the door, praying for Fannie to change her mind. Praying for God to intervene and stop her. But they got in the car and drove away.

She wanted to scream and cry, but a strange calm settled over her. It was as if some part of her mind disconnected from her emotions. She became dead inside. The pain was too deep for tears.

She turned back into the house, then went to the bedroom she would share with Joseph and took off her wedding dress. Carefully, she folded it away. She would wear it again only when her body was dressed for her burial. She put on one of her everyday dresses that had been brought over by her attendants and then she sat down on the sofa in Joseph's living room and waited for him to come in.

At midnight she gave up trying to stay awake and went to bed. When she woke just before dawn, she was still alone.

Joseph raised his head and rubbed his stiff neck. He'd slept slumped over his desk in his office. He hadn't ac-

tually slept. The night had been more a series of fitful
rest, terrifying dreams and an even more terrible reality.
He had tried to pray, but he found no comfort in speaking to God. God wasn't listening.

He rose stiffly and walked to the front of the barn.
Smoke rose from the chimney of the house. Anne must
be up. He leaned against the doorway and closed his
eyes. It didn't stop him from seeing the mess he'd made
of their lives.

He should have gone to her last night. He should have
tried to comfort her, but he didn't know how. She had
married him for Leah's sake and now Leah was gone.
His grand idea to build a family had turned into a trap
for Anne. She didn't have the baby she loved and she
was stuck with a husband she didn't love, either. The
irony was a bitter pill to swallow first thing in the morning. He hadn't gone to Anne last night because he was
a coward. He was afraid she would turn him away. And
he didn't know if he could survive that.

"I was beginning to worry about you."

He jerked upright. She was standing a few feet away
looking sad and yet still beautiful in the early-morning
light. She wore a dark blue dress with a black apron.
Somber colors for a somber day. "I'm sorry, Anne."

"I know. This isn't what we bargained for, is it?"

"*Nay.* It isn't. I'm going to milk. You can go home if
you want. We'll think of what to tell people later."

"I am home, Joseph."

"I meant you could go to your own house if you
wished."

She folded her arms tightly across her middle. Her
chin quivered as her head came up. "I know full well
what you meant. We are wed. A promise is a prom-

ise, but promises can be broken. Our vows cannot be unspoken. They were made before God and man. I'm your wife."

"Leah was the reason for those vows. Now she's gone. I knew better than to love that child." He couldn't bear to be reminded of what he'd lost. The child he loved, the sister he would have given anything to help, his dreams of a family, of a wife who could learn to love him. They were all ashes in his mouth. He turned away and began walking toward the barn.

"I miss her, too. My heart is breaking, the way yours is breaking, because I love her, too," Anne yelled. "All we have left is each other."

He spun around. "Would you have married me if you knew Fannie was coming back for Leah?"

She pressed her lips tightly together, unable to answer him. She didn't have to. He already knew the answer. "Go home or stay. It makes no difference to me."

"We have to start somewhere, Joseph."

"I know. I'm just not ready to do that yet." He walked away without looking back.

He was in so much pain. Anne knew he was suffering and she was powerless to help. She understood the pain of losing a child. Not once but twice. Time and faith in God's mercy were the only things that would heal Joseph's wounds. And hers.

She returned to the house and walked into the living room. Leah's crib with its bright quilt sat where it had been yesterday. Yesterday it held a happy, grinning baby girl. Today it held only memories.

Anne ran her hands along the smooth wooden rail. Great care had gone into creating it. The owner would want it back. There would be children and grandchildren to use it and that was a good thing. Love should be passed down in families, too.

She opened the drawers of the dresser and took out the outfits that Leah had worn. She held them to her face, but they had been washed. They didn't hold her baby's scent. They smelled of fresh air and sunshine, just as they had when she took them off the clothesline. She sat down on the floor and gathered them into a pile on her lap. The tears came then and there was no stopping them.

She didn't know how long she sat there crying, but she felt Joseph sink down beside her. He gathered her into his arms and held her as she wept. His tears mingled with hers. They were two souls broken by grief. Where did they go from there?

Chapter Twenty-One

When their tears were spent, Joseph rose to his feet, wiped his face with his hands and went to the crib. "Do you want me to put these things away?"

"I can do it for you. I know how hard it is to put away a child's things. I remember packing away the quilt I made for him was the hardest thing for me."

"Whose quilt?" He asked without looking at her.

"My son's."

"Your son?" Joseph was clearly bewildered. "You had a child?"

"I tried to tell you the day you proposed, but you said it didn't matter. I was grateful that I didn't have to share my shameful story with you, but I want you to hear the story now."

"All right."

"I was seventeen and in love with the son of the banker in the town near where I lived in Ohio. I was incredibly foolish and naive. I make no excuse for myself. I knew what we were doing was wrong, but I loved him so much. When I told him I was pregnant, everything changed. I thought we would marry. I was badly mistaken. He didn't want to be a husband or a father. He had plans to go away to college, and he wasn't going to give that up for a silly Amish girl. He wanted me to place our baby for adoption."

"He was a man without honor."

"He was a frightened boy pressured by his parents. I forgave him long ago. My mother was the midwife in our community. She understood, but my father did not. I had shamed him. He wanted nothing to do with me or my child. I was sent to live with my mother's sister. She knew of a childless Amish couple who would love my baby and raise him as their own. It was a heart-wrenching decision, but I finally agreed. That's why I know how hard it must have been for Fannie to leave Leah with you. My heart ached for her. I also know how joyful it was for her to see and hold her baby again."

"I don't wish to talk about my sister. So you gave your child up for adoption?" The timbre of his voice didn't change. Did he disapprove of her actions as he did his sister's?

"I never got the chance. There were complications. My mother did not call the ambulance. My son was born dead because the cord was wrapped around his neck."

"Like Rhonda's babe." His tone softened.

"Very much like that, only *Gott* called my son home. He showed mercy to Rhonda and Silas by sparing their child. I wish I knew why my little Mathias couldn't stay with me. *Gott* has His own plan and we cannot comprehend His ways, but He will have to explain that to me when I stand before Him."

"I'm sorry for all you endured. Now to lose Leah, too. It's not fair."

"We can endure with *Gottes* help. That is why you

can't lose faith. *Gott* brought the two of us together because of Leah. His plan has not changed, even though ours have. I will be a good wife to you. I will fulfill my wifely duties. I will honor and obey you all the days of my life, but… I think we both need time to heal."

She folded her hands together and stared at the floor. "There is a spare bedroom here. I will use that unless you insist otherwise."

Amazed by how calmly Anne spoke about the suffering she had endured, Joseph could only stare at her. Her faith was unwavering. He couldn't say the same. In spite of everything, she had found the strength to go on, to move ahead and to help others by bringing their babies into the world when she had been denied a child of her own. She was a remarkable woman.

He didn't know what to say to her but he knew what he wanted. He wanted a true wife, not a wife in name only.

He wanted Anne. But on her terms.

He wanted her to come to him with love in her heart, not because it was her duty. However long that took, he would wait. Because deep in his soul, he knew she was a woman worth waiting for. The one chosen by God to be his helpmate for life. The woman he had grown to love.

He cleared his throat. "The spare room will be fine. It's never used."

She drew a deep breath. *"Danki."*

He moved to stand in front of her. Placing his fingers under her chin, he raised her face until she was looking at him. "We were friends before the wedding, Anne. Leah brought us together, but we became friends because of who we are. Not because of her. I want us to be friends now."

A half smile turned up the corner of her lip. "Does that mean you won't make me milk your goats?"

"No, you still have to do that, wife."

Her smile widened. "You make it hard to be your friend."

"If it was easy, everyone would do it."

"I reckon we'll need to be friends if we are to have any kind of marriage at all."

He was glad she could see it that way. For now. "We'll make the best of it. Shall I help you put away these things?"

She touched his arm. "Only if you want to do it."

"I didn't get to say goodbye to her. Maybe this will help."

"We'll pray for her. For both of them."

"I'll pray for Leah, but I'm not sure I can pray for her mother."

"You will. Time heals our wounds even if the scars remain. Leah may yet come back to us, if only for a visit. We can't know what the future holds. Cutting ties with Fannie will cut our ties with Leah, too."

"I know you are right, but I can't condone my sister's choices. It is not an easy thing to shun a person I love, but I do it out of that love. She must see the consequences of her actions and the harm she has caused."

He began picking up the clothes scattered on the floor. Together they packed them away in boxes and stacked them in the crib to be returned to their owners. Later that afternoon he drove the wagon up to the door and loaded Leah's things into it. Anne came out to watch him. He offered his hand. "Would you like to come to town with me?"

She shook her head. "I have enough to do here. I still have things I need to bring over from my place."

"All right. I'll be home for supper. What are we having?"

Crossing her arms, she pretended to look annoyed. "What do you care? You like everything, including pickled okra. You'll like what I put in front of you and you won't complain."

"Spoken like a good wife." He smiled, although he didn't feel like it. He appreciated her efforts to cheer him up. He had tried to do the same for her. It was harder than it looked. They both missed Leah terribly. There was a hole in the fabric of their relationship. He prayed it could be mended.

Driving into town, he had time to contemplate his spunky wife and wonder if she would ever come to care for him. She was used to her independence. He didn't want her to give it up. The last thing he wanted was for their marriage to be a burden to her. He wanted it to be a joy.

He delivered the furniture and other items to Naomi at her home. She was shocked to learn that Leah was no longer with them. He asked her to visit Anne soon. "She is going to need someone to talk to about losing Leah."

"I know she will. I'll be out tomorrow. Bless you both."

The coming night loomed large and awkward when he returned home. They ate a simple supper of bread and cheese and parted company in the center of the living room, where Joseph wished her a good-night. He hoped it would be a better night for her. It wouldn't be for him.

Early the next morning, he drove out to see Calvin Miller. It took a considerable amount of haggling, but he headed for home with Pocahontas tied to the back of his wagon. The pony would be his wedding present to Anne. He knew how much she liked the lively, well-trained little mare and how much she needed a fast buggy horse to get her to her deliveries in time.

She was leaving the henhouse with a basket of eggs in her hand when he drove into the yard. Her eyes lit up with delight when she saw Pocahontas. "Has Calvin decided he can spare her for a few more weeks? That's *wunderbar.*"

"You don't have to return her. She's yours now." He stepped down from the wagon.

"You mean you purchased her for me?" Anne's puzzled expression made him chuckle.

He walked around to the rear of the wagon and untied the mare. He led her up to Anne. Taking the egg basket from her, he placed the lead rope in her palm. "She is my wedding gift to you. I don't want my wife being late for a birthing, and Daisy deserves to retire in peace."

Tears glistened in Anne's eyes. "I don't know what to say. This is very kind of you."

Her practical side quickly asserted itself. "How much did old man Miller charge you for her?"

"You don't want to know."

She opened her mouth to argue, but he forestalled her by holding up his hand. "This bargain is done. I promise that from now on, I will consult you on any purchases because it is your money, too, and we need to manage it wisely. But Pocahontas is a gift."

Anne stroked the horse's nose. "She is one I will cherish, and doubly so because she came from you."

Maybe now was the time to make plans for the future so it didn't feel as if they were simply waiting for Leah to return when she might not. "Next week will be Thanksgiving. I was wondering if you had any plans."

The light in her eyes faded. "Not this year."

"Do you have something you normally do? Somewhere you go? I know a lot of Amish folks enjoy getting together for the *Englisch* holiday."

"I like to invite the families of the babies I've delivered that year over to celebrate. It was something my mother started doing. It's fun to see how the *kinner* have grown."

"Why aren't you doing it this year?"

"Because."

"That's not a reason."

"Because I know you don't like company and crowds. Besides, I don't feel like celebrating now."

It touched him that she was willing to put aside something she enjoyed for his sake. He could surely do the same. "You should invite them, anyway. I would enjoy having a few families at my place for a day."

"Are you sure?"

He knew she loved visiting. Her friends were important to her. She liked people. She especially liked their babies. Maybe having some around in her home would get her to thinking about having children of her own. With him. "I can always go hide in the barn if it gets too rowdy. My office has a lock on the door."

"It does? Why?"

"Beats me. The door came with a lock installed."

"Have you ever used it?"

"Only to prevent Chester from eating my record books."

She grinned, but it quickly faded. "Are you sure you want to do this? People won't be expecting newlyweds to entertain them."

"We've been the unexpected couple from the start. I don't think we should change now. Most newlyweds travel to visit relatives in the months after they wed. You don't have much family. I don't have any…"

He stumbled to a halt. Her eyes filled with sympathy. He drew a deep breath. "Besides, who will milk the goats if I'm not here? I think a Thanksgiving Day feast is exactly what we need to celebrate our marriage."

He smiled, hoping he had convinced her he would enjoy it. He wouldn't, but for her sake, he would pretend to have a wonderful time. Anne deserved things that would make her happy. If it was within his power, he could give her those things. He wanted her to think kindly of him. It occurred to him exactly what he needed to do.

He was going to court his wife.

Anne went through the motions of preparations for Thanksgiving. She welcomed anything to keep her mind off missing Leah, but the baby was never far from her thoughts. She knew the same was true for Joseph, but they were both determined to move forward with their lives. He was as busy as she was, cleaning up the farm, painting his barn. When he wasn't busy with his own projects, he was helping her. As the days passed, their awkwardness eased and their teasing friendship returned.

She hand-delivered two dozen invitations and found many of her families were hoping she would still hold her annual gathering in spite of getting married. All but one family agreed to come, including Rhonda and Silas. Everyone insisted on making it a potluck meal so that Anne and Joseph wouldn't be saddled with the expense of another big dinner so soon after their wedding feast.

Anne scrubbed his house from top to bottom, washing windows and floors. She beat rugs and polished every inch of the furniture. The only room she didn't clean was his bedroom.

Although she was the one who had suggested separate bedrooms, she had secretly hoped he would dismiss her request. It had hurt when he'd agreed. He'd made it clear that he didn't want her, that he didn't love her. Leah had been the only reason he'd proposed. He wanted a mother for his child. Not a wife. She'd known that going in.

Anne was grateful for his friendship, but she wondered how long she could hide the fact that she was deeply in love with him. She longed to tell him the truth, but the fear that he didn't want her love kept her silent. For now, she could hope that his feelings would grow from friendship into something more. If she confessed her love and found he wanted only her friendship, she might die of shame. How pathetic was it to fall in love with another man who didn't want her?

Sometimes, when she caught Joseph staring at her, she thought she saw a deeper affection in the depths of his gray eyes, but he never spoke of it. Maybe she only imagined it.

The evening before Thanksgiving, when Joseph was getting ready to start the evening milking, Anne slipped into her coat and walked out with him.

He gave her a quizzical look. "Where are you going?"

"To help you milk."

"I was there the last time you tried. It wasn't a pretty sight."

"Ha! All I need is a little practice."

"Are you sure you want to try it again?"

"I'm sure."

"Okay, come on." He held out his hand and she took it. It was only a small step forward in their relationship, but she cherished it nonetheless.

Chapter Twenty-Two

The buggies began arriving at ten o'clock in the morning on Thanksgiving. By noon Joseph's house was overflowing with laughing, chattering couples and their babies. Ten families in all had accepted Anne's invitation. The kitchen was awash in mouthwatering aromas. *Hingleflesh*, the roasting chicken, *grumbatta mush*, or mashed potatoes and gravy. There was creamed celery, fried sweet potatoes, macaroni and cheese, and peas. On the counter were pumpkin and lemon sponge pies and trays of cookies. Occasionally, one or two of the older children attempted to sample some, but they were quickly herded out of the kitchen.

Joseph found himself surrounded by young men who were happy to tease him about his recent nuptials. He smiled at their jokes and tolerated their ribbing, never letting on that he and Anne still had separate bedrooms.

Anne was in her element. Several times during the day, he caught her eye and she gave him a bright smile, the first one in days. These women were her friends and she enjoyed being the hostess. At one point in the late afternoon, he noticed she was missing from the group.

Some of the families were getting ready to leave and he knew she would want to say goodbye. He cornered Rhonda. "Have you seen Anne?"

"She took the baby into the other room to change him for me."

"Danki," he said, going in search of his missing wife. Joseph opened the door to her bedroom and saw her seated in the rocker, holding Rhonda's infant snuggled against her chest. Her cheek lay on the top of the baby's head. A single tear rolled from the corner of her eye.

She looked up. "I miss her so much. My arms are empty without her."

He came and knelt in front of her. He laid his hand on the baby's head. "I miss her, too. I can't stop thinking about her. Is she okay? Is Fannie taking good care of her? I'm afraid I will wonder what has become of her for my whole life."

"I'm sorry that you married me in haste and are stuck with me now." Another tear slipped down her face.

His heart ached for her. He moved his hand to cup her cheek. "Oh, Anne, please don't say that. I am *not* sorry that I married you."

"Do you mean that?" Her eyes begged him for the truth.

He struggled to find the words that would convince her. "I mean it with all my heart. Perhaps this was God's plan for Leah all along. She was our matchmaker. I would not have gone looking for a wife otherwise."

Anne nodded. "I would've never considered you husband material if not for her."

A glow of hope centered itself in his chest. "Husband material? Do you think you can mold me into a man who will make you happy?"

"*Nay*, I cannot do that. I would not change a single thing about you. You already make me happy."

He wanted that to be true, but he knew he was no prize. "I am not as handsome as Micah. Nor as witty or charming."

"But you have something he doesn't have."

"One hundred goats?" he asked, trying to coax a smile from her. It worked.

"Even if he acquired two hundred goats, he would still not possess what you already hold."

"And what is that?"

"My heart and my love."

Happiness exploded in his heart and sent a lump into his throat. He didn't deserve her love.

She looked down. "I didn't mean to burden you with this so soon. I know you don't love me and that's okay. I was going to wait until you came to care for me, too, before I spoke."

Her gaze rose to his face. "But then I thought what if I lost you as I lost Leah and I never told you that I loved you. I couldn't stand that."

Anne stroked the baby's head and let the infant curl his fingers around her pinkie. It helped to hold another baby. At first she didn't think it would, but Leah had taught her that she could love more than one child. Joseph had shown her she could love more than one man, even if he didn't love her in return.

Joseph cleared his throat. "Anne, if I possessed nothing else in the world but your heart and your love, I would be the richest man on earth. I love you, too."

Her eyes widened in wonder. "You do?"

He bent toward her and kissed her forehead. "I think I've loved you since the day you hit me with a tomato."

She gave him a wavery smile as joy unfurled in her heart. What had she done to deserve such a wonderful man? "If that is what it takes to get your attention, I'm going to plant a lot of tomatoes in the spring."

He grinned, but then his smile faded and his eyes grew serious.

Joseph knew he had to make a complete confession. This would be the start of their true marriage. From now on, there could only be honesty between them. "Darling, I tricked you into marrying me."

"I don't understand."

"The bishop said he would take Leah away if I didn't find a wife. He said he would give her to a childless couple to raise. I couldn't bear to lose her. I knew how much you loved her, and I used that love to convince you to marry me. Can you forgive me for that?"

"There is nothing to forgive. We both loved her."

The bedroom door opened and Rhonda came in. Joseph rose to his feet and curbed his need to show Anne just how much he cared. He would bide his time for now, but when they were alone he would pour out his heart to her.

Rhonda said, "Silas is getting ready to go home. I thought I should collect my baby before we leave."

"I reckon I have to give him back." Anne kissed the top of the baby's head and handed him to her mother. She and Joseph followed the young mother outside, where her husband had their buggy hitched and waiting for her.

A car drove in and stopped beyond the buggy. The driver-side door opened and an *Englisch* woman stepped out.

"Roxann," Anne cried and rushed toward her. The two women embraced. "Joseph, come and meet my friend Roxann Shield. She is the nurse-midwife I have been telling you about."

Roxann nodded to him. "It's a pleasure to meet you."

"Our Thanksgiving meal is over, but there is plenty left to eat. Come in." He tipped his head toward the house, realizing that he had enjoyed the day visiting with people he knew and even those he didn't. There would be more get-togethers in their future. His future. One with Anne by his side and God willing, children of their own around them.

"Actually, I've just come to deliver a package," Roxann said.

"A package?" Anne gave her a puzzled look.

"It's really two packages." She leaned down and spoke to someone in the car. "I brought you this far. The next step is up to you."

The passenger-side door opened and a woman stepped out. Joseph realized it was Fannie. And she held Leah in her arms. She glanced at Joseph and then looked down. *"Hallo, brooder."*

He took a step back, too stunned to speak.

Anne could barely believe her eyes. Leah was here. God had given her the chance to see her beautiful baby again. Anne glanced at Fannie. Why was she here? And why was she with Roxann? Anne turned to Joseph. She could not invite Fannie in without his consent. He had declared that his sister was dead to him and he was the head of the house.

"Why are you here?" he demanded.

Fannie turned to Roxann. "Maybe this was a bad idea."

"No, I think this was the best idea you have had in a long time. Give him a chance," Roxann said.

Anne looked to her friend. "Roxann, what's going on?"

"Fannie can tell you. Go ahead."

Staring at the ground, Fannie began speaking. "After Johnny dumped me, I was desperate. He took all our money. I stole some stuff and got caught. That's when I wrote the second letter to Joseph. The judge gave me probation instead of jail time. I met Brian there. He was on probation, too. We hit it off, or so I thought."

Roxann looked to Joseph. "Brian was on probation for domestic abuse. He hit his previous girlfriend."

"I didn't like the way he talked to you," Joseph said.

Anne struggled to quell her mounting excitement. At least he was speaking to his sister. "How did you meet Roxann?"

"You gave me her name. I thought I was pregnant again, so I got an appointment with her. You said she would see me for free. I had just left Brian. I was worried he'd hurt Leah. I think I finally wised up about guys like him. I don't know why I always find them."

Roxann smiled at Anne. "By the way, you owe me one hundred and seventy-five dollars for an office visit."

"I'll write you a check." Anne lowered her voice. "Fannie, are you pregnant?"

She nodded. "Johnny is the father. It's dumb, I know, but I just want someone to love me. Someone to hold."

Anne held out her arms. "We love you and your babies."

"You don't even know me."

"I know you," Joseph said. "And I have always loved

you. *Willkomm* home, little sister. Promise me you will stay as long as you need."

Tears rolled down Fannie's face. "That might be a really long time." She flew to her brother's arms and Anne gave thanks to God for His kindness.

"Can I have my old room?" Fannie asked when she stopped crying.

"I have a few things of mine in there, but *ja*," Anne answered. "Roxann, please come in and I'll fix you something to eat."

"I don't mind if I do. It was a long ride." Roxann followed Fannie inside.

Joseph put his arm around Anne. "That leaves us with just one problem."

"I know."

"We only have one bedroom left."

"I realize that." Her cheeks grew hot.

"I'm willing to share my space with my wife. Are you ready to come home?"

She threw her arms around his neck. "I've never been so ready in my life. *Gott* has granted us a great gift."

"He has, but there is one more thing I need."

"What?"

"A kiss, Mrs. Lapp. I need to find out if my wife is a good kisser."

Anne glanced toward the house. They were still alone if she didn't count the dozens of goats watching them over the fences. "I have no idea if I'm a good kisser, but I'm willing to practice until I get it right."

"*Goot* girl." He proceeded to pull her close and kiss her tenderly.

Joy flooded every fiber of her being. She put her

arms around his neck and drew him closer. "I can see I'm going to need a lot of practice."

"Tonight. But right now I want to go hold my baby girl."

"Me, too." They linked arms and entered the house with joyful hearts.

Epilogue

Early March

"We've got twins!" Anne shouted to Joseph.

"Twins? I'm coming." He jogged across the pasture to her side. A young doe was nursing two brown-and-black kids with white stars on their foreheads and long floppy ears.

"*Goot* girl, Jenny. Two nice little *bubbels*." He patted her head as she nuzzled her newborns.

"Is this the last of them?" Anne wiped her hands on a towel and gazed out over the greening pasture dotted with does and wobbly kids. A hedge of honeysuckle was blooming on an old rock fence nearby and the air was sweet with the scent.

"Jenny was the last one. We have fifty-two new goats. Your own milk herd in another two years."

She smiled at the love of her life. He still liked goats better than most people, but that didn't include herself, Leah or Fannie. They were truly his family now. "We're going to need fifty new goats if we expand into cheese making. Are you sure you want to do that?"

"Fannie knows what she's doing. You have to admit she's made some fine cheeses. If she thinks we can find an organic market, I'm willing to give it a shot."

"She's worried she'll disappoint you."

"I'll make sure she knows my love isn't tied to any success or failure. It's always there."

Anne kissed him on the cheek. "I love you."

"So you've told me."

"I haven't told you today."

"You did. Before breakfast, during milking, after milking and after lunch. Four times today, five counting right now."

"You're counting how many times I tell you that I love you?"

He pulled her close to him. "Every one. I want to remember them all."

Cupping his face between her hands, she gave him a quick peck on the lips. "I only count your kisses."

He chuckled. "How many are we up to?"

"Two thousand and seventy-one."

"No wonder my lips are tired." She swatted his shoulder and stepped away, but inside, she was smiling.

He looked over the pasture. "I'm glad we are done birthing for the year."

Was this the right time? Maybe it was the best time. "Actually, we aren't done."

"*Ja*, Fannie will have her new baby in June and then we will be done."

"There will be one more. On about October 22, by my calculations."

She watched his face. Understanding suddenly dawned on him. "You? We? Us? We're pregnant?"

She nodded. "We are. Are you happy?"

He pulled her close. "You have no idea how happy you have made me. *Gott es goot.*"

"*Ja*, He is." She closed her eyes and collected kisses number two thousand and seventy-two, seventy-three and seventy-four.

After that, she lost count as his love swept her away to gorgeous bliss surrounded by the fragrance of honeysuckle on a green hillside of Pennsylvania overlooking her home.

* * * * *

Plain Pursuit

ALISON STONE

Thanks to my awesome agent, Jennifer Schober, who stuck with me on this long and winding road to publication. Your faith in me kept me going.

Thanks to Allison Lyons, my editor, who championed my work from the beginning. I'm thrilled we finally get to work together.

Thanks to my fabulous critique partners and good friends, Amanda Usen and Barb Hughes. You guys always keep me on track, especially when I get carried away with the suspense and forget that it's a romance, too. To Roxanne, I miss your insightful critiques and sharp wit.

Thanks to Professor Karen M. Johnson-Weiner, who generously answered my questions about the Amish. Any errors I've made are mine alone.

Thanks to my mom and dad for providing a childhood home filled with lots of love and laughter. Thanks for making financial sacrifices to send all five of your children to wonderful schools. It laid the foundation for all my successes in life. Thank you for that gift.

And thanks to my husband, Scott, and our four children, Scotty, Alex, Kelsey and Leah. If you want something bad enough and you're willing to work hard, dreams can come true. Thanks for helping me make my dream come true. I love you guys, always and forever.

Then Peter came to Him and asked,
"Lord, how often should I forgive someone
who sins against me? Seven times?"
"No, not seven times," Jesus replied,
"but seventy times seven!"
—*Matthew 18:21–22*

Chapter One

The pungent odor of manure and smoldering wreckage clogged Anna's throat. As she coughed, she tented
her hand over her eyes to shield them from the lowering sun. Stalks and stalks of corn swayed under brisk
winds, masking the point of impact where the single-
engine plane plummeted into the earth. An unmistakable desire to scream overwhelmed her. She clamped her
jaw to quell her emotions. She had to hold it together for
now. Swallowing hard, she tried to rid her mouth of the
horrible taste floating in the air. Across the country road
from her parked vehicle, first responders fastened the
straps to secure the crumpled plane to a flatbed truck.

Turning her back, she flattened her palms against
the window of her car. She closed her eyes as the world
seemed to slow to a crawl. Tears stung the backs of her
eyes. Her brother was dead. She was alone.

Anna turned around and leaned back against her car.
She ran a hand across her damp forehead. It was unusually hot for early October in western New York. The
heat rolled off the asphalt, scorching her cheeks. The
bold blue numbers *977* stood out on the tail of the plane,

remarkably unscathed among the heap of metal. Her brother had sent her a photo of the plane a few weeks ago. He had been so proud of his purchase. She had thought he was crazy. Pressing a hand to her mouth, she realized she had never responded to his email. She had been so wrapped up in her job as a high school counselor at the start of a new school year. Now it was too late to tell him anything.

Her brother had always been there for her when it truly counted. Now only one thing remained for her to do. She closed her eyes. *Dear Lord, please welcome my brother into Your arms.* A tear tracked down her warm cheek.

"Anna Quinn." A male voice sounded from behind her. Swiping at her wet cheeks, she glanced over the hood of her car, surprised to see a tall gentleman striding toward her with a confidence normally reserved for those in law enforcement. Her legs felt weak and she took a deep breath to tamp down her initial trepidation. His dark suit fit his broad shoulders impeccably but seemed out of place among the uniformed first responders dotting the countryside. The intensity in his brown eyes unnerved her.

"Yes, I'm Anna." Dread whispered across the fine hairs on the back of her neck, but she kept her voice even. Her brother was dead. How much worse could it get? Foreboding gnawed at her insides. Past experience told her it could always get worse.

"I'm Special Agent Eli Miller." She accepted his outstretched hand. Warmth spread through her palm. Self-aware, she reclaimed her hand and crossed her arms tightly against her body. Thrusting her chin upward, she met his gaze. The compassion in his brown eyes almost crumbled her composure. She wondered fleetingly what it would be like to take comfort in his strong arms. To rely on someone besides herself.

Heat crept up her cheeks when she realized he was waiting for some kind of response. "You called me about the crash," she said.

The call was a blur, yet she had recognized the soothing timbre of his voice. She had barely gotten the name of the town before she hit End and sat dumbfounded in the guidance office where she worked sixty miles away in Buffalo. She had left without explaining her emergency to anyone in the office.

Anna's chest tightened. "How did you know to call me?"

The deep rumble of the flatbed truck's diesel engine fired to life, drawing the man's attention. The corners of his mouth tugged down. "Your brother asked me to call you."

Anna wasn't sure she had heard him correctly over the noise of the truck as it eased onto the narrow country road. She tracked the twisted metal of her brother's plane on top of the flatbed truck until it reached the crest of the hill. Then she turned to face him. Goose bumps swept over her as the significance of his words took shape.

"When…?" She hesitated, her pulse whooshing in her ears. Had she misunderstood? Was her brother in a hospital somewhere? A flicker of hope sparked deep within her. "When did Daniel ask you to call me? My brother's…dead?" Rubbing her temples, her scrutiny fell to his suit, his authoritative stance. The world seemed to sway with the cornstalks. "You told me he had been killed."

Concern flashing in his eyes, the man caught her

arm. "Yes, I'm sorry. I didn't mean to mislead you. Your brother died in the crash." He guided her to the driver's side of her vehicle and opened the door. "Here. Sit down."

Anna sat sideways on the seat, her feet resting on the door frame. "When did you talk to my brother?" She stared at the agent's polished shoes, trying to puzzle it all out. Finally, she met his eyes. "Was he in trouble?"

"Your brother and I talked last week." Special Agent Eli Miller rested his elbow on the open door. "Daniel told me to call you if anything should happen to him." He seemed to be gauging her expression for a reaction.

Anna scrunched up her face. "If *anything* happened?" She pointed to the field. "Like if he was killed in a plane crash?"

"I don't think he could have predicted that, but yes, he asked me to call you." He reached into his suit coat pocket and pulled out a worn business card with a familiar logo on it. She straightened her back. Years ago, after she had landed her first job as a high school counselor, she had dropped the card into a care package for her brother stationed in Iraq.

"Daniel gave you that? I don't understand." She rubbed her forehead, wishing she could fill her lungs with fresh air—air without this horrible smell.

"He wasn't only worried about his own safety." He never lifted his pensive gaze from her face. "He was worried about yours."

"*My* safety?"

"Has anything out of the ordinary happened lately?"

Anna bit her bottom lip. Her mind's eye drifted to the strange note she had found on her car after school last week. She shrugged. "Someone left a note on my car.

It was nothing." She struggled to recall the exact words on the note. "I think it said, 'You're next.'"

"Did you report it?"

Anna laughed, the mirthless sound grating her nerves. "No…I'm a high school counselor. A few faculty cars had been egged the week before. That's all it was." She scooted out of the car and brushed past him, turning her back to the crash site. "I took the job to help kids. If I ratted them out every time they looked at me sideways, they wouldn't trust me." Goodness knew where she'd be if her high school counselor hadn't reached out to her.

"Anything strange besides the note?" The concern in his voice melted her composure.

Tears blurred her vision and she quickly blinked them away. "Other than the occasional disgruntled student— who is harmless, I can assure you—I live a pretty boring life."

"Is there anyone you want me to call for you?"

"No," she whispered, staring over the cornfields. An uneasiness seeped into her bones. Her brother tended to be the paranoid one, not her. But she couldn't dismiss it. History told her things weren't always what they seemed. "Can I see your credentials?" Anna met his assessing gaze; flecks of yellow accented his brown eyes. She turned the leather ID holder over in her hands. *Special Agent Eli R. Miller.* It seemed legitimate.

"You met my brother in person?" She studied him, eager to read any clues from the smooth planes of his handsome face. She wanted to ask: Did Daniel seem okay? Was he thin? Dragging a hand over her hair to smooth the few strands that had fallen out of her ponytail, she was ashamed she didn't know the answers. Ashamed she had grown estranged from her big brother.

Dear Lord, please forgive me. Let me find peace through this nightmare.

Special Agent Miller hiked a dark eyebrow. "Yes. We talked briefly a week ago. I had some questions concerning his return to Apple Creek."

Anna jerked her head back. "I don't understand. He was in Apple Creek working on his photography. Why would the FBI be concerned about my brother's whereabouts?" Foreboding mingled with the acrid fumes hanging in the air.

"Your brother went to Genwego State University, right?"

"Yes." She furrowed her brow. "He dropped out his senior year. What does that have to do with anything?"

"I'm working a cold case. I've been reinterviewing people who lived in the area ten years ago."

"Was my brother able to help you?"

"No. But when I met with him, he was worried about his safety and yours. I had a sense he was somewhat relieved I had contacted him."

"Do you think I'm in danger?"

They locked eyes. He seemed to hesitate a moment before saying no.

She reached into her car and pulled out her purse. She dug out a new business card. Holding it between two fingers, she offered it to him. "May I trade you?"

He accepted the new card and handed her the old one. She flipped it over. In her handwriting on the back she had written: *I'm only a phone call away.* The faded ink was water-stained, but the message was clear. Yet the phone calls between her and her brother had become few and far between.

As she slipped the old business card into a pocket of

her purse, the *clip clop clip* of what sounded like a horse reached her ears. She froze as a horse and buggy made its way along the country road. A man in a brimmed straw hat gently flicked the reins, urging the horse on. Tipping his hat, he seemed to make direct eye contact with the FBI agent as he passed.

Outlined against the purple and pink hues of the evening sky, the buggy maintained its steady progress until it crested the hill and disappeared. Anna made a full circle, taking in her surroundings, including the vast cornfield that greeted her brother's demise. She had been so focused on the crash site—on her distress—she hadn't noticed a neat farmhouse at the top of a long driveway across from the cornfields. A white split-rail fence ran the length of the property. A buggy, the same style as the one that had passed, sat next to the barn a hundred feet or so from the house. The early-evening shadows muted the details, but she realized something she had missed in her distracted state. "An Amish family lives here."

Special Agent Miller nodded, seemingly unfazed. Obviously he wasn't likely to miss such specifics. Besides, he had been in Apple Creek before now.

"My brother's plane crashed on an Amish farm? Ironic." A nervous giggle escaped her lips. "The very community that shuns most technology has one of man's modern marvels plummeting to earth on their soil."

Awareness heated her face when she found him regarding her with a quizzical look. "I'm sorry. I tend to talk too much when I'm upset." Her gaze drifted back toward the crash site, hidden by the tall cornstalks. "Thank God no one on the ground was hurt."

Special Agent Miller nodded but didn't say anything. His economy of words wore on her patience. Fisting her hands, she resisted the urge to slug the information out of him.

Crossing her arms, Anna narrowed her gaze. It wasn't beyond a law enforcement officer to lie to get what he wanted. She had learned that the hard way. "Why are you really here, Special Agent Eli Miller?"

The pain in Anna's eyes spoke volumes despite her display of false bravado. Eli refused to add to her burden, but his conscience didn't allow him to flat-out lie, either. "As I said, your brother's name came up in regard to a ten-year-old cold case." The words rang oddly distant in his ears. This wasn't exactly *any* case.

"Is…was—" she quickly changed tense "—Daniel in some kind of trouble?" Her pink-rimmed hazel eyes pleaded for the truth.

"Ma'am." A baby-faced police officer emerged from the cornfield carrying a green garment. "I understand you're the deceased's sister." Nodding, Anna's eyes widened. "This was in the plane." He held out what looked to be an army jacket.

She grabbed the garment and hugged it to her chest. "Thank you." The officer tipped his hat, respectful of her loss.

"We need someone to identify the body." The officer tapped his fingers nervously against his thigh.

Anna dropped her head and covered her mouth with her hands. "I don't know…."

"Where's the sheriff?" Eli asked. "I thought he'd be out here."

"No, sir, I'm handling this one." The officer tucked his thumbs into his belt and looked at Anna. "We really need you to identify the body, Miss Quinn."

Growing impatient with the officer's insistence, Eli stepped forward, partially blocking Anna in a protective gesture. "I knew the deceased. I'll do it."

Anna lifted her head. "This is something I need to do." Her voice broke over the last few words. "Where…?" Her gaze drifted toward the cornstalks as if she imagined traipsing through the field and finding her brother's bruised and battered body on the ground.

The officer's wary gaze moved to Eli, then back to her. "The morgue is at Apple Creek Hospital. I can take you. It's getting dark and it's easy to get turned around on these country roads."

"Let me drive you." Eli placed his hand on her trembling arm.

Anna nodded, the corners of her mouth pulling down. "Is it okay if I leave my car parked on the main road?"

Eli took her keys, their fingers brushing in the exchange. Anna's eyes snapped to his and he smiled reassuringly. "Let me move your car off the road."

After he moved her vehicle, he guided her with a hand at the small of her back to his SUV parked in the Amish family's yard. No one was outside the neat farmhouse. Just as well. He had all the information he needed for now. The officer in charge had informed him no one on the ground had been hurt in the crash. *Thank God*.

Eli opened the car door for Anna. Her long lashes brushed her porcelain skin as she ducked into the vehicle. With his hand still on the door handle, his focus drifted to the familiar farmhouse. A young girl emerged from the house, her pale blue gown rustling around her ankles as she sprinted across the grass toward the building next door. The Amish girl reached the neighboring house without so much as turning her bonneted head. Longing for a simpler life filled him.

Squaring his shoulders, Eli strode around the front of the vehicle. The case he was working on had never been easy. The death of Daniel Quinn was an unexpected complication. But even though he was dead, Eli still had to get answers. For the family. For himself.

Chapter Two

"So, Special Agent Eli Miller, what cold case did you talk to my brother about?" Anna had waited until her FBI escort had pulled out onto the road. For a moment back at the farmhouse he had seemed slightly distracted, as if he had something more on his mind than the plane crash. Her shoulders sagged. She squeezed her purse in her lap and held it close. Tears blurred her vision.

He flicked a gaze in her direction, then turned his attention back to the road. "Call me Eli, please." His mouth curved into a small smile, transforming his profile from the serious FBI agent to someone…well, someone not so serious. She ran her pinkie fingers under her eyes. She wasn't partial to men in law enforcement, but her emotional state made her vulnerable to a handsome man with a friendly smile regardless of his chosen career.

Heat crept up her neck and she turned to stare at the cornfields rushing by outside the car window. Instinctively, she was leery of those in law enforcement. Yet Eli's eyes radiated warmth, a kindness, so unlike her father's penetrating glare when he was looking for an excuse to punish her. She blinked a few times to dismiss the memory.

"Are you going to tell me about this cold case?" Anna asked again.

Eli seemed intent on staring straight ahead at the road. "The cold case stemmed from an old case—a five-year-old Amish girl was kidnapped from Apple Creek." His knuckles whitened on the steering wheel.

"Did they ever find her?"

"No." The single word came out clipped.

"Why did you talk to my brother?"

"He was a student at nearby Genwego State at the time."

"You contacted him just because he was a student at the time?" Anna shifted in her seat to look at him directly, fingering the locket on her necklace.

"When the child disappeared, a lot of college fraternities were in Apple Creek doing a pub crawl." A muscle worked in his jaw, but he kept his full attention on the road. "You know, when they come into town and go from one bar to another? Back then at least five bars dotted Main Street. All but one have closed down since. We hoped someone might have seen something."

"Ten years later?" Disbelief edged her tone.

Eli nodded. "It happens. Sometimes someone remembers something they didn't think was important at the time. Did Daniel ever mention the incident to you?"

She shook her head, scrambling to remember. "Ten years ago...I was starting college. That's the fall Daniel dropped out and enlisted in the army. He never mentioned anything about an Amish girl's disappearance. Should he have?" Her stomach hollowed out. At the time, she had found it puzzling her brother had quit college so close to graduation, but he assured her he had a plan.

"Well—" Eli adjusted his grip on the steering wheel "—let's take one thing at a time." He didn't say it, but she knew what he meant. Right now, she had to identify her brother's body.

Anna slumped into the leather seat and leaned her head back. Before long, the silos, barns and cows were replaced by neat homes and sidewalks as they approached the center of Apple Creek. The last bit of sunlight lit the trees, whose leaves had turned a crimson red and yellow, providing a picturesque landscape. If the circumstances of her arrival had been different, she might have enjoyed the scenery.

Eli slowed his vehicle at a stop sign. Churches occupied two of the four corners of the intersection. Her mind drifted for a moment and she wondered if her brother had maintained his faith after all these years. He had been the one to first drag her to church when they had ended up in a foster home. In church she had found peace and comfort despite the turmoil surrounding their lives.

Silently she said a prayer, asking God to give her strength to deal with the task at hand. Closing her eyes briefly, a quiet calmness descended on her. When she opened her eyes, she noticed hitching posts in front of several of the stores on Main Street. Only one space was actually occupied by a horse and buggy. How peculiar to live as if from another time. Despite having lived in the Buffalo area her entire life, she had never realized the Amish had settled in the countryside little more than an hour away.

Eli drove a few minutes longer, then flicked on the directional and turned into a driveway marked by a large *H*. The small-town hospital was merely a single-story brick building that might have been mistaken for a school if not for the hospital sign out front.

Sensing Eli's gaze, Anna laced her fingers and twisted her hands. In a few minutes she'd have to identify her brother's body. Graphic images formed in her mind. "I don't know if I can do this."

"Come on." He pushed open his door. "I'll be with you the entire time." He came around to her side of the vehicle and helped her out. Streetlamps chased away the gathering dusk.

"Why are you doing this for me?"

"Because it's the right thing to do." With a hand to the small of her back he guided her toward the hospital. Each and every detail—the chipped paint on the bench, the no-smoking sign, the fallen leaves littering the sidewalk—came into sharp focus, as if she were witnessing it all from above.

The automated glass doors whirred open. A sterile, disinfectant-like scent assaulted her. A gray-haired lady in a pink jacket lifted her gaze in mild interest. Eli flashed his credentials and the elderly woman nodded without saying a word.

Eli strode toward a door marked Stairs and opened it for her. "Down one flight." Anna's shoulder brushed his broad chest as she scooted past him into the stairwell. A cool draft floated up from the floor below, sending a chill skittering down her spine.

"I'll be with you the entire time," Eli reminded her, placing a reassuring hand loosely on her waist.

The clacking of her heels on the linoleum became the focus of her attention. Not Eli's comforting presence. And certainly not the task waiting for her.

Reality in the form of a white placard with black lettering slapped her in the face. Morgue. She sucked in a quick breath, then swallowed hard. Nausea licked at her throat.

When they approached a second door, Eli caught her wrist, stopping her in her tracks. Suddenly, she was hyperaware of his touch, the intensity in his gaze. "You don't have to do this. I met your brother. I can identify him." The sincerity in his brown eyes weakened her resolve.

She opened her mouth, then snapped it shut. She glanced at Eli, then back at the door leading to the morgue. "I have to do this. Daniel's my brother."

Eli nodded. "Okay." His hand slipped down to hers. He gave it a squeeze but didn't let go. The small gesture gave her comfort. "Are you ready?"

Anna turned toward the morgue entrance, then back toward Eli. His features softened and the beginning of a smile tipped the corners of his mouth. The shield around her heart shifted a fraction. She had been alone for so long that she didn't know how to rely on anyone.

"Let's go." Eli pushed open the door leading into a large room. The legs of the stainless steel tables came into view. Her focus shifted from the table legs to the gray linoleum at her feet. Cool, heavy air floated along the floor, licking at her ankles. Eli ran his thumb gently across the back of her hand. "Ready?"

Closing her eyes, she filled her lungs. Would anyone ever be ready to identify a loved one's body? An image flickered across her brain. Her beloved mother, her long blond hair cascading over the pillow in the casket. The beautician had tried her best, she really had, but no one could do her mother's makeup as well as her mother.

She used to sit at her vanity every morning perfecting her hair and face, wanting to look beautiful for Father.

The mere thought stirred old fears and insecurities. Anna let go of Eli's hand and crossed her arms. She drew her shoulders to her ears, trying to shake the chill.

"Anna?" Eli's concerned voice broke through her trance. From one nightmare to another. Slowly, she opened her eyes. She forced herself to lift her eyes to the form draped in a white sheet. Her lips thinned into a straight line and she stifled a sob. Out of the corner of her eye, she noticed Eli nod to the only other man in the room. He peeled back the sheet, revealing her brother's face. Bright fluorescent lights cast an unnatural pallor on his whiskered jaw. Darkness pushed on the periphery of her vision. Her heart raced.

Dear Lord, get me through this. Give me strength.

Anna slid her gaze across her brother's features, allowing a numbness to dull the ache in her heart. Her brother's cleft chin, the subtle bump in his nose—the one she shared—and the flat pane of his forehead. Cold, hard reality set in. Her big brother was dead.

Buzzing filled her ears. All the colors came into sharp focus. Blinking a few times, she struggled to concentrate on her brother through her watery gaze, knowing this would be the last time she'd ever see him. Tonight she'd sign the paperwork to have the funeral home pick up his body for cremation. *Dear Lord, help me.* After she cleaned out his apartment, she'd go back to Buffalo and inter him next to their mother.

"It's him," she croaked out. "That's my brother, Daniel Quinn." She turned and buried her face in Eli's shoulder and cried, really cried, for the first time since she had received the news.

"Okay. It's over now." Eli made a soft hushing noise next to her ear, smoothing his hand down her hair.

"I'm sorry." Anna lifted her face and brushed at her tears. Heat burned her cheeks. She had no business seeking comfort from this man. An FBI agent. A stranger. Cupping her cheeks, she stepped back.

"Let's get the papers signed and get you out of here," Eli said.

After Anna took care of the paperwork at the morgue, Eli guided her up the stairs to the main lobby. Before they reached the exit, a clamor came from down the hall. The double doors leading to another part of the hospital swung open, then bounced off the wall. A tall, well-dressed man strode in. His facial features contorted in obvious pain. He held on to a woman at her waist. Her wailing and sobbing scraped across Anna's already fried nerves, and she froze by the stairwell to let them pass.

"Beth," the man cooed in the woman's ear. He ran a hand down her blond hair, pulling it back from her face. "Please," the man pleaded, apparently unsure of how to handle the woman's grief.

Eli put his arm around Anna's shoulders and pulled her close. It seemed the most natural thing to lean into him. To accept the comfort he was offering. "Let's get you out of here," he whispered.

The woman stumbled forward. A groan escaped her lips. As her companion guided her toward the exit, her unfocused eyes drifted to Anna and Eli. Her head snapped up. "Who are you?" Her words slurred as if she had been drinking. She slapped at the tears trailing down her cheeks, wearing off her smooth foundation.

"I'm sorry. I don't think you know me. I'm not from

Apple Creek." She struggled to keep her voice from shaking. Eli's grip tightened around her shoulders.

"You're *his* sister." The coldness in the woman's eyes chilled Anna to the bone.

"I'm sorry...." Anna swallowed hard, confusion clouding her brain.

"Mrs. Christopher," Eli said, "now is not the time."

"Get out of my face." The woman pinned Eli with her steely gaze. The two apparently knew each other. With lightning speed, the woman reached out and brought her palm against Anna's cheek with a resounding smack. "Your brother dragged my baby onto that plane. She wasn't supposed to be there." A tear dripped from her quivering chin.

"Mrs. Christopher, please, everyone is hurting here." Eli tucked Anna behind him.

Anna's mind whirled as she stood dumbfounded, her hand pressed to her stinging cheek. Her mouth worked but no words came.

Mrs. Christopher's eyes narrowed into hateful slits. "My baby girl is in there." She jabbed her long manicured finger toward the double doors but didn't turn her head. "They don't know if she's going to make it."

"I am so sorry." Anna's chest grew heavy.

"You will be," the woman said. "I will make sure of it. Your brother was reckless. He had been drinking. Someone saw him at the diner with a beer. *Before* he took my baby up in his plane."

Anna's heart stuttered. She struggled to catch her breath. The conversation seemed to wind down in slow motion. She slipped her hand around the crook of Eli's arm, grateful for the support.

Eli led her past the grieving couple. The man—speaking for the first time—hollered after them. "Special Agent Miller—" disdain evident in his tone "—I suggest you keep Miss Quinn away from us. Her brother has destroyed my family." He lowered his voice. "It would be best if she took care of her business and left Apple Creek immediately. Our family has suffered enough without her here as a constant reminder."

"I wish Tiffany well," Eli said, his voice tight. "Miss Quinn has experienced a terrible loss of her own. If you'll excuse us."

Anna locked gazes with Mr. Christopher. Fury shot from his eyes. The fine hairs on the back of her neck prickled to life, convincing her if she didn't leave town, he'd make her wish she had.

Outside the hospital's main entrance, a black limousine straddled the ramped pavement. Tom Hanson, the driver, leaned against the hood and read the newspaper under the artificial light, seemingly unaware he was being observed. The Christophers were the only people pretentious—and rich enough—to have a chauffeured limo in Apple Creek. Mr. Christopher had created a cable-industry empire and located it in his hometown. The company had satellite offices all over the East Coast but kept their main headquarters in rural Apple Creek. Eli suspected they enjoyed the "big fish in a small pond" cachet it afforded.

Despite Beth and Richard Christopher's angry display in the lobby, Eli's heart ached for them. All the money in the world couldn't buy them happiness if their family was ripped apart. He hoped Tiffany pulled through.

Once inside his vehicle, Eli shifted in his seat. The

yellow light from the parking lot lamppost cast Anna's face in deep shadows. "Are you okay?"

Anna's pink lips pulled down at the corners. "Did you know about the poor girl who was on the plane with my brother?" An accusatory tone laced her question.

"Yes." Tense silence hung heavy in the air.

"Why didn't you tell me?"

"I didn't want to burden you."

"You couldn't hide it from me forever." A dark line creased her forehead. "I know you don't know me, but I'm not a fragile woman. Don't hide anything from me. Not when it concerns my brother."

Eli glanced toward the main entrance of the hospital but didn't say anything. Tom opened the back door of the limo and the Christophers disappeared inside.

"How did those people know I was Daniel's sister?"

"Probably because you're with me."

Covering her face, she sighed her frustration. "Don't they realize this is the last place I want to be? There's so much I need to do before I can go home."

Eli reached across and touched her delicate hand, drawing it away from her face. He was secretly pleased when she didn't pull away. "I can help you."

"Why would you help me?"

Because your brother is the last solid link to Mary's abduction. He turned away, afraid he'd chase her off if he told her the truth. He stared at the SUV logo emblazoned on the center of the steering wheel until it blurred. "I'll be in town for a few weeks. I'm here if you need me." He met her gaze.

Anna nodded, skepticism evident in the delicate lines around her eyes. Tipping her head back against the headrest, she yanked the rubber band from her hair, allowing her chestnut hair to fall in loose curls over her shoulders. For the briefest of moments, he wondered if her hair felt as silky as it looked. "Can you take me back to my car?"

"Sure." Tugging at his tie with one hand, he turned the key in the ignition with the other. They drove through the center of Apple Creek. Most of the businesses were closed for the night. When they reached the country road, his headlights cut through the blackness. Silence stretched between them as Eli struggled with how much he should tell Anna about his suspicions regarding her brother. Daniel was dead, so nothing could hurt him now. But what about Anna? She seemed fiercely loyal to him. He wrapped his fingers tightly around the steering wheel. She had suffered enough for today. From what he knew of her childhood through his investigation into her brother, she had suffered enough for a lifetime.

He'd tell her the truth tomorrow.

When they finally reached the crash site, Eli turned into the driveway rutted with wagon wheels and horse hooves. Anna's car was parked on the lawn where he had left it. Sighing heavily, she tucked a strand of hair behind her ear. "Where is the nearest hotel?"

They glanced at each other and a slow smile spread up her pretty face, no doubt anticipating his answer. "Um, all the way back in town." Eli laughed.

"Exactly what I thought." She lifted her hair from her forehead and held it there. Her shoulders slumped. "I just want to grab something to eat and go to sleep."

"What about staying at your brother's apartment?"

Anna shook her head. "I'm not ready to go there. Not yet." She lowered her voice. "That would mean facing all his…stuff."

Eli's eyes drifted to the outline of the farmhouse. "I

need to stop in here. Then we can figure out where to grab a bite and a place for you to sleep, okay?"

Anna jerked her head back. "Isn't it too late to drop in unannounced?"

"Come on." He got out and met Anna around the front of the vehicle.

A cool breeze blew her hair softly around her shoulders. Only a hint of the scent of burning wreckage clung to the night air. She hooked a strand of her hair with her pinkie and slid it away from her face. The bright moon lit on her hesitant features. "It seems really late. Maybe we shouldn't bother them."

"Watch your step." He held out his hand and Anna put her slim hand in his. "Come on. It's fine." Her cheek brushed against his shoulder as they navigated their way across the uneven lawn. A clean scent of coconut from her hair drifted to his nose.

Slowing his pace, he reached down and boldly tipped her chin toward the sky. "I bet you don't see those in the city."

"Wow, I don't think I've ever seen so many stars." He stole a glance at the wonder in her eyes and bemoaned the circumstances surrounding their meeting. Another time, another place, perhaps. "There seems to be a certain peace out here. No traffic noise. No nothing."

Eli wrapped his hand around the smooth railing leading up the steps. "It is a peaceful existence. A lot of work. No modern conveniences. But the Amish don't clutter their lives with a lot of distractions. The Amish have a saying, 'To be in this world, but not of this world.'"

"Are you sure this can't wait until morning?" Anna whispered. "Don't they go to bed early?"

"It's only eight-thirty."

"I know, it's just…" She let her words trail off.

"You're uncomfortable."

Anna scrunched up her nose. "I've never met anyone who's Amish." She glanced down at her clothes. "I mean, am I dressed appropriately?" She lowered her voice to barely a whisper, and she tugged at the cardigan covering her sleeveless top. "And I was really hoping to freshen up soon. Do they have indoor plumbing?"

Eli laughed. If only she knew. "Yes, they have indoor plumbing." He gestured toward the window where a soft glow emanated. "And lights. You won't have to fumble around in the dark. They're just not hooked up to the grid."

"The grid?"

"They don't use electricity. But there are plenty of other independent sources of power."

Anna seemed to consider this for a moment. "It's incredible, really, that people still live this way."

Eli leaned on the railing. "We won't be long. I just want to make sure they're okay."

Her tired gaze drifted to the street. The moonlight glinted off her vehicle's windshield. "Okay."

He rapped on the door before she could change her mind. Who was he kidding? He had to do it before *he* changed his mind. Sweat slicked his palms. The door opened slowly. Beautiful brown eyes met his. A smile broke wide on the woman's face. "Abram! Abram!" she called, glancing over her shoulder. "Come quickly."

Out of the corner of his eye, Eli sensed Anna watching him. He was glad for the shadows. He yanked his tie out of habit as the space suddenly felt close. The door swung all the way open. The woman's long gown rustled in the evening breeze. The hair poking out from under her *kapp* seemed grayer than he remembered. Her bright eyes met his. Covering her mouth, she stepped onto the porch, the kindness in her eyes familiar.

"Eli, you're home."

Chapter Three

Anna watched transfixed as the Amish woman welcomed them. Eli's lips curved into a small smile, but a hint of hesitancy flickered in his eyes. "Anna, this is my mother, Mrs. Mariam Miller."

"Hello, Mrs. Miller. Nice to meet you." Anna did a horrible job hiding her surprise.

"Please call me Mariam." She took Anna's hand in her callused one. "Welcome." His mother glanced over her shoulder. "Your father must be in the barn with Samuel." She spun on her heel. "Let me get him."

Eli reached out and caught his mother's arm. "Wait. How are you? The plane crash this morning must have been a shock."

Mariam fidgeted with the edge of her cape. "Those poor people. Do you know how they are?"

Anna's cheeks grew warm.

"I'm afraid the pilot died. His passenger was the youngest child of the Christophers, Tiffany. She's in the hospital." Eli placed a reassuring hand on the small of Anna's back.

"Oh, dear." His mother's eyes grew wide. "Katie Mae

does some housekeeping for the Christopher family. I wonder if she knows…."

"I can talk to her if you'd like," Eli said.

"I hope we're not stopping by too late." Anna found herself studying the space, suddenly fascinated to find herself inside an Amish home. Two oak rocking chairs sat in the middle of a room with wall-to-wall oak hardwood floors. The wood continued halfway up the wall and stopped at the chair rail. The room had a scarcity of knickknacks. Her mind's eye flashed to the assortment of crystal trinkets her mother had collected with reckless abandon. Her childhood home had never lacked for *stuff.* A lump formed in her throat and she pushed the thought aside.

"I'm glad you came." Soft frown lines accentuated Mariam's mouth. "Did the plane crash bring you here?" She gathered her apron in her hands. "The noise. It was horrible." Tears filled the corners of her eyes.

"Yes, I'm afraid it did." Eli momentarily found Anna's hand by her side and gave it a quick squeeze. Anna held her breath, relieved he didn't explain that her brother was killed in the crash. In her exhausted state, she feared any outpouring of sympathy would send her crumbling.

"Do you need a room for the night? I could check with your father. I'm sure under the circumstances it would be acceptable." Mariam stepped deeper into the entryway and called, "Katie Mae, please come here."

"I don't want to cause any trouble." Eli slipped his car keys into his pocket.

Mrs. Miller seemed to study her son's face. "I suppose your brother, Samuel, won't mind having a bunkmate." She hesitated a fraction. "You weren't planning on sharing a room?"

Embarrassment flushed Anna's cheeks. She imagined that the Amish views on premarital cohabitation ran toward the conservative. "We're not…" She glanced at Eli for help, but apparently they didn't know each other well enough to have their signals worked out.

"My brother was piloting the plane that crashed." She swallowed hard. "I just met Eli today." There, she said it out loud. The reality of her words crashed over her. Biting her lower lip, she hoped to keep her emotions at bay.

Mariam's eyes grew wide. "I am so sorry. Do you need to contact your family? The Jones family down the road has a phone."

Anna closed her eyes briefly. She couldn't find the words to say she didn't have any family. Not anymore. "It can wait," she lied.

A hint of confusion flashed across Mariam's face. Eli's shuttered expression gave nothing away, yet something niggled at her brain. Why hadn't he asked about her family earlier?

A young woman, probably in her late teens, appeared in the hallway. She had on a calf-length dress in a beautiful shade of blue that matched her eyes. Her flawless skin was untouched by makeup. A loop of brown hair poked out the side of her bonnet. The strings on the bonnet dangled by her chin. When her eyes landed on Eli, she smiled broadly. She covered the distance between them in a few short steps and wrapped her arms around his neck. Her cheeks blushed a pretty pink and she quickly stepped back, running her hands down the front of her dress. "Hey, big brother." Her eyes sparkled.

"Hey, Katie Mae."

"So nice to see you. I just got home from work."

"Still working for the Christophers, I hear."

Katie Mae rolled her eyes. "Yes. I'm supposed to do light housework, but half the time I'm watching the grandchildren. They are a handful."

A small smile lifted the corners of Eli's mouth. "I'm sure you handle them just fine." He hesitated a moment, as if weighing his next words. "I imagine it was a little chaotic over there today."

"Oh, dear, yes. Thank goodness Tiffany wasn't killed in that horrible plane crash. Mrs. Christopher is beside herself. Her mother didn't even know she was on the plane until the sheriff showed up at her door to tell her about the crash."

"How horrible," Anna said.

Eli made the introductions between the women, then turned to his mother. "So, Father's still out working in the barn? It's getting late."

"He and Samuel are checking on Red." Katie Mae's voice grew quiet. "He's getting old."

"I brought Red, an Irish setter, home when he was a puppy." A faraway look settled in his eyes. "Must have been more than twelve years ago."

"Why don't you show Anna the extra room upstairs?" Mariam motioned to her daughter. "I'll go discuss the arrangements with your father."

Katie Mae led Anna up the wooden stairs to a bedroom down a short hallway. "Can I get you anything?"

Anna glanced around the tidy room. The furnishings were sparse but clean. A beautiful quilt in shades of blue and green covered the bed. A lone calendar was tacked to the wall. "This is fine. Thank you."

"The bathroom is at the end of the hallway. I will put some clean linens on the chair." The young woman's blue gown rustled around her ankles, revealing black laced boots. "If you'd like, I'll make you some tea and a little something to eat."

"Thank you."

Katie Mae paused at the door, and curiosity lit her face. "Is my brother courting you?"

Anna shook her head. "Oh, no. We just met today."

The young woman frowned. "Too bad." She shrugged. "He could use someone in his life. He's too tied up in his job… Well, your tea will be downstairs." She turned on her heel and disappeared, leaving Anna mildly amused by the question.

Anna flopped down on the bed and closed her eyes. She nearly groaned when she remembered she'd have to retrieve her suitcase from her car. She had packed for a week, knowing she'd have to take care of her brother's apartment in Apple Creek and other details.

"Are the accommodations okay?"

Anna sat up and adjusted the hem of her shirt. Eli leaned on the door frame, a strange look on his face. He had shed his suit coat and rolled his white shirtsleeves to his elbows. Realizing she was staring, she dropped her gaze.

"Oh, man, you're a lifesaver." She stood, relieved to see her suitcase at his feet.

"I try." He stepped into the room, brushing past her, and set the case on the trunk at the foot of the bed. She was keenly aware of him sharing the small space. "I still had your car keys from this morning." Eli tossed them on the dresser. "I'll let you get settled." He turned to leave.

"Wait."

He paused in the doorway and glanced over his shoulder.

"I appreciate all you've done for me today." She held up her palms. "Including this room. But tomorrow I'll go to the motel, because I really don't think I could stay at my brother's place. It would just be too hard." She bit her lower lip.

"One day at a time." The kindness in his eyes warmed her heart.

She tilted her head, studying him. "You grew up here? You're Amish?" She blurted out the questions on the tip of her tongue. She had no right to be intrusive, but she couldn't help herself.

Smiling, he pivoted on his heel. Dark whiskers colored his square jaw. "There is nothing to tell. I was born into the Amish community, but I am not Amish. I left before I was baptized."

Anna narrowed her eyes. "And your parents are okay with that? I thought if you left, you were shunned for life or something."

Eli stepped back and leaned against the windowsill. He undid the knot of his tie. Pulling one end, he unlaced it from his collar, then he ran the silky material through his fingers. "They tolerate the occasional visit, but I'm careful not to overstay my welcome. I don't want to cause them any trouble." He looked like he wanted to say more but didn't. "My parents were disappointed I didn't choose to stay. All Amish parents dream of their children accepting their way of life."

"But it wasn't for you?"

He folded the tie accordion style and gripped it in one hand. He looked up and met her gaze. "It's complicated." He crossed the room and adjusted the brightness on the lamp. "Do you have everything you need? There should be a flashlight in the drawer, too."

Unable to hide her amusement, she shrugged.

"A few less modern conveniences than you're used to?"

"How'd you guess?" She arched an eyebrow.

"The light is fueled by a propane tank in the night-stand."

Anna jerked her head back, marveling at the inge-nuity.

"Are these accommodations okay with you? I didn't want to offend my mother when she extended the invi-tation. I think you'll find it far more comfortable than the Apple Creek Motel." He stuffed his hands into his pockets and crossed his ankles.

"It's fine. Thanks. Really, you've been too kind."

He pulled out his cell phone. "You won't get reception here, either. If there's someone you need to contact at home, a boyfriend, maybe, we can go to the neighbors. I don't mind driving you." Was there a glint of expecta-tion in his eyes, or was she imagining it?

"No. There's no one." A pain stabbed her heart and she sat back down on the edge of the bed. Then realiz-ing how pathetic she sounded, she added, "I'll update work next week."

"I'm sorry about your brother," Eli said. "It's hard to lose someone close to you." He spoke the words as if from experience, but she figured she had pried enough already tonight.

"I can't believe he's gone." She ran her hands up and down her arms. "I dread going to his apartment. It's going to be hard to pack away his things." Once again tears burned the backs of her eyes. "My brother had called me a few times recently, but I never called him back." Her voice cracked.

Eli left his perch at the windowsill and sat next to her on the bed, pulling her hand into his. "Take it one day at a time."

Their eyes locked. An emotional connection sparked between them. The walls of the bedroom seemed to close in on her, and she closed her eyes to stop the swaying. Exhaustion was catching up with her.

"I avoided my brother's calls because I couldn't deal with him and the demands of my job. He seemed so different after the war. Paranoid. I used to tell him he reminded me of Mel Gibson in *Conspiracy Theory*." She ran a shaky hand over her mouth. "Remember that movie?" She bowed her head. "I'm so ashamed. I spent my life helping the students at school but I couldn't take five minutes to answer a call from my brother."

"Don't beat yourself up. You didn't know." He squeezed her hand.

Her mouth twisted in skepticism. "But if I hadn't avoided him, I *would have* known something was wrong. Now I'll never have another chance to talk to him. To tell him I love him."

Bowing her head, she covered her face and fought her emotions. Eli placed his solid hand at the back of her head and pulled her into his chest. Sitting on the edge of the bed, she settled into his arms. A mixture of laundry detergent and his aftershave filled her senses.

"Eli—" Anna sat upright. A man with an unkempt beard and blunt-style haircut stood in the doorway "—I need to talk to you downstairs." His cool manner and stare tightened Anna's gut.

"Father," Eli said, his tone even, "nice to see you. This is Anna Quinn." He turned to Anna. "My father, Abram Miller."

The man gave her a curt nod. "If you'll excuse us, I'd like to talk to my son in private."

After his father left, Eli angled his head and brushed his thumb across her cheek. "You okay?"

Anna forced a smile. "You better go talk to your father."

A man of few words, Eli's father descended the stairs and headed outside to the porch. Eli flinched when the screen door slammed against its frame. He caught his father's profile against the backdrop of the night sky. His father was a commanding figure and Eli knew he'd talk when he was ready to talk.

With work-worn hands wrapped around the rail, his father stared out into the distance toward the crash scene. "I never understood man's need to fly. It seems to go against nature." He hesitated a moment before adding, "I pray the man is in God's hands now."

Eli bowed his head. It had been a long time since he had said a prayer. Not so much because of disbelief, but because of apathy, distraction and his job. He scrubbed a hand across his face. Wasn't that part of the reason why his parents—and the entire Amish community—set themselves apart? So they wouldn't be distracted by the outside world and instead could focus on God? Under the night sky, the fields seemed to stretch forever. The Amish believed the agricultural life was as close to God as you could get.

"Anna's brother died in the crash." Eli leaned back in the rocker. The wood felt cool through his thin dress shirt. His grandfather had made these chairs when Eli was a boy. He had been fascinated watching his grandfather work.

"Your mother told me." Abram faced his son, his features heavily shadowed. "But you have been in Apple Creek often over the past month."

"Yes, but never overnight. I drove back and forth to Buffalo." Eli was reluctant to share too much information with his father. They lived in different worlds. "If our staying here is going to cause problems, I'll take Anna to the motel in town."

Abram lifted his hand. "I suppose the bishop will understand the circumstances surrounding your *temporary* stay." His emphasis was not lost on Eli.

"Thank you." He wrapped his fingers around the smooth arms of the rocker. "How did you know I've been in town recently?"

"Isaac Lapp mentioned he saw you in town." *Figures.* The same age as Eli, Isaac had been courting his sister, Katie Mae, almost ten years his junior. Isaac had left Apple Creek to work on a ranch out west years ago, only to return to fully join the Amish faith about eighteen months ago. His family owned the Apple Creek General Store in town and had welcomed him back with open arms.

And Isaac liked to talk.

"You're chasing a ghost." Abram's statement startled Eli. His father never asked about the investigation that had consumed Eli for the past ten years.

"I have new leads."

"You need to let your sister rest."

My sister. Ten years ago, his sweet sister Mary had disappeared while in town with him. She was only five at the time and he was eighteen. She had been his responsibility. Guilt and anguish sat like rocks in his gut. "I can't."

Under the white glow of the moonlight, his father's

eyes flashed. "You are wasting your life. You need to forgive the man who did this."

"You say you have forgiven him, but you have not moved on. Last time I stopped by, you were still leaving Mary's chair empty at the table."

"Your mother…" His words trailed off. Eli waited for his father to continue, but he didn't.

"Dat…" The word felt strange on his lips. "I didn't come here to fight. I came here because I have unfinished business."

"Your unfinished business is a constant, painful reminder to your mother of everything we have lost. We need to have faith and trust in God that Mary is now in His care. Does Anna know you are investigating her brother?" Abram's pointed words hit their mark.

Eli looked up with a start, then glanced toward the screen door. "Did you hear that from Isaac?"

"Isaac had told me to keep an eye on Daniel Quinn because he had been taking photographs in the area." Abram pointed to the cornfield across the way. "This is the same man who died today?"

Eli nodded.

Abram's hand dropped to his side. "Daniel spent a lot of time taking photographs. Claimed they were for a book or some magazine or some such. He seemed respectful. He only took photos of the property. He knew we didn't want to be photographed." Abram fingered his unkempt beard. "Isaac thought we should be aware of who was wandering our property."

Eli scratched his head. "Who else knows I am investigating Daniel?" His mind raced with the implications.

"No one else in the family as far as I know. I told Isaac not to scare the women with his gossip. The next time Daniel had come around, I had asked him to please respect our privacy. I thought it best he not take photographs on our farm anymore."

"How did he respond?"

"He complied. He was always polite. Seemed like a sincere young man," Abram said. "I can't believe this man hurt a child. I am reluctant to believe Isaac." His voice grew low. "It's hard to comprehend such evil."

The pain in his father's eyes tore at Eli's soul. His father rarely mentioned his youngest daughter, Mary.

Eli glanced toward the door, hoping Anna was still upstairs. "Father, we can't discuss this now. I don't want to jeopardize my investigation."

Abram crossed his arms over his chest and leaned back against the railing. "You have not chosen our way of life, but I raised you better than this."

"I am not going to stop looking for the truth." Frustration and anger warred for control.

"Truth?" Abram's bushy eyebrows shot up. "Then don't lie to Daniel's sister. Tell her your suspicions."

"I only met her today. I owe her nothing." The harsh words scraped across his nerves. Had he become so single-minded in his focus that he had lost all sight of others' feelings? Anna's trusting eyes came to mind. It had always been about finding the person who hurt Mary. He never imagined his prime suspect would have a family of his own who might be destroyed by his investigation.

Eli softened his tone. "You'll never understand my choices, but there are things I have to do for my job."

His father's lips drew into a straight line. The Amish were not selfish people. They didn't make choices based on personal preferences and desires. They made decisions for the good of the entire community.

He met his father's gaze. "I have to do it for Mary."

Chapter Four

Dressed in sweats, a T-shirt and a hoodie, Anna stuffed her feet into her running shoes and tiptoed downstairs. A recurring nightmare had her up before dawn and she thought she'd go crazy inside the small confines of the sterile room. No television, no radio, no electronics. Nothing to distract her. She opened the front door, surprised to find it unlocked. Stepping onto the front porch, she took in the Miller's barn and the dense foliage on the surrounding hills. The first hint of pink colored the sky. The sun hadn't yet poked out over the trees.

A quiet rustling made her glance over her shoulder at the house. For all she knew, the Miller women were up preparing breakfast already. The men were probably in the barn doing their early-morning chores. Not ready to face anyone yet, she jogged down the porch steps and stopped by the road to stretch. A soft wind blew across the cornfields, sending a hint of acrid smoke in her direction. A tightness squeezed her chest.

Focusing all her attention on the ground directly in front of her, she tipped her head from side to side, easing out the kinks. Determined to exercise away her mount-

ing stress, she started her jog on the left side of the road,
facing traffic. However, she didn't expect to see any cars
at this early hour in the country. As her sneakers hit the
pavement, she tried to get into a rhythm. But the image
of her brother's cold dead body in the morgue seeped
into her brain only to be replaced by more graphic images of her dead mother and father.

She pumped her arms harder. The steady incline of
the road forced her to concentrate on her breathing, the
placement of her feet, her stride. Soon, her thoughts
cleared. She crested the hill and sidestepped some
horse manure in the road. A horse and open wagon approached. The combination of the brim of his hat and
the dim early-morning light shadowed the driver's features. He waved as he passed. Befuddled, she ignored
his greeting and kept running, feeling rude.

The first hint of sun became visible over the tree-
tops. Sweat trickled down her temples. Lost in thought,
she realized she had gone much farther than she anticipated. Slowing her pace, she looked up and down the
long country road. She crossed to the other side to face
the nonexistent traffic as she made her way back.

City habits die hard.

When she reached the road in front of the Miller's
home, she leaned over and braced her hands on her
thighs, trying to catch her breath. She found herself staring at the cornstalks. She glanced toward the quiet farmhouse, not detecting any activity. But surely they were
all up by now. Sucking in a quick breath, she stepped off
the road into the soft soil. She held out her arm to push
aside the cornstalks. Their sweet smell tickled her nose,
and she pinched her nose to stop the threatening sneeze.

Pushing her way through the stalks, she realized she

should have followed the beaten path made by the rescue workers. When she reached the clearing, she froze. A small crater of dark soil marked the spot where her brother had met his fate. Tiny white dots danced in front of her eyes. Covering her mouth, she backed away as her stomach heaved. Out of the corner of her eye, she saw a dark shadow flicker between stalks. Training her gaze on the form, she sensed her fight-or-flight response kick in.

She spun around and plowed through the stalks. Each of her frantic steps was met with a rustling off to her right. Her heartbeat ratcheted up in her chest. Stalks whacked her face. *Please help me, Lord.* Sensing she was losing ground, she spun back around to face her potential attacker, but she twisted her ankle on the uneven earth and bit back a yelp. Two strong hands gripped her upper arms. A blood-curdling scream died on her lips when she glanced up to find Eli's concerned gaze on her.

"Thank goodness you're here." Her breath came out in ragged gasps.

"I came outside to look for you when you didn't answer my knock on your bedroom door. What's wrong?"

"Were you walking through the cornstalks?"

"No, I just saw you when you lost your footing." He narrowed his gaze. "What's going on?"

"Someone…" Anna swallowed hard. "Someone was in there."

"Are you okay?"

Unable to find the words, she nodded. He pointed to the house. "Go wait up there while I check it out."

Anna nodded and jogged toward the house. Her ankle seemed fine under her weight. She reached the top step and her rubbery legs went out from under her. Dropping down on to the top step, she wrapped her arms around her middle and leaned forward, her eyes locked on the cornfield.

After what seemed like forever, Eli appeared and strode toward her. Her heart rate had returned to normal. "I didn't see anything." He narrowed his gaze. "What exactly did you see?"

"I…" Her shoulders dropped. "I don't know. Maybe I was imagining things." She pushed a hand through her hair. "Maybe I'm as paranoid as my brother."

Eli planted one foot on the bottom step of the porch and leaned his elbow on the railing. "You've had a lot to take in." He offered her his hand and she pushed off the step to stand next to him.

"My nerves are shot." Her laugh came out high-pitched and grating.

"Why did you go into the field?"

"I thought it would help me move past this nightmare if I saw the spot where his plane went down." She had always regretted not returning to her childhood home after her mother's murder. "I guess it was stupid."

"No, it's just that your brother was worried about you." He glanced back toward the fields. "Until I figure out why, I want to keep an eye on you."

Anna climbed a step to gain some distance. She didn't know whether she should be flattered or annoyed. "I can take care of myself. I've been doing it for most of my life."

Eli pinned her with his gaze. "Humor me, would you?" When she didn't answer, he added, "Come on. Let's go inside. My mother is making breakfast."

"Mind if I clean up first?" He held open the screen door for her. She ran up the stairs, aware of Eli watch-

ing her. Now *he* was worried she was in danger. *Had*
someone been following her in the fields? Shards of ice
shot through her veins.

Despite the unseasonably warm October weather,
Anna threw on a thin cardigan and capris, compelled to
cover her exposed flesh. Anything less and she would
have felt severely underdressed—disrespectful even—in
this Amish house. Besides, she couldn't shake the chill
from her encounter in the cornstalks.

When she finally wandered downstairs to the kitchen,
she was quickly ushered to the breakfast table. Mother
and daughter in their long gowns, hair neatly pinned
underneath their bonnets, moved in a practiced rhythm.

"We trust you had a good sleep, Miss Quinn," Mariam said, never once slowing from the hustle and bustle
of preparing breakfast.

"Yes, thank you." The lie flew from her lips. It was
easy because Eli's mother never met her eyes. Anna
rolled her shoulders, trying to ease the kinks in her back.
A bead of sweat rolled down her back in the close quarters of the kitchen. The cooking stove gave off immense
heat.

"Are you okay?" Mariam's soft voice snapped her out
of her reverie. "Please have a seat."

Unable to find her voice, Anna nodded and pulled
out the closest chair.

"No, please, sit in this one." The older woman pointed
to another chair. Mariam smoothed her hand across the
top of the empty chair and slid it back into place.

Anna sat and leaned into the slats of the wooden high-
back chair. A fragrant aroma wafted from the stove.
Her stomach growled. Until then, she hadn't realized

she was hungry. A moment later, Eli strolled into the kitchen dressed in blue jeans and a dark-blue golf shirt.

"Feel better?" The intensity in Eli's gaze unnerved her and she nodded. He pulled out a chair across from hers and sat down. The silence stretched between them.

Nervous energy finally got the best of Anna. "I thought I'd drive by my brother's apartment today. Clean out his things."

"I'll go with you."

"That's not necessary." She blurted out the words on reflex, despite knowing he'd insist. "I don't want you to go to any more trouble than you already have."

"I'd like to see if I can find anything at your brother's apartment that might answer why he was worried." Eli seemed to be selecting his words carefully. His mother placed a bowl of scrambled eggs on the table and smiled but didn't say anything. "I have two weeks of vacation. I arranged it yesterday afternoon with my supervisor."

Anna took a small spoonful of scrambled eggs, then pushed them around her plate with her fork. "For your cold case investigation?" Out of the corner of her eye, Anna noticed Mariam watching her son with keen interest. "Why did you have to take vacation for a case? Isn't it part of your job?"

"It's kind of a personal project." Eli's lips flattened into a thin line. Anna flicked a gaze toward his mother standing by the stove.

"Do you think my brother's worries had anything to do with your investigation? It's not likely, right? He didn't know anything." Dread washed over her as they locked gazes, an unreadable emotion in his eyes. Shaking his head, he cut a sideways glance toward his mother.

She took a bite of scrambled eggs despite the knot in her stomach.

A teenage boy dressed in a blue shirt, pants with suspenders and a straw hat burst in through the back door. Despite a scolding from his mother, he raced from one window to the next.

"Hey, Samuel, what's going on out there?" The legs of Eli's chair scraped across the hardwood floor as he stood up.

The teenager leaned on the window's ledge and peered out. "There's a big truck with a long pole on it. One of the English is carrying something big on his shoulder and they're coming this way. *Dat* told me to get in the house. To tell *Mem* and Katie Mae to stay put."

Eli strode toward the front door and yanked it open. When Anna reached his side, she was struck by the hard expression on his features. Eli was a formidable man. A cold chill ran down her spine despite the warm breeze.

A camera crew stood a few feet from the porch steps. A well-coiffed woman with a blond bob and a microphone in hand took a step forward, doing a quick check of her shoes as if she had stepped in something. "Can we speak to someone regarding the plane crash?"

Eli glared at her until she lowered the microphone and gestured to her cameraman to turn off the camera. She pointed the mic at Eli. "Do you live here?" She rearranged her lips into a phony smile. "Help us out here. I need some footage for the evening news."

Eli jerked his chin toward the street. "Take footage from the road. This is private property."

"We'd like to interview someone. We're working several angles." The woman persisted. "At first we thought it was a cruel twist that a plane crashed in the middle of an Amish field. Two different worlds colliding." Her lips quirked. "And, I think a lot of people would be surprised to learn of the thriving Amish community in western New York."

"They can read about it in the guidebooks." Eli started to close the door. The woman raised her voice. "We learned Tiffany Christopher was critically injured in the crash. I'm sure you're aware they're a prominent family in this area."

Anna froze and held her breath. She had the sensation of standing on the ocean's edge about to be clobbered by a giant wave. The reporter's focus turned toward her. "I was told the pilot's sister was in town."

Eli held his hand in front of Anna protectively.

"Do you know—" the reporter consulted her note-pad "—where we could find Daniel Quinn's family? His sister?"

Seemingly in an effort to intimidate, Eli moved toward the reporter. "I *asked* you to leave."

The reporter tilted her head. "I thought maybe we could get a comment from the sister. To clear his name."

Tiny white dots floated in Anna's line of vision. "What are you talking about?"

"Mr. and Mrs. Christopher have alleged the man piloting the plane was unstable. That he had suffered from post-traumatic stress disorder and was drunk when he took the plane up with Tiffany on board." The pounding of her heartbeat in her ears nearly drowned out the reporter's allegations. "I understand there was a history of violence in his family."

Panic pierced Anna's heart. She stepped forward and wrapped her hands around the smooth railing for stability. "My brother died in the crash. Let him rest in peace." Tears clogged her throat, making it difficult to speak. She didn't want her family's tragic past splashed all over the news *again*.

"Your brother?" The reporter's eyes lit up, but she obviously already knew who Anna was. "Would you be willing to go on camera?"

The implications ran through her mind. She didn't know anyone in this small town. Maybe if people knew she was here they'd help her piece together what her brother was doing in Apple Creek that had him spooked.

Keenly aware of the camera trained on her, she inhaled deeply. Daniel wouldn't have risked his life by drinking before flying. None of this made sense. She wished she could rewind time. If only she had kept in touch with her brother.

Anna walked down the porch steps and stared straight into the camera. "My brother, Daniel Quinn, died in the plane crash. If anyone knows—" she started over "—if anyone knew my brother, please contact me." After she rattled off the digits of her cell phone number, Eli placed his firm hand on her shoulder. If his touch was meant to be a warning, it came too late.

An internal voice scolded her for announcing her cell phone number on a newscast, but right now she didn't care. She had nothing to lose. Worse case, she'd get a new cell phone number after things calmed down. "I want to talk to anyone who saw my brother early yesterday morning or the night before his flight. Or anyone who had ties to my brother while he was in Apple Creek."

She was desperate to shed some light on his frame of mind. Had he gone off the deep end with his conspiracy theories? Twin ribbons of shame and grief twisted around her heart. Daniel had always looked out for her. He'd even saved her life when she was twelve years old. Tears burned the backs of her eyes. It was too late for her big brother, but she owed him this much—to clear his name in death.

"Was it a scheduled flight?" The woman's hawkish eyes shifted from hers to Eli's and back.

This time Eli answered. "Neither Miss Quinn nor I have any information regarding the investigation. You'll have to talk to the sheriff." He lifted his chin. "Now, if you'll please respect the privacy of the family who lives here, we'd appreciate it."

The reporter lowered her microphone and offered her business card to Anna. "If you'd like to do a full interview, please call me." She pursed her lips. "I'm sorry about your loss."

"Thank you." A dark part of Anna's heart suspected the reporter took pleasure in other people's misfortune. It made for good news.

Eli's solid hand rested on her shoulder. She resisted the urge to lean into him for support. After the news crew crossed the road and started filming the crash site, she looked up at him. "Do you think I made a stupid mistake?"

"Sometimes you have to go with your gut."

A mirthless laugh escaped Anna's lips. "You don't know me very well. I'm not one to shoot from the hip."

Seeming to regard her carefully, he rubbed a hand across his whiskered chin. "Will getting answers help you sleep better at night? Bring you peace?"

She searched his brown eyes, feeling an unexpected connection as if he understood her pain. "I hope so," she whispered.

Eli brushed a knuckle across the back of her hand, the motion so quick she thought she imagined it. "You're not convinced?"

Anna shrugged. She turned and climbed the steps, the wood slats of the porch creaking under her weight. Katie Mae appeared in the side yard and placed a wicker basket on the grass. Bending at the waist, she lifted a wet dress and pinned it to the clothesline. Anna stood transfixed as Eli's younger sister completed the chore. Three rows of garments in subtle hues of gray, bright blue, dark blue and lavender weighed down the lines. Something about the simplicity of the chore, the repetitiveness of it, appealed to Anna. Could peace be found in the simple things?

Anna swept a strand of hair out of her eyes. Nothing about her life had ever been simple.

After the commotion outside the Miller's farmhouse, Eli drove Anna to her brother's place. On the drive over, she finally got the nerve to ask the question that had been haunting her since the reporter first brought it up. "You met my brother. He sometimes gets crazy ideas, but he didn't seem unstable, did he? Had he been drinking?" Her voice cracked over the last word. Their father had been an abusive alcoholic.

Eli ran the palm of his hand across the top of the steering wheel, never taking his eyes off the road. "I can't say he was drinking, but he was agitated. He was worried about you."

"It doesn't make sense. Does any of this have to do with your cold case?" Anna was afraid of his answer. No way had her brother been involved with a child's disappearance. But she had to ask.

Eli cut her a sideways glance. "I don't know. He was reluctant to tell me what he knew, if anything. He seemed afraid." She sensed Eli wasn't telling her the entire truth.

The car came to a stop at the intersection. As frustration welled inside her, a sign on the lawn of one of the churches at the corner came into focus. *No Jesus, No Peace. Know Jesus, Know Peace.* Slipping her hands between her knees and straightening her arms, she wondered why she couldn't instinctively shut off her worries and rely on God. Only her faith could get her through this.

Curiosity nudged her. "Growing up in an Amish community, faith was a big part of it, right?" The entire concept fascinated her. "Do you still go to church?"

Anna studied Eli's profile. A muscle worked in his jaw. He gave her a measured stare. "What is the old saying? Don't discuss religion and politics."

"I didn't mean to offend you."

He stared out the windshield. The silence between them grew thick with tension. Obviously she had touched on a sore subject. About a half mile past the center of town, they turned into the driveway of a well-maintained home. Pots of yellow and purple mums lined the porch steps. Large windows overlooked the front yard.

Eli navigated the driveway until he reached the back of the house. He jerked his chin toward a three-car garage and a set of steps hugging one side of the structure. The furthest bay was open. "Your brother rented the garage apartment." He parked and climbed out. Anna joined him around the front of the vehicle.

A man about her brother's age stepped out of the open garage, wiping his hands on a dirty rag. Something flashed in his eyes when he saw Anna. His unshaven face and buzz cut made her think of her brother's appearance when he got off the plane six months ago from his service in the Middle East. The man wore oil-stained jeans and a ripped T-shirt. It appeared they had pulled him away from his work.

"You must be Daniel's sister," he said, his voice gruff. "I'd see the resemblance even if Eli hadn't contacted me to tell me you were on your way." He stuffed the rag in his back pocket. "Sorry. That was horrible what happened to him. I hear my cousin Tiffany's putting up a good fight, though."

Anna's eyelids fluttered. "Oh, I'm sorry. Tiffany is your cousin?"

The man gave her a solemn nod.

"Did you know my brother well?" she asked, eager to get any information she could.

He jerked his thumb toward the steps. "Daniel rented out the garage apartment. He was busy on some photography project." He narrowed his gaze. "I think he was putting photographs together for a book or something. People seem to be fixated on the Amish." He hooked one thumb through his belt loop. "It's beyond me."

"Did he tell you about his project?" Anna asked. Her gaze drifted to Eli, who stood off to the side with his hands loosely crossed over his broad chest.

"Yeah, he seemed eager to wrap up the project and move on all of a sudden. I figured he needed to finish the job to get paid." He rolled his eyes. "There's not much to do in this town."

"Do you have the key?" Eli asked. "Anna would like to see her brother's apartment."

The man reached into his pocket and pulled out a ring filled with keys. "Sure, man."

"I'm sorry I didn't catch your name," Anna said as they moved toward the stairs leading to the second-story apartment.

"Tom Hanson."

Something jogged in her memory. "Did you know my brother from when he went to college in the area?" Something about the way he was staring at her—almost through her—unnerved her.

"A little bit. He and my cousin Chase, Tiffany's brother, were tight." Jangling the keys, he scrunched up his face, thinking. "They were in the same fraternity at Genwego. I wasn't the college type. I went to trade school. I do pretty good as a handyman and jack-of-all-trades for my aunt and uncle."

"Tiffany Christopher's parents?"

Tom nodded. "My mom and Aunt Beth are sisters. My mom married some loser and moved up to Buffalo a bunch of years ago. Aunt Beth and Uncle Richard have always looked out for me."

Anna glanced at the main house, her chest growing tight. "Is this…their house?" She should have thought of that the minute he introduced himself as Tiffany's cousin. She imagined the back door swinging open and Mrs. Christopher emerging, fury in her dark eyes.

Eli smiled gently and mouthed the words, *It's okay.*

"*Doctor* Richard Christopher, Senior, lives here. He's like a grandfather to me. I hang around in case he needs anything." He held up his hands. "Ah, don't worry. I'm the black sheep of the family. It's my Uncle Richard that runs this town. I'm just another one of their servants." He smirked. "Long story." He shrugged. "Actually, I don't mind. It's steady work. Good pay. Not much else going on jobwise in the booming metropolis of Apple Creek." Tom separated a key from the ring. "Here."

Eli took it from him. "We'll keep this. I'll return it in a few days after Anna goes through her brother's things."

Anna's attention shifted to the stairwell leading to her brother's apartment and she suddenly felt light-headed. Eli flashed her a concerned glance and she forced a smile.

"I think I should hold on to that key." A deep line marred Tom's forehead.

"It's fine," Eli assured him. "It's the beginning of the month. Daniel's paid up to the end, right? I'll hold on to the key."

"I guess so." Tom stuffed the key ring back into his pocket.

The wood creaked under their weight as they climbed the steps. At the top landing, Eli had reached out to insert the key into the lock when the door swung inward. Anna's heart plummeted. Eli held out his arm to stop her forward momentum. "Wait here."

She covered her mouth to stifle her shock. Papers littered the floor. A lamp was upended. Couch cushions had been tossed across the small space. Anna's shoulder hit the door frame, her knees having gone weak, and she fell to the floor.

Chapter Five

❧

Eli crouched down in front of Anna and helped her to a seated position. Her legs seemed to go out from under her. "You okay?"

Giving him a sheepish smile, she nodded and leaned her shoulder on the door frame. "I felt a little light-headed. I'm fine. Give me a minute."

Eli studied her face, before saying, "Stay here. I'll be right back." He carefully stepped around the items scattered across the floor of Daniel's apartment. He didn't want to destroy anything that might be evidence. A quick canvass told him whoever had done this was long gone. Frustration simmered below the surface. The break-in convinced Eli that Daniel was more than paranoid. With Daniel's death, Eli feared he might never find the truth. He might never know what happened to Mary.

Eli crossed the room to a small desk in the corner. With the eraser end of a pencil, he shifted through the material. Best he could tell, someone had riffled through everything. When he was here talking to Daniel last week, the apartment had been orderly, meticulously so.

A photo of a run-down shed bracketed by two willow

trees caught his attention. "Your brother had an eye for photography." He glanced over his shoulder. Anna had gotten to her feet and stepped into the room, her eyes wide, her arms wrapped around her middle. A ribbon of compassion twisted around his heart. He couldn't deny the connection he felt with Anna. He turned his attention back to the desk and examined the photo.

"He loved photography." Her voice held a wistful tone. "It was his escape. It doesn't surprise me that he came to the countryside to capture its beauty."

"What was he trying to escape?" He turned around to face her.

Her features seemed shuttered. "We had a rough childhood."

He knew about their childhood, at least all the information available in the files. He had dug into Daniel's past during his investigation into Mary's disappearance. But he knew Anna would shut down if he told her he already knew about her tragic upbringing. He'd hoped she'd mention it first. "Anything you want to talk about?"

Lowering her eyes, she shook her head. She waved her hand dismissively. "No one wants to hear a sob story."

"Try me." He rested his hip against the desk and wrapped his fingers around its smooth edge.

She sat on the arm of the couch and braced her hands on her knees. "I'm only telling you this because it might help you understand my brother."

He nodded but didn't say a word.

If her eyes were lasers, she'd have burned two holes in the floor. "When I was twelve, my father shot and killed my mother…then himself." She ran her pinkie finger under her eye. "That's the CliffsNotes version."

She clasped her fist in her hand. "My brother has been my only family since. He was my protector. He watched over me in the foster system."

Her jaw quivered, but she shrugged as if it were no big deal. "My parents' deaths and his years at war shaped my brother. He was quirky—a little paranoid—but he had a huge heart." She met Eli's gaze with watery eyes.

She ran a hand down her ponytail and dragged the end over her shoulder. "Nothing is easy, is it?" Standing, she sighed. "I just want to pack up his stuff, but now—" she lifted her palms "—this mess." Grief etched her features. "It's as if the world is conspiring to keep me here."

"I'm sorry about your family." Eli took a step forward, but Anna held up her palm.

"I'm fine…. It's old news."

Eli nodded. The hurt in her eyes told him it would never be old news.

"Let's just figure this out so I can go home as soon as possible."

"Whatever you want." Eli studied her for a minute. She forced a smile before wandering over to some framed photographs on a shelf above the TV. Turning his focus back to the desk, he tamped down the urge to comfort her. He had a job to do.

Eli noticed a square, dust-free spot where Daniel's computer had been. Something niggled at his brain.

"What do we have here?" Sheriff Chuck Blakely stepped into the room, something crunching under his boot.

"Tom call you?" Eli crossed his arms and strode toward the door. He didn't want the sheriff's interference. Ever since Mary's disappearance, the local sheriff's office and the FBI had not had the best relationship. There were accusations of incompetence and withholding information on both sides long before Eli joined the FBI. A basic turf war. It also didn't help that the sheriff's son was in the same fraternity as Chase and Daniel at Genwego State at the time of Mary's disappearance. All ranks had closed around Blakely's son.

"Yeah." The sheriff released a long sigh. "Looks like someone did a number on this place." The sheriff pointed to Anna. "You're Daniel's sister. The one on the television." His tone scraped across Eli's nerves. The two men had butted heads more than once over the years.

The sheriff scanned the room. "Best I figure, someone knew about the crash, knew the apartment would be empty and decided to break in."

"Daniel hasn't been in Apple Creek long." Anna frowned. "I doubt many people knew where he lived."

The sheriff raised an eyebrow. "Small town. People always seem to know everyone else's business." He narrowed his gaze at Anna. "The bad guys watch the news, too. They take advantage."

Anna's cheeks grew red. She rubbed the hollow of her neck with trembling fingers. "Maybe I shouldn't have talked to the reporter."

Eli touched her forearm. "You only spoke to the news this morning. I'm guessing this happened overnight."

"After what the reporter said…" Anna's words trailed off, seemingly oblivious to Eli's reassurances. "I wanted to know more about what my brother was doing while he was here in Apple Creek."

Sheriff Blakely scoffed and tucked in his chin. "Like I said, Miss Quinn, it's a small town. Special Agent Miller and I have been watching your brother."

Anna's eyes widened. "Why? Is it illegal to take photographs?"

"No," Sheriff Blakely said, "but Special Agent Miller thinks he might have had something to do with the abduction of—"

"That's enough, Sheriff." A knot tightened in Eli's gut. This was not the way he wanted Anna to find out her brother was under investigation. Her glare landed squarely on Eli. "*You* have been investigating my brother? I thought you were interviewing a lot of individuals who happened to be in Apple Creek ten years ago. But you were targeting him."

"Yes, he was under investigation." Eli gritted his teeth, anger pulsing through his veins. Sheriff Blakely was going to destroy what little trust he had established with Anna.

"Your brother had an uncanny tendency to be in the wrong place at the wrong time." The sheriff couldn't keep his mouth shut. "It was only a matter of time before we found enough evidence to arrest Daniel and charge him for the ten-year-old case."

Anna watched Eli with accusatory eyes. Her pulse jumped in her throat. "There is no way my brother would hurt anyone. Never mind a child."

Eli bowed his head briefly, then met Anna's gaze. Out of the corner of his eye, he knew the sheriff was watching him. He'd have to pick his words carefully. "I'm still trying to put all the pieces together. I'm trying to figure out the extent of your brother's involvement." He wasn't ready to tell Anna the missing girl was his sister. He supposed they both had their share of secrets they'd have to reveal in due time.

Eli turned to the sheriff. "I'd like to talk to Anna in private."

The sheriff stood firm, his eyes growing dark. Then they softened. "Miss Quinn, you'll have to file a report of what's missing in your brother's apartment."

"I don't know what he had." Anna's voice was shaky, distracted.

"You'll have to do your best. Stop by the station." The sheriff strode out of the room, leaving Eli to face Anna.

Anna collapsed onto the only cushion remaining on the couch. "There is no way my brother had anything to do with that missing child."

In a haze of confusion, Anna lowered her gaze. A photo of her brother on the end table caught her attention. Her heart lurched, and tears blurred her vision. She reached over and picked it up. He was about twelve and she was nine. They had huge smiles on their faces and leaves stuck in their messy hair.

Thoughts swirling, she set the photo down and fingered the gold lighter next to it. Tingles of realization blanketed her arms. This was her mother's lighter. And the end table used to be in their grandmother's house. Pressing her fingers to her temple, the world seemed to close in around her.

She rose to her feet and brushed past Eli. She heard his voice but couldn't make out the words. Unable to hold back the tears, she ran down the steps and kept going. She twisted her ankle on the loose gravel and quickly regained her footing. When she reached the main road, she turned toward town.

Tears streamed down her cheeks. Her lungs burned as she briskly walked in the direction she had come. She decided she'd call a cab when she reached town, then collect her things from the Millers' home. She'd find a motel room, clean out her brother's apartment and stay away from Eli. He was using her. He couldn't be trusted. *Just like her father.*

Adrenaline tunneled her vision. How could he think her brother had something to do with the disappearance of a child? Life's circumstances made her brother a lot of things but not someone who hurt children. *Never.*

Her limbs went weak when the general store came into view. Swiping at her tears, she stepped off the curb. Screeching tires sent needles of icy terror coursing through her veins. Out of the corner of her eye she could see a car barreling toward her. Turning away from it, she dove toward the curb and landed with a scraping thud on her left side. A whoosh of warm air lifted her hair as the car sped by. Searing pain shot to her left knee and elbow.

Get the license plate number!

She pushed up on her elbow and winced. Whipping her head around, a pair of designer shoes blocked her view of the departing vehicle. Anna's gaze traveled upward to the woman's shocked face. "Oh, dear, are you okay?"

Anna scooted to a seated position on the curb, her face warm from a mix of embarrassment and pain. She gave her knee a cursory look. Her insides did a little flip. "Did you notice the car?"

The woman tented her hand over her eyes and looked down the street. "I'm afraid not." She pointed to a large window of a ladies clothing store behind her. A partially dressed mannequin stood shamelessly on display. "I was working on the display when I heard tires screeching.

All my attention was focused on you lying in the street." She pouted her pink lips. "I'm sorry."

"Are you okay?" A man called as he ran across the street holding on to his straw hat. He held out his hand to help Anna stand. Her knee throbbed when she put weight on it. "What happened?"

"Some guy came flying out of nowhere and almost hit her." The excited woman signaled with her arms.

Anna brushed off her pants, putting all her weight on her right foot.

"Come over to the general store. I'll get you some bandages and you can clean up. We'll call the sheriff." Hooking his thumb in one of his suspenders, the man let his gaze wander the length of her. She assumed he was assessing her injuries.

The sheriff wasn't exactly on the top of her list of people she wanted to call. He had had such a smug look when he accused her brother. She dismissed the image. What could the sheriff do anyway? No one saw the car. It was probably some college kids on a joyride. *And I wasn't paying attention when I stepped into the street.*

Anna took off her cardigan and glanced at her elbow. Little black bits of gravel dotted her scraped-up skin. "Yuck," she muttered under her breath. "Do you have water at the store?"

"Sure, come on." He offered his hand. "Do you need help?"

"I think I'm okay." Favoring her right foot, Anna did her best not to hobble across the deserted street. In her distracted state she had foolishly stepped out in front of the car without looking. Heat swept up her neck and cheeks. What an idiot. She could have been killed.

The man walked ahead and held open the door, bells

jangling against the glass. "There's a chair near the register. Have a seat. I'll get you some water."

"Thanks. Um—" she hesitated for a second "—is there a cab company around here?"

A bemused smile curved his lips. "No." He crossed to the back of the store and grabbed a water bottle from the shelf. Handing it to her, he cocked an eyebrow. "I could give you a ride home on my wagon." A twinkle lit his eye. "Unless it's too far."

Anna sat down and accepted the bottle of water. "Thanks anyway. I'll figure something out." She stretched her bruised leg and suddenly second-guessed her decision to run out on Eli.

The man smoothed a hand down his suspenders, studying her. "You're Daniel Quinn's sister." He lowered his gaze. "I'm sorry about the accident."

"Thanks. But—"

"I saw you on TV," he interrupted before she had a chance to finish. He lifted a finger to his lips. "Shhhh… don't tell anyone." He pointed to the front window. "Sometimes I linger over my coffee at the coffee shop down the street so I can watch TV." He leaned back on the counter. "I'm Isaac Lapp. My family owns the store."

Anna twisted off the cap from the water bottle and took a long drink. "Did you know my brother?"

"He came in the store once in a while. I knew him a bit from his college days, too." Isaac shrugged a shoulder. "I was in my running-around days then. We had some fun. But lately, Daniel had been focused on his photography. We didn't have much in common anymore." He flicked the brim of his hat.

"I suppose not." With everything else clattering in her brain, it was outside her imagination to guess how

Amish people spent their spare time. She figured they didn't regularly hang out with—what did Eli's brother call them?—ah, the *English.*

The bell hanging from the front door jangled. Eli stood in the doorway, a pinched expression on his handsome face. No doubt the excitable lady across the street had directed him to her whereabouts.

"I bet he could give you a ride in his car." Isaac pointed to Eli. "You know Anna Quinn here? Her brother was the one you've been asking questions about."

Eli closed the distance between them, shooting daggers at Isaac with his eyes. When his gaze met hers, his brows snapped together. "What happened?"

Anna examined her elbow, cognizant of Eli, who had crouched down in front of her, resting a hand on her knee for support. "I wasn't paying attention and stepped in front of a car. It was stupid. I got a little banged up when I jumped out of the way. That's all."

Eli gently inspected her elbow, his warm fingers trailing the uninjured flesh near the pebbles stuck in her arm. Her traitorous heart did a little flip-flop. "Did the car stop?" She shook her head. "You get the license plate or a description?"

"I was too busy with my face-plant." Anna pulled her arm away and stood up, brushing past him. She yanked the pant leg of her capris up to inspect her knee. Losing her balance, she leaned forward, resting her palm on Eli's broad chest. Their eyes locked and lingered a little longer than she had intended. Fire in her cheeks, she glanced down, focusing all her attention on her knee. It looked pretty much the same as her elbow. Just great.

Anna examined a nearby shelf. "Can I have those bandages?"

"Sure." Isaac pulled out some things from behind the counter.

"Did you see anything?" Eli asked Isaac.

"Nope, just heard the commotion. I was around back taking some boxes to the Dumpster. Sorry." Isaac crossed over to the shelf, grabbed a second water and offered it to Anna. "Maybe you should pour this over your knee. It will clean it up a little until you can get home."

"Thanks."

Isaac took off his hat and hung it on a peg. "Can I get you anything else? Want me to call the sheriff?"

Anna's eyes met Eli's. He was the first to speak. "No, I'll look into it." He wrapped his hand around Anna's waist. "Let's go." Her wounds ached, but they were bearable. "I have a first aid kit in the car."

"Suit yourself." Isaac stepped behind the register. Anna reached into her purse and pulled out her credit card. Isaac held up his hand. "We don't take credit cards."

"Oh."

Eli opened his wallet and pulled out a twenty.

Isaac waved him off. "Forget about it. I'm just glad I could help."

"Thank you." Anna forced a smile. "I think the sooner I get out of Apple Creek the better. So far I haven't had a very pleasant stay."

Isaac seemed to regard her for a moment as Eli nudged her forward. "How about you, Eli? You plan on hanging around Apple Creek much longer?"

"I have some time off." One side of Eli's mouth slanted into a grin, but the smile didn't reach his eyes.

Isaac pushed out his lower lip, seeming to give it some thought. "I guess I'll be seeing you around." His dark eyes landed on Anna. "I'm real sorry about your brother. You'll probably make arrangements and then be on your way, I suppose." Isaac leaned back and crossed his arms. "Most people don't hang around Apple Creek for long. It's plain too quiet."

"Thank you for your help. I do have a lot to do." The water sloshed out of the bottle as she moved toward the door. "I better go before I make a mess in your store."

"I suppose you won't be looking for that cab anymore." Isaac's words competed with the bells clacking against the door.

With Eli supporting her, Anna hop-walked onto the sidewalk. She wheeled around, gritting her teeth against the sudden pain shooting up her leg. She leaned in close, resisting the urge to pound her fist against his solid chest. "You used me to get to my brother." She struggled to catch her breath. Her heart beat wildly against her ribs. "You wanted access to his apartment. You wanted to search his things. And you couldn't legally do that unless I invited you to come into his apartment."

"I told you at breakfast that I wanted to see if I could uncover anything in his apartment."

"You never told me you planned to use whatever you found *against* my brother."

"I don't want to argue on the sidewalk." Eli cupped her right elbow and guided her toward his SUV parked by the curb.

She yanked her elbow away from his grip. "Someone broke into my brother's apartment. What do you think they were looking for?"

"I don't know." She couldn't read the expression in his eyes. Was he still holding something back?

The tiny hairs on the back of her neck prickled to life

when a new, horrible thought took hold. "Do you think his plane crash was an accident?"

He let out a heavy sigh. "I don't know. I called a friend in the FAA to check out the plane."

"Oh, no, this is unbelievable."

"Let's not jump to conclusions just yet." He gently nudged her toward his vehicle again. "We need to clean your wounds so they don't get infected."

The flesh on her elbow was torn up and discolored. Her stomach did that little queasy thing again. "Have you ever done this before?"

"Cleaned a wound?" He slanted her a glance as if to say, "Trust me."

But she didn't trust him. Not by a long shot.

Eli yanked open the back door of his SUV and held out his hand. "Have a seat."

Anna narrowed her gaze and squeezed past him, obviously not ready to forgive him. He couldn't blame her. Holding on to the door for support, she lowered herself on to the backseat. She grimaced as she examined her elbow. "I think it looks worse than it is," she said.

Without asking her permission, he gently took her wrist and extended her arm. A soft gasp escaped her lips. He poured the water over the wound and she winced. "When we get back to the house, we can do a better job of this."

Anna scratched her head with her free hand. "Maybe I should find someplace else to stay. It will be easier for me to handle my brother's affairs without worrying you'll try to use something against him."

Eli stepped back and rested his elbow on the door frame. He had totally botched this. Just because they both had painful pasts didn't make them kindred spirits. He sighed heavily. "I'm looking for the truth. Don't you want to know the truth? Even if it hurts?"

Hiking up her chin, a look of determination lit her hazel eyes. "I know the truth. My brother would never in a million years hurt a child."

"You said yourself you had grown apart over the years." He poured more water over the wound.

Anna wrenched her arm free and scowled at him. He held up a hand. "Before you make your case, let me get the first aid kit." He grabbed the white box from the back of the SUV and found her pacing the sidewalk. She flinched every time she stepped on her left foot.

"We may have grown apart, but I know the type of person he is…was." Anna stopped and squared off with him.

"I know you loved your brother, but we don't always know a person's heart."

"I don't believe any of this."

Eli held up the kit. "You gonna let me help you?"

Anna bowed her head and sat back down on the edge of the seat. She held still as he wrapped her arm with a clean bandage and clipped it in place.

"Pull up your pant leg." Eli twisted off the cap of the second water. Anna held her leg out so he could run the cool water over the wound without getting the inside of the vehicle wet.

"Man, that's cold." Anna shivered. "Tell me, why my brother? I thought there were lots of fraternity guys in Apple Creek that evening." He supported her foot on his upper thigh as he wrapped another bandage around the wound.

As Eli put the clip on the bandage to keep it in place,

he sensed her growing unease. She planted her foot on the curb and levered herself out of the car. He grabbed her forearm as she tried to brush past him, but she jerked away. "You weren't on this case in the beginning, were you?" she asked.

"No." He pinned her with his gaze, wondering when she was going to put two and two together and realize the missing Amish girl was his sister. "I took the case over from an agent who retired."

"You're going off his theory then?"

"He was a solid agent." Eli walked around the back of the vehicle and tucked the kit away in his trunk. He rejoined Anna by the side of the car.

Anna crossed her arms and stepped toward him. A soft breeze blew a lock of hair that had escaped her ponytail across her face, sending an alluring scent his way. "How did they narrow their list of suspects?" Her eyes sparked. "My brother made your short list of suspects because the FBI was aware of his troubled past. The FBI knew he had been considered a suspect in my parents' deaths."

Eli nodded. He forced his shoulders back and tried to erect a wall around his emotions. This tactic had served him well over the years as he dealt with tragic cases. But when it came to this case, anger and hurt easily pierced the wall.

Don't make it personal. An emptiness sloshed in the pit of his stomach. That line had been crossed a long time ago when it came to this case.

Yet he owed her some information. "The sheriff and the FBI agent at the time of the child's disappearance did know about your brother's background."

"You're just like the police who initially investigated

my parents' deaths. They couldn't imagine that one of their own killed his wife. You knew my father was a police officer, right? He used that authority to control my mother. To control us. After his death, his *brothers* tried to pin it on Daniel, the so-called troubled teen. But you want to know the truth?" She dragged the side of her shaking hand across the bottom of her eye. Her voice wobbled. "He saved my life the day my parents were killed." Anna stared off in the distance. "If he hadn't locked me in my room that day, I would be dead, too."

Chapter Six

Anna stuffed her hands in the pockets of her capris and drew her arms in close. She shuddered, suddenly feeling terribly exposed on the sidewalk in front of the general store.

"Let's get you something warm to drink. There's a coffee shop…" His words trailed off, and she followed his gaze.

"Ah, what do we have here?" Mrs. Christopher glared at them with hardened features.

Eli seemed to regard her for a moment. "Good morning, Beth. How is Tiffany?"

The woman's gaze faltered for a moment. She smoothed a hand down her long blond hair. "My Tiffany is still in a coma, but the entire town has her in their prayers. She *will* get better. It's just a matter of time." She sniffed and angled the sharp lines of her chin. Clutching her purse close to her body, she said, "I wanted to stop and get Tiffany her favorite candy for when she wakes up."

"Glad to hear it," Eli said. "Please let me know if you need anything. Do you still have my number?"

Beth glared at him with disdain. "I don't need anything from you." Her gaze shifted to Anna. "I understand the garage apartment was broken into."

Emotions Anna couldn't quite name narrowed her throat. "Yes, I'm afraid so."

"That's rather unfortunate." Mrs. Christopher seemed to notice Anna's bandage and paused for a moment. She wiggled her fingers and widened her eyes. "It's always something, isn't it? I'll need you to have your brother's things out of the apartment as soon as possible. I have another renter. I can't have people thinking it's empty, an easy target."

"I thought my brother had paid until the end of the month."

Beth flicked her hand in a dismissive gesture. "Daniel had a verbal agreement with my son. I'll gladly refund the balance of his rent." She took a few steps toward the general store and glanced over her shoulder. "Please, clear out his things."

"You've got to be kidding me," Anna muttered, shaking her head. "She's heartless."

"Come on, let's get some coffee."

They walked the block to the coffee shop, ordered their drinks and settled at a table by the window. Anna took a few long sips of her café mocha, letting the liquid warm her insides. "I guess I better clean out Daniel's apartment right away."

Eli reached over and brushed a thumb across the back of her hand. "I'll help you."

She pulled her hand back and placed it in her lap. "How can I trust you?"

"I'm sorry." Eli tapped his thumb on the handle of his mug. "I didn't tell you right away about the investigation because the timing wasn't right. You had only learned about your brother's death."

Looking at the ceiling, she hoped to stop the threatening tears. "I'm tougher than I look." She gave him a faint smile and a tear spilled down her cheek.

"Oh, yeah?"

His playful tone made her laugh. "I don't like to talk about the day—" she lowered her voice to barely a whisper "—my father killed my mother, but…." The need to explain propelled the conversation forward.

"You don't have to talk about it. I read the case files." The compassion in his voice made her resolve slip. He knew all the intimate details of her tragic past. Details she had carefully hidden from everyone in her life. It was easier to shut people out. Pretend she didn't have this horrible past.

Pulling her hands into her lap, she narrowed her gaze at him. "I have to tell you. If I don't, you'll twist it around to use it to suit your case. That's what the police did. I can only imagine how the police reports read. They turned everything around to protect my father."

Anna took another sip, letting the warm liquid flow down her throat. "That night, my mother woke me up when it was still dark out." Outside the coffee shop, a horse trotted by, pulling an open buggy carrying a young Amish woman. She blinked away the blurry image. "Mom had told me to hurry up and pack a few things. She had finally decided to leave my father. I had been begging her to do it for ages. Now that she had finally made the decision, we didn't have much time. My father—" she struggled to say the word without tasting the bile in her mouth "—was due home from the midnight shift soon."

Anna tilted her head from side to side, trying to ease the stiffness between her shoulder blades. Nerves tangled in her belly under Eli's intense gaze. "I got up and threw a few things in a suitcase. Then I heard shouting coming from the kitchen. My father had arrived home early."

Anna's gaze shifted to Eli, then back to the street. It would be easier to tell the story without seeing the concern in his brown eyes. "My father had been pushed over the edge."

"You don't have to tell me any more," Eli whispered in a soothing voice. "I know what happened. It's too hard for you."

She traced a finger along the rim of the cup. "No, the reports don't tell the whole story. The reports were filled out by my father's friends on the force…the good ol' boys club."

"But the truth about your father killing your mother then himself eventually came out."

"The accusations did a number on my brother." She pursed her lips. "The reports can't possibly tell the entire story." Running her fingers through the end of her ponytail, she turned her gaze on him. "That morning, I heard my mother pleading with my father, so I tiptoed into the kitchen." The scene unfolded in her mind like a made-for-TV movie. "My father was yelling at my mother." Spittle shot from her father's mouth. "He told her she had no right to leave. He had something in his hand."

Anna smoothed her hand along her hair, the long-ago day replaying with gut-wrenching clarity. "I was about to confront my father." Her eyes locked with Eli's. "I *hated* my father. He was a chameleon, you know? One minute he was so sweet and the next he'd smack the smile off your face.

"Before I had a chance to confront him, my brother grabbed my arm, dragged me to my bedroom and locked me in. He made me promise I wouldn't try to come out until he came to get me." A shaky breath escaped her lips. "A few minutes later my father pounded on my door. Screamed at me to come out." She ran a hand under her nose. "I heard my mother hollering at him. I slipped into my closet and sat on the floor. I can still see the trim from my dance costume draping down in my line of vision, the walls shaking around me as my father pounded the door. But I didn't come out."

Anna stared out the window with a faraway look in her eyes. She fiddled with a locket around her neck and her shoulders drooped, as if she were drawing into herself while she retold the details of that horrific day.

"The rest is a blur." She narrowed her gaze as if searching her memories. "I heard my father walk back down the hall, yelling for my brother. I heard a shot, then another." She ran her hands up and down her arms. She finally turned to meet his gaze. Hurt resonated deep in her hazel eyes. "The silence that followed was deafening. I sat on the floor of the closet for an eternity. I thought my brother was never coming back. Finally, I heard a knock. My brother whispered my name through the door." A tear ran down her cheek and plopped on to the table. "I was afraid to unlock my bedroom door in case it was a trick…but it wasn't a trick.

"My father killed my mother, then killed himself. Daniel had tried to stop my father, but he was only a kid himself. When my father threatened to kill Daniel, he had no choice but to hide."

Eli couldn't imagine the terror she had lived through that day. He wanted to reach out and pull her into an embrace, but he hardly knew her beyond the words in a report filed a long time ago. He had successfully kept a professional distance from the people in the tragic reports he read day in and day out. Until today. If only their circumstances were different.

"If Daniel hadn't locked me in my room and hid himself, my father would have killed us all."

"I'm sorry." His words were all he had to offer.

Closing her eyes briefly, she twisted her threaded fingers. "And you think because my brother was exposed to such violence that he repeated the cycle?" The frustration was evident in her voice.

He owed her honesty. "Yes. It's a theory."

"No way. Daniel had been a bit of a hellion when he was growing up. But after my parents died, he was my guardian angel. He protected me the entire time we were in foster care. I would have been lost without him."

Eli slumped back in his chair and ran a hand across his whiskered chin. He had to dig deeper. Get everything out in the open. "There were reports that perhaps your brother had been the one to fire the gun, killing your parents."

"That was all fabricated. The cop who first responded was a friend of my father's." Her eyes glistened with tears. "He tried to get my brother to confess."

"Why did your brother drop out of college?"

Anna shrugged. "I don't think he ever fit in. He decided to enlist in the army. I don't know."

"He dropped out right after the Amish girl went missing." *The Amish girl. My sister.* Eli neglected to tell her that, though. *So much for honesty.* The air was already thick with emotion and he wasn't quite ready to let her see the pain in *his* soul.

"That doesn't make him guilty." Her pink lips curled into a grimace. Suddenly her expression softened and her eyes grew wide. "It makes sense if he dropped out due to the stress of the investigation. Daniel went through a lot when they interrogated him after my parents died. Who would want to go through that again?" She ran a shaky hand across her mouth. "But he never once mentioned anything about this girl's disappearance to me. He must have been worried it would be pinned on him." She bit her lower lip. "Remember how paranoid he could be?"

Eli leaned forward, resting his elbows on the table. "I think Daniel knew something about the child's disappearance." What part Daniel played in it was still up for debate. And now that he was dead, Eli feared he might never solve the case.

Anna leaned back in the chair and crossed her arms. "What *exactly* did Daniel say when you met with him last week?"

"He seemed skittish. He claimed he was in Apple Creek for a photography project. And like I said, he was worried about his safety and yours. "Eli ran a hand across the back of his neck. "I knew I'd have to earn his trust before he talked, so I didn't push. Now I'm afraid it's too late."

"Daniel didn't trust many people." A mirthless laugh escaped her lips. "He came by it honestly after everything he'd been through. I have no idea why he'd be worried about me. I live a very quiet life." Her brow furrowed. "However, I have a had a run of bad luck lately."

She shook her head as if dismissing the notion. "Maybe I'm becoming as paranoid as he is."

"I'd like to keep a close eye on you."

Her eyes widened. "No, I'm fine."

Eli held up his hand to quiet her protest. "I believe he knew something, and now that he's gone, I'd like your permission to search his things."

Red splotches flared on her cheeks. "If I do that, you'll use anything you might find against him. You don't really care if he's guilty. You just want to close your case. Gold star for Special Agent Miller. Move on to the next case."

A muscle worked in his jaw. "Do you really believe that?"

She arched a brow. "My father was in law enforcement. He didn't leave me with the best impression of the profession."

"Someday you're going to have to trust someone. I'm asking you to trust me."

Anna stilled and stared at him but didn't say anything.

Eli continued. "Ten years ago, Daniel belonged to a fraternity on campus. A couple of the seniors, your brother included, were rumored to have sent a few freshmen on a mission, like tipping a cow. But in their twisted version, it involved harassing the Amish."

"This all ties in with the girl's disappearance?" The color drained from her face.

"The buggy that had transported Mary to town was found about a mile away, overturned in a ditch. The FBI figured something had spooked the horse, sending it bolting away with Mary inside. Sugar—the horse—had to be put down." Eli cleared his throat.

"But what about the child? What happened to her?"

"Never found." Eli fought to keep his tone even. "Last time she was seen was inside the store. No one saw her outside the general store. Perhaps she climbed back into the wagon on her own before the horse was spooked." He rubbed a hand across the back of his neck. "We haven't been able to put all the pieces together."

"But you do think my brother was involved?"

Eli quickly glanced over his shoulder. They were the only customers in the coffee shop. "Yes, but he wasn't the only one."

"Chase Christopher was one of his fraternity brothers." Anna placed both of her palms on the table and sat ramrod straight.

"Exactly."

"That explains Mrs. Christopher's disdain for you."

"I'm good at making friends." He smiled.

"I can see that. So you're investigating Chase, too?" The hope in her voice squeezed his heart. He so wanted to give this woman good news. Something to hang on to.

Eli plucked at the napkin crumpled on the table. "The Christopher family is very powerful. Mr. Christopher hired the best lawyers for his son."

Anna slumped back in her chair and crossed her arms. "Figures."

"The sheriff's son was also in their fraternity."

"And he was untouchable, too." Anna rested her forehead in her hand.

"The sheriff made it difficult, but the FBI kept pushing. Both Chase and the sheriff's son had rock solid alibis."

"And my brother?" The air grew heavy with tension. "Did he have an alibi?

"None of his fraternity brothers vouched for him. He

claimed he was taking photos by the lake. I fear the truth may have died with your brother."

Anna tilted her head. "I'll help you find the truth. If Daniel was involved with something stupid that went bad, he would have come forward a long time ago. I know my brother."

"People make stupid decisions all the time. They get trapped." Eli snapped his fingers. "And in a flash, one decision, then another changes the course of his life. Then he doesn't know how to go back."

"Even if my brother knew something, he wouldn't have waited ten years."

"It's hard to know what someone would do under pressure." Eli met her gaze and his heart went out to her. How would Anna handle not only the death of her brother, but also the news that he may have been involved in a horrible crime?

"My brother is levelheaded under the worst of circumstances. He proved that to me when my father killed my mom. I just can't…" She seemed to be deep in thought. "Wait." She leaned back and dug her cell phone out of her purse. "My brother left me a voice mail a week ago. I saved it. Something about it didn't make sense, but I dismissed it. I thought it was another of his conspiracy theories. He said he was taking photos, working on a new project." She looked up. "He needed help."

"Was it unusual for him to reach out to you?" He leaned forward and tried to read the screen of her cell phone, but it was too far away.

"Daniel never asked for help." She shrugged. "Well, at least not before he went to war. He was always the one who helped me. In the message his voice sounded strained." She twisted her lips. "I dismissed it, figuring I'd deal with it later. I'd had a rough week." She smoothed a hand down her ponytail. "I should have called him back."

She traced her finger along the rim of her coffee mug. "I just wanted to flop on the couch, watch some television and veg out." She lifted her watery gaze to meet his. "You know, I counsel students for a living. When my own brother needs me, I check out."

Eli squeezed her hand but didn't say anything.

She held up a finger in a wait-a-minute gesture. "I have to power the phone up. I turned it off because I wasn't getting a signal at your parents' house." She glanced at him briefly, then back down at her phone. "His voice mail said to check my email. He knew I'm not good about checking my personal email account." After a minute, she clicked on the screen a few times. Her features grew slack and she held out her phone with a shaky hand.

He put his hand under hers for support and read an email message.

Anna ~ tried to send important photos. Taking too long to upload! Will bring them to you. Flying up this afternoon. Some crazy stuff going on. Need to see your smiling face and lie low for a bit. Be safe.
Luv ya ~ D

"Did he try to send the photos again?" Eli's nerves hummed with anticipation.

She flicked her index finger across the touch screen. "No, no other emails from him." She rubbed her temples. "I wish I knew what he was talking about." She collapsed against the back of the chair, a haunted look on her face. Suddenly she bolted upright. "Did they get everything from the plane?"

Eli nodded.

"There was no luggage? No camera? Daniel said he was going to bring the photos to me."

"No, nothing other than Tiffany's purse. The sheriff already returned it to her father." Excitement buzzed his nerve endings. He understood where she was going with this. Maybe Daniel did have proof. Maybe Daniel had photos. Maybe that's what someone was looking for at his apartment.

"Did you notice a camera in his apartment or maybe from the plane crash?"

"No. Daniel was traveling light. I think they only planned on going up to Buffalo for the day. And I didn't notice his camera in the apartment."

Anna jumped to her feet. "I have Daniel's jacket in my car. Maybe he had a USB flash drive with photos in his pocket." She tilted her head. "It's worth a shot."

Eli's nerves hummed the entire drive. As they crested the hill near his family's farm, he pressed the brake, slowing for a buggy, its orange triangle in stark contrast to the black body, one of the Amish's concessions to a modern world. Two young boys not more than two years of age sat on the floorboards behind the seat, seemingly oblivious to the car following them.

"That doesn't look safe. Look how easily they could fall out." Anna sounded horrified. A short lip on the platform of the buggy and one black bar about halfway up were the only restraints keeping the boys inside.

"Theirs is not a world of car seats and lawsuits."

"But still," Anna said. Eli watched the one boy reach

across and snatch something from the other boy's hand. The second boy seemed unfazed. They wore sky-blue shirts, suspenders and hats. Something tugged at his heart. He missed the simplicity of growing up in this community.

Drumming her fingers on the door, Anna huffed in frustration.

He cut her a sideways glance. "They live and think differently than we do."

"It's not that. I'm anxious to see if Daniel left anything in his jacket."

"I don't want to go around the buggy on this blind hill."

Anna pulled her hands into her lap and twisted her fingers. "I know."

"We're almost there." The Amish woman at the reins guided the buggy a little closer to the side of the road. "I used to hate when a vehicle approached my buggy." Eli flexed his fingers around the steering wheel. "Some of the college kids used to beep their horns and swerve close, hoping to startle the horse."

"Really?"

"We…the Amish—" he quickly corrected himself "—just want to exist peacefully. It's increasingly difficult as the outside world encroaches on their way of life." Eli carefully pulled out and around, giving the buggy a wide berth. He waved in greeting, but the woman on the buggy didn't acknowledge him. A short distance up, Eli turned onto his family's property.

"Where's my car?" Anna leaned forward, straining to see through the windshield, her eyes scanning the horizon. She sagged against the seat. "Oh, that's right, you moved my car."

"Out of respect for my parents. It's acceptable for the Amish to ride in a vehicle even when they can't drive, but my father is pretty strict. And always worried about appearances. No sense setting him off by parking your car in front of his home. Sometimes the neighbors talk." He tipped his head. "Even in an Amish community. They're still human."

"But surely the neighbors would understand it's not their vehicle."

"Yes, but whenever I come around, I try to be discreet. The bishop has suggested to my parents that I may not be a good influence on the younger men in the district. I don't want to cause my parents any additional grief."

"I don't have a childhood home to go back to, either," she muttered. Her voice had a faraway quality that worked on the shield surrounding his heart.

Eli drove his SUV around the back of the barn. The vehicle rocked over the ruts of the narrow wagon wheels. How many times had he ridden the horse and buggy to this point? Then he'd have to take care of the horse. Taking the key out of the ignition and climbing out seemed so simple in comparison. Yet sometimes he missed the steady beat of the horses' hooves, the wind whistling past his ears and nothing on his mind but the task at hand.

"You coming?" He blinked at Anna's voice. She gave him a quizzical look and aimed her key fob at her car. The lights flashed.

Walking alongside the vehicle, he tensed when he noticed the back passenger window was smashed. Pink blossomed on Anna's cheeks and she shook her head.

She peered inside, careful to hold her hands away

from the shards of glass clinging to the door frame. "Daniel's jacket was in the backseat." She straightened. "Now it's gone."

Eli tented his hands over his eyes to block the late-afternoon sun. The only thing that broke the endless tract of fields was the occasional farmhouse or barn. In the distance, someone worked the field guiding a team of horses. "I don't get it. No one knew the car was back here. You can't see it from the road." He rubbed the back of his neck. "Unless someone saw me move it."

Anna crossed her arms. "Why would someone steal Daniel's jacket?" She opened the back door before he had a chance to stop her. She reached in and pulled out a piece of paper. She looked up, fear in her eyes. "This note says, 'You're next.'"

Eli's gut twisted. Was someone else looking for the same thing they were? Did someone else know Daniel had incriminating photos? *If* he had incriminating photos. Once again, a potential revelation about his sister's disappearance was pulled out from under him. Something sinister lurked in this town and someone was determined to keep it under wraps.

Daniel's concern for his sister came to mind. "I don't like this one bit." Eli scratched his head. "I think you should go back to Buffalo until I figure out what this all means. I have a couple weeks off from the bureau. I'll continue the investigation. But I want to know you're safe."

"Buffalo isn't that far away. Why do you think I'd be safer there?" Anna flattened her palm against her forehead, her eyes glistening with fear. "This is the same note I had on my car in the school parking lot. The same handwriting. I thought it was a stupid prank from the students."

A long brittle silence stretched between them before Eli spoke. "Daniel was afraid for your safety. Maybe someone had threatened you hoping it would scare Daniel into stopping whatever he was doing."

"What do you think he was doing?"

"I think either he had evidence in the missing child case or he was close to uncovering it."

Anna's eyes brightened. "So this means he's innocent." Her words came out in a rush.

Eli touched her forearm reassuringly. "Maybe. But it could also mean your brother was going to confess and take someone down with him." He slammed his fist against the frame of the door. A section of glass rained down the side of the car. "I don't like this. I'd feel better if you went back to Buffalo. I will have someone keep an eye on you there."

"Why can't you protect me?" A timid smile played on her lips even as tears filled her eyes.

"Oh, come on. I don't have time to babysit you."

Her eyebrows shot up. "Babysit? Are you serious? I can help go through my brother's things. I can help you find whatever it is these guys are after."

"I can't risk that." Eli tilted his head from side to side, trying to ease the growing tightness in his neck. He wanted nothing more than to keep her close. But he couldn't deal with losing anyone else close to him.

"Why come after me?"

"You're Daniel's sister."

Anna held up her palms as if to say "And…?"

"I've investigated many crimes. The bad guys don't always have logical reasons. And unfortunately, sometimes we don't know their motives until after they're caught." Eli opened the back door and examined the inside of her vehicle. Glass littered the backseat and floor. As far as he could tell, the only item they had taken was Daniel's jacket. "Maybe they think you have something they're looking for. Maybe photos?"

Anna's eyes grew wide. "We have to find the photos. I just know they'll prove Daniel's innocence."

Shaking his head, Eli muttered something she couldn't quite make out. "Listen, if you're going to stay in Apple Creek, I want you to stay here at my parents' house so I can keep an eye on you."

"I don't want to bring trouble to your family."

The thought had crossed his mind. "I'll be staying there, too."

Anna shrugged, seemingly resigned. "What now? Do we call the sheriff?"

"No. The sheriff has been a detriment to this investigation. The Christophers are powerful people in this town. I wouldn't be surprised if they have the sheriff under their thumb. And there's the issue of the sheriff's son."

"And Chase Christopher. He's still on your short list of suspects?"

"He had a rock solid alibi, remember?"

"You don't sound convinced." Anna crossed her arms. "It doesn't make sense. If my brother was the fall guy, why make threats against me after Daniel's dead? It only proves that someone else has something to hide."

"I was thinking the same thing." He plowed a hand through his hair. "I'll look into it myself. Tomorrow morning, I'll go back to Daniel's apartment and sort through his things and see if we can find anything. There has to be something there." He pinned her with a gaze. "And they don't want you to find it."

"I'm going with you to my brother's apartment." Her pinched features radiated her distrust.

Eli pulled out his cell phone, then remembering the lack of reception, slipped it back into his coat pocket. "I'm going to drive into town and make a few phone calls. Give me your phone."

Anna furrowed her brow but handed it to him.

"I'm going to program my phone number into your phone in case you need me. But if it's a true emergency, call 9-1-1. They have the capability to track your location if necessary."

"Good to know." Anna's casual words belied the fear in her eyes. "But it's not going to help me out here. There's no cell reception."

"It will be okay," Eli assured her. "Let's get you inside."

They started to walk across the lawn toward the house when Anna caught Eli's arm. "Wait. What about little Mary's family? Maybe one of them is out for revenge. Maybe they hate me because they think my brother hurt their little girl? Wasn't Isaac blabbing around town that the FBI was investigating Daniel?"

"Isaac likes to gossip. But no, it's not Mary's family." His answer came out clipped. Certain.

"No. Just no?" Anna's voice went up an octave. "How can you be sure?"

Eli looked down into Anna's eyes and tamped down the emotion brewing below the surface. "Because Mary was my little sister."

Chapter Seven

Anna's hand flew to her chest. "Oh, no...why didn't you tell me?" Her mind churned to reframe everything he had told her up to now.

A muscle in Eli's jaw twitched. "I try to maintain some professional distance. It's hard. Most people know my history. Apple Creek is a small town, so I don't have to tell anyone." He pointed toward the barn on his parents' farm. "Let's go in there so we can talk in private." Without waiting for her response, he strode into the barn. Anna had no choice but to follow.

Slits of sunlight streamed in through the walls of the barn, creating pockets of light and darkness. It would be completely dark before long. The earthy smell of hay reached her nose. She was surprised to see a tractor parked in the corner of the barn, its large wheels void of rubber.

"Over here." Eli gestured with an open palm to a hay bale.

Anna sat and the coolness seeped through her khaki capris. Running her fingers along the edges of the bandage on her knee, she waited for Eli to speak. He paced the small space in front of her. "Mary was only five years old the day she went missing." His fists tightened at his side. "My mother had asked me to run into town to get something. Our family was hosting worship service the next day so everyone was busy with preparations. Little Mary had come running over to me, begging to go along."

He stopped and lowered himself on to the hay bale next to hers. "On the buggy ride into town, Mary was chatty, telling me everything going through her mind." A small smile played on his lips as he talked about his little sister in a wistful tone. Anna's heart ached for him. She reached over and rested her hand on his solid forearm.

"How old were you?"

Eli met her gaze. "Eighteen."

Leaning forward, he rested his elbows on his knees. "I've replayed the events over and over in my head. We went into the general store and she wanted to look at the candy display near the front. I went in back with Mr. Lapp, Isaac's father, and we sorted through the supplies my mother needed for the communal meal."

Bowing his head, he threaded his fingers through his hair. Her hand slipped from his arm. "I don't know how long we were in the back of the store, but when I came out front Mary was gone." Clenching his jaw, he turned away from her. "And so was my horse and buggy."

Anna rested her hand on his back, his strength evident under her touch. "I'm so sorry."

"I should have never taken my eyes off her." Despair dripped from his voice.

"It's not your fault." He flinched.

"I was responsible for her."

For the first time, Anna realized why she was instinctively drawn to this man. They shared a deep pain. He understood the heartache haunting her each day.

The creaking of the barn door hinges captured their attention. Red, the family's Irish setter, ambled in followed by Samuel. Moving directly to Eli, the aging dog pushed his nose onto his former master's lap and was promptly rewarded with getting his ears fluffed. "Hey, buddy. How ya doing?"

Samuel started to back out. "I didn't mean to interrupt."

"No, it's okay," Eli said. "How are you?"

"Good." Samuel shrugged, as if embarrassed. "I was going to get Red his dinner." He gestured to a bag of dog food propped in one of the stalls.

Eli pushed to his feet. "I'll do it."

"Okay, then I'll get cleaned up for dinner." He took a few steps toward the door, then spun back around. "*Mem*'s probably going to be wondering if you'll be staying for dinner."

Eli flicked a glance at Anna. "What do you say?"

Tiny butterflies flitted in her stomach. "That would be nice, thank you." She'd never admit it to Eli, but she hoped to get to know his family a little better, to help shed some light on the type of man he was. Then a part of her wondered why she cared. As soon as she had things settled in Apple Creek, they'd be going their separate ways.

"Hey, Samuel, did you see anyone around here earlier today? Someone broke the back window of Anna's car."

Samuel narrowed his gaze. "No, I was busy in the fields most of the day. We're harvesting the corn for feed."

The somewhat familiar half-smile pushed up one

side of Eli's mouth. "Okay. Well, tell *Mem* we'll be in shortly."

Samuel turned and strode out of the barn. "He seems so serious. Is that the Amish way?"

Eli seemed to consider her question for a moment. "He took Mary's disappearance quite hard, too." Eli crossed over to where the dog food was stored. Bowl in hand, he scooped in some of the food. The chore was punctuated by pats and hugs to his beloved pet. He obviously loved the dog. He glanced over his shoulder at her. "Samuel is Mary's twin. They had been inseparable."

Anna's heart tightened. "I can't imagine."

Eli patted Red's head, then left him to eat.

"You miss it here, don't you?" Anna asked.

"Some things, but I could never go back."

A little part of her was relieved. As long as Eli was part of her world, there was hope for more. Yet she feared she was confusing empathy and compassion for feelings of closeness.

"You became an FBI agent to help find your sister's abductor?"

Eli settled back down next to her on the hay bale. "The FBI got involved right after my sister's disappearance. The agent in charge had sympathy for me. I admired him. Not long after, I left home, studied hard and was admitted to college." He ran a hand across his jaw. "It was a long journey. I had a lot of catching up to do. At the time, I only had an eighth-grade education."

"Really?"

"The Amish don't value education the same way we do. They fear it could lead the youth away from their homes." Red noisily slopped up his dinner a few feet away. "The FBI agent pitied me and took me under his wing. The goal of becoming an agent kept me focused. Then working as an agent propelled me forward. Guilt is a powerful motivator. I could have been destroyed by it."

Anna understood guilt. She often wondered how different things would have been if she hadn't convinced her mother to leave her father. Had coming home and finding his family packing been the final straw? Maybe she should have just dealt with it and left home as soon as she turned eighteen. Instead she had embarked upon a campaign to convince her mom to leave her father, not wanting to abandon her. Anna's pleading and her mother's decision had sealed their fate.

"Even though I haven't made an arrest in my sister's disappearance, I've helped a lot of other people along the way." Red strolled over and curled up at Eli's feet. He reached down and stroked his fur. "I guess that counts for something."

Anna brushed the back of her hand across his whiskered cheek. "It counts for a lot."

He reached up and caught her hand in his. Their gazes lingered. Something she couldn't quite name hung, unspoken, between them, softening her heart. A sad smile played on his face in the dim lighting. "I can't rest until I figure out what happened to my sister."

After dinner Anna helped Mariam and Katie Mae clean up the dishes despite their protests that they didn't need any help. Eli had run into town to make some phone calls. She tried not to think about everything that had transpired today. She just wanted a few minutes to quiet her mind. The routine of doing dishes provided that. When the dinner dishes were dried and put away, Mariam invited Anna to join her in the sitting room.

Anna leaned back into the deep rocker and rested her scraped-up leg on a wooden footstool. She had cleaned the wounds out more thoroughly before dinner. Her knee throbbed a little from standing in the kitchen for so long, but other than that she figured she'd survive.

Sitting across from her, Mariam picked up her embroidery. The even up and down of her hand as she worked the needle through the fabric was mesmerizing. The quiet ticking of the battery-powered clock filled the silence. This was such a different existence than the life she lived in Buffalo, where she often had the radio or television on for background noise.

Anna wondered a little guiltily if Mariam knew of the suspicions surrounding her brother. If she did, she didn't let on. An urge to assure the dear woman her brother had nothing to do with her daughter's disappearance almost overwhelmed her, but she decided not to spoil the mood.

"It's so quiet here. Peaceful."

Mariam nodded. "How are you doing, Anna? You have suffered a terrible loss."

Weariness weighed heavily in her chest. "I'm fine."

Mariam nodded, then examined the design in her fabric. Setting her project aside, Mariam rocked slowly back and forth in her rocker, a faraway look descended into her eyes. "You only met my Eli yesterday?"

Anna gripped the smooth handles of the rocker. "Yes."

The corners of Mariam's pale lips turned down. "That surprises me. I would have guessed you've known each other longer. You seem—" she seemed to be searching for the right word "—comfortable with each other." Mariam waved her hand in dismissal. "I suppose it's just as well…" She let her words trail off. "My heart longs for him to come home."

"To return to the Amish life?" The words flew from Anna's lips before she was able to call them back.

Blushing, Mariam picked up her project and guided the needle through the fabric. "I want to know that he's okay. It would give me a measure of peace." She lifted her gaze to meet Anna's, a plea in her eyes.

The next morning was Sunday. Feeling uncomfortable in his own skin, Eli followed a half step behind Anna up the steps of Apple Creek Community Church. How she picked this one over the church across the street was a mystery to him. He supposed it had to do with the time of the church service.

"I don't know how you talked me into this," he muttered. "Is this what you and my mother were conspiring about last night? To get me back to church of some kind?"

"No, this is strictly for me." Anna bowed her head, her long chestnut hair flowing in loose curls over her shoulders. "I need to go to church this morning to pray from my brother. Sometimes I get so caught up in the trials of life, I forget to lean on my faith." Her voice cracked over the last few words. Immediately regretting his flippant attitude, he caught her hand and gave it a quick squeeze.

"And to pray for Tiffany's recovery," she added as she pulled on the large wooden door leading into the church.

Eli quickly reached around her and grabbed the wrought-iron handle. She smiled her thanks and brushed past him as they entered the foyer. He realized this was the first time he had ever been in a church building.

Growing up in an Amish community, they worshiped in barns and homes, a throwback to the days of fearing persecution.

Anna slipped into a pew at the back of the church. In the quiet moments before the service started, Eli tried to recall one of the prayers he had memorized as a child, but he couldn't focus. He was eager to get back to Daniel's apartment and go through his things thoroughly. Maybe they'd find something they had missed, perhaps the photos.

Anna's shoulder brushed his as they scooted along the polished wood of the pew to make room for another family. He couldn't figure out how this woman he had just met two days ago had convinced him to attend a church service. No other woman had ever had this kind of influence over him. Her long lashes swept her smooth skin as she bowed her head in prayer. She was absolutely beautiful.

And your job is to keep her safe. Period. A harsh voice snapped him out of his daydream. And if the investigation continued on the track he suspected, she'd never forgive him for accusing her brother of hurting his sister. His shoulders sagged and he settled back in the pew.

A sharp clacking drew Eli's attention toward the center aisle. Beth and Richard Christopher strode into the church, her heels sounding against the hardwood floor, their eyes straight ahead. Next to him, Anna's face grew red. "It's okay," he whispered.

"Coming here was a bad idea. I had no idea this was *their* church."

Eli reached over and touched her knee. "I think technically it's God's church."

A quiet giggle bubbled from her lips. Warmth coiled around his heart.

A few moments later, the minister took the altar and led the congregation in prayer. Anna stood silently next to him while everyone around them joined in. When the song finished, the minister greeted the congregation.

"This is a glorious Sunday and we owe much thanks to the Lord. Our prayers have been answered. I have wonderful news this morning about Tiffany Christopher, a young member of our church, who as most of you know had been in a horrible plane crash. She has regained consciousness. Praise God."

Eli's gaze locked with Anna's.

"Please continue to pray for her complete recovery. We welcome her parents here this morning. Let us pray." After a slight pause, the minister added, "Let us also pray for the young man who perished in the crash. I understand he was new to our small town. May he find eternal peace."

Eli waited until the quiet reflection was over before he whispered into Anna's ear. "I hate to do this to you, but we have to go."

A vertical line appeared between Anna's brows, but she didn't argue. They slipped out of the church. "What's going on?" she asked as soon as they were outside.

"If Tiffany is awake, we need to talk to her right now. While her parents are still in church."

"Do you think they'll let us in to see her?" Anna's insides twisted into knots. Part of her was afraid of what she'd learn from Tiffany about her brother. But deep in her heart, she knew he had nothing to do with Mary's disappearance.

"Yes. I may have to tell them it's official FBI business, but they'll let me in."

"Is it official FBI business?"

"I'm FBI and it's important to me."

Anna nodded and swallowed a lump in her throat, deciding not to force the issue further. "I don't know if I can do this. I'm not very good in hospitals." Her grandmother had already been in frail health when her mother had died, so she couldn't take in her orphaned grandchildren. Less than a year after Anna's mother was killed, her grandmother lingered for three weeks in the hospital before dying.

Outside the ICU wing, Eli cupped Anna's shoulders. "I want you to stay outside the room near the nurses' station. I'll go in and talk to Tiffany." He raised an eyebrow and seemed to try to read her thoughts. "Are you okay?"

Anna waved her hand in dismissal. "Fine. Just not a fan of hospitals." She shrugged. "But who is, huh?"

Eli nodded, pinning her with his intense brown eyes. "We don't know what kind of shape Tiffany's in, so don't count on anything. She may not be able to talk to us."

Anna nodded in understanding. Leaning an elbow on the counter at the nurses' station, she watched Eli approach Tiffany's bed. She had a clear view through floor-to-ceiling windows. The area was filled with quiet chatter, subtle beeping and the occasional squeak of a nurse's sneaker against the shiny linoleum.

Tiffany opened her eyes and blinked a few times when Eli approached. She wore a look of confusion on her pretty face. Anna understood why her brother may have been attracted to her. Tiffany's gaze seemed to drift past Eli and land on Anna. Lowering her eyes,

Anna felt like she had been caught gawking. Her heart rate kicked up a notch.

When she lifted her gaze, Tiffany pointed a shaky hand, tubes and tape attached, at her. Eli turned around and nodded. He came to the door of the hospital room. "Tiffany's a bit out of it, but she wants to see you."

"Me?"

"Apparently she recognized you from a photo in Daniel's apartment."

Anna struggled to find words. Eli took her hand and led her into the room. Tiffany lay back on her pillow, her eyes tracking Anna's movements.

A small smile pulled at the corners of Tiffany's mouth.

"I'm Daniel's sister, Anna." Tiffany seemed very frail underneath the thin hospital blanket. "How are you feeling?"

Tiffany's forehead creased. "I'm just glad to be here. Time will tell." The young woman's eyes drifted toward the window. "I'm sorry about Daniel. He was a really nice guy."

"Thank you." Eli stood close behind Anna, providing much needed moral support. "Do you know what Daniel was up to recently?"

Tiffany dragged a shaky hand across her mouth. "He liked to take photographs."

Anna glanced up at Eli. There had to be more to it.

"Was he doing anything more? Was he looking for something?" Eli asked. Anna could tell he was being careful with the questions, but he kept glancing toward the door, making her even more nervous. She wondered how long they had before her angry parents showed up.

Tiffany scrunched her lips. She seemed to be struggling with a decision.

Anna took a risk and covered Tiffany's hand with hers. "You can't hurt Daniel now. Please tell us if you know anything."

The young woman sighed heavily. "He seemed obsessed with the disappearance of Mary Miller. I don't know why."

"He didn't say?" The eagerness in Eli's voice mirrored her own emotions.

"No. I figured he was going to do a feature on the story with photographs."

"How did you meet Daniel?" Eli asked.

"He came by the house looking for Chase, but my brother was out of town. He travels a lot for work." Tiffany rolled her eyes. "The all-important *family* business." She coughed. Eli stepped around Anna, picked up the water from the bedside table and held the straw to her mouth. She took a few sips. "I told Daniel I had an interest in photography and we started hanging out." Tiffany gave them a watery smile. "I thought he was cute and so different than a lot of the boys my mom tries to fix me up with. At first I just lied about liking photography. But his enthusiasm for it was contagious."

"Where were you going on Friday morning?" Anna asked.

"To see you. He was worried. He said you hadn't answered any of his calls. He hadn't taken his plane up in a while. He figured we could take a short trip to Buffalo."

The email suggested he had been flying to see her but having it confirmed made her feel even worse. She crossed her arms.

Tiffany shrugged a thin shoulder. "I tagged along at

the last minute. I thought it would be fun to shoot some photos from the plane. I'm sure my mom was shocked when she learned I had been in a plane crash. I told her I was going shopping with a friend. Once I recover, she'll probably kill me for lying to her." Tiffany laughed.

"I'm sure they're just thankful you're going to be okay." Eli set the cup of water back down on the table. "Did Daniel have his camera with him on the plane?"

"Yes. He never went anywhere without it."

Anna rubbed her forehead, wondering where the camera was now.

"Did Daniel ever catch up with Chase?" Eli glanced at the clock on the wall. The church service would be ending soon.

"Yes. Once he stopped over to see me and Chase was home. They went outside to talk, so I didn't hear the entire conversation. But he was obsessed with something that happened when they were in the fraternity. He wouldn't tell me." Tiffany's voice grew soft. She started coughing again and tears ran down her cheeks. Eli grabbed a tissue from the bedside table and handed it to her. Her cough subsided. "They were arguing. Chase was telling him to leave well enough alone."

"Do you know what he meant by that?" Anxiety sent chills up Anna's spine. Eli had mentioned his sister went missing during the fraternity's rush week.

"Do you know if their argument had anything to do with my sister's disappearance?"

Tiffany's eyes widened. "Goodness, no. My brother is a lot of things, but he'd never hurt someone. Not physically. I know Daniel was obsessed with Mary's disappearance, but I never even considered they might have been arguing about that." She narrowed her eyes. "Chase was going on and on about how fraternity brothers always looked out for one another. He is big into that fraternity stuff. Chase was a legacy. My dad belonged to the same fraternity." Tiffany scrunched up her nose. "If only Chase would be as loyal to me."

"Why do you say that?" Eli handed her a second tissue.

"I went to college and earned a business degree, but Chase edges me out of the family business every chance he gets. And my parents haven't been much help. My father won't address the issue. And my mother has always favored Chase. Must be a firstborn thing."

Tiffany curled her lip. "My mom thinks a worthy career aspiration is to become a trophy wife. Like her. She brags she hit pay dirt when she met my dad."

"What did your parents think about you hanging out with Daniel?" Eli locked gazes with Anna. Anticipation charged the air as she waited for the answer.

"Let's just say he wasn't exactly husband material." Tiffany coughed. "Who cares? We were just enjoying each other's company." She looked up at Anna. "Your brother was a nice guy. He spoke often of you, Anna. It was obvious you guys were close."

They had been close once. Anna put her hand on top of Tiffany's. "Thank you." She gave the young woman a quivery smile. "Thank you," she repeated.

Eli squeezed her shoulder. "We'll let you sleep, Tiffany." He put his business card on the table next to her bed. "Call me if you remember anything else."

Tiffany nodded and then sank deeper into the pillows. "I will."

Chapter Eight

An oily scent hung in the air at the airplane hangar, reminiscent of the crash scene. Anna drew in shallow breaths and said a quick prayer, hoping the rescue workers had overlooked Daniel's camera or a USB flash drive among the wreckage. If Daniel had brought his camera, like Tiffany said he had, where was it?

When they rounded the corner, the twisted metal of her brother's plane rested on a tarp in the far corner of the hangar. Anna gasped and pressed a hand to her chest. She thought she had been prepared to see it again. Blinking rapidly, she spun around to face the wide opening of the hangar, to take in the brilliant blue sky, to settle her raw emotions.

Eli gently placed a hand on the small of her back and she stiffened. "Why don't you hang back here? I'll search the plane."

Anna plastered on a smile. "I'm fine, really." Her gaze drifted over the twisted heap that was once her brother's pride and joy. Tears burned the back of her nose.

"You don't have to be brave. I'm here." She lowered her gaze to the floor, but when he touched her arm, she was forced to meet the tender look in his eyes. "I can search the plane."

Their gazes lingered for a moment before she closed her eyes and gave him a curt nod. "I have to do this."

"Okay then. We do it together." Eli's hand slid down her arm and his fingers intertwined with hers. "Okay?" he whispered, squeezing her hand. The scent of his after-shave tickled her nose and she smiled, suddenly calmer.

When they reached the wreckage, Eli released her hand. "Let me peek inside." He rested one foot on the metal frame and glanced over his shoulder. "The sheriff said they didn't find anything in the cockpit. They may not have noticed something small like a flash drive if they weren't looking for it. I can't imagine they'd over-look a camera."

Please, God, let us find something. Anything. Anna walked around to the other side of the plane and leaned in, resting her hand on the cool metal, almost afraid to touch anything. The hangar was eerily quiet. No one else seemed to be around. Anxiety had her ready to jump out of her skin. Anyone could have had access to this plane. It sat in the middle of an unsecured hangar in the heart of cow country. Had someone else already been poking around? The same person who'd broken her car window and stole Daniel's jacket?

"Watch the broken glass and sharp metal," Eli said.

She double-checked the placement of her hands, then continued to scan the cockpit. "It could be anywhere." If it existed at all.

The sound of footsteps echoed across the expansive hangar. Anna looked up to see a man walking toward them with a clipboard. Eli greeted him warmly. "Anna, this is Tim Gardner with the FAA." Eli turned back to Tim. "I didn't realize you'd make it out here so quickly."

"I did it as a special favor for you." Tim clapped Eli on the shoulder.

"Thanks. Have you had a chance to look at it?" Eli asked.

"Just finished going over it a few minutes ago. Must have been in the main office when you two strolled in." Tim looked down at his clipboard, then back at Eli. "I'm going to have to take some of the parts in for teardown, but my gut tells me someone tampered with the plane's engine."

"What—" her voice cracked "—are you saying?"

"I'm still investigating, but I'm afraid your brother's plane may have been sabotaged."

All the blood rushed from her head. She blinked back the white dots clouding her vision. Eli's solid hand on the small of her back grounded her. "Someone killed my brother?" she muttered, flattening her hand against her stomach. Her worst fear was realized.

"I'm real sorry about your loss." Tim gestured with the clipboard. "I'll finish this report and get back to you."

"Thanks." Tim strode toward the office.

The deep rumble of a small plane vibrated through the shell of the hangar. A sleek jet taxied to the outside of the hangar. A black limousine she hadn't noticed before sat on the tarmac. "Who's that?" she shouted over the roar of the engine. The hot air swept her hair back from her face.

Eli tented his hand over his eyes. He seemed to tense as the stairs on the plane popped out and a man appeared at the door. The man seemed to regard them for a moment before nodding in their direction. A second man followed him down the stairs.

Anna was surprised to see Tom Hanson step out of the driver's side of the limousine and walk around to open the back door, allowing Mr. Christopher, Tiffany and Chase's father, to step out. She saw a hint of long blond hair inside the limo. *Mrs. Christopher.*

"Maybe coming here wasn't such a good idea." Anna twisted her fingers, trying to tamp down her nervous energy.

"We're fine. Chase Christopher must be coming home to see his sister."

"Who's the other man with him?" Anna whispered.

"Bradley Blakely, the sheriff's son. He works with Chase. They went to college together." He ran his hand down Anna's arm. "They were all fraternity brothers."

Chase took his father's outstretched hand. His father gave him a hearty clap on the back. The men talked briefly before Mr. Christopher and Bradley climbed into the limo. Chase strolled over to Eli and Anna.

"To what does Apple Creek owe the visit of Special Agent Eli Miller?" Chase cocked an eyebrow. "I thought you left your backwoods way of life for the big city."

Eli tipped his head toward the wreckage. "The plane crash." He seemed to let his words sink in. "I hear your sister is doing better."

Anna couldn't make out Chase's eyes through the dark lenses of his sunglasses. "Yes, she is. Thank goodness." His brow furrowed over the top of the frames. "So, I imagine you'll be leaving soon."

Anna wrapped her hand around Eli's elbow. His muscles tensed, but he didn't say anything.

Chase seemed to be looking in her direction, but she

couldn't be sure. "You must be Anna Quinn." She assumed he had seen her on the news. "Sorry about your brother. If there's anything the Christopher family can do, let me know. We were fraternity brothers. Fraternity brothers always take care of their own."

Anna narrowed her gaze at him. "Thank you." She hesitated a fraction. "I understand you talked to my brother recently."

Chase seemed to jerk his head back ever so slightly.

"What did you talk about? Did he tell you why he returned to Apple Creek?" Anna hated the desperation in her voice.

Chase plowed a hand through his thick hair. "Wasn't he photographing the Amish for a coffee-table book?" He shrugged. "My job has me traveling like crazy. We really didn't have a chance to catch up. I mean, nothing more than a quick conversation. I understand he and my sister were friendly." He bowed his head slightly. "Thank goodness she wasn't killed. She has a long recovery in front of her."

"Chase—" Mrs. Christopher strode toward them, her high heels clacking on the cement floor of the hangar "—your sister is expecting us."

Chase gave them a cool smile. "My family is waiting." He started to walk away, then he turned back around. "Do you plan to have a service for Daniel? I'd like to attend."

"I haven't had a chance to plan it. I still have to take care of my brother's things."

Mrs. Christopher wrapped her hand possessively around her son's arm. "I would appreciate it if you cleared out your brother's things soon." She narrowed her gaze. "I think it would be cathartic if you boxed everything up and donated it all to charity. You need to move on with your life." She patted her son's arm. "I could have Tom take care of it. This really must be horrible for you." Her unusually smooth forehead failed to convey the right touch of sympathy. "Why delay the inevitable?"

"No, thank you. I'd like to go through my brother's things myself."

"Tom really wouldn't mind. Just say the word." She glanced up at her son. "Come on."

"Let me know when the service is." Chase gave her a thin-lipped smile.

Anna watched them climb into the vehicle. The limo made a U-turn and the back window slid down. Something in Mrs. Christopher's blank expression made icy fear course through her veins.

Eli took Anna's hand as she stepped over the trampled cornstalks at the site of the crash. They had struck out at the hangar and with the second search of Daniel's apartment. No flash drive. No camera. *Nothing.* Anna couldn't shake the dread that had descended on her after their visit to her brother's crumpled plane.

Squaring her shoulders, Anna steeled herself for the site in front of her—the place where her brother's plane crashed. Unable to tear her eyes away from the scorched earth, she wondered what her brother's last thoughts were. Closing her eyes, she covered her mouth to stifle a sob.

Anna bowed her head and offered a quick prayer that her brother no longer suffered. That he was at peace. That she and Eli would find peace. That they both would find the answers they needed. She stole a glance at Eli as he walked slowly, flashlight in hand, searching the charred earth. Determination fueling her, she stepped forward, the stalks crunching under her feet.

The sun hung low in the sky. Something about the shadowy fields made the hairs on her arms stand up, and it had nothing to do with the accident. Or maybe it had everything to do with it. All around her, the land seemed to stretch forever, yet the stalks of corn closed in on her.

Anna joined Eli in crisscrossing the area. The beams of the flashlights were aimed at the ground. Eli reasoned that the light would bounce off the metal of a flash drive or camera, making it easier to find now versus in the bright sunshine.

Anna directed her flashlight at the damp soil. "You think my brother found something and someone wanted him dead?"

"I'm afraid so." Eli bowed his head and swatted at his neck. "And based on recent events, I think they're still looking for it." Something in his tone made her look up. He grabbed her forearm, his eyebrows drawing together. "I don't want you out of my sight."

His possessive touch sent a flush of tingles racing across her flesh. Apparently sensing her unease, he let go and the lines around his eyes softened. "I don't want anything to happen to you."

Averting her gaze, Anna made a show of slapping at a mosquito on her arm. She quickly changed the subject. "Let's search the area before it gets any later."

The bent cornstalks crunched under Anna's tennis shoes. Her eyes tracked the beam of the flashlight. Eli trudged forward and looped back the other way, both of their heads bowed. After about thirty minutes of crisscrossing the site and a little farther beyond, Anna plopped down, completely oblivious to the damp earth seeping through her pants. She hugged her legs to her chest and watched Eli continue the fruitless search. He had a look of determination. A look of a man possessed.

Hopelessness overwhelmed her. "We're not going to find anything, are we?" She held up her palms. "It could be anywhere."

Eli sighed heavily. "It's not looking good."

Anna scratched her forehead. "We don't know if the photos are of any value. My brother didn't give me much to go on in the email."

Eli plopped down next to her, bumping her shoulder. "I'm not giving up on this."

Anna rested her elbows on her knees. "I know. We have to find the truth."

A crunching sound came from behind them. Eli scrambled to his feet and shone a flashlight in the direction of the noise. A young man, his eyes shadowed by a wide-brimmed hat, approached. He seemed to be looking past her to Eli. No, he was staring at an empty space. *The crash site.* His haunted look unnerved her. It took her a minute to recognize Samuel, Eli's fifteen-year-old brother.

"Hi, Samuel." Eli lowered the beam of his flashlight, sending the features of his brother's face into darker shadows. He strode over and clapped his younger brother on the shoulder. "How's it going?"

"Do you think he went to heaven?" Samuel's question startled Anna.

"He is at peace," Eli said, his tone convincing.

Closing her eyes, Anna prayed silently. *Please let him be at peace.*

"I better go before *Dat* comes looking for me. I have chores."

"Wait," Eli called to his brother. His kindness toward his little brother reminded her of her own brother. Pressing her fist to her lips, she felt hollow inside. "Did you see the plane crash? You're usually outside doing chores...."

Anxiety spurred her to her feet. She swiped at her damp jeans, her eyes intently focused on Samuel. His brown eyes grew wide. Anna couldn't help but wonder if this was what Eli looked like when he was growing up in the Amish community.

Samuel tugged on the brim of his hat, shading his eyes. "I was walking from the barn when I heard a loud noise." The boy looked up and gestured with his hands, like wings of a plane. "I saw a plane close. Closer than I've seen the other planes when they use the Apple Creek Airpark." He had a faraway look in his eyes. "It made a horrible sputtering sound. The wings clipped a few trees before it hit...." His gaze dropped to the scorched earth. "I ran over in this direction."

Anna's heart squeezed. Hearing about her brother's last minutes of life tore at her heart. The terror he must have experienced.

"Did you tell anyone what you saw?" Eli asked.

"No. *Dat* told us not to talk to the English coming to gawk at another man's misfortune."

Eli leaned over to meet the boy eye-to-eye. "There's nothing to be afraid of. Did you tell *Dat*?"

"No." Samuel stared in the direction of the crushed stalks as if reliving the moment.

"Did you approach the plane?" Anna's pulse thudded in her ears.

"He...he—" Samuel pushed his hat up and scratched his forehead "—he was hanging upside down." His eyes grew red. "All I could think about is how the Amish aren't supposed to fly."

"You saw him?" Anna nearly crumbled to her knees. She feared she wouldn't hear his response over the whooshing in her ears.

"I need to go. *Dat* will be looking for me." The teen turned and ran off, not answering her question.

Anna watched him disappear through the cornstalks. "Do you think my brother suffered?"

"It happened so fast."

"Your brother seems troubled. I think he's not telling us everything." As a counselor, she had experience with kids in crisis.

"It had to be hard to witness an accident like that."

"But why didn't he speak up sooner?" She tried to soften the edge in her voice. "He saw the crash. Maybe there's more he's not telling us. He said he saw my brother." Why did this give her hope? Her brother was dead. Nothing changed that.

"You don't understand. The Amish are reluctant to get involved in what they consider English problems. I'll talk to him later. He might be reluctant to talk in front of you." Eli closed the distance between them and took her hand. "He's entering a tough stage in his life. My parents will be encouraging him to get baptized. But as a young man, he'll be tempted to explore the outside world."

Anna's mouth bowed into a small smile. "I suppose that's why they don't like you hanging around. You're an example of the outside world."

Something akin to hurt descended into his eyes. "I'm going to search the area one more time."

Anna lifted her face to the sky. The sun had fully set and a million stars dotted the night sky, making her feel small. The crunch of Eli's footsteps on the dried cornstalks floated back to her. She was glad she wasn't alone.

Eli adjusted the knob on the lamp and the light grew brighter. He sat on the edge of the bed, exhausted but not quite ready for sleep. He had hoped to talk with Samuel this evening but couldn't find him. He supposed his little brother was out in the barn tending to Red. He'd give him more time before he forced him to talk about the crash. They'd catch up at some point because they were sharing the same sleeping quarters.

Scrubbing a hand across his face, he yawned. At home, he would have flopped down on the couch and channel surfed until his mind numbed into oblivion and sleep stole over him, even if temporarily. Despite having grown up in an Amish home, he had quickly grown accustomed to modern conveniences. And mind-deadening technology.

With nothing but silence to keep him company, his thoughts drifted. Eli had been a dutiful son his entire childhood. The day Mary disappeared, he had prayed and prayed for her safe return. Two days later, when Mary's bed was still empty, he decided God was not a merciful God. Right then and there he abandoned his plain ways. The only time he found peace over the years was when he was absorbed in a case, helping some victim or their family find closure. The only way he would find true peace would be when he solved Mary's case.

His father cleared his throat. Eli snapped his attention toward the door. "Will you take a walk with me, Eli?" Abram asked.

Eli followed his father through the kitchen, grabbing his coat from the hook on the way out. The cloudless night afforded him a view of a million stars. In the city, light pollution drowned out the crisp view of the stars. The stillness here was peaceful as long as he didn't let his thoughts get in the way.

Abram walked toward the barn and Eli followed, knowing his father would tell him what was on his mind when he was ready. He slowed by the barn door and turned to face his son. "The plane has been cleared away from our fields."

"Yes, they didn't waste any time." A dark line furrowed his father's brow. "I thought that would make you happy. You'll be able to finish harvesting the corn for feed."

"Nothing about this situation makes me happy."

Eli bit his lip, knowing better than to argue with his father. "Are you anxious for me to go?"

"Son, we never wanted you to leave in the first place. *You* made your choice."

"I did. And I made the decision before I was baptized." There was no reason for his family to shun him. That was reserved for baptized members who turned their backs on the Ordnung, the set of Amish rules that governed their community. By shunning wayward members, the Amish hoped they'd see the error of their ways. Yet returning home for Eli had never been the same. He'd never be fully welcomed. He could see disappointment in his father's eyes and hurt in his mother's. And he was never encouraged to stay long. He didn't want to get his parents in trouble with the bishop. The Amish set themselves apart for a reason. There were too many distractions and temptations in the outside world.

"I know." His father angled his head so the brim of his hat shadowed his eyes. "We miss you, son, but we have to be careful. Your mother heard talk in town. The bishop thinks we are too tolerant of your visits." Abram's voice grew quiet. "And ever since your arrival, Samuel seems agitated. He admires you and I fear he's curious about your way of life."

Abram ran a hand down his beard. "Samuel has been venturing into town. I'm not sure who he is visiting. He seems to have taken a liking to Isaac, but I fear Samuel might want to explore the world like Isaac did."

"I will see what I can find out."

"Thank you." Abram squared his shoulders. "And I think for your own peace of mind, it's time for you to let Mary go. Until then, you'll never find peace."

Eli tried to relax his clenched jaw. "I can never let her go. I have to find answers."

"What if those answers lead to Daniel Quinn? Justice is not for this world anymore. Can you live with hurting Anna? She is blameless in all this."

"I have to find the truth. It was my fault Mary disappeared. I should have never let her out of my sight."

"It's not your fault." His father's voice was stern.

Eli's throat closed around his grief.

"We have forgiven whoever took our Mary. We don't want anyone else to be hurt."

Eli's grief shifted into anger. "No one has been arrested." He had grown tired of having this argument with his father.

"It doesn't matter. We have forgiven him. I have faith Mary has found peace. And we are at peace with our forgiveness."

But the ever-present pain he always saw in his mother's eyes revealed something perhaps his father was unwilling to accept. His mother may have proclaimed her forgiveness, but her eyes radiated the pain of a mother who has lost a child.

"You cannot come into our home and continue this hunt. It serves no purpose."

"Someone has to pay."

"Retribution is not our way."

"Father, didn't you love your Mary?"

Abram took a moment before speaking, his eyes heavily shadowed, but Eli noticed his lips trembled. "A father loves his children."

"Then how can you forgive so easily?" *Especially when I have not been able to forgive myself.*

Chapter Nine

Anna splashed cold water on her face, then patted it dry with a towel. The linens smelled of fresh air, unlike any scented detergent. She was grateful Eli's family allowed indoor plumbing because she had learned that not all Amish communities did. She yanked the clip from her hair, letting it cascade down her shoulders. Leaning close to the mirror, she pressed on the flesh under her eyes. The dim light from the oil lamp in the bathroom did nothing to help her appearance, yet it accurately reflected how she felt. Tired, drained, exhausted. The weight of the world on her shoulders.

With her small overnight bag in hand, she tiptoed down the hallway to her room, hoping she wouldn't run into anyone. As she neared the top of the stairs, she heard voices floating up from the sitting room. Curious, she wanted to go see who it was but felt underdressed in her T-shirt and cotton pajama pants. She lingered at the top of the stairs.

"Sorry to stop by so late. I only now heard about the horrible accident," a woman said, her voice shaky, older perhaps.

"Oh, Sara, you could have waited till morning. How is your daughter?"

The woman sighed. "The trip seems longer each time I take it. I so wish she lived closer. But her husband was determined to settle nearer his parents."

Anna slipped to her bedroom and dropped the toiletries on the dresser. She grabbed a sweatshirt out of her suitcase and jammed her arms into it. Smoothing a hand over her hair, she descended the stairs. She was about to make her presence known when she heard Mariam speak.

"God tells us to lay our worries in his hands, but I am filled with concern for my son Samuel." A mix of anxiety and shame laced Mariam's voice.

Anna thought about Eli's younger brother, the stress on his face when they saw him in the field this afternoon.

"He's always been quiet. Too quiet. I fear he's never gotten over losing his twin." Her delicate tone belied the gravity of her words.

"Poor Mary." The older woman tsk-tsked.

"My faith in God has sustained me." Mariam's voice was barely a whisper. "My faith is strong, but so is my motherly instinct. We are losing him."

"I know how hard it was for you when Eli left." The older woman's voice grew quiet. "I hear he's staying here."

"Oh, only for a day or two. He's here because of the crash." Anna's heart squeezed at the defensiveness in Mariam's voice.

"Some of the neighbors are talking."

"Let them talk," Mariam said in what Anna suspected was a rare display of defiance. "God will never forgive me for not trusting in His plan, but I've already lost two children. I can't lose a third. Abram doesn't want to discuss it. I think he fears we are inviting trouble."

Anna pulled her sleeves down over her hands and stifled a shudder. Clearing her voice, she stepped into the entryway of the sitting room. "I'm sorry to interrupt."

Mariam jumped to her feet. "I didn't realize you were awake." She held out her palm to the older woman. "This is my aunt Sara."

Anna nodded. "Hello." Embarrassment heated her cheeks. "I don't mean to pry, but why do you think you will lose Samuel?"

Mariam seemed to regard the older woman for a moment. Sara lowered her gaze and folded her hands in her lap. "He is approaching *Rumspringa*." Anna gave her a confused look, so Mariam explained. "His running around time. He'll have a chance to explore the outside world, relax the rules a bit, before he commits to the Amish way. Before he is baptized. He so reminds me of Eli. I fear he might look to the outside world to search for something he thinks he's missing here."

Mariam fidgeted with the fabric of her apron. She looked up with steely resolve. "He loves his brother so. Any words from him may be encouragement to leave the Amish."

"I don't think Eli would encourage him to leave his home."

Mariam lifted her palms. "I have said too much."

Sara stood and Mariam followed suit.

"Nice to meet you, Sara."

Sara nodded, then she turned to her niece. "You should talk to Abram about your worries."

"You're right." Mariam bowed. "I will talk to him when he gets in." She twisted her hands. "He and Samuel have been spending a lot of time in the barn with Red. Poor creature."

A stiff breeze blew in through the open window. Anna tucked a strand of hair behind her ear. The chirp of crickets filled the air.

Sara paused in front of Anna and gave her a pointed glare. "English life can be hard."

Anna crossed her arms, then let them fall to her side. "I'm sure everyone has their moments."

"My husband told me about your family."

"Sara—" Mariam's tone held an urgent quality "—Anna's brother died in the plane crash."

"I am sorry for that. But do you think it's wise she stay here?"

Anna's cheeks burned hot. "What do you mean? It's only temporary. Surely no one will have issue with that."

"The sheriff stopped my husband when he was in town today." She smoothed her hands down her skirt. "He thought we should know who was staying in our community."

"What did the sheriff tell you?" Anna bit her cheek, realizing her initial distaste for the sheriff was well founded.

"He told us about your poor mother...." No doubt, the sheriff had told her how her father killed her mother. How her brother was suspected in hurting Mary.

Grateful for the dim lighting, Anna tipped her head back to hold off the tears blurring her vision. "I will move to a motel first thing in the morning." The thought of staying at her brother's apartment after someone broke into it unnerved her. "The last thing I want to do is cause your family any more trouble."

"You don't have to leave." Mariam said, her voice

barely a whisper. "I am sorry I made you feel like you had to leave. Considering the circumstances—" Mariam met her aunt Sara's perplexed gaze "—I'm sure no one in the community would fault us for welcoming the English into our home during their time of need."

Sara pursed her lips. "It's late. I must be going." Sara slipped out the door. By the starlight Anna could see the older woman climb up into a buggy. A man flicked his wrists and the jangle of the harness and the crunching of the wheels on the gravel competed with the calls of the night critters.

Mariam sighed and lowered herself into the rocker, seemingly defeated. It was obvious she didn't have a stomach for conflict. "Abram and I already knew your brother was under investigation regarding our sweet Mary before my aunt arrived. We didn't know, however, about your parents. I'm sorry. I have been too wrapped up in my own worries." Mariam's eyes brightened. "None of this affects our feelings for you. We forgive whoever took our Mary."

Anger flashed below the surface. "I don't need your forgiveness, Mrs. Miller."

Mariam bowed her head. "I didn't mean to offend you." She got up, crossed over to the window and slid it shut, cutting off the cacophony of night critters. Without the cool evening breeze, the walls pushed in.

Anna turned to Mariam, who was standing motionless. "I'm sorry to have caused your family so much turmoil. I will be sure to leave in the morning." She didn't want to stay where they'd be looking at her, pitying her. She had had enough of that as a teenager—the whispers in the hallway in high school, the taunts, the pointing and staring. Kids were cruel.

Yet her heart went out to Mariam and her family. She was a school counselor, so maybe she'd be able to help Samuel with his feelings of loss. She couldn't turn away from a lost soul. "Perhaps I could talk to Samuel. I work with teenagers every day. Maybe I can help him come to terms with his feelings."

Shaking her head, Mariam wrung her hands. "That won't be necessary."

"What won't be necessary?" Abram stood in the doorway. His face was hidden in shadow, but the angry edge to his question left no room for interpretation.

Anna started to speak, but Mariam interrupted, her voice quiet in submission to her husband's authority. "Anna and I were having a chat. She has a lot on her mind since her brother's accident."

"Is everything okay?" Eli strolled up next to his father.

Mariam squared her shoulders and hiked her chin. "Everything's fine. I must go check on Katie Mae." She brushed past her husband.

Abram watched his wife stride out of the sitting room without a word. His eyes then landed on Anna. "We don't want our children to have undue influence from outsiders. You'd be wise to remember that."

Anna shoved her feet into her tennis shoes and ran outside. The wooden door slammed against the door frame, sending her nerves into overdrive. The tragedy from her past had caught up with her. Even out here on this Amish farm. A world away. She filled her lungs with the sweet country night air. Streaks of billowy clouds floated across the moon. The earthy smell reached her nose. Taking in the beautiful display calmed her rioting emotions, even if only a fraction.

She knew she couldn't go back inside just yet. The walls would surely close in on her. As she strolled toward the barn, the silhouette of a young Amish man and his dog came into view. She glanced back toward the house. No one would be the wiser if she happened to talk to Samuel. Maybe she could help. She pulled the sleeves of her sweatshirt down over her hands and strode faster toward the barn as the young man disappeared inside. Her tennis shoes kicked up the occasional pebble.

The red barn stood adjacent to the rows and rows of corn. The barn door yawned open. She peered inside, but it was heavily cloaked in shadows. "Samuel." Her call was met with silence and her muscles tensed. "Samuel, it's Anna. I want to talk."

"About what?" Samuel stepped into the opening, a serious look on his face. Ice formed in her veins.

"Your mother is worried about you."

Samuel's brow furrowed. "It is not our place to worry. We must trust God's plan." His words held a trace of irony. Had he been eavesdropping on her conversation with his mother through the open window? She didn't accuse him for fear of chasing him away.

Anna dug deep. "Maybe God brought me here so you'd have someone to talk to." Samuel hitched an eyebrow in obvious skepticism. "It's okay to talk about something when it's bothering you."

"I know what your brother did." His words grew hard, his tone that of someone much older than his fifteen years.

"My brother didn't hurt your sister if that's what

you're thinking." It took a lot of control to hold her voice steady.

"The sheriff thinks he did." He tugged on the brim of his hat. "Isaac thinks he did." His words held a challenge. "And Eli has been investigating him."

Anna flinched. His words cut her to the core. "I know you're hurting, but I know my brother. He would have never hurt a child." She rubbed the sleeves of her sweatshirt. "When I was twelve, my parents both died." She didn't bother explaining the gory truth. "My brother was all I had. He took care of me. He wasn't perfect, but he was good at heart. And that's what counts."

Samuel stood frozen in place, glaring at her while Red disappeared deeper into the barn.

"He even took me to church." Guilt nagged at her conscience. "But I'm not out here to talk about my brother. I want to talk about you."

A rustling came from the dark confines of the barn. Unfamiliar with the agricultural life, Anna couldn't decipher it, but it seemed to pique Samuel's interest. "Is everything okay?"

"I'm worried about Red. She's getting old."

"I never had a pet. Always wanted one, though." She searched his face to see if she was reaching him. Samuel scratched his head, seemingly bored.

"Your mom is concerned you will leave home like Eli did." Samuel jerked his head back, as if the thought surprised him. "If you heard the stories around town about my parents, you might think that beyond this farm is a big bad scary world." Anna held up her palms and looked around. "A lot of English might agree. But I can't tell you that. You have to make your own decision. If things are bothering you in here—" she pointed to her heart "—you won't be able to automatically fix them out there." She pointed toward the country road. "You have to work on what's inside first."

She couldn't make out Samuel's eyes shadowed by the brim of his hat. "I can't believe my parents are allowing you to stay in our home. Your brother ruined everything." His voice cracked.

Anna's breath hitched. "I plan to find a motel in the morning."

"It would be best if you left Apple Creek all together."

"Who told you I should leave Apple Creek?"

"Isaac." Rounding his shoulders, Samuel turned on his heel and disappeared into the darkened barn.

"Samuel…Samuel, come back here." A loud thud vibrated from deep in the barn. Concern blossomed in her chest.

"Samuel?" No answer. Goose bumps blanketed her skin.

The hay crunched under her feet as she stepped into the barn. Slivers of moonlight leaked in through the wood slats. She recognized the outline of a tractor and another door opening toward the fields.

"Samuel?" She found herself whispering. The loft creaked. An uneasy sense of hyperawareness coursed through her. The scent of dry hay filled her nostrils. A sprinkling of something rained down on her shoulders. "Samuel, are you up there? Please, let's talk." A dark shadow filled her field of vision. Something slammed into her head, driving her to the ground. Her head hit the hard-packed earth and her final awareness was filled with icy panic for Samuel's well-being.

Chapter Ten

We don't want our children to have undue influence from outsiders. Abram's words rang in Eli's ears as he watched Anna storm past him and out the back door. His father had been speaking to Anna, but the full implication of his message landed squarely on Eli's shoulder. *He* was the outsider. He was the one his father feared would have undue influence on his children. He watched his father hang his hat on the hook by the door. Intuitively, he already knew this, but to hear it spoken with such clarity was like a knife to the heart.

Had Eli been deluding himself? Did he really believe that when he found Mary or her kidnapper he'd be welcomed home the hero? *No,* he'd forever be the outsider. The Amish way was to forgive.

But not their own.

As long as he refused to come back into the fold, he'd never be forgiven. They saw his need for justice as a form of revenge. In their eyes, revenge only got in the way of redemption. Because he turned away from the church, his parents feared for his soul. Now they feared for their other children. He ran a hand across his whiskered jaw.

His father put his hand on the banister at the bottom of the stairs. "Good night."

"I must find out what happened to Mary. You know that. It's something I have to do."

Abram bowed his head, as if gathering his thoughts. "You were raised to do what is right for the common good. I did not raise you to pursue personal goals. You must be humble. Accept God's will."

Eli curled his fingers into fists. God's will had not dictated his sister's disappearance. It had been the evil hand of man. He bit back a retort. He knew he'd get nowhere. He had been living in the outside world for over ten years now. He didn't know how to rein in the emotions that sliced through him. "This is hardly a personal goal. I need to know what happened to Mary. I cannot rest until justice is served. For Mary's sake."

Abram climbed one stair and glanced over his shoulder. "Do you think you will be happy then?"

Eli rubbed a hand across the back of his neck. He doubted he'd ever be happy. Nothing would bring back his little sister. He stared after his father as he climbed the stairs.

Feeling caged, Eli strode onto the back porch, holding the door so it wouldn't slam in its frame. Having seen Anna go out the back door, he had expected to find her on the back porch. Mild concern whispered across his brain. He started to cross the yard when he heard barking coming from the barn.

When he reached the barn, Red was barking wildly. Eli's heart stopped when he saw Anna's thin frame sprawled out on the barn floor.

"Anna." He ran the short distance and dropped down beside her. "Anna." He pushed away the hay bale resting on her shoulder. "Can you hear me?" He pressed his fingers to her delicate throat. When he found her pulse, he released the breath he hadn't realized he'd been holding.

He slipped one arm under her legs, the other under her arms and picked her up. She was light, delicate. Something inside him stirred. Why did he feel so protective of her? *Forever the champion of the underdog?* He smelled the coconut scent of her shampoo. He felt the steady up and down of her chest as he carried her. He turned to bring her into the house when a shadow appeared in the doorway. He froze for a fraction before he realized it was his younger brother.

"What are you doing here? Did you see what happened?" Eli asked, a sharp edge to his tone.

Samuel stood stock-still, his features unreadable in the dark shadows. "Is she dead?"

"No." Losing patience, Eli pushed past him. "Let me get her into the house."

Eli rushed with her toward the house. Tendrils of awareness whispered across the back of his neck. He turned around on the porch and stared into the darkness, certain someone was staring back.

Unfamiliar voices stirred Anna from a restless sleep. No, wait, she didn't remember going to bed. The events of last night emerged as if from a slowly lifting fog. *The barn...?* She forced her eyes open. A pounding thudded under her skull with the effort. Blinking against the light, she recognized Eli's concerned face.

"Hey there." A small smile turned up the corners of his mouth. The edge of the bed dipped where he sat.

"You had us all scared." He ran his warm finger across her forehead.

Pain seared across her brain as she moved her gaze around the room. Mariam and Abram stood in the far corner and young Samuel hung back by the door. "What happened?" she asked through her parched lips.

Eli tucked a strand of hair behind her ear. "I was hoping you could tell us."

Closing her eyes, she thought back to the last few moments she remembered. "Something fell on me. I think it was a hay bale from the loft." She leaned up on her elbow and a sharp pain shot up her neck.

Eli adjusted the pillows under her head. "Relax. We need to take you to the hospital. Make sure nothing is broken. See if you have a concussion."

With her eyes closed, Anna held up her hand. The last place she wanted to go was the hospital. "Let me rest a few minutes. I think I'm fine."

"Did you see anyone?" Eli asked. Anna realized for the first time that he was holding her hand and rubbing the pad of his thumb gently across the back of her hand. Something warm coiled around her heart. No, he was simply offering comfort because that's the kind of man he was. Shame she met the right man at the wrong time.

"I…" She opened her eyes and strained to see Samuel's expression as he stood in the doorway. His mouth was drawn into a grimace. She had to earn his trust. Her eyes moved to Abram. A pain scratched across her brain with the sudden movement. Maybe she did have a concussion. She squinted. Eli's father seemed to be studying his youngest son. She could only imagine the intense pressure this boy felt as he moved into adulthood with the expectation that he be baptized. Or risk becoming an outsider.

"No," she lied, "I didn't see anyone. I wandered into the barn and before I knew what happened, something fell on me." Her eyes met Eli's. "Is it unusual for things to fall off the barn loft?"

It was Abram who spoke up, his voice tight. "We may be Plain People, but we take pride in our work. We do not stack things such that they might fall and injure someone."

Anna ran a hand across her forehead. "I didn't mean to imply…" She stopped talking. Each word pinged her aching brain.

"We will let you rest." Mariam led Abram and Samuel from the room. Eli hung back, still sitting on the edge of the bed, holding her hand.

"You spoke to Samuel before you were injured," Eli whispered, not bothering to frame it as a question.

Anna nodded, immediately regretting the movement. "Your father wouldn't have approved. I need to gain Samuel's trust to help him. He seems angry." She rubbed her temple. "Or maybe sad. He hasn't dealt with the loss of his twin sister." Her chest grew heavy with the real-ization. "And thanks to the town gossips, he thinks I'm the sister of the devil himself."

Flashlight in hand, Eli climbed the wooden ladder to the barn loft. The smell of hay melted the years away. When he was a kid, he'd climb up here to play hooky from his chores—only long enough to read a few pages, not long enough to get scolded by his father. It seemed impossible the memories belonged to him. A young Amish boy. A lifetime ago. He shoved aside the past and focused on the task at hand.

The shaft of light from his flashlight illuminated the

old wood beams and hay bales. No sign of anything pre-
cariously close to the edge. Stepping farther onto the
loft, he tested his weight on the beams. A lone hay bale
sat near the back along the wall. As he approached, his
flashlight lit on a small pile of cigarettes stubbed out on
a flat rock. He ran his hand over the back of his neck,
wondering if Samuel had taken to smoking, a habit not
quite banned by the Amish but certainly frowned upon.
The elders looked the other way, praying the young and
foolish would give up the vice once they were baptized.
He'd have to talk to his little brother, not that he'd listen to him.

They all had bigger issues right now.

Had Samuel accidentally knocked a hay bale over the
edge and now was afraid to speak up? Afraid he'd be
scolded for smoking or for hurting Anna?

He was about to turn on his heel when a crumpled
piece of paper among the loose strands of hay caught
his eye. He picked it up and flattened it on his thigh. It
was a page torn from a yearbook or maybe downloaded
from a website. It only took him a second before he
saw it—a portrait of Miss Quinn, School Counselor.
His heart kicked up a notch. He directed his flashlight
around the space, looking for something, but he wasn't
sure what. Crouching, he tried to get at the same level
as the smoker would be using the rock as an ashtray.

That's when he saw it. A knot in the wood. He peered
through the hole it formed. From this position, he had a
clear view of his parents' home and the window of Anna's bedroom. His gut tightened. This hadn't been an
accident. Someone was determined to run Anna out of
town, or worse. If not for dumb luck—or perhaps the
grace of God—they may have succeeded tonight.

Daniel's concerned face flashed in his mind. "Watch out for my sister," he had warned the week before he died. Had someone threatened to hurt Anna if Daniel didn't stop whatever he was doing? But why try to hurt Anna now that Daniel was dead? Maybe they were concerned Anna wouldn't rest until she uncovered whatever her brother had.

Tucking the paper into his back pocket, he climbed down from the loft. He did a quick canvass of the barn and nearby property before making his way across the yard to the farmhouse. He found Anna sitting up in bed, her hand on her forehead and her face pale.

"Are you okay?" He frowned. Without waiting for an answer, he slipped his arm around her waist. "Come on, I'm taking you to the emergency room. You might have a concussion." Grimacing, Anna eased her legs out of bed and didn't argue with him.

Definitely not a good sign.

Eli tapped on the glass of the triage station in the emergency room that served the rural community. It was a far cry from the hustle and bustle of a city E.R. All the same, the composed nurse looked up at him and rolled her eyes. The nurse had obviously dealt with anxious loved ones hundreds of times. "Sir, you'll have to wait your turn. We had a car accident come in." The nurse gave him a pointed glare, then went back to the computer screen in front of her.

He sat down next to Anna in the orange plastic chairs arranged in a narrow U facing a television mounted on the wall. "I'm sorry. You holding up okay?"

"My stomach seems to have settled, but I have one horrendous headache." She squinted up at him before closing her eyes. He flicked his gaze to the harsh glare of the fluorescent lighting.

Eli glanced at the triage station but forced himself to sit tight. He was used to taking control, having his way. But even he couldn't justify pushing Anna ahead of a car accident victim. Glancing down, he noticed her trembling hands. Without asking for permission, he reached over, took her hand and pulled her toward him. He slipped his arm around her shoulders and let her rest her head on his chest. It felt right. But nothing good could come from falling for this woman. He had given up everything to find Mary and he didn't plan on stopping now. And if her brother was involved, their relationship would be doomed from the start. *How could two people ever get past that?*

He smoothed a hand down her hair, unable to resist the silky feel of it. For now, he'd have to settle for pretending.

"Well, well, well…" A familiar, yet smug, voice sounded from behind him. Eli turned to find the sheriff standing there, his lips twisted into a sardonic grin.

Eli gently shifted Anna out of his embrace and stood to face the sheriff. He crossed his arms. Why did it always feel like a turf war with this man?

"Are you here because of the car accident?" Eli asked.

"Not my jurisdiction."

Cocking an eyebrow, he waited for the sheriff to continue. "I'm here on a courtesy call," he finally said.

"Courtesy call?" The first twinges of escalating anger coursed through his veins. Was the sheriff following him?

"The Christophers called me. They would like to clear out Daniel's apartment." The sheriff leaned around Eli to get a look at Anna. Resting her elbow on the back of the chair, she supported her head in her hand.

"How did you know we were here?" Eli asked.

"Stopped by your parents' farm." The sheriff jerked his chin toward Anna. "What happened?"

"She bumped her head. I want to get her checked out. See if she has a concussion." Eli didn't want to clue the sheriff in on what he'd found in the loft, not yet anyway. He had come too far to lose control now. Ten years ago when Mary went missing he had seen firsthand how protective of an investigation the sheriff had become. As if bringing in outside help was an affront to his manhood. Besides, in this small town, the sheriff was a little too close to the Christophers.

"Bumped her head?" The sheriff stepped around Eli and approached Anna. All of Eli's defense mechanisms kicked into high gear. He needed to protect her from this bully. That's what the sheriff was. On the day Mary disappeared, he had tried to bully Eli into saying things that weren't true. Tried to accuse him of racing his buggy. Losing control. Hurting Mary. Even now the thought of it nearly snapped his thin thread of control. He had been too young, too naive to stand up to the man back then. Not anymore.

"Anna fell and bumped her head. We're seeking medical help. End of story." He glared down at the sheriff. "We will clean out Daniel's apartment by the end of the month. You can let the Christophers know."

The sheriff grimaced. "I want to hear for myself how Anna bumped her head." The sheriff pushed back his shoulders and narrowed his gaze. "As you well know, your family's farm is in my jurisdiction." A threat laced his tone.

Eli's and Anna's gazes met. She must have read something in his eyes because she said, "It was stupid really. I wanted to see the horses and when one of them backed up, I jumped out of the way and slammed my head on the stall door." She shrugged, but the light-hearted gesture came off as strained.

"Eli, maybe you can check with the nurse while I talk to Anna alone." Eli was more than familiar with domestic abuse protocol. To isolate the parties so the victim can request help. Why would the sheriff take that approach? He knew he and Anna had only met recently. Unless he was trying to isolate Anna to intimidate her. To coerce her into going back to Buffalo. For some reason, Anna seemed to be a thorn in the Christopher family's side and the sheriff was always quick to protect them. And his own son who was a close friend of Chase Christopher's.

"You heard the lady. She told you she injured herself in the barn. Let her be. She's in a lot of pain."

The sheriff seemed to regard them for a moment. "I understand Daniel's body is scheduled for cremation tomorrow. You plan on leaving soon?"

Anna rose to her feet. Pain etched her features from the effort. "Sheriff, I need to clean out my brother's apartment and take care of a few things first."

"It would be best if you cleared out of the Christopher's property as soon as possible."

Eli watched the sheriff leave the E.R. Anna placed her hand on his forearm. "Why didn't you tell the sheriff the truth about my accident?"

"I don't trust him. I don't know who he's talking to and I don't want it to affect the investigation." He patted her hand, then turned and led her back to her chair.

Anna sat down slowly, wincing with the motion. "What is the truth, Eli?"

Eli dug a piece of paper out of his jeans' pocket and unfolded it. Anna stared at the crumpled paper. A crease cut her face diagonally, giving her a warped look. "That's my staff photo from the high school yearbook." She looked up to meet Eli's gaze, and apprehension filled her eyes. "Where did you find that?"

"In the barn loft." He reached out and captured her hand in his. "It seems someone was watching you from the loft. I don't think they had planned on hurting you in the barn, but they took the opportunity when you happened to be in there."

"But why?" Her mind swirled with the possibilities.

"Do you have any enemies in Buffalo?" Eli asked, brushing a strand of hair from her face. "It wouldn't take much for them to follow you here."

Splaying her delicate hands, she said, "I'm a school counselor. Sure, I have the occasional angry student, but nothing out of the ordinary." Her hands curled into fists as she met his gaze. "This has to do with my brother, right? He found something that might incriminate someone in Mary's disappearance. Now they want me to go home so I don't uncover whatever information he had. Then they can pin Mary's kidnapping on him. Case closed. Nice and neat."

Eli scrubbed a hand across his face. "You could be right. But it doesn't add up. Now that Daniel's gone, as long as these attacks continue, it only proves that someone else has something to lose if we find whatever it is Daniel had."

"Obviously, they're desperate enough to take the

chance. If we never figure out what Daniel had uncovered, the truth could remain buried forever."

Eli nodded. "And if someone's desperate, they won't stop—"

"You think someone will kill me if I don't leave well enough alone?" Fear flashed in her hazel eyes.

"I won't let that happen."

Chapter Eleven

"Thanks." Anna accepted the water from Eli and ran her free hand across the smooth grain of the arms of the rocking chair. The ache in her head had died down to a dull roar now that they were back at the Miller's home. Yet another painful thought whispered across her brain. *Someone killed Daniel, and now they're out to get me.*

Eli leaned forward in his rocker, a concerned look in his deep brown eyes. "I'd feel better if I could watch you for a little bit before you go to bed." The doctor said she had a mild concussion.

"I don't think I could sleep if I tried."

Eli stared straight ahead as if deep in thought. She studied his strong profile. She had only known him a short time, but his mere presence calmed her nerves. Having witnessed firsthand the destruction her father—a police officer—rained down on her family, she had vowed she'd never fall for anyone in law enforcement. She believed the difficulties of the job had turned her father into an evil man. And because he was a police officer, her mother had nowhere to turn.

Maybe she had been wrong.

She sipped the cool water. Eli was different. Wasn't he? She witnessed his compassion, his gentleness, his love of family even though they considered him an outsider. Her father could be the sweetest guy, too. He was never as contrite as he was the day after he brutally beat his wife. Her gaze drifted to Eli's strong hands. She had never seen them raised in anger. Maybe he *was* different. Her heart ached. He had a family right here, but they kept him at arm's length. She had none.

"Is it tough to be back here?" Immediately heat blossomed in her cheeks. "I mean…you grew up in an Amish community. This was your home. It's obvious your mother loves you dearly." His father was harder to read, but she imagined he cared for his eldest son in his own way. "Have you ever regretted your decision to leave? Have you lost all faith?"

Eli shifted in his chair to face her, the smooth planes of his features void of emotion. "The day my little sister disappeared was the day I lost faith."

"Maybe you would find peace if you went back to your faith."

Half his mouth curved into a grin. "Do you really see me as returning to the Amish way of life?"

A laugh bubbled up from Anna's lips. Pain scraped against her brain. "Ouch." She rubbed her forehead gently. "I didn't necessarily mean for you to go back to being Amish. But haven't you ever considered joining another church? Maybe it would bring you some peace. I know it did after my mother was killed." Pain sliced her heart even after all these years.

Eli braced the arms of his chair. "I'll find peace when I arrest the evil person who took my sister."

"What if that never happens?" she whispered.

"I can't think that way."

Silence stretched between them. Anna let her thoughts drift. An ache throbbed behind her eyes. "The sheriff is eager for me to leave town."

"It sure seems that way. The Christopher family is putting the screws to him." A muscle twitched in Eli's jaw. "That's how things sometimes work in small towns."

Anna searched his face. "Maybe I should leave. Take my brother's remains and go home." Part of her wanted him to ask her to stay. Another part of her wanted life to go back to normal.

Eli's lips thinned into a straight line. He pushed to his feet and crossed to the window, pulling back the single panel covering it. The silence stretched for too long. Unease prickled the back of her neck. She needed answers as much as he did.

When he turned around, she struggled to read his eyes in the dim light. Time seemed to come to a screeching halt as the back of her throat ached. "It would be safer if you left."

His unequivocal answer slicked her palms with sweat. She ran them across her thighs, struggling to stay composed. "I'd hate to bring danger to your family. I'll check into the motel in town."

Eli sat down and leaned in close, running a knuckle across the back of her hand. "You should go back to Buffalo. Out of harm's way. I'll have someone keep an eye on you for a while. Till I know this mess has blown over."

She sat up straight and narrowed her gaze. "You still have doubts about my brother. If I leave, it will be easier for you to put a neat little bow on your investigation." She regretted her words even as they poured from her mouth. She lowered her voice. "I have to know the truth."

She started to stand and Eli reached out and caught her hand, forcing her back down. His words came out even and soft, barely audible above the frantic pulsing in her ears. "I want the truth, too."

The anger drained out of her. Tears stung the backs of her eyes and she couldn't contain them this time. Tear after tear trailed down her face. Eli reached out and dragged the pad of his thumb across her cheek.

She gently pushed his hand away. "I can't stay here. I can't put your family at risk. But I can't go home yet."

Eli stared at her with a distant look in his eyes. "You need to get a good night's rest. How are you feeling?" He reached out a hand.

"I'll be fine." She accepted his hand and stood up. A wave of pain swept over her, but she stifled a grimace.

"We'll figure things out in the morning. Come on." He wrapped his arm around her waist and they turned to go upstairs. In the doorway, Samuel held a camera by a long strap.

"Where did you get that?" Eli brushed past Anna.

Samuel stretched out his arm, letting the camera dangle. Eli reached for it, but Samuel jerked away. "It's for Anna."

Taking the strap, Anna's heart raced. She turned the cool metal over in her hands. It looked expensive. Slowly she lifted her head to meet Samuel's expectant gaze.

"Your brother gave it to me." With his mussed hair and nightclothes, Samuel seemed far younger than his fifteen years.

"I don't understand. Is this...?" With trembling fingers, she flicked the camera's on button but nothing happened.

"The morning of the accident..." Samuel's voice

floated through a long tunnel. She stepped backward. The back of her legs hit the chair. She plopped down, not taking her eyes off the teenager. "I saw the accident. When I reached the plane, he was bleeding pretty badly from his head. I almost ran away. I wanted to get the neighbors. They have a phone. I wanted to call for help." He scratched his head, leaving thick, dark tufts of hair standing on end. "But the man was trying to tell me something. I couldn't make out the words. He tossed the camera toward me." Samuel pointed to it with a shaky finger.

"My brother was conscious after he crashed?" Disbelief edged her words.

Samuel nodded. "I was afraid. I didn't know what to do."

Eli placed his hand on his brother's shoulder. "It's okay. Tell us what happened."

"I don't want to get in trouble." Samuel studied the floor.

"Why would you get in trouble?" Eli leaned down to meet Samuel eye-to-eye.

"Isaac gave me a radio a few months ago and *Dat* found it. I promised him I wouldn't use any banned items."

"You understand this is different?"

Samuel stared blankly at him. "I knew it was wrong, yet I let my curiosity get the best of me. I wanted to see how the camera worked." He lowered his gaze. "I couldn't figure it out."

"Did my brother say anything?" Anna's face had grown ghostly white.

"He was moaning. I thought he said, 'Mary.'" He shrugged, a poor attempt at acting nonchalant.

"Mary? Are you sure?" Eli struggled to keep his tone even.

Samuel stared off in the distance. "That's all he said. *Mary.* I thought maybe the girl in the plane with him was named Mary, but when I learned later her name was Tiffany, I got scared because then I thought maybe he was talking about our Mary." He looked up with watery eyes. "Why would he be talking about our sister?" His face crumpled in confusion.

Eli squeezed his brother's shoulder. "You did the right thing by giving us the camera."

"You won't tell *Dat* I had the camera, will you?" Samuel spoke in a whisper, his lower lip trembling.

Eli patted his brother's shoulder reassuringly. "No one needs to know you had this. The important thing is you came forward now." He narrowed his gaze. "Did you tell anyone about the camera?"

Samuel bowed his head and dragged his bare foot across the floor. "Well, I didn't exactly tell anyone. But I did ask Isaac if he thought having a picture taken was really going against the Bible. He asked me why I cared so much because it wasn't like I'd ever have one." He slowly lifted his head.

Samuel glanced at Anna, a look of contrition on his face. "I'm real sorry about running away from you. It's my fault you got hurt in the barn. You would have never been in the barn if I hadn't run through there."

"It wasn't your fault." She flicked her gaze momentarily to Eli. "You can't blame yourself."

Samuel fisted his hands at his side. "I can't deal with any more guilt."

"What are you talking about, Samuel?" Eli asked.

Samuel looked at him with hesitant eyes. "The day Mary disappeared, I was teasing her. I pulled off her *kapp* and yanked her hair. She went with you because she wanted to get away from me." His shoulders rounded and he sobbed. "It's all my fault."

"No, that's not true." Eli grabbed both his brother's upper arms in a reassuring brace. "You were just a kid. You were only five years old."

Samuel's eyes grew wide. "But don't you understand? If I hadn't been a pest, she would have been helping me dust off the benches for the worship service in the barn. She wouldn't have been with you in town. Because of me, my whole family was destroyed."

Chapter Twelve

The next morning, Eli slipped behind the wheel of his SUV and glanced over at Anna. She cradled Daniel's camera in her lap as if it were a baby. He reached across the center console and patted her knee. "Once we get new batteries, we'll know what's on there."

Anna nodded. "I know. Do you think my brother gave the camera to Samuel because he didn't want someone to get ahold of it?" She traced a finger along the top of the camera and glanced out the window. "Do you think having this puts us in danger?"

"The thought crossed my mind. We'll have to keep it low key." Eli reached behind the seat and pulled out a small black canvas bag. "Put it in here."

Fidgeting with the zipper of the bag, Anna finally got it open and placed the camera gingerly inside. "If Daniel had photographic evidence, why do you think he didn't tell you?" He noted the apprehension in her voice.

Eli ran his hand across the top of the steering wheel. "I don't know. Maybe he was paranoid it would make him look guilty." A quiet groan left her lips. "Don't borrow trouble. Wait and see."

"You said the FBI was all over his fraternity, right? I bet my brother had his suspicions. He came back to uncover the truth himself."

"Possibly." He tilted his head to try to get a read on her emotions. "But why not stick around in the first place? Why drop out and enlist in the army?"

She sighed, obviously exasperated. "Because you guys—" She seemed to catch herself. "The FBI was narrowing in on him because of his past. Who better to accuse than a guy who had once been under investigation for his parents' deaths? He chose to enlist instead of waiting around. I know he's innocent."

"Let's find out what's on that camera." He gave her a weak smile before turning the key in the ignition. Suddenly he heard Katie Mae calling from the front porch. She waved, then ran full speed toward the car, her blue dress flapping around her legs. He opened the power window and waited for her to reach them.

"Can you drive me into town?" she asked, hope glistening in her eyes. "I was about to hitch the horse to the buggy when *Mem* mentioned you were driving in." She squinted up at the sky. "Dark clouds are rolling in."

"*Mem* knows you're going with us?" Eli asked. He didn't want to be accused of being an undue influence on his little sister, even though many Amish were allowed to ride in cars. He hated to admit how much his father's words bothered him.

Katie Mae looked toward the house and waved, presumably to their mother who he imagined was standing at the kitchen window. His little sister jumped into the backseat of the car. "The fabric for my wedding dress is in at the general store."

Anna shifted in her seat. "When are you and Isaac getting married?"

Katie Mae's face grew bright red. The Amish did not talk about engagements like people in the outside world. It was a formal matter to be taken seriously. It was not marked with wedding showers and bachelorette parties. "We haven't been published yet." Katie Mae adjusted the *kapp* on her head, the way she always did when she was nervous.

"The custom is for young Amish girls to make their own wedding dresses. So, Katie Mae is going to work on it well ahead of time to assure she's done when she and Isaac decide it's time." Eli looked into the rearview mirror and winked at his sister. He wished he could muster genuine enthusiasm for this union. He still thought of Isaac as the wild teenager who only recently returned to Apple Creek. He had since been baptized, but something about him bugged Eli.

What was Isaac thinking giving Samuel a radio?

Isaac still kept his car parked at an abandoned barn on the edge of Apple Creek. He claimed he didn't drive it, but Eli saw him once last month driving late at night. He put the car into gear and dismissed the thought. *Who am I to judge?*

"He's been courting me awhile." Katie Mae lowered her voice. "But we aren't supposed to talk about it. He visits me on Sunday evenings. That's where I was last night. He usually escorts me home from the singings." His little sister's face split into a wide grin, unable to hide her excitement. A bride was still a bride, he imagined. He, too, had been sweet on someone before Mary was kidnapped. He sometimes wondered what happened to Rebecca. Last he heard, she married a man from another Amish community and had a handful of children.

An unexpected emptiness tore at his soul. He realized something for the first time—he wanted a wife, children and something more in his life than this constant emptiness. He caught Anna's eye. A smile brightened her beautiful face and he was relieved she couldn't read his mind. Mentally shaking his head, he pulled onto the country road, doubting he'd find peace in anything until he found justice for Mary.

Once in town, Eli parked in a small lot between the general store and the diner. He picked a spot that didn't have a hitching post. He pushed open the door, thinking about how the past and the present fought for prominence in this small town. The past and present warred for position in his life, too. Katie Mae and Anna joined him around the back of the vehicle.

"After we stop in the general store, let's get something to eat at the diner," Eli said.

Katie Mae smiled. "Sounds good." She seemed especially cheerful today. Eli's chin dipped to his chest and he studied the ground. Should he speak up about his reservations about Isaac? Would his father even listen? Did he have any right to interfere with her future?

As always, when Eli went into the general store, the memories from that fateful day swept over him. Anna went to the counter and asked Mr. Lapp for AAA batteries while Katie Mae chatted happily with Mrs. Lapp, her future mother-in-law if all went as planned. After they made their purchases, they left the store, the bells clanking against the door and the sound jarring him. He had been too distracted the day Mary disappeared

to hear any bells announcing anyone else's presence—
or Mary's exit.

The three of them made an unlikely trio as they
crossed the parking lot to the diner. They found a booth
in the corner and placed their order. They were the only
patrons in the diner, so Eli wasn't worried about hiding
the camera. They sat quietly while Anna fidgeted with
the camera for a few moments as she figured out how
to load the batteries. He considered offering her help,
but she seemed intent on the task.

Once the batteries were in place, she turned on the
camera. A sense of anticipation charged the air. A quiet
chime confirmed it had power. Anna glanced up, apprehension creasing her forehead. "I'm almost afraid
to look."

"What are you looking at?" Katie Mae asked as the
waitress returned to the table with three coffees.

"This is my brother's camera. I can scroll through the
photos he took on it." The corners of Katie Mae's lips
tugged down. "I'll show you in a minute."

Sitting next to Anna, Eli saw the digital display. Anna
clicked a button and Tiffany's smiling face filled the
screen. Then one of Daniel making a goofy face. Anna
ran her finger over the glass. She scrolled through the
photos. Images of farms and silos and silhouettes of
Amish children flashed by. His claim that he was working on a book of Amish photographs seemed to be legitimate. Then an image filled the screen, and Eli inhaled
sharply.

A photo of an Amish *kapp* in Daniel's hand.

"Stop," Eli said, his heart thumping in his chest. He
took the camera and brought it to his face to examine
the image. He clicked the zoom button. The *kapp* had

jagged gray stitching around one edge. The handiwork had been done by a child. *My Mary.* Tears burned his throat. She had been so proud of the work, even when their mother corrected her for using the wrong shade of thread. But the little girl didn't care. It had been one of her first attempts at sewing.

But what brought him chills, even more than the familiar stitching, was the embroidery in the corner. *M.M.* His sister had carefully stitched her initials. The letters were surprisingly neat considering her age. Their mother had overlooked this minor transgression. Despite the fact that some Amish women sewed their initials on a handkerchief or corner of a dress pocket, which would be hidden by their apron, they would never monogram their *kapp*.

Lowering the camera, he looked over at his sister, who was sipping her coffee and watching him with interest. If he said anything now, Katie Mae would surely run home and tell their father and mother what he had found on the camera.

Anna's warm hand settled on his arm. He looked up and met her gaze. "Are you okay?" He nodded. Eli blinked a few times and scrolled through the photos. Prior to the image of the man holding his sister's *kapp* he had seen a series of photos of an old run-down cottage or cabin of some sort. He stared intently at the screen, wondering if Daniel had found his sister's *kapp* near the cabin.

"What's so interesting?" Katie Mae's voice came from over his shoulder. "Can I take a look?"

Eli tilted the camera so his sister could see the image of the cabin. He didn't want to shock her with the image of their little sister's *kapp*.

"My brother was taking photos of the countryside." Anna gave his forearm a reassuring squeeze. He wondered what she'd made out of her brother holding the *kapp*. Did she realize it was Mary's?

All sorts of questions crowded his mind. Where did Daniel find it? Was he going to implicate others? Where was it now? He rubbed his forehead. His mind raced.

"I know that cabin." Katie Mae startled him.

Leaning back, he looked up at his sister. She slid back into the booth across from him and took another sip of coffee. If not for the Amish clothing, her chattiness and excitement could have been mistaken for any other teenage girl in America. He wished for so much more for his sister. The world had a lot to offer her. He gritted his teeth. Who was he to brand one way of life better than another?

"You know where Daniel was when he took this photo?" he asked.

Katie Mae arched a pale eyebrow. "Yes. That's on the edge of the Christophers' lakefront property." She hitched a shoulder. "The one they use sometimes in the summer." She twisted her lips. "Never understood why people need two homes. The house they have in town could squeeze in all of the Millers and their cousins."

Eli's heart raced. Maybe this was the clue he had been working ten years to find. He struggled to keep his voice calm. "Is it next to the main house?" From looking at the photo, he couldn't imagine the Christophers would have allowed anything in their possession to have fallen into such disrepair.

"Oh, no…" Katie Mae's eyebrows shot up. "It's a good hike from the main house. One day in early spring, I had been put in charge of little Joey and Patrick, the

Christophers' grandchildren, while their mother had her nails done. I tried to clean the house with them underfoot, but they had too much energy. I took them out for a walk and they kept going and going. Didn't even mind me when I called for them to come back. Lucky I kept up with them."

"This cabin is through the woods? Could you find it again?"

Katie Mae nodded. "It's near the lake. North of the main house."

"How do you know it's the same cabin?" Anna's brows drew together.

Katie Mae held out her hand and Eli handed over the camera. She squinted at the image, then handed it back, as if she were passing a hot potato. Perhaps she feared being seen in public with a camera. She pointed from a distance at the image. "See the broken railing?" Eli examined the photo. Sure enough, the horizontal rail was broken and resting at an angle. "I was thinking *Dat* would have fixed that rail the minute it broke."

Anxiety made it nearly impossible to stay seated in their small booth. He had to find this cabin and Mary's *kapp*. He fisted his hands.

He had to find Mary's body.

"You sure we're heading in the right direction?" Eli's deep voice broke the tension-filled silence.

"Yes." Katie Mae, her face inches from her backseat window, watched the scenery intently.

It was now late afternoon and Anna wished she hadn't pushed aside the hamburger at the diner. When Katie Mae had excused herself to use the bathroom, Eli had explained his suspicions about the bonnet—or *kapp* as he called it—leaving Anna nauseous. Now, a sinking feeling told her this wasn't going to be a quick trip to the cabin. She anticipated it as much as she dreaded it. Could this be the day they finally cleared her brother's name? Or the day the last nail was hammered into his coffin?

Coffin.

The cold word made all the blood rush from her head. She'd have to make arrangements for the proper burial of her brother's remains as soon as she returned home.

Up ahead, a dark purple-gray cloud moved in from the west, its edge pushing against the bright blue sky. A crack of lightning split the dark cloud. Anna counted. *Twenty-five.* A dull rumble sounded in the distance. A charge of anticipation tickled the back of her neck. Generally, she loved a good storm, but not today. She'd rather visit the run-down cabin under bright skies. She bit the inside of her cheek. Her stomach ached. Maybe she wasn't hungry after all.

Katie Mae tapped on the window, drawing Anna's attention again. Eli's sister sat in the seat behind her brother, an intense expression on her pale face. "Turn here. That narrow lane." Eli slowed and turned left onto a gravel road. Anna was impressed the young girl had remembered the directions.

As if answering her question, Katie Mae said, "We came down this lane and walked back on the side of the road. It was a lot quicker than trampling through the woods again. I had to get the boys home before their grandmother realized how far we had gone. I didn't want to lose my job." Katie Mae propped her elbow on the door and rested her chin on her fist. "I was hired to clean, not watch the kids. But Mrs. Christopher always seems overwhelmed when the grandchildren visit. And

Chase's wife tends to bring the boys over to their grandparents' home a lot when Chase is traveling. Then she disappears, too."

Anna tapped her fingers on the center console, realizing they were getting close to the cabin in her brother's photos. As much as she wanted to clear his name, she feared finding something incriminating. What if witnessing their father murder their mother had shifted something in his personality? What if he had been warped enough to hurt a child? Eli reached over and covered her drumming fingers with his hand.

She cut him a sideways glance. "Sorry, I can't help it."

"Let's take it one step at a time, okay?" Eli smiled, the small gesture warming her heart.

Anna nodded, unable to form words. The tips of her fingers began to tingle and she sent up a silent prayer. *Dear Lord, please help me get through this.*

As they drove deeper into the woods, the thick canopy of tree branches swallowed them. The thick foliage and the clouds rolling in made it seem later than it really was. She ran a hand up and down her bare arms, wishing she had grabbed a sweater.

Up ahead a downed tree blocked the road. Eli slowed the vehicle and leaned forward, narrowing his gaze.

"We're going to have to park here and walk the rest of the way. It's not too far," Katie Mae said, pulling on the door handle.

They all climbed out of the SUV and assembled around front. Anna glanced down at her bare arms. She wasn't exactly dressed for a trek through the woods.

"We need to follow the road a little farther." Katie

Mae hiked her dress and climbed over the thick tree trunk in the road. She strode ahead, as if on an adventure.

Eli grabbed Anna's hand. "Let's get moving. We don't have a lot of time. From the looks of it, rain is on the way." Without saying a word, Anna took his hand. He guided her over the tree and stuck close by as they trudged about a half mile. Anna tried not to make a big show of it, but every few feet she had to swat at the mosquitoes feasting on her flesh. Only Katie Mae chatted about this and that as they made their way deeper into the woods.

When they reached a small clearing, a cabin came into view. Large sections of roof tile were missing. A wicker chair sat upended in the yard. The railing was broken, like the one in the photo. Anna's knees grew weak. She was retracing Daniel's steps. Had they lead to his death?

The rich smell of damp soil reached her nose. The entire scene was dreary. She held her elbows tight to her sides and clasped her hands in front of her.

Eli's gaze swept over her. "You're getting eaten alive." He ran the back of his knuckle across her cheek. "There's even one here." His touch lingered. It was a completely innocent gesture, but she couldn't deny the growing attraction melting her insides. A smile played on his lips as if he knew the effect his touch had.

"I should have brought you back to my parents' house. You don't need to be out here."

"No, I'm fine."

He lifted a skeptical eyebrow. "Okay, let's go then." He started walking again and Anna followed. His sister had already reached the cabin. "Wait up, Katie. Don't go inside until I have a chance to check it out."

Nostalgia pulled at Anna's heart when she heard the protectiveness in Eli's voice. That's how Daniel had always been to her. Protective. Now it was her turn to look out for her big brother one final time, if only to protect his reputation.

"Don't be such a worrywart." Katie Mae climbed onto the porch and peered through the window. "No one's around." She had all the confidence of a young girl who had lived a very sheltered life. Now that Anna thought about it, it was a wonder her parents allowed her to have a job off the farm working for the Christophers. She thought the Millers would want to keep their only surviving daughter close at all times. But that wasn't the way they lived. She had heard something once from a devout Christian that worrying was showing your lack of faith in God. Anna fisted her hands and squeezed, wishing she could learn from them. Worrying was a favorite pastime of hers.

Visible through the small breaks in the branches, lightning continued to light up the sky. Thunder rumbled overhead. A rush of water rustled the leaves. Eli wrapped his arm around Anna's shoulders and started jogging. Katie waited for them under the porch's overhang. Head down, Anna ran alongside Eli, aware of his clean scent. Prior to Eli, she couldn't remember the last time she had been under the protective arm of a man. Her heart shifted. *Be careful,* a voice inside her head whispered. *This man has the power to destroy the reputation of the only family you ever really had.*

Anna shivered against Eli's arm. He squeezed her shoulder, the only physical contact he'd allow himself. As much as he sought justice for Mary, he feared finding his answers at the expense of this beautiful woman. Not exactly the foundation to build a relationship on. Glancing toward the cabin door, he found his sister staring at them with a huge smile.

"Excuse me." Eli dropped his arm from around Anna's shoulder and brushed past his sister. He tested the door handle. It was unlocked, which made things easier for him, but it also begged the question—who else had access? *Who didn't?* Teenagers probably used the deserted cabin as a hangout. "Wait here while I check things out."

Anna's eyes flared wide, as if she didn't trust him. Or did he detect a hint of fear? Her shoulders sagged in acquiescence. "Okay, but hurry." She swatted at something on her ankle. "I'm getting eaten alive out here."

He stepped into the cabin. The trapped stale air mixed with pine assaulted his nose. A few beer cans littered the table next to the couch. An opened bag of chips sat on the cushion. He walked over and picked them up. The expiration date on the bag was two weeks ago.

"Can we come in?" Katie called from the doorway.

"One sec." Eli did a quick sweep of the cabin, the two bedrooms, the bathroom and the closets. Whoever had been here wasn't here now. Perhaps Daniel had been the last person here. And they all knew what happened to him. Eli made his way back to the front door and pulled it wide-open. "Come on in."

Katie Mae breezed into the room and flopped down on the couch, the fabric of her full skirt landing in a swoosh. "I got a rock in my shoe." Yanking at her boot, she worked at the laces without much regard for anything else.

Anna stepped into the middle of the room, her thin

arms around her middle. Her eyes grew wide as she took in her surroundings. He imagined she was thinking the same thing. Daniel had been here and he had Mary's *kapp*. Eli scrubbed a hand over his face, fearing the answers he had been so close to finding may now elude him forever.

"Where do we start?" Anna looked at him for guidance. He was about to answer when a huge clap of thunder made her jump. "Wow. That was close."

A torrential downpour pounded the roof while tree branches clawed at the walls. "We'll take our time here so we don't have to walk back through this weather."

"You don't think anyone will find us here trespassing?" Anna asked, concern lining her pretty features.

"Are you kidding?" Katie Mae spoke up. "The Christophers haven't used this place in years. I heard them say as much when their grandchildren asked about it." She lowered her voice. "Then they admonished the boys to never venture so deep in the woods. They said it wasn't safe." She pursed her lips. "And guessing from the way they take care of this place, I imagine they're right."

"We're fine," Eli reassured Anna. "I called Dr. Christopher, Chase's grandfather. He owns this property. He gave me permission to look around. Told me there's nothing but cobwebs at *that old place*."

Eli strode over to the kitchen and opened and closed drawers and cupboards. His stomach sloshed with dread. He half hoped and half feared he'd find Mary's *kapp*. But even if he did, what would it prove? Without saying a word, Anna strolled around the cabin, looking on bookshelves and under cushions.

Katie Mae busied herself picking up the empty beer

cans. She held one to her nose and scrunched her face. "What are you guys looking for?"

Eli caught Anna's eye. "Something Daniel had."

Katie Mae didn't ask for clarification and went back to tidying up.

Anna approached Eli as he crouched and pulled out the contents of the closet in the bedroom. "You really don't think we'll find anything here, do you?"

Eli sat back on his heels and scratched his forehead. "I don't know what to think. Your brother obviously found my sister's *kapp*—" he looked over Anna's shoulder to make sure his sister was out of ear's reach "—and he was standing outside this cabin when he took a photo of it. I'm trying to put together the pieces."

"Maybe it was his form of insurance." Anna knelt down next to him. "He was afraid and by taking the photo, he wanted us to know he found the bonnet here." Anna looked at him with hopeful eyes. He knew she really wanted him to believe Daniel was innocent in all this. He wasn't convinced. Even if others had been involved, it didn't automatically make Daniel innocent.

Anna covered Eli's hand with hers. He flipped his hand over so their palms touched. His gaze lingered on her face. He leaned over and wiped at a black smudge on her cheek. "I wish we had met under different circumstances."

A small smile curved the corners of her pink lips. "Me, too."

Closing his eyes, he cupped her soft cheek and pressed his forehead against hers. "You think this was God's plan?" The scent of her fresh shampoo swirled around him.

She whispered, "I wish I knew His plan."

He savored the moment a fraction longer, then pulled away and helped her to her feet. "I've fallen away from my faith, but I want to believe God has good things in store for you."

Nodding, she averted her eyes. Pink colored her cheeks.

"Let's see if there's anything to be found in this place." He strode away, ignoring the pain evident in her hazel eyes.

Chapter Thirteen

Anna closed her eyes, willing away the swirling panic. The quiet moment she shared with Eli seemed like a dream. Now the musty smell permeating the run-down cabin made the walls close in. Breathing in and out slowly, she stood rooted in place.

Eli opened and closed the drawers in the dresser, each one banging shut a little louder. The frustration rolled off him in waves. "I don't know where to start," he muttered.

Anna sent up a silent prayer that the truth didn't mean destroying the warm feelings she had for her big brother. She wouldn't be able to live with that. Forcing a tight smile, an idea took shape. "The photo was taken outside with the cabin in the background. Maybe we should search outside." She flicked her gaze to the windows. Heavy rain sluiced down the panes, making it impossible to see outside. "If only it weren't raining."

"Hopefully it will let up soon." He sighed. "I'm afraid anything outside will be gone by now." Eli paced the space in front of the bed. "But Daniel had to find it someplace where it had been kept safe for ten years." A line creased his forehead. "Where would you hide something around here to keep it safe?"

Anna rubbed her cheek. "Floorboards. Attic. A secret compartment in the wall."

Eli turned from searching a cabinet along the wall and smiled at her. A twinkle lit his eyes, a welcome change from the intensity she had witnessed only moments ago. She shrugged, heat warming her cheeks at his slow perusal of her face. "I watch a lot of crime shows," she said in her defense.

"Nothing wrong with that." Eli strode out of the bedroom, tilting his face toward the ceiling. She did the same. No sign of an attic or a basement anywhere. He turned around and faced her. "We can't start tearing up the floorboards. I can't abuse Dr. Christopher's trust like that. Maybe if a few boards are loose, we can peek."

"Why would you have to tear the floorboards apart?" Katie Mae asked.

Eli hesitated, as if debating whether to tell his sister about Daniel's discovery. "Sit down, Katie."

The strings from her bonnet dangled around her chin. "No, you're scaring me." Her eyes grew bright. "Is this about Mary?"

Eli nodded.

"I knew it. That's what brought you back to Apple Creek." Katie's face grew paler.

He reached out and took his sister's hand. Anna stared as time slowed to a crawl. Eli's words came out even, calm. "Daniel took a photograph of Mary's *kapp*."

Katie Mae backed up and sat down on the sofa. Her brows snapped together. "How do you know it's hers? It could be anybody's."

"Remember when she tried to sew the seam herself and she added her initials?"

Katie Mae nodded but didn't say anything. The steady drum of rain slowed to a trickle.

"Let's go outside and get some air," Eli said, reaching for his sister's hand.

Anna heard him quietly ask his sister if she was all right. Katie Mae answered with a slow nod.

After the passing rain shower, dusk had gathered quickly, creating long shadows in the corners of the cabin's front porch. Katie Mae brushed at her skirt as if she was shaking away the dust.

The mud sucked at Anna's tennis shoes as she made her way across the property to where Eli stood. Anna turned around and framed the cabin in her sites. "I think Daniel must have been standing near here when he took that picture." Her brother loved nature. He loved capturing what other people tended to not see. But what had brought him all the way out here? What had led him to this cabin?

Eli searched the area. "The ground is wet but overall pretty solid. I don't see that anything was buried out here."

"If that *kapp* was Mary's, where is it now?" Katie glared at Anna accusingly.

"Exactly what I'm wondering." Eli seemed to be picking his words carefully. "Why didn't your brother turn it in immediately?"

"He feared it would make him look guilty." The words tumbled out one after the other. That was the only explanation that made any sense.

Eli ran a hand across his mouth. "He had the chance

when he met with me. But he didn't. Or he could have called the sheriff."

The sheriff's smug face came to mind. "He didn't like the sheriff."

"I imagine that's true. The sheriff came down hard on him ten years ago."

Anna planted her fists on her hips. "The sheriff investigated a lot of fraternities in town the day Mary disappeared. The only reason he focused on my brother was because of the rumors surrounding my parents' deaths." Her anger heated her ears. "My father's wrath infected my family long after his death."

"Okay, we do know your brother had Mary's *kapp*." He shifted his weight and seemed to be taking in the surroundings. "Where is it now?"

Anna swatted at another mosquito.

"I think I saw bug spray near the sink." Katie Mae had strolled to the edge of the clearing and was staring at the lake. A few rays of sun poked through the clouds close to the horizon.

"Be careful near that cliff, Katie Mae," Eli called. His sister nodded and moved back from the edge.

Going insane from the itching, Anna started to walk toward the house. "I'll be right back." She couldn't figure out why the bugs weren't bothering Eli or Katie Mae. She supposed it was because she had the most exposed flesh. She scratched at her arms and her ankles. It was maddening.

The first porch step creaked under Anna's weight. Once again, when she opened the cabin door, the thick musty smell assaulted her. It seemed the shadows had grown longer in the short interval since they had left. A shiver crawled across her skin. She glanced over her shoulder and saw the beam of light from Eli's flashlight bouncing around the property. Nightfall was coming fast. Pushing back her shoulders she swatted at yet another mosquito and made her way inside. It would only take a second. In and out.

Anna stepped into the room and stopped. Her heartbeat kicked up a notch. She had the distinct sense she wasn't alone. She backed up and reached for the doorknob. A figure emerged from the shadows on the other side of the room. With a sweat-slicked palm, she tried to turn the door handle but her hand slipped off. She tried to scream but couldn't find her voice.

Dear Lord, help me.

The figure stood there, staring at her, but she couldn't make out his features in the darkened room. He made a sudden move toward her. Against the dim light filtering in through the windows, she discerned the distinct shape of a hat with a broad brim. She stood transfixed, her legs like jelly, before she willed herself to move. She bolted toward the back exit. Dizzy from the surge of adrenaline, she leaned heavily on the door. Her fingers found the handle and she yanked it open.

Thank God.

She stepped onto the back porch and ran to a nearby crop of trees, trying to determine the best path to make her way around to Eli. Footsteps on the back porch made her blood run cold. She dipped behind a tree and crouched down. *Dear Lord, please protect me.* She squeezed her eyes shut. *Watch over Eli and Katie Mae.*

Silence stretched for what seemed like an eternity. She lifted her head, her rasping breaths joining the cacophony of night critters. An explosion ripped through the night air. She buried her face in her arms. A searing heat whooshed across the back of her neck. Her heart plummeted. *Oh, no.*

Orange flames shot out the windows, consuming the cabin in greedy licks.

An explosion made Eli spin around. Icy dread coursed through his veins when he saw the cabin in a ball of fire. *Anna!*

Katie Mae had flattened herself against a tree, a hand over her mouth. He clutched his sister's arms. "Are you okay?" Katie nodded. The flames reflected in her terror-filled eyes. "Stay here. Don't move. Do you understand?"

Katie Mae nodded.

Breaking into a full run, he approached the front of the cabin. The heat from the fire pushed him back. The bright glow of the flames made the surrounding area black as night. He heaved from the exertion. Adrenaline pumped through his veins. "Anna! Anna!" he screamed.

No answer. The entire woods had turned silent.

Black smoke clogged his lungs. Bending at his waist, he braced his hands on his knees. His pulse thrummed in his ears. He strained to hear. He wanted something—anything—to indicate Anna was okay.

Okay, God. I haven't come to You for much lately, but if You are really out there, I need You now. Don't let me down. Please send Anna safely to me.

The crackling of dried beams split the night air. The cabin was going up like a tinderbox. No way could anyone survive.

Please God.

Panic made his heart race. Frantically, he pointed his flashlight to the black edges of the yard. He strode around to the side of the cabin, searching for an alternate way in. The beam from his flashlight bounced off a side window.

"Anna! Anna!"

Exploding glass made him jump back. The flames licked the edges of the window.

Please God, help Anna escape. Help me find her in time.

Despite the roaring in his ears a calmness descended upon him. He strode around the back of the cabin as if driven by some unseen hand. He had to push aside overgrown shrubs and low tree branches to make his way to the back door.

A twig snapped and he whirled his flashlight around. Anna stepped out from behind a tree, and she held a hand up to block the beam from his flashlight. Relief flooded his system. He pulled her into a fierce embrace. Glancing up, he whispered, "Thank You, God." He leaned back to look at her. The oranges flames glinted in the whites of her eyes. "You are okay, aren't you?"

Anna nodded and buried her face in his chest. "I got out before the explosion. I hid behind a tree."

The taste of charred wood coated his dry mouth. *Thank you.*

"What happened?" He traced her cheek with the pad of his thumb. Tears left tracks on her sooty face.

"There was a man in there." She swiped a hand across her wet cheek. "He ran toward me, but I got around him and escaped out the back door."

Eli ran a protective hand down her arm. "Did he touch you?"

"No." Her fair skin glistened from the heat of the fire.

His eyes drifted toward the inferno. "I didn't notice anyone leaving through the front."

"No, he followed me out the back. That's why I hid." She released a long shaky breath. "Hiding probably spared me getting hurt from the explosion."

"I shouldn't have brought you here." Obviously someone wanted them to stop investigating Mary's disappearance. He couldn't live with losing someone he cared about. *Not again.* The realization nearly knocked the wind out of him.

Anna narrowed her gaze. "I wanted to come with you, remember? I have as much at stake as you do."

Shaking his head, he plucked his cell phone from his back pocket. No signal. *Figures.* "We'll have to hike back to the car and get help. You think you can manage?" Anna took a step, testing her legs. He grabbed her elbow to steady her, his gaze scanning the darkened woods around them. *Katie Mae.* Sweat trickling down between his shoulder blades, he strode as fast as he could, guiding Anna by her elbow. He sent up a silent prayer of thanks when he saw Katie Mae standing exactly where he had left her.

"What happened?" Katie Mae's whisper was barely audible over the crackling of the timber.

"Do you think we should look for a hose? I'd hate for the trees to go up," Anna said.

"No, we wouldn't stand a chance with a hose. I hope the drenching rain we had earlier will buy us time to call the fire department."

Eli held Anna's forearm tightly as they made their way down the path. He kept his flashlight beam pointed ahead, aware of his sister leading the way. The weight of his gun in its holster provided a measure of comfort.

Whoever did this hadn't gone far. They were probably still in the woods nearby. Watching them. If they had been desperate enough to blow up the cabin, they wouldn't hesitate to come after them as they made their way across the rutted path to his vehicle.

A million stars dotted the sky as Eli climbed out of his SUV. He had called the fire department as soon as he had gotten cell phone reception—which happened to be where the car was parked. Then they stopped at the sheriff's station to give a full report. Eli told Katie Mae not to tell their parents about Mary's *kapp*. He didn't want his parents to worry and he didn't want the information to get out. Not yet anyway.

After seeing Anna and Katie Mae safely home, he drove to the closest neighbors with a landline. He didn't have the patience to drive back into town to get cell phone reception. He made a few quick phone calls to work associates in Buffalo, then rushed back to his parents' house, uneasy that he had left Anna out of his sight.

He slipped off his mud-caked shoes at the back door and gave his mother a weary smile.

Mariam looked up from her meal preparations. "She's upstairs cleaning up." His mother answered his unasked question. "Katie Mae told me there was a fire?" Her brow furrowed in confusion.

"It's a long story, *Mem*. But I'm going to take Anna somewhere else to stay. It's too dangerous for her here." His hand instinctively went to his gun. He could protect himself. Now he had to protect Anna. Someone didn't want them to uncover the truth. "I'm afraid staying here isn't a good idea." He glanced around the tidy but plain kitchen, starting to understand how the simple life left room for so much more. His job—his responsibilities—weighed heavily on him. "I can't do that to you and Father. You've already been through so much."

Mariam placed the wooden spoon down on the counter and turned around slowly. "I already spoke with your father. You must stay as long as you are in town." His father would have never extended the offer personally, but his mother's words spoke volumes.

Eli rubbed the back of his neck. He had already called in a few friends from Buffalo to provide extra security. Whether he and Anna stayed here or not, he wanted someone keeping an eye on his parents' property. No one was going to get to his parents' house without raising a red flag.

"Thanks." Eli patted his mother's hand and she met his gaze with a tired smile. "Maybe it would be best if I kept an eye on things here, too. I'm going to check on Anna."

Eli climbed the stairs and stopped outside Anna's bedroom. The soft glow from the lamp flickered through the crack underneath the door. He knocked quietly. He heard a muted shuffling, then saw a shadow under the door. A second later, her clean, pale face shone up at him. Her hair was wrapped in a white towel, and she had on a T-shirt and gray pajama bottoms.

Feeling his face redden—something he wasn't accustomed to—he stepped back. "I'm sorry. I wanted to make sure you were okay."

Anna stepped aside and held out her arm, welcoming him into her room. He crossed over to the window. Under the bright moon, he could see the landscape. The barn loomed as an imposing figure across the yard. Someone had been stalking Anna from its loft. Despite his mother's insistence, maybe staying here wasn't the best idea. Indecision dogged him. He glanced down at his cell phone for the time. His reinforcements should be here soon.

He turned around to face Anna. Something he didn't dare acknowledge stirred in his heart, but he dismissed it as his protective instinct. Nothing more. "I talked to the chief of the fire department. They have the fire contained. He thinks one of the propane tanks on the back porch blew."

Anna nodded but didn't say anything. "There's something I didn't tell you."

Eli narrowed his gaze. She sat on the corner of the bed. "The person I saw…"

"The person in the cabin?"

"Yes." The look in Anna's eyes was tentative. She seemed to be searching for the right words. "I didn't want to say anything in front of Katie Mae, but he's Amish."

A pounding started behind Eli's eyes. He slumped against the windowsill. "Why do you think that?"

Anna pulled the white towel from her head. Her curly hair spilled out around her shoulders, leaving wet spots on her dark-blue T-shirt. "I saw the outline of his—" She touched the crown of her head. "It had a brim, like the hats the Amish wear."

Eli pushed a hand through his hair. "That can't be." Anna met him with an unwavering stare but didn't say anything. "The Amish don't believe in violence. They are conscientious objectors. They never resort to violence." He realized the ridiculousness of this generalization. The Amish were people, too, who made good and bad choices. They had free will, just like everyone else.

"I'm just telling you what I saw," Anna said through gritted teeth.

"Maybe in the confusion…" He stopped arguing when he met her steely gaze of determination.

"The person in the cabin was wearing an Amish hat." She lowered her voice. "Maybe he wanted me to think he was Amish." Narrowing her gaze, she seemed deep in thought. "But I don't think he was expecting me. I surprised him. Maybe I'm grasping at straws, but I think he was looking for something." She scratched absent-mindedly at a red mark on her arm. "Who knew we were going to the cabin?"

"Only Dr. Christopher. Chase's grandfather. I called him. He's a good man. When he was still practicing medicine, he often treated the Amish for little or no fee. He owns the property and I wanted his permission to search it in case we found anything. Otherwise, if we found evidence, we wouldn't be able to use it in a court of law."

"Why would he give his permission?"

Eli shrugged. "I suppose he didn't think we'd find anything."

Anna nodded slowly. "Maybe Dr. Christopher told someone…or someone overheard the conversation."

Eli rubbed his jaw. "Tom Hanson lives with him. I'll talk to him."

Anna stood and crossed to the window. The scent of her hair coiled through him and against his better judgment, he took a step closer. The only indication she was aware of his proximity was the faint blush of pink blossoming up her neck. She stared out the window, her arms hanging loosely at her sides. He reached out and twirled a wet strand of hair around his fingers. Boldly, he cupped her cheek with his other hand and turned her face toward his.

"You scared me today," he whispered, his voice hoarse.

A thin line, barely visible in the flickering glow of the soft light, creased her forehead. He traced the line with his finger, then let it drop to the softness of her cheek. "I reached out to God when I couldn't find you during the fire."

A small smile played on her lips.

He lowered his gaze before lifting it to meet hers. "Sometimes He does answer our prayers."

She blinked slowly as his finger moved down to tilt her chin. Leaning in, he brushed his lips chastely against hers, testing her resolve. He pulled back and studied her face. Her dark lashes rested against her pale cheeks.

Under different circumstances.

Something stirred deep within him. She smelled of lotion and soap. Her freshly scrubbed face had never been more beautiful.

It was Anna who broke the spell swirling around them. She bowed her head, then stepped back from his touch. She crossed her arms over her T-shirt, as if embarrassed. "We're both under a lot of stress." Her clear hazel eyes locked with his. He wanted to tell her it was more than that. That he had started to care for her deeply. But could she ever trust him when he still had doubts about her brother's involvement with Mary's disappearance?

"Anna—"

A rapping at the door startled them. They stepped guiltily apart. "Come in," Anna said, her voice scratchy.

The door creaked open. Abram stood in the doorway, a stern look on his face. He waited for his father's scolding as if he were a teenager again. But the scolding never came. "Two men are downstairs. I believe you called for them."

Anna followed Eli downstairs, her hand skimming the top of the railing. Light-headed, she didn't trust her legs to support her. The sweet sensation from his tender kiss had affected her like no other. Could she be falling for this man? She didn't even want to imagine that complication. Maybe her emotions stemmed more from loneliness now her only family was gone. She hated that needy part of her. She had always been so independent.

Unexpected longing twisted around her heart. Wouldn't it be nice to have someone to rely on? She rubbed her temples. Her thoughts suddenly shifted. Someone to let her down? To hurt her? To leave her?

At the bottom of the stairs, two men dressed in jeans and dark golf shirts greeted Eli. He shook their hands and introduced them to Anna and Abram. Abram didn't appear too welcoming.

"I invited Dominic and William to help me keep an eye on things," Eli said, his gaze trained on his father.

Abram hiked his chin. "We have had enough of the outside world to last us a lifetime." Cutting his gaze toward his son, he continued, "This is my home. You should have asked before you invited these men here."

Eli stared resolutely at his father. "You would have said no."

"Then I think you'd understand why I find this disrespectful. You have never respected our ways. You made that abundantly clear when you left Apple Creek. You can continue your way of life but not under my roof. If you ever decide to join us fully in baptism, we will welcome you with open arms." Abram's tone was sharp, angry. Although he had always been stern, Anna had never heard him raise his voice. Out of the corner of her eye, she noticed Eli wince.

"Father, I respect your position. However, Dominic and William are with a private security firm. I have hired them to patrol the premises until we can figure out who has been trying to hurt Anna." Eli slid his hand across the small of her back. She resisted the urge to lean into him, to find strength in him. "I promise you they will not interfere with your way of life." Eli seemed to pick his words carefully.

Abram's mouth flattened into a grim line and his shoulders shifted. It seemed as though he might walk away without saying anything more. She sensed this was how Eli's father dealt with his rebel son. Guilt and silence. Didn't these men know they were the only family they'd ever have?

It was then that Mariam stepped into the foyer. "I have trust in God to protect my family. I also trust Eli knows what's best in this situation." She looked at her husband, pleading with her eyes. "If he deems it's necessary to have these two men here as extra eyes and ears against the evil that is out there, I ask you to please reconsider, Abram." Anna detected fear in Mariam's voice.

"The small bedroom near the back of the house is available for when they need to rest. It's not much, but it has a cot." Abram turned and walked away.

"Thanks," Eli called after his father. Lowering his voice, he added, "I respect your home, *Mem*. Dominic and William will rotate rounds. I want to make sure my family is safe."

Anna's heart tightened in her chest from a twinge of

jealousy. Even though he was estranged from them, he still had a family to protect.

Mariam retreated to the back of the house to join her husband. Mariam had effectively gotten her way while still deferring to her husband. Anna hung back, her arms crossed over her T-shirt, suddenly feeling very conspicuous, as Eli walked outside with Dominic and William. But curiosity got the best of her. She stepped out onto the porch and listened to the men talk. It was decided they would both watch the property but then alternate shifts when they got tired.

Clutching the hem of her shirt, she scanned the darkened yard. Was someone out there now? Watching? An idea slammed into her and she found herself forcing her shoulders back. Her comment would have to wait. She didn't know these two new men and didn't want to share her thoughts in front of them.

A horse neighed loudly near the road. Squinting, Anna made out the outline of a wagon turning toward the house. The Amish man hopped off and Anna tracked his movements as he strode toward them. The image from the cabin of a man—Amish hat perched on his head—solidified in her imagination. Should she be suspicious of all Amish men? The idea seemed preposterous. There must be hundreds of men in this community alone who wore these wide-brimmed hats.

She found herself stepping back, ready to retreat into the house. She glanced at the three strong men standing next to her, guns strapped to their bodies. If she couldn't feel safe now, would she ever? Maybe if she went home...? Away from whatever danger lurked here in Apple Creek.

She couldn't run forever.

Dominic was the first to come down the steps, one hand hovering over the handle of his gun. Anna's heart jackhammered in her chest. Eli seemed to shift, blocking her view, a protective gesture. "Hold up, there," Dominic said in a deep voice, one that commanded authority.

"What's this all about?" Anna recognized the male voice. She peered around Eli to see Isaac leaning casually on the post at the bottom of the steps. "Something else going on I don't know about?" A look of amusement graced his narrow face as the corners of his mouth quirked into a grin.

"Isaac, we have a lot going on here. Maybe you can pay a social visit to my sister another time." Eli crossed his arms over his broad chest.

Isaac cocked his head in obvious confusion. "Samuel came running over and left a message with *Mem* about some kind of accident. That Katie Mae was shaken up. You can't tell me I can't see Katie Mae."

A muscle worked in Eli's jaw, but Anna doubted Isaac noticed. He seemed to be filled with more self-confidence than the other Amish men she had met in the community. Maybe his hubris stemmed from his experience in the outside world. Worldliness the other Amish men lacked. Worldliness he'd have to lose if he wanted to fit in with these humble people.

A niggling tugged at the base of Anna's brain. She prayed Katie Mae came to her senses before she settled down with Isaac. Surely there was someone better suited for her.

Eli glanced toward the house, then stepped aside. "I'll tell Katie Mae you're here." Apparently this was not a battle he wanted to take on.

Dominic and William brushed past Isaac and strode

toward their vehicles, out of place on this farm time had forgotten. Presumably they were going to devise a plan on how to protect the Millers' home—and her. A sour taste made her flinch. Her gaze drifted to the cornfields across the road, but all she could see was darkness.

"So," Isaac said in a lazy lilt, "I hear the Christophers' cabin went up in ball of fire." His lips tugged down at the corners, but his eyes seemed bright, intrigued. "You narrowly escaped?"

Anna regarded him quietly, her eyes moving to his hat. Anger bubbled up quite unexpectedly. "What do you know about it?"

Isaac frowned and cupped his hands over his chest as if he were offended. "Only what Samuel shared with me. He said you almost got blown up while Katie Mae and Eli were outside."

The memory of the flames licking at the back of her neck made the fine hairs stand on edge. "I'm all right now. Thanks for asking." She hated the bristle in her voice. Maybe this was Isaac's way. He reminded her of a bored gossip.

A moment later, Eli returned, holding open the screen door. "Katie Mae's in the kitchen."

Isaac tipped his hat at Anna, then went inside. Anna rubbed her arms, trying to dispel the coolness of the evening. "Do you think…"

"What?" Eli pressed.

"Do you think Katie Mae will be happy with Isaac? She seems so innocent and he's… I can't put my finger on it."

Eli's eyes shimmered in the moonlight and a deep rumble of laughter filled the night air. She couldn't help but giggle in response. The day's events had made her punchy. "What's so funny?" Her cheeks grew warm.

"He's always rubbed me the wrong way, too. I figured I was being the overprotective big brother." Eli playfully ran the palm of his hand along her forearm, her flesh tingling under his touch.

She shrugged. "He unnerves me." She lowered her voice to barely a whisper. "What's his story?"

"You already know he's been courting Katie Mae for almost a year now. I imagine sometime soon they'll be publishing their engagement." His tone was solemn. She supposed it frustrated him he had little say in what happened in his sister's world.

"He seems much older than she."

"He is. He's my age. He left the Amish way of life for a few years. Came back I'd say eighteen months ago." Eli took Anna's hand and led her to one of the straight-back chairs on the porch. She slowly sat down, the cool wood chilly through her thin pajama bottoms.

"And he was welcomed back? Just like that?" Anna snapped her fingers. "I thought the Amish were strict."

"Oh, they are." Eli ran his palms along the smooth arms of the chair. "But if you repent, if you ask for forgiveness, they will welcome you back. Haven't you been listening to my parents? They lay the guilt on thick, hoping eventually their methods will wear me out. That I'll return and be baptized." He leaned toward her. She smelled the subtle mix of charred wood and his after-shave. Her stomach did a little flip-flop at his proximity. "A family welcomes back a wayward son, relieved he now has a shot at eternal salvation."

"Has a shot?"

"Ah, the Amish do not assume salvation is guaranteed. They are a humble people. But the best chance of going to heaven is living a good life within the rules of the Amish church or the Ordnung."

"Did you really reach out to God today?" Anna asked, keeping her gaze trained on the darkened yard.

"Yes." Eli let out a long breath. "Maybe you can teach an old dog new tricks." She detected a smile in his voice.

Closing her eyes, she pushed her feet against the wood planks, making the chair move in a subtle back and forth motion. Was her faith as strong as she proclaimed? Had she truly trusted God to lead her through this troubled time? Where did she stand when it came to eternal life?

What if I had met my Maker today in the explosion?

Chapter Fourteen

The next morning, Anna got up early, unable to sleep. She rolled out of bed and pulled back the curtain. Orange and pink streaked the country sky, promising a beautiful day—at least in the weather department. Her burdensome worries already weighed her down.

Trust God.

She sat down on the edge of her bed and shrugged, shaking off the chill of the early morning. Footsteps and clattering dishes indicated the Miller women were up and preparing for the day. A twinge of shame jabbed her. She felt lazy stretching and wiping the sleep out of her eyes. She missed her quiet apartment. The solitude in the morning. The time to pull herself together before she had to face other people.

She wished she had the freedom to go for a morning run, but she knew that was out of the question. It wasn't safe and besides, she needed to rest after her concussion. She smoothed a hand over her mussed hair. Would returning to Buffalo be an end to her troubles? Wasn't that what someone wanted? For her to go home and stop pushing this investigation?

Yet Eli would continue to push.

She did have to return to her job in Buffalo. Her students were counting on her, and they were approaching the end of the first marking quarter. She sighed heavily, wondering what had happened to the bonnet in the photo. Dread snaked its way through her body. She pushed back her shoulders in quiet determination. She had to stick it out a few more days and help Eli clear her brother's name, realizing Eli's goal was not necessarily to clear her brother's name, but to find his sister's kidnapper.

Getting down on her knees and resting her elbows on the quilt, she closed her eyes and tried again. *Dear Lord, help me do right by my brother. Please bring closure for the Miller family. May they find peace in knowing what happened to their dear Mary. I will work hard to trust Your plan. Amen.*

Anna swiped at a tear trailing down her cheek. She pushed to her feet. A thin rim of orange peaked over the trees in the distance. She watched silently as the sun rose higher in the sky. Grabbing jeans and a T-shirt out of her suitcase, she tiptoed to the bathroom to get ready for the day. She ran a brush through her wet hair, then checked her face in the mirror. She looked pale without her makeup but otherwise fine. She smoothed balm on her lips and headed downstairs.

She found Katie Mae cooking at the kitchen stove. "Morning," Anna said.

Katie Mae looked up with a pinched expression on her face. Without saying a word, she gave Anna her back and returned to stirring something on the stove. The curt greeting left Anna unsettled. She glanced out the window. In the driveway sat one of the cars of the men who had arrived to protect her. She figured he couldn't be far.

"Isaac thinks it's time you left." Katie Mae's quiet, angry words cut through the silence.

Anna turned around and found Eli's little sister glaring at her. The oatmeal from her spoon plopped onto the hardwood floor. "Your parents invited me to stay." She understood Katie Mae's concern but couldn't figure out why she had turned on her overnight. Maybe the explosion at the cabin had profoundly affected her.

Katie Mae frowned and tossed the spoon into the pot, then stepped toward Anna. She spoke in a hushed voice. "That is their way. They don't like confrontation." Katie pointed at one of the men, now leaning on his vehicle. "You have brought these men here who are patrolling our peaceful farm." She lowered her eyes. "We all could have been killed in the explosion."

"I'm sorry." Anna rubbed her temples. The first hint of a headache scraped across her brain. "I wish I knew who was behind this."

"Isaac thinks things would go back to normal if you went away."

A fire grew in her chest. "What do *you* think, Katie Mae?"

Katie Mae looked Anna in the eyes, the spark no longer there. "Isaac says your brother took our Mary. He doesn't understand why Eli doesn't declare the case closed now that your brother's gone."

Katie Mae's words pierced her heart like a dagger. "What do you think?" Anna repeated, this time more softly.

The girl crossed to the kitchen table, pulled out a chair and dropped down. She fingered the strings on her bonnet, then folded her hands in her lap. After what appeared to be an internal struggle, Eli's sister looked up at her, an apology in her eyes. "I like you, Anna. You are good for my brother... I was so scared yesterday."

Anna sat across from Katie Mae. "You and me both."

"Eli is driven. He won't rest until he finds out what happened to Mary." The young woman bowed her head. "I am more like my parents. I have forgiven whoever did this. I want to move forward." A tiny smile graced Katie Mae's pale lips. "I don't believe your brother had anything to do with my Mary. He's your family and if he was anything like you, it's not possible. You are so kind."

Anna's heart felt full. "Thank you."

"Besides, that would just complicate things between you and *my* brother." Katie Mae's chin dipped down. "I see how he looks at you."

Nerves tangled in Anna's belly. "Eli and I have bigger concerns than worrying about our relationship." A quiet laugh escaped her lips. "The only relationship we have is to find out what my brother was doing in Apple Creek." She reached across and touched Katie Mae's hand. "You were nine when Mary disappeared?"

Katie Mae nodded, pulling her hand away from Anna's and folding them in her lap. "Oh, Mary loved Eli. Tagged along with him everywhere."

"I felt the same way about my brother." She fought the threatening tears. "I have to believe he's innocent."

Katie Mae smiled, a tenderness touching her eyes. "I hope you find what you're looking for."

Heavy footsteps on the back porch drew their attention. Katie Mae jumped to her feet and started stirring the oatmeal. "The men will be coming in from their morning chores for breakfast."

Anna stood. "Can I help you?"

A small smile flitted at the corners of Katie Mae's

mouth. She gestured with her elbow to the fruit sitting on the counter. "Can you cut the cantaloupe?"

Anna picked up the sharp knife and cut through the melon on the wood cutting board. She was surprised to see Eli stroll in, sweat glistening off his forehead. She had assumed he was still in bed. Hay stuck to his T-shirt. A few tufts of hair stood up. Warmth blossomed in her chest, and Katie Mae's words floated back to her: *I see the way he looks at you.*

"You got up early." She returned her attention to slicing the melon.

"Thought I'd get my morning workout in and help with chores. Kill two birds with one stone." His voice sounded husky this morning.

Her heart fluttered and heat warmed her face. She focused intently on cutting the fruit into small slices. Samuel stomped in behind his older brother. He tossed his hat on a hook by the door. Katie Mae made a shooing gesture. "Go clean up for breakfast."

Eli passed by, brushing his hand gently across her arm. She froze with the knife poised above the fruit, trying to quell her rioting emotions. She looked up to find Katie Mae staring, her mouth sloped in an I-told-you-so expression.

Anna's face was on fire. Things had gotten far too complicated in this supposedly simple world.

Eli plunked down at the breakfast table—in the same seat he had sat in as a child. He glanced up to find two sets of expectant eyes on him. He had the niggling sense he had walked in on a conversation he wasn't supposed to hear. Katie Mae had a faint smile on her lips. She filled a coffee mug and handed it to Anna. "I believe Eli likes his coffee black."

Eli bit back a smile of his own when he noticed Anna's confused look. She cut a sideways glance to his sister, who then nudged her gently toward Eli. Anna gave a slow nod in understanding, then walked over and set the coffee mug down, the ceramic clanking against the pine table, the dark contents swishing out the sides. She lifted a perfectly groomed brow. "Don't get used to this," she said, barely above a whisper. A twinkle lit her eye.

He reached out and brushed his hand across hers. "Oh, I could."

Leaning close so her long curls brushed his shoulder, she whispered close to his ear. "You live in the English world now, buddy."

He reached up and gently yanked on a curl, releasing the fresh coconut scent of her shampoo. Her hazel eyes widened and she stepped back, her hair slipping out of his fingers. He winked at her. He woke up this morning so incredibly grateful that Anna hadn't been hurt—or worse—yesterday in the fire. Now, he wondered more than ever if, after this mess was cleared up, they had a shot at getting to know one another better. It seemed like the fates had a horrible sense of humor if they conspired for him to fall for Anna.

The fates? A quiet voice whispered across his brain. *Perhaps you should put more faith in God.*

A pounding at the front door snapped him out of his reverie. He pushed back from the table and held out a protective arm to stop Anna and his sister. "Let me get it." Ignoring him, Anna followed him to the front door, where they found the sheriff. Dominic, one of the security guards, stood nearby at the bottom of the porch steps.

"What's going on, Sheriff?" Eli asked. Anna slipped her hand around the bend of his arm.

The sheriff focused his narrowed eyes on Anna. "We need to talk to her."

"About what?" Eli covered Anna's hand and squeezed.

"It seems the fire at the Christopher cabin was arson."

Anna straightened her back. "I already told you I saw someone in the cabin before the explosion."

The sheriff tipped his hat. "Are you sticking to your story?"

"I—" Anna started to protest when Eli squeezed her hand in a gentle warning.

"Is Anna in some kind of trouble? Does she need a lawyer?" Eli recognized a fishing expedition. He didn't understand the sheriff's angle. This went beyond the usual turf war between locals and the FBI.

The sheriff took the slightest step back, indicating he wasn't ready to make an arrest. "You might want to call yourself a lawyer, Miss Quinn."

A quiet gasp escaped her lips. "It's okay," Eli whispered.

The sheriff reached into his pocket and pulled out a plastic bag. Inside was a gold item. Anna reached for it with a shaky hand, but the sheriff pulled back the bag. "You recognize this, Miss Quinn?"

Anna looked up at Eli, helplessness reflected in her eyes. "It's my mother's lighter."

"Any idea how your mother's lighter ended up in the charred ruins of the Christopher cabin?"

Eli spoke first. "Anna did *not* set that fire. I was there. She barely escaped the explosion when the propane tank went." The memory of the fireball twisted his insides. "No way."

The sheriff tipped his head. "Are you sure? How well do you know her?"

Eli didn't like the way he said the word *her*. "I know Anna Quinn well enough. She'd have no reason…" A hint of doubt whispered across his brain. *To protect her brother. To destroy any possible evidence in the cabin?* But risk her own life? She had already escaped out the back of the cabin.

"No way," he repeated.

The sheriff stuffed the lighter in his pocket. "We got a solid print off the lighter. I've contacted the State Department of Education." He smiled smugly at Anna. "I'm checking to see if your employment fingerprints are still on file."

"But…" Anna seemed to struggle to find words. "I saw a man with an Amish hat run out the back of the cabin before it exploded."

"Convenient. You know how many men around here are Amish?" The sheriff turned on his heel and walked down the steps. "Besides, they sell those hats down at the general store. *If* you actually saw someone else there."

Anna's face grew ashen white. "Why would I blow up a cabin?" She threaded her fingers through the ends of her hair. "My hair got singed. Why would I almost kill myself in the process?"

The sheriff turned around. "To hide evidence that proves your brother kidnapped and murdered Mary Miller."

Eli swallowed back his revulsion. "What are you talking about?"

"Isaac told us about the photos of Mary's bonnet. He

also said you were alone in the cabin before it went up."
The sheriff cocked an eyebrow.

Eli gritted his teeth. A cold rage welled up inside him.
Katie Mae must have fed Isaac all sorts of information.
"I think Anna knows more than she's letting on."

"No, that's—" Anna started to protest and Eli held
up his hand to stop her.

"Sheriff, I was there. Anna did not start the fire."
He tried to tamp his anger simmering under the surface. "Don't bother coming back here unless you have
an arrest warrant." Eli wrapped his arm around Anna's
shoulder and pulled her close.

"Trust me, I will," the sheriff hollered over his shoulder. "I told you the Quinns were nothing but bad eggs. If
I were a betting man, I'd say she knows what her brother
hid up there at the cabin and destroyed the evidence before we had a chance to find it."

The sheriff strolled over to his cruiser and climbed
in. He made a show of taking a few notes before turning his vehicle around and leaving. Anna sagged against
him. He ran his hand down the length of her arm. "Don't
worry. He's full of bluster." He forced a smile in a display of levity he didn't feel.

How well do I know Anna?

As if reading his doubts, Anna slipped away from him
and dropped into the rocker on the porch. She slumped
against its hard back. He crossed to her and leaned back
against the rail. She looked up, steely resolve mixed with
something he couldn't quite name glistening in her eyes.
"My fingerprints are on that lighter."

Eli narrowed his gaze. "There are probably a million fingerprints on it. How long ago did your mother
pass away?"

"No, you don't understand. I touched it recently."

* * *

Anna's heart beat wildly as Eli parked his SUV in front of Daniel's garage apartment. The last time she had seen her mother's lighter was at Daniel's place a few days ago. Someone must have come in after them and taken the lighter from the table next to his couch.

Tom Hanson met them in the driveway. Eli slammed the car door shut and towered over Tom. "Anyone else stop by? Who else has a key to this apartment?"

Tom lowered his eyes, then quickly glanced toward the street. "I have another one on the key ring. And the last renter never returned the key when he moved out." He shrugged. "Who knows how many keys are floating around out there? It's not like we have a high crime rate. Most people don't even lock their doors around here."

"I locked it after Anna and I left. You go back in there?"

"No and as far as I know, no one else has." He shook his head to reinforce his answer. The tips of Anna's fingers tingled.

"What about the back door leading from the apartment directly to the inside of the garage?" A muscle twitched in Eli's jaw.

"No one uses that door." Tom pulled a rag out of his back pocket and wiped his hands.

"Are you afraid of something, Tom?" Eli crossed his arms and stepped toward the man.

Tom's eyes grew wide. "Of course I'm not afraid of anything. I have it pretty good around here. Living in grandpa's house. I don't need any trouble from you."

"We're not looking to cause trouble."

Tom nodded. There was something about him. He

seemed…fearful. "I got nothing to hide. I have a good job. Don't go stirring the pot."

Eli clapped Tom on the shoulder. "Okay, well, we'll lock up when we leave. You'll let me know if anyone else comes around?"

Tom nodded again. "Grab Daniel's stuff while you're here. My aunt Beth has been on the warpath. She wants it all gone."

"We know, the sheriff told us."

"Sorry about that." Tom looked genuinely contrite. "The Christophers are used to getting their way." A gruff laugh escaped his lips. "I don't want to give her a reason to kick me to the curb. I like my job."

Anna swallowed a lump in her throat. "We've had a lot going on. Give me a few days and I'll get his stuff." Her gaze traveled to the staircase. "The furniture came with the apartment?"

"Yes, most of it anyway. You have to remove his personal stuff. You know, his clothes in the drawers and maybe throw out whatever you don't want. I'd feel bad going through his stuff. Your brother was a good guy." Tom frowned, as if giving it thoughtful consideration. "I mean, the few times I saw him."

"I'll do that. Do you know where I can get some boxes?"

Tom's face brightened, as if he were eager to please. "There are some in the basement." He turned and started toward the house. "I'll get them for you."

Eli and Anna climbed the steps to the garage apartment. Now that the initial shock of her brother's death had worn off, she was struck by how sparse his living conditions had been. One of the few personal items he had was the framed photo of the two of them. This time she picked it up and dropped it into her purse. She pushed a strand of hair behind her ears. "I wish I hadn't lost contact with Daniel. Maybe things would be different now."

Eli searched each drawer of the desk. "Don't beat yourself up."

Anna nodded. If anyone understood regrets, it was Eli.

He closed the last drawer. "Where did you see the lighter?"

"Over there." She pointed to the end table next to the couch. All but one cushion was still on the floor. She recognized the table as one that used to sit in their childhood family room. It had seemed out of place even then in her parents' perfectly maintained home. She ran her fingers along the edge. "The lighter was sitting on this table. My mom always kept it next to the couch." She clenched her hands. "One of her vices. Besides my father." She bit out the last words.

Her eyes dropped to the lip of the table. The marble top was removable. Anna and Daniel used to hide papers and tiny items in the small space between the marble and the wood frame. She removed the lamp from the table and set it on the floor. Wedging her small fingers between the marble and wood, she worked it up. Eli slipped in next to her and lifted the heavy marble.

White fabric in a plastic bag stood out in stark contrast to the dark maple wood. White dots danced in her line of vision. Glancing over her shoulder, she found Eli staring in disbelief. Sliding in next to her, he scooped up the bag and turned it over in his hands. Moving as if in a trance, he dropped down on to the couch. The cushion released a spray of dust that hung in the stream of sunlight shining in through dirty windows. Anna dropped to her knees in front of him and slid her hands under his. "Mary's bonnet?"

He nodded. Through the bag he thumbed the pale gray stitching against the white garment. "She was learning to sew." A muscle in his jaw twitched. The rims of his eyes grew red.

A buzzing started in her head. "How did it get in there?"

Eli took Anna's hands in his, moved her aside and stood up. She narrowed her gaze, trying to read his emotions. He paced the small space. "Daniel must have found her *kapp* and didn't know how to come forward with it. He had to know the initials embroidered on it stood for Mary Miller. But why didn't he show it to me when I met him?" His hands curled into fists.

"Maybe he was afraid he'd look guilty. Remember how paranoid he was? He wanted time to figure out who hurt Mary." It was the only thing that made sense right from the beginning.

Eli plowed a hand through his hair and stopped pacing, turning to face Anna. "Let's go pay another visit to Tiffany. Maybe she's up for talking longer. Maybe Daniel confided in her after all."

"Wait." Anna held out her hand. "Are you okay?"

Eli glanced down at the *kapp*. He couldn't believe he held it in his hand. He remembered the day Mary had proudly sewn the string back on after she tore it climbing the back fence. His chest tightened. "This is the first solid clue I've had in Mary's disappearance."

"Do you think my brother had something to do with it?"

The pleading look in her eyes toyed with his rioting

emotions. "Sit down." Tears gathered in the corners of her eyes as she sat down on the couch and he sat on the corner of the coffee table. Their knees brushed briefly before she angled them away.

"I don't know."

A tear escaped and slid down her cheek. Anna's shoulders visibly sagged. She lowered her eyes, her long lashes brushing against her fair skin. He struggled to catch a decent breath. Reaching out, he captured her hands when it looked like she wanted to flee. "Hear me out." Her eyes grew hard and locked with his, challenging him. "Your brother knew *something*. I don't know if he uncovered it because of the photos he was taking. Perhaps he stumbled onto something and didn't know who to trust. It's obvious the sheriff is protective of the Christopher family. And his own son."

Anna pulled her hands out of his grasp and crossed her arms over her chest. Her thin frame shuddered. "Or—" he ran a hand across his jaw, regretting the pain he was causing her "—he had firsthand knowledge of what happened to my sister and he came back to Apple Creek to set things right. He wanted to make sure he rounded up all the players so everyone involved would be punished." He held out Mary's *kapp. Poor sweet Mary.* "I can't figure out how he found this in the first place."

All the color drained from Anna's face. "You're right, we should talk to Tiffany again."

Eli glanced down at the *kapp* and ran his hand across the plastic bag protecting it. "I should probably contact my office, let them know what we have."

"What about the sheriff?"

Eli knew Anna didn't like the sheriff any more than he did.

He thought of Abram and Mariam, whose hearts would be torn anew when they learned what they had found. He ran a hand across the back of his neck. Wasn't this what he had worked for all these years? Too many unanswered questions remained. He wanted to be the one to tell his parents.

He stood and offered his hand to Anna. "The sheriff can wait. Let's talk to Tiffany."

Before they reached the hospital, Eli called his contact at the hospital to make sure Tiffany didn't have any visitors. Even with the reassurance she was alone, Anna's nerve endings hummed to life. The last thing she wanted was a run-in with someone from the Christopher family.

Tiffany's condition had improved, so she had been moved out of ICU. When they reached her room, they found her sitting up in bed chatting on her cell phone. When Tiffany noticed them, she froze. "I have to go," she said into the phone, then pulled it away from her ear. She held the cell phone between her palms and stared at them.

"Hi, Tiffany." Anna stood tentatively in the doorway. Tiffany waved, the beginning of a smile on her pale lips. "How are you feeling?"

The young girl raised her bandaged arm. "Besides my broken arm and leg? I'll survive. I think they're sending me home soon, but I'm going to require help getting around."

"I imagine your family—"

Tiffany waved her hand, cutting her off. "My family can afford to hire a nurse to help me. They don't want anything to cut into their lunch and shopping time."

Anna suddenly felt sorry for Tiffany. She wanted to

reassure her that her parents cared, then she thought of her own parents. Her mother cared, but not enough to get herself and her family out of harm's way. Something pinged her conscience. Was it really fair to blame her mother? Her father had a hold on her. She had been trapped.

"We wanted to talk to you again about your time with Daniel," Eli said.

Tiffany looked up, tears welling in her blue eyes. "I don't know what to tell you."

"You said Daniel was fascinated with the Mary Miller case. What *exactly* did he say?" Anna wrapped her hands around the cool metal of the bedside rail.

Tiffany stopped fingering the edge of her bedspread and glanced over, meeting Anna's gaze. "Why?" She lowered her voice. "Did he actually find something?"

"What was he looking for, Tiffany?" Eli asked. "Don't let his death be in vain."

Tiffany's eyes widened. "What do you mean?" Her brows furrowed. "You're scaring me."

Eli looked at Anna, as if asking for permission. "We have reason to believe the plane was sabotaged."

The color of Tiffany's face matched the crisp white hospital linens. With a shaky hand she clutched the sheet to her chest. "I was on that plane." Her eyes moved rapidly, as if she was remembering something. "In the final minutes he was scrambling to keep it in the air. He was rambling that someone messed with the plane. He was in a panic."

Anna's gut tightened. "Did Daniel ever tell you he suspected someone was out to get him?" She hated to ask, knowing it made her brother sound unstable.

Tiffany pulled her hair back off her face but didn't say anything.

"Please, Tiffany, if you know anything..." Anna urged.

Tiffany worked her bottom lip. "Daniel told me he thought my brother and a few other guys at the fraternity had something to do with the little Amish girl's disappearance." The way she referred to Mary seemed impersonal. Tiffany must have realized it because her attention darted toward the door, then to Eli. "He was obsessed with your sister's disappearance."

"What made him suspect his fraternity brothers?" Eli's voice sounded even, unaffected.

"He heard them arguing the night your sister went missing."

"You didn't believe him?" Anna's knees grew weak. She dropped into the vinyl chair next to the bed. Eli touched her shoulder.

Tiffany shrugged. "I didn't. I'm sorry I didn't tell you everything before. My brother can be a jerk...but hurt a child?" She brushed a tear from her cheek. "Chase has two young boys of his own. I didn't want to cause trouble for him. Some of Daniel's ideas seemed so out there."

"Did he tell you what he overheard?" Eli squeezed Anna's shoulder.

"After the guys in the fraternity argued, he said they went up to my grandfather's cabin. Daniel didn't go with them." She twisted her lips. "Daniel was obsessed with searching the place, but if he found anything he never told me." Her brow furrowed. She lowered her voice. "*Did* he find something?"

Eli and Anna locked gazes. Anna leaned forward and touched Tiffany's hand, but Eli was the first to speak.

"For your own protection, I don't want to tell you anything more than you already know. Do you still have my business card?" Tiffany nodded slowly. "Don't tell your family we were here. But if you hear anything else, will you let me know?"

Fear etched lines around Tiffany's eyes. "Did Chase hurt your little sister?"

"I don't know."

"Will you find out?" Tiffany asked, a hard set to her pale blue eyes. "My mother always made excuses for him. If he was involved, maybe once in his life, he'll have to take responsibility for it."

Eli nodded. "Rest. Call me if you need anything."

As they walked down the hospital corridor, Anna turned to Eli. "How do we prove Chase was involved?"

"We still need to connect the pieces. It's a long shot, but I'm going to send Mary's *kapp* to FBI forensics. Maybe they can get some DNA from it. Meanwhile, I can track down the fraternity brothers. If they know we found evidence, maybe one of them will crack. It's only a theory. But it's the best one we have."

Eli reached out and took Anna's hand. Her heart went out to him. "There's one more thing."

Her limbs suddenly felt heavy. "What?"

"You need to leave Apple Creek."

"I want to help you. Clear my brother's name. And I still have to clean out his things from the apartment."

The fight was draining from her. They had argued about this a million times before, it seemed. She dragged a hand through her hair. "Maybe it's time I went home and put my brother to rest. Maybe this will give me some sense of peace so I can return later and deal with his things." She looked up and met his gaze. "Promise me you'll be fair, no matter what you discover."

"I promise." He squeezed her hand. "Thank you."

Eli sat at his parents' kitchen table while Mariam stood at the sink nervously wringing her hands. She obviously sensed this visit was like no other. Samuel had been sent out to the field to get their father. Katie Mae sat across from him while Anna went upstairs to pack her things. Because Mary's *kapp* had been found in Daniel's possession, Anna claimed she wasn't comfortable joining them when he broke the news.

A cold knot fisted his gut. The only moment Eli dreaded more than this one was when he had to face his parents for the first time after Mary's disappearance. He exhaled sharply and bowed his head. *God, please give me the words to tell my parents.*

A quiet calm settled over him. He opened his eyes and looked around the neat space. His parents were God-fearing. They didn't deserve any of this. *Who did?*

"What's this about?" Mariam asked for the second time since they had arrived. She leaned against the stove and fiddled with the folds in her apron.

Eli stood and reached for his mother's hand. She took it tentatively and he guided her to a seat. "Let's wait for *Dat*."

Mariam's gaze drifted to Mary's empty seat. She ran her fingers along the smooth pine of the long table, her eyes filling with worry. He'd do anything to take this pain from his mother.

Heavy footsteps sounded on the back porch. In unison, everyone's attention swung to the back door. First Samuel appeared in the doorway. He hung his hat on the hook, then walked over and stood by the counter. He seemed reluctant to sit down. Then his father strode through the door. Abram's eyes grew wide, then he seemed to catch himself. He slowed, taking in the scene in front of him.

It was Mariam who spoke first. "Sit, Abram. Eli has news."

Abram wore a mask of stone. He took off his hat and hung it next to Samuel's on the hook by the door. He strolled over to where they had gathered and pulled out his seat, the chair legs scrapping across the floor. Everything seemed to play out in slow motion.

When his father finally sat, Eli slipped the clear plastic bag with Mary's *kapp* from Anna's bag resting against his chair. He pushed it toward his father and mother. A quiet gasp escaped his mother's lips. She pressed a trembling hand to her mouth. The hurt in his mother's eyes tore at his heart.

His father's lower lip quivered. He reached out and ran a wrinkled hand across the bag. "It is a child's *kapp*." His voice lifted in a slight lilt, but there was no doubt in his eyes.

Eli nodded. "We found it today."

"It's Mary's." His mother's words came out in a painful sob. Tears burned the back of Eli's eyes. "And Mary?" The hope in his mother's face was too much to bear. "Did you find our sweet Mary?"

Eli struggled to find the right words. "I didn't find Mary."

Abram pushed back and stood. He slapped his palm on the table, his body shaking with rage. "Why do you bring this here and say it's Mary's? It could be any child's."

Mariam reached for the bag and pulled it toward her. "It is Mary's." Through the bag she traced the ragged gray stitching his little sister had taken great care with. And the initials his sister had stitched.

Abram picked up the chair and slammed the four legs down with one loud thud. "We must have faith in God. It is a fool's errand to keep after this ten years later. We must forgive and move on." Fear blended with his anger.

Katie Mae found her voice, albeit soft and tremulous. "Where did you find this?"

Eli stared at the white garment. "In Daniel Quinn's apartment."

"Anna's brother hurt our Mary?" Katie Mae's voice rose into a near screech. "Daniel was here. On our farm. Taking photographs." Covering her face with her hands, she crumpled into soft sobs.

"I'm trying to figure it out." Eli glanced toward the kitchen door, wondering if Anna could hear the conversation. "Anna is upstairs packing her things. I've arranged for Dominic to take her home. It will be better for everyone."

Mariam folded her hands on top of the table. "We must have forgiveness in our hearts. We cannot blame her for her brother's actions. She is hurting now." The Amish's ability to forgive was remarkable.

"*Mem,* she needs to go." Eli rose and turned to find Anna standing in the doorway with her suitcase in hand. Pink rimmed her hazel eyes.

Katie Mae stood and approached Anna, her hands twisted in the folds of her dress. "I forgive your brother."

Anna's eyes grew wide and filled with tears. Her mouth opened, then snapped shut. Her knuckles whitened on the handle of the suitcase. "I'm sorry about

Mary. But I don't believe my brother did this. I think he was trying to help solve the case because he suspected—"

Eli gave her a curt nod, indicating he didn't want her to say anymore.

Anna covered her mouth. "I am so sorry for your loss."

Mariam sat at the table and nodded, a single tear trailing down her cheek. Abram stood silently in the corner. Both of his parents seemed transfixed by the child's *kapp* in the center of the table.

Anna crossed the kitchen and stopped by the door, her back to them. Her shoulders rose and fell, her chestnut brown curls flowing down her back. Slowly, she turned around. "I know my brother could have never hurt your child." She hiked her chin and drew in a shuddering breath. "I will keep you all in my prayers."

She turned and left. The screen door closed with a resounding thwack. Eli forced himself to stay seated for a moment longer, knowing Dominic would keep her safe until he could go to her. For now, he had to be here for his family.

Anna stepped onto the porch, and the cool evening air hit her fiery cheeks. The whisper of doubt regarding her brother was going to kill her. How could she move forward if they never found the truth? Yet she knew Eli was right. She had to leave town for now. She took some consolation in knowing she'd return to her high school students. Her mind needed the distraction.

And finally, she could inter Daniel's ashes next to their mother's. She bit her lower lip and pushed the thought aside.

Filling her lungs with the fresh country air, she crossed the yard. She'd miss this place. Dominic opened the back door of his black SUV and Anna tossed her bag in. Her car was still at the shop getting the window replaced. She figured the car was ready, but Eli insisted she ride with—she flicked a glance at her chauffeur's bulging biceps—the Hulk. Eli said he'd have someone drop her car off at her house in Buffalo in a few days. She held on to the small hope that *someone* would be Eli.

As she walked around to the passenger side, she heard Eli calling her name. She turned to see him jogging down the steps and across the lawn. Her mood buoyed.

Dominic climbed into the car and closed the door, presumably to give them privacy. Eli took Anna's hands in his. "I'll keep you posted."

Pursing her lips, she nodded. "I hope you find the truth. I need to know my brother's innocent."

Eli squeezed her hands but didn't say anything. Not exactly a ringing endorsement for her brother's innocence. "It was great to meet you. I wish it had been under better circumstances." His words seemed stilted.

"Is this goodbye?"

"I want to know you're safe. I know Dominic will take care of you while I investigate things here."

Anna's gaze drifted to the cornfields behind him. Much of the corn had been harvested for feed. The scent of earth filled her nose. Finally finding her nerve, she leaned in and brushed a kiss across his smooth cheek. He smelled of soap and aftershave. "Goodbye, Eli," she whispered in his ear.

He swept his thumb across the back of her hand. "Goodbye, Anna."

Chapter Fifteen

With an unfocused gaze, Anna stared over the fields as Dominic pulled onto the road. Gently, with the pad of her finger, she traced the spot where Eli's whiskers had brushed her face. If only they had met at a different time, under different circumstances, she might have finally been willing to let down her guard. To give someone a chance. Even someone in law enforcement. But as long as there was an inkling in Eli's mind that her brother was guilty of hurting his sister, they'd never have a future.

The SUV crested the hill and eventually fields gave way to more frequent houses. Anna glanced at Dominic. He stared straight ahead. Unfortunately he wasn't the chatty type. She could have used the distraction.

As they approached the center of Apple Creek, her cell phone rang. She pulled it out of her purse. Her brows furrowed. "Hello."

The man on the other end of the phone cleared his throat. "Yeah, Anna. It's Tom Hanson."

"Hi, Tom." She sensed his apprehension. "Is something wrong?"

"I hate to do this to you, but my aunt Beth, uh, Mrs.

Christopher, is determined to get rid of your brother's things. She told me to put it all out by the curb tonight." A pounding started in the back of her head. A long pause floated across the line. "And tomorrow's garbage pickup."

Looking out the window, she realized they were driving farther out of town. A warning voice whispered in her head. *Don't lose what little connection you have to your big brother.* "Any chance you can put the stuff in a corner of the garage for now?" She cut a sideways glance at Dominic. "I'm busy now."

"My aunt's pretty mad. I don't want to lose my job over this."

Anna worked her bottom lip. She sensed Dominic looking at her. "What's wrong?" His deep voice startled her.

"Hold on," she said into the phone. Turning to Dominic she said, "The Christophers are going to throw my brother's things out."

"Tell him to store them. Eli wants you out of Apple Creek." *Eli wants you out...* Dominic's words hurt more than they should have.

"Please, it will only take a minute." She thought about her grandmother's end table, and her brother's photographs were like a window into his soul. What Mrs. Christopher considered junk were the only things she had left from her family.

When Dominic didn't say anything, Anna put the phone back to her ear. "I'm not far. I'll be there in a few minutes. Can you meet me at his apartment?"

"I'm here now. See you in a few."

Anna tossed the phone into her purse. "Dominic, we need to make a quick detour."

"No way. Eli told me to get you out of Apple Creek."

"It will take five minutes. My brother's apartment is just down the road. Turn around, please."

Dominic huffed and slapped the steering wheel. When he slowed the vehicle and did a three-point turn in the middle of the road, Anna's shoulders sagged. "Thank you."

They drove back through Apple Creek toward Daniel's garage apartment. She pointed to the house. "Turn in here." The sun had set and long shadows gathered in the corners of the long driveway. "Pull around back and park near the steps. It should only take a few minutes to load up. Tom says he already put things in boxes."

Dominic threw the gear into park. "If Eli gets wind of this, he'll have my head."

"He won't ever know," she said conspiratorially.

Dominic muttered under his breath, then pointed to the steps hugging one side of the garage. "Your brother's apartment is up there?"

"Yes."

"Okay." Her bodyguard turned and glared at her. "You stay put. Stay inside the vehicle. Give me your cell phone." She handed him her phone and he punched in a few numbers, programming his number directly into her cell. "Call me if you see anyone. Got it?"

Anna swallowed hard. Icy fear pricked her skin. All they were doing was picking up her brother's things. So why did she suddenly feel like they were on a covert mission?

Tom appeared at the bottom of the steps. He waved them over. "You hear me?" Dominic said in a commanding voice. "Stay put. I'll get your brother's things."

Dominic climbed out of the vehicle, then paused in the open doorway. "Take the keys. Just in case."

Anna's mouth grew dry. They were picking up a few things, she reminded herself. *Just getting a few things.* She hoped he remembered the end table and the framed photos. Leaning back against the cool leather of the seat, she tried to relax.

She watched as Dominic followed Tom up the steps. From her vantage point she could see them enter the apartment. A moment later, Dominic came out and put a box on the landing. He went back into the apartment. Anna tapped her fingers on the armrest of her door. She glanced down at her cell phone. Nervousness raked across her flesh when time seemed to stretch with no sign of Dominic or Tom.

She leaned forward. *Where are you?* Her fingers brushed against the handle, but Dominic's stern warning whispered across her brain. *Stay put.* She stared at her cell phone and waited ten minutes before dialing Dominic's phone number. No answer.

Her heart jackhammered. She glanced down at the keys in her hand. She could leave and go get Eli, but what about Dominic? She suddenly felt foolish. Dominic was probably helping Tom move something and couldn't get to his phone. She waited a few more minutes, then dialed his number again. Still no answer.

A whisper of dread made the fine hairs on the back of her neck stand at attention. She shook the phone in her hand, willing it to ring. Maybe she should call Eli. And tell him what? That she convinced Dominic to ignore his instructions? A new wave of apprehension washed over her. Even if she wanted to call Eli, he didn't have cell phone reception at his parents' home.

Despite the fluttering in her chest, she unlocked the passenger door and pulled the handle. The dome light snapped on, bathing her in stark white light. She tried to shake the fear pulsing through her veins. She slipped out of the car and closed the door with a quiet click.

The deep hum of something mechanized made her pause. The garage door rumbled open. A mixture of relief and apprehension twined up her spine. Maybe they had used the back entry to carry some stuff out through the garage. Anna walked around to the back of Dominic's vehicle to pop the rear hatch. She was already out of the vehicle so she might as well help.

Soft steps crunched on the gravel driveway. She spun around to see Mrs. Christopher standing there with a sour expression on her face. Anna pressed a hand to her chest. "Oh, my goodness, you scared me. I'm picking up Daniel's things right now. We'll be out of your way shortly." She hated the breathless quality of her voice.

Mrs. Christopher narrowed her gaze. "Come with me."

Anna moved back around to the passenger door of Dominic's vehicle, suddenly wishing she had taken his advice and stayed safely inside.

"No, over here." Mrs. Christopher jaw clenched as she tilted her head toward the garage.

"I don't understand. A friend of mine is helping Tom bring my brother's things down." She glanced toward the steps, willing Dominic to appear.

That's when Anna saw the black object in Mrs. Christopher's hand. Anna's heart plummeted to her shoes. She blinked in confusion as she tried to process everything.

"Walk."

"Where…?"

Mrs. Christopher jammed the gun against Anna's rib cage. "The garage. Go."

Anna's gaze shifted to the stairs.

"No one is coming to help you," the older woman said. "Get in the driver's side."

Anna's eyes slid across the fancy sports car. "You want me to drive?"

Mrs. Christopher seemed mildly amused. "I can't very well drive and keep an eye on you." The way she waved the gun around made Anna wince. "Get in. I don't have time for this nonsense."

Anna did as she was told. She climbed into the driver's seat and her knees hit the steering wheel. Out of the corner of her eye, she watched Mrs. Christopher walk around the back of the car. She took that moment to slip her cell phone out, dial 9-1-1 and hide it under the front seat. Her heart beat wildly in her ears when Mrs. Christopher got in the passenger's side.

"What were you doing?" The older woman's blue eyes flashed rage.

Anna's panicked thoughts mercifully tended toward survival. "I needed to adjust the seat. My knees…." She lifted her knee to bang against the steering wheel.

Silence stretched between them. Anna clenched her jaw. Mrs. Christopher leaned forward, keeping the gun trained on Anna. *Please don't let her find my phone.* As if an answer to her prayer, Mrs. Christopher leaned back. "It's the button on the side."

Anna reached down with her left hand and found a few buttons. She raised, lowered and moved her seat, pretending to be clueless, but she really was buying time. Hoping Dominic would suddenly appear.

"Hurry. It's time to go."

Not wanting to tempt fate, Anna pushed a button to start the car. Gripping the gear stick, she put it in drive and drove out of the garage.

"Drive and don't do anything stupid or—" she jerked her thumb toward the trunk "—you're not the only one whose life is at stake."

A horrible realization took hold. Had she somehow overpowered Dominic? As unreasonable as that seemed, a mental image of Dominic stuffed in the trunk came to mind. As she eased the car forward, she glanced around for Tom. No sign of him, either.

Her eyes dropped to the gun. With regret, Anna realized even if this crazy person was a bad shot, she had a pretty good chance of hitting her in this small space.

"Where are you taking me?"

"To get the answers you've been dying to get."

Chapter Sixteen

"I'm taking you to the cabin. That's where the problem began…and ends." Mrs. Christopher sniffed.

"I don't understand. Why me?" Anna tracked the gun out of the corner of her eye.

"It didn't have to be this way. If only your brother had left well enough alone."

"My brother's dead. I bet you messed with his plane."

Mrs. Christopher chuckled, low and slightly amused. "You highly overestimate my willingness to get my hands dirty. But, yes, I did arrange it. Once I learned he had photographs, I had to find them. And you and your boyfriend just wouldn't quit."

"You won't get away with this. Eli will find you." *Please, Lord, let Eli find me in time.* She prayed the sheriff's office was tracking her 9-1-1 call on her cell phone neatly tucked under her seat. She only wished she had the time to tell the dispatcher her emergency. *Please, please, please let them investigate the call.*

Mrs. Christopher lowered the gun slightly and laughed. "No, he'll be coming after Tom Hanson. Not me. I'm a well-respected member of Apple Creek." She covered her mouth in mock surprise. "Your bodyguard never saw me. He didn't know what hit him. And, oh, dear, someone stole my car. Tom—the black sheep of the family—never could be trusted."

Mrs. Christopher sat up straighter in her seat. "Here, turn here."

Anna slowed the vehicle and turned up the familiar narrow road leading to the cabin in the woods. The vehicle rocked over the deep ruts and Anna wondered if the sports car would make it without getting stuck. Her gaze shifted to the gun. She wished Mrs. Christopher would move her finger away from the trigger. One deep rut and it would all be over.

The large tree still blocked the road. Mrs. Christopher's face was shrouded in shadows, but Anna suspected she hadn't anticipated this obstacle. "Get out."

Anna did as she was told. A breeze rustled the leaves, sending a whisper of dread across her goose-pimpled skin. Her gaze cut to Mrs. Christopher climbing out the other side. A momentary thought flashed through her mind. *Run.* She glanced down at her sandals, realizing she had a better chance of getting shot than getting away.

Dear Lord, let Eli find me in time.

Mrs. Christopher came up behind her and jabbed her in the back. Anna's head bounced forward. "Stop stalling. Get moving."

Moonlight poked through the branches. *Maybe I should run.* The gravel crunched under their unsteady steps. Mrs. Christopher wrapped her thin fingers more tightly around Anna's forearm, as if reading her mind.

"What happened to Mary?" If this was it, Anna wanted answers.

"What are you talking about?" Mrs. Christopher squared her shoulders, seemingly indignant.

"That's what this is all about, right? Something happened to Mary and the Christopher family wanted to pin it on my brother." It was the most logical conclusion.

"My son Chase has been in trouble since the day he was born." She pushed Anna forward again. "It only got worse after his father left."

Anna's mouth grew dry. "His father? I thought you and Mr. Christopher were still married."

"Yes. Chase is my husband's stepson."

"But they share the same last name?" Her mind whirred with the possibilities. A mosquito bit her cheek and she swatted at it.

"Richard would never adopt Chase, but he didn't argue when I legally changed my son's name to his. The Christopher name opens doors." In the dark, Anna imagined her captor hiking her proud chin. "Despite growing up in a privileged home, Chase tried to slam every single door shut. If my husband knew half the things Chase was involved with, he would have dumped him—dumped me—a long time ago." She stopped and turned, leaning close to Anna's face. A craziness lit her eyes. "I worked hard to get to this station in life. To have *everything* I could possibly want. I'm not going to let some ungrateful kid of mine ruin it for me. Or some nosy do-gooders."

Arching an eyebrow, Mrs. Christopher twisted her lips. "It's a shame really. Chase is a brilliant boy. He just doesn't think things through. I thought if Daniel's apartment was cleaned out, you'd have no reason to stay. I wanted you out of our lives."

Anna tried to take a step back, but Mrs. Christopher dug her thin fingers into her arm.

"Keep walking." The woman's energy level seemed to ramp up when the dark shadow of the cabin ruins came into view. The scent of charred wood reached Anna's nose and the memory of the inferno made her palms slick with sweat. Mrs. Christopher trudged past the cabin toward the tree where Daniel had taken photos of the bonnet. A dreadful thought whispered across her brain. *Does Mrs. Christopher know where Mary's body is buried?*

Instinctively Anna slowed her pace, and once again, Mrs. Christopher pushed her forward. "Come on." They reached a clearing. The ground dropped off and the lake stretched out in front of them. The moonlight glinted off the ripples. A soft breeze lifted the hair away from the clammy skin of her neck.

Dear Lord, please protect me.

Mrs. Christopher gestured with her gun down to the water. "You want to know what happened to Mary. You can join her."

Eli parked his SUV behind a sports car on the rutted road leading to the cabin. He had no idea what to expect when he drove out here. The dispatcher had told the sheriff about a dropped call from Anna's phone. The sheriff didn't waste any time contacting Eli. When Eli couldn't reach Anna or Dominic, he pulled some strings at his home FBI office to track the GPS on her phone. The signal was coming from right around here. He aimed the beam of the flashlight into the vehicle. It was empty. He'd have to call the plates in, but for now, he had to find Anna.

A thumping noise rattled the trunk. His pulse spiked. *Anna.* He yanked open the door and leaned into the backseat, feeling along its top for a lever. The seat flopped forward. He flashed the beam of his flashlight and froze when he found Tom Hanson lying on his back with his mouth, feet and hands bound. Eli ripped the silver duct tape from the startled man's face.

"Give me your hands," Eli commanded. Tom pushed his bound hands through the opening. He cut the ropes with his pocketknife. "Can you pull yourself through?"

Groaning, Tom grabbed hold of the folded seat and pulled. Eli grasped his forearms and backed out of the car. After some awkward rearranging, Tom climbed out and sat on the front seat, his bound feet dangling out of the car.

"Where's Anna?" Eli squinted in the direction of the cabin but couldn't see past the tree cutting off the road. He bent over and cut the last of the ropes from Tom's ankles.

"That woman is crazy," Tom said. "She tricked me."

Eli glared at Tom. "What woman?"

"Aunt Beth. She's absolutely crazy. She promised me if I took care of things, I wouldn't have to be her lackey anymore." A sheen of sweat glistened on Tom's forehead.

"What things?" A knot formed in Eli's chest.

"I had to protect Chase." Tom scratched his head with reckless abandon.

"Which meant stopping Daniel from revealing what he found."

Tom rubbed his wrists where the ropes had dug into his flesh. "I only meant to scare Daniel. I didn't want anyone to die."

"So you sabotaged his plane?" Eli asked in disbelief.

"Yeah, well...."

"How did you think he'd survive a plane crash?"

"I didn't think. I just did what my aunt told me to do. She nearly went over the edge when she learned Tiffany had been in the plane. She wasn't supposed to be with Daniel that day." Tom glanced up at him with a contrite look on his face. "In the end, she got so desperate she had me wear an Amish hat while I set the cabin fire and plant the lighter to make it look like Anna was trying to destroy evidence."

Eli wanted to throttle this simpleton but realized now was not the time. "I need to find Anna *now*. Where is she?"

"Aunt Beth showed up at Daniel's apartment. The big guy—"

"Dominic?"

"Yeah, I guess. He was with Anna." Tom rubbed his wrists. "The big guy came up to the apartment to pick up Daniel's stuff. *She* wanted it gone." He raised an eyebrow. "But now I think she wanted to lure Anna there." His jaw worked. "My aunt had become unraveled. She snuck up behind Dominic and bashed him over the head with her gun. He went down in a heap." He curled his nose. "Never seen a big guy go down so hard. I don't think he's dead, but he's going to have a whopper of a headache." He scratched his head and winced. "I can relate."

Eli ran a hand across his mouth, his patience evaporating. "Where *is* Anna?"

"I don't know. My aunt asked me to come down into the garage through the back stairway. You know the one that leads directly into the garage? When I got down to the garage, she had her trunk open. Next thing I know, she *bashed* me." He rubbed his head. "Lights out." He lifted his palms. "And here I am."

Eli pointed at Tom. "Stay here. I'll deal with you later." He turned and jogged toward the cabin.

Dear Lord, guide me. Let me save Anna.

A stiff wind gusted off the lake, nearly drowning Mrs. Christopher's words.

"Why did you hurt Mary?" Anna asked, her voice shaking.

"My son—" the older woman's lips thinned as if she were holding back her temper "—is not a strong man. I blame myself. I always catered to him." The moonlight glinted in the whites of her eyes.

Something by the tree line caught Anna's attention. She captured Eli's gaze and held it. Her legs almost went out from under her. *Thank You, God.* Eli held a finger to his lips.

"One night, Chase and a bunch of his fraternity brothers were drinking. The Blakely boy had borrowed a Taser from his father's trunk. He's the sheriff's son, you know. All they meant to do was have a little fun. Show off. Maybe scare the horse a little. All the other guys went into a bar and Chase… I don't think he even touched the animal. Just activated the Taser in front of the horse's nose.

"He didn't know the Amish girl was in the buggy." Mrs. Christopher's gaze grew vacant. "Chase said she didn't make a sound. He saw her head pop up at the last minute and she looked at him with wide eyes. She saw Chase."

"The child had a name. Mary Miller," Anna said through clenched teeth.

Mrs. Christopher seemed to consider this for only a moment. "Chase called me, blubbering. He was always calling me, looking for me to solve his problems. He had followed the buggy in his car. When the buggy crashed, the Amish girl tumbled out. Chase put her in the car and I told him to meet me here. He was completely panicked. She must have hit her head because she wasn't breathing by the time I got to her. I told him not to tell anybody." Mrs. Christopher ran a finger along her lower lip, as if reliving the night. "When I got here, I sent my son away."

"What did you do?" Anna's eyes grew wide with the realization, keenly aware of Eli listening from a few feet away.

"It was perfect." She ignored her question, as if fascinated by her own story. "As long as everyone kept quiet, no one ever had to know. We could go on living as we were accustomed." A quiet sob fell from her lips, the first sign of any remorse. "Your brother didn't need to get involved. He wasn't even there that night. But he suspected something. I think he overheard his fraternity brothers arguing. He couldn't leave well enough alone.

"I had to do it. It was the only way to protect my son. To protect me." The proud woman's jaw was set in determination. "I threw Mary's body off this cliff. Her stupid bonnet got hung up on a branch. I was afraid if I threw it after her, it would float on the surface. So I stuffed it under a floorboard in the cabin. I should have buried it somewhere, but the ground was too hard. I didn't have any tools," she muttered, as if realizing the one mistake that had unraveled all her plans.

Mrs. Christopher gave her head a curt nod, as if snapping out of her reverie. She trained the gun on Anna's chest. "Now it's your turn."

In a flash, Mrs. Christopher dropped to the ground. A primal cry rang out from the otherwise dignified woman. Anna backed away from the edge, her legs crumbling underneath her. Anna knelt on the ground as Eli pulled Mrs. Christopher's arms behind her back and put on handcuffs. He dragged her to a seated position away from the ledge. He grabbed her gun and tucked it into his waistband.

Under the moonlight, Mrs. Christopher's face grew hard. She glared at Anna. "You ruined everything."

"Thank God you found me." Her heart filled with joy.

Eli cupped her cheeks and pressed his lips against her forehead. "I tracked the GPS on your phone. Smart girl."

Eli stood and pulled Anna up with him. She buried her face into his solid chest. "I've never been happier to see anyone in my entire life," she said.

He brushed his finger across her cheek. "Me, neither."

Mrs. Christopher rocked back and forth and moaned something unintelligible.

"I am so sorry about Mary," Anna said.

"Me, too." Eli tucked a strand of hair behind her ear and a slow smile spread across his face. "Thank God you're safe. Are you okay to walk on your own?"

"Yes," Anna whispered. "Do what you have to do with her."

Eli leaned over and grabbed the woman by her arm, bringing her to her feet. His features hardened. "Come on. We have some other people to track down."

"Leave my son out of this," Mrs. Christopher screeched at the top of her lungs. "It's Tom Hanson's fault. He's an idiot. He screwed everything up. If he had only followed my instructions exactly…"

The entire walk back to the car, Mrs. Christopher

wailed and moaned. When they got closer to the road, the red and blue lights from the sheriff's cruiser lit the area. Tom Hanson was already in custody. Eli handed Mrs. Christopher to the sheriff.

"You need to send a unit over to Daniel Quinn's apartment right away. A friend of mine was knocked unconscious by Mrs. Christopher." Eli's stomach twisted and he sent up a silent prayer for Dominic.

Eli waited for the sheriff to finish his call, then said, "Thanks for not dismissing Anna's 9-1-1 call. You saved her life." He brushed a mosquito off his forearm. "Sheriff, we need to talk to your son about the night my sister disappeared."

The sheriff's brow furrowed. "Why?" Then his features softened. His shoulders sagged. "I will bring him in first thing in the morning."

"With your okay, I'd like to pick up Chase Christopher tonight."

The sheriff nodded.

Anna rested her hand on Eli's back and leaned into him. Wrapping an arm around her shoulders, he pulled her closer. Her entire body relaxed. "Finally, justice for Mary," she whispered.

Epilogue

It felt good to be back in Apple Creek after a few weeks away. Most of the cornfields had been harvested, changing the appearance of the landscape. Slouching in the passenger seat of Eli's car, a million thoughts floated through her mind.

Eli had finally gotten the answers he had been looking for. Chase and Beth Christopher had been arrested for their roles in Mary's death. Tom Hanson was also in custody.

Eli had told her how Tom had owned up to sabotaging Daniel's plane and setting the cabin on fire with the hope of destroying any possible evidence against Chase. From his jail cell, Tom was spilling the rest of the family secrets. Under his aunt's instructions, he had been stalking Anna. He watched her from the barn loft, trailed her in the cornfield and nearly ran her over in town. Mrs. Christopher had hoped to chase Anna out of town, counting on Eli to pin Mary's disappearance on Anna's brother. In her eyes, Anna was the only one with a stake in proving Daniel's innocence. When Anna wouldn't leave, the threats escalated. A cold chill ran down her spine.

The sheriff's son had cooperated fully. He didn't have knowledge of the crime, but he had lied about Chase's alibi at the time Mary went missing. If only he hadn't been intimidated by the Christopher family all those years ago, the Miller family would have found the answers they needed.

And Anna had her answer, too. Daniel was innocent.

"How is your family doing?" she finally asked, breaking the silence.

"My parents' propensity for forgiveness is incredible. They are at peace."

"How is Dominic?"

"Mostly embarrassed. Mrs. Christopher had caught him with the butt of her gun from behind, knocking him out." Eli ran his palm along the steering wheel. "Thank God she didn't shoot him."

Anna glanced over at Eli. "How about you? Have you found peace?"

"I'm working on it. I've gone to a few church services over the past few weeks." Half of his mouth slanted into a wry grin. "I'm a work in progress."

"Good. Good." Anna wrapped her fingers around the smooth vinyl of the armrest between them.

"I'm sorry I wasn't there for your brother's service," Eli said, never taking his eyes off the road. "I had to be in court."

Anna waved her hand in dismissal. "I understand. I had his ashes buried next to my mother's. It felt good to have some closure. And your family had a service for Mary?" They never found Mary's body, but at least they found peace in having some answers.

Eli nodded. "Yes. Buggies lined up as far as the eye could see. It provided healing for all of us."

"And Samuel and Katie Mae? How are they?" She watched the trees rush by outside her passenger window, feeling like she was asking him twenty questions. But there were so many things she still wanted to know.

"Samuel is coming around. He's always been so quiet. But he seems more content. I don't think my mother has to worry about him leaving. He seems committed to sticking around." He shrugged. "He's sweet on an Amish girl who lives on a neighboring farm. Time will tell.

"Katie Mae and Isaac officially announced their engagement."

Anna's eyes widened. "Really? Are you happy about that?"

Eli made a deep noise in his throat. "What do I know? I had a long conversation with Isaac recently. Maybe I judged him too harshly. He claimed he was abrasive with me because he feared I'd talk Katie Mae out of marrying him. It was a defense mechanism. He does seem to love her."

"You're turning into a softie." Anna patted his knee, then pulled her hand away. "How is Tiffany?"

"She's on the mend. She has a ways to go both physically and mentally. It's a lot to deal with, learning your brother and mother are capable of such evil. At least she has her father. Mr. Christopher knew nothing about the incident. He'd been too busy working and building his empire."

Eli turned his vehicle up the narrow road leading to the cabin. The search crews looking for Mary's body had cleared the tree from the road. They reached the burned-out cabin and Eli stopped the vehicle. They climbed out.

Anna opened the back door and grabbed the bouquet of wildflowers.

Red lifted his head, seemingly content to rest on the backseat. Eli brushed past Anna and hooked Red's leash. "Come on." He patted the dog's head, and he jumped out of the car.

They followed a zigzag path to the clearing. Red sniffed everything in his path. Eli wrapped the leash tightly around his hand when they reached the cliff, and Anna leaned forward and glanced down to the chilly lake waters. Although the dive team had not been able to find Mary's remains, the Millers' strong faith gave them peace. It had been ten years, and they finally had answers. What they had always known was still true—their beloved daughter was in heaven.

"Would you like to say a prayer?" Anna asked.

Eli bowed his head, reached out and captured Anna's hand. "Dear Lord, thank You for letting me find justice for Mary. Please let all those hurt by the cruel acts of that day find peace." He squeezed her hand. "Thank You for the gift of Mary's life, however short."

A brisk wind whipped up across the lake and Anna pulled her coat tighter, the wildflowers brushing her nose. Eli wrapped his arm around her shoulder and held her close. Red sat down next to her feet. "And thank You, Lord, for bringing Anna into my life. I am truly thankful for my blessings. Amen."

Warmth blossomed in her chest. She handed Eli half of the bouquet and together they tossed them. The wildflowers rained down on to the surface of the lake. They watched in silence as the colorful flowers bobbed and dipped, floating out toward the horizon.

Eli turned Anna to face him, searching her face with intense eyes. "I don't want to lose you."

"I...don't..."

Eli touched his finger to her lips. A smile pulled on the corners of her mouth and joy filled her heart. "If you'll have me, Miss Anna Quinn, I'd like to court you." Her insides tingled.

She cupped his face with her hands and kissed his cheek. He grabbed her wrists in one of his and planted a firm kiss on her lips.

After a moment, he pulled away, a question in his eyes. Anna couldn't contain her smile.

"Can I take that as a yes?" Eli asked.

"Yes!" Anna threw her arms around his neck and squeezed. "I'd love for you to court me."

Red jumped up, resting one paw on Eli's thigh and the other on Anna's waist. Laughing, they both fluffed the Irish setter's ears. "You want in on this, too, huh?" Eli asked.

Red barked, then dropped down. Spinning in a tight circle, he settled back in at their feet.

Anna pressed her cheek to Eli's chest and he wrapped his strong arms tightly around her. The sweet scent of the crisp fall air filled her senses. She tried to memorize every detail of the glorious moment. *I am truly blessed.*

Eli pressed a kiss to the crown of her head. He leaned back and tucked a strand of hair behind her ear, leaving a trail of warmth under his touch. "Ready?"

She nodded. "Ready."

* * * * *

Love Inspired®

Save $1.00

on the purchase of any
Love Inspired®,
Love Inspired® Suspense or
Love Inspired® Historical book.

Available wherever books are sold, including
most bookstores, supermarkets, drugstores
and discount stores.

Save $1.00

**on the purchase of any Love Inspired®, Love Inspired® Suspense
or Love Inspired® Historical book.**

Coupon valid until March 15, 2016. Redeemable at participating retail outlets in the
U.S. and Canada only. Limit one coupon per customer.

52613353

5 65373 00076 2   (8100)0 12127

SPECIAL EXCERPT FROM

Love Inspired®

*As a young woman seeks a better life for herself
and her son in Amish country, will she find happiness
and love with an Amish carpenter?*

**Read on for a sneak preview of
A HUSBAND FOR MARI,
the second book in the new series
THE AMISH MATCHMAKER.**

"That's James," Sara the matchmaker explained in English. "He's the one charging me an outrageous amount for the addition to my house."

"You want craftsmanship, you have to pay for it," James answered confidently. He strode into the kitchen, opened a cupboard, removed a coffee mug and poured himself a cup. "We're the best, and you wouldn't be satisfied with anyone else."

He glanced at Mari. "This must be your new houseguest. Mari, is it?"

"*Ya*, this is my friend Mari." Sara introduced her. "She and her son, Zachary, will be here with me for a while, so I expect you to make her feel welcome."

"Pleased to meet you, Mari," James said. The foreman's voice was pleasant, his penetrating eyes strikingly memorable. Mari felt a strange ripple of exhilaration as James's strong face softened into a genuine smile, and he held her gaze for just a fraction of a second longer than was appropriate.

Warmth suffused her throat as Mari offered a stiff nod and a hasty "Good morning," before turning her attention to her unfinished breakfast. Mari didn't want anyone to get the idea that she'd come to Seven Poplars so Sara could find her a husband. That was the last thing on her mind.

"Going to be working for Gideon and Addy, I hear," James remarked as he added milk to his coffee from a small pitcher on the table.

Mari slowly lifted her gaze. James had nice hands. She raised her eyes higher to find that he was still watching her intently, but it wasn't a predatory gaze. James seemed genuinely friendly rather than coming on to her, as if he was interested in what she had to say. "I hope so." She suddenly felt shy, and she had no idea why. "I don't know a thing about butcher shops."

"You'll pick it up quick." James took a sip of his coffee. "And Gideon is a great guy. He'll make it fun. Don't you think so, Sara?"

Sara looked from James to Mari and then back at James. "I agree." She smiled and took a sip of her coffee. "I think Mari's a fine candidate for all sorts of things."

Don't miss
A HUSBAND FOR MARI
by Emma Miller,
available February 2016 wherever
Love Inspired® books and ebooks are sold.